The Hundred-Towered City

It stared at them with yellow eyes as it raised two huge hands with long fingernails.

'Jack?' cried Annie. 'What is it?'

The strange little creature seemed about to spring at Annie when someone from behind it gave it an enormous kick and sent it flying through the air. It howled hellishly as it went, ending up on the gutter of a roof. It shook a gnarled fist at the children, but then it was gone, over the rooftops, amongst the forest of chimneys.

The two children turned to thank their rescuer, only to see a huge figure in a black cloak. It was impossible to tell whether his features were kind or hostile in the rapidly descending darkness, especially in that lightless alleyway. All they could make out was a big, brutish and bulky shape blocking their way.

'Oh heck,' muttered Jack, his heart racing.

BY GARRY KILWORTH

The Knights of Liofwende

Spiggot's Quest

Mallmoc's Castle

Boggart and Fen

Attica

Jigsaw

The Hundred-Towered City

The Hundred-Towered City

Garry Kilworth

www.atombooks.co.uk

ATOM

First published in Great Britain in 2008 by Atom
This paperback edition published in 2009 by Atom

A CIP catalogue record for this book
is available from the British Library.

ISBN 978 1 90565 405 5

Typeset in Bembo by Palimpsest Book Production Limited,
Grangemouth, Stirlingshire

Printed and bound in Great Britain by
CPI Mackays, Chatham ME5 8TD

Atom
An imprint of
Little, Brown Book Group
100 Victoria Embankment
London EC4Y 0DY

An Hachette UK Company
www.hachette.co.uk

www.atombooks.co.uk

For fellow writer Mike Stone
whose assistance and encouragement
over the years has been greatly appreciated

ACKNOWLEDGEMENTS

My grateful thanks to Petr Kotrle, my sometimes Czech translator and our excellent host when my wife and I visited the Czech Republic, for reading an early draft of this novel and offering valuable advice. It hardly needs to be said that any errors regarding Petr's wonderful country remain absolutely my own.

PROLOGUE

Jack's dad was a wacky inventor, his mother was a dotty professor of economics, his sister was too snooty and clever for her own good, and his younger brother was a constant pain in the neck. Jack was convinced he was the only reasonable, normal person in the house. He was at the moment helping Roger, his father, in their basement, which served as Roger's workshop. Jack wasn't assisting his dad out of any sense of duty, but because he knew if he was anywhere within the call of his sister, he would have to give her a hand with vacuuming the bedrooms of their Victorian house. Jack hated housework.

'Hand me the small torque wrench,' said Roger, from underneath the veteran motorcycle he was rebuilding. 'It's the shiny one with the black grip.'

Jack did as he was told, saying conversationally, 'I might join the army when I leave school. Or the navy.'

If he was expecting an argument from his dad, he got it typically in the form of mild sarcasm.

'Why not the Royal Air Force? You can kill more people with bombs dropped from a jet plane.'

'It's not all about killing people. You learn to do a trade.'

'And what trade would you like to excel at?'

Jack had recently been impressed by a television advertisement, aimed at young men who liked action and adventure.

'I dunno – telecommunications?'

Roger nodded and banged his head on the exhaust pipe.

'Ouch!' He sat up and rubbed his temple, then looked at his son. 'All right. Go ahead. Join the army and communicate. Then perhaps we'll get some communication out of you when they let you come home on leave. Your mother says all you do these days is grunt at her when she asks you a question.'

Jack shrugged. 'She always asks such daft things.'

'Like what?'

'Like "How did your football kit get so dirty?" What am I supposed to say to that? "Well mum, I don't know. We played in this enclosed white dome, with a sparkling clean floor and white walls. I'm mystified by how mud got on my shirt."'

'There's no need for sarcasm. You don't hear me using it.'

'Ha!'

'What's that supposed to mean? Pass me the flathead screwdriver. No, that's a Phillips. The flathead's the one with the straight tip. Thanks. So you think I'm sarcastic?'

'Only all the time.'

'OI! YOU TWO! DAD? CAN I HAVE A BIT OF TOAST?'

The yell came down from above, from the mouth of Davey, Jack's younger brother.

Roger sighed and said, 'I swear that young man was born with the voice of an elephant. Go and tell him all right.' He rose from the floor, covered in grease. 'Your sister's probably finished the housework by now, so you needn't worry about coming back.'

2

Jack gave his father a hurt look. 'Dad, whatever do you mean?'

'You know what I mean, mister.'

As well as being a brilliant inventor, Jack's dad Roger Kettle was a motorcycle enthusiast. Being British, he especially liked those bikes of old – the Vincent Black Lightning, the Ariel Arrow and most of the BSA models – which his own father had ridden in his youth. So naturally, having invented a time-travelling device, Roger chose to attach it to a veteran motorcycle in order to disguise its true purpose from prying eyes.

Roger was a brilliant man. He was one of those people who locked themselves into their workroom and had to be bullied or coaxed out for meals. When he was in the middle of an invention, he slept on a sofa-bed in the basement. This time he had surpassed himself. Having read all there was to read about the feasibility and theory of time travel (which many scientists thought impossible), Roger went off and followed a line of discovery all his own. That was what he always did. He listened to what others had written, so he knew what the laws of science said, then thought his way along a completely different path.

His reward here had been to discover that time did not travel in a straight line, but was a spiral groove, as on an old-fashioned vinyl record. To travel in time all you had to do was jump from one groove to the next, if a device could be made in order to accomplish this feat. He couldn't help himself once he had come across this amazing discovery and simply had to tell his family, who all thought it was fantastically mind-boggling, even Mum, who occasionally became impatient with these strange scientific explorations of her husband, which it had to be said very often produced quite extraordinary but valueless inventions.

Roger's mind blazed with triumph when he made this discovery. Feverishly, he worked for two whole years on a device which enabled the user to hop across the grooves. The device was quite small, about the size of a mobile phone, and fitted easily into Roger's favourite machine. The motorcycle could still be used as an ordinary motorbike as well as a time machine.

A sidecar was added for the use of extra passengers.

'You understand what we're doing here, Jack?' Roger said to him, as Jack climbed the stairs. 'I'm building a *time machine*.'

Jack smiled inwardly at his father's attempt at a drama.

'Sure, Pop. A time machine. Brilliant. I've read heaps of stories about time machines. Read a new one only the other day.'

Roger went a bit sniffy. 'H.G. Wells was the original,' he said, rather predictably. 'All the others are copies as far as I'm concerned. Oh, here's your sister. Coming to help, Annie?'

Annie, one year younger than Jack, had poked her face around the doorway above. She screwed up her nose.

'As if,' she replied. 'I'm off out, Dad. OK? Going to the cinema with Josie.'

Even before Roger replied she was back to texting on her mobile.

'You might learn something,' he suggested.

'I already know everything.' She flounced away.

'Women!' muttered Roger. 'Thank the Lord there's only two of 'em in this house.'

Jack grinned. 'We outnumber them.'

After Jack had sorted out Davey, he went back to the serious business of helping with the time machine, which was nearing completion. He did little more than hand spanners and calipers to his father, but he loved the fact that he was in on a new and great invention. Time machines had been talked about for a very long while and now his father – *his* father – was close to producing one. Roger had often said that science fiction hardware was fantasy one day and fact the next. 'Witness the geostationary satellite,' he had told Jack, 'first fictionalised by Arthur C. Clarke and later becoming fact. Now there are satellites up there for television and telephones and you name it.'

'Where are we going first?' asked Jack, handing his dad a set of Allen keys and marvelling at the shiny machine under construction. 'Or should I say *when*?' He spoke as if it were to be a Sunday outing, a picnic in the country or a trip to the beach.

'We? You're going nowhere, young man. Much too dangerous. We might have the machine but we know nothing about the travel or what might happen when we arrive. There are all sorts of unknown hazards, from ending up in a terrible situation – the middle of a battle, for instance – to catching the plague on landing. No, we have to proceed with caution, Jack. I will do some short-hop experiments and we'll see where things lead us from there . . .' Both Jack and Roger looked up at a sound from the doorway. Ten-year-old Davey stood there, eating toast and covered from head to foot in foul-smelling slime.

'Hi!' said Davey brightly. 'I fell in the compost pit. That's dangerous, that is. You should have a cover on it, Dad. People could get killed.'

'The compost pit is behind the garden shed. You can't fall in it unless you climb over the fence. Were you climbing on the fence?'

Davey made no reply, crunching his burnt toast.

'If your mother sees you up here like that,' said Roger, '*you'll* be toast. Get to the bathroom, chuck those clothes in the basket and shower before she comes in. Uh-uh, there's the door now. Quick.'

Davey scuttled away. A female voice floated down the stairs. It was Kate, Jack's mum.

'Anybody in? Someone come and help me get the shopping out of the car. It's heavy.'

'I'll go,' said Jack. 'If Davey goes, he's dead.'

Roger nodded, absorbed by his task once more.

After dinner that night, Kate settled down in front of the family computer, researching the family tree. She had been doing this for months now, but complained that she was stuck for a branch of the family that had lived in Prague at the turn of the last century. When she learned that her husband's latest invention was a time machine, she said in a surprised voice, 'Really? You're kidding.'

'No,' he replied seriously, 'a time machine.'

'Good heavens.'

Kate reflected on this amazing news, but was so used to her husband's inventive genius she soon got over her shock.

'All right then,' she told him firmly. 'You can take me back to the early 1900s. I need to get to the Prague Record

Office before it was burnt down in 1904. There are some documents that no longer exist, which were lost in that fire.'

Roger raised his eyebrows at this.

'I'm not sure, dear. I'll need to test the time machine before we all go traipsing off on our own particular jaunts.'

'Of course you will, darling, but once you have . . .'

By the end of the following month, Roger had already done several short-hop experiments, with wonderful success. He'd even taken each of the children, one at a time, on a short trip. Then he had tried some longer leaps back into the past. He had taken on board the idea that his machine could also be made to change its geographic position on the planet, as well as go back in time. He spent long hours working out the physics on paper, then modified the device.

Now he could travel back to nineteenth-century India, or pre-First World War One Germany, to gather the feel of the real history of those periods and places.

Roger had discovered that going much more than 150 years into the past was not good for his body's constitution. Something biological happened when he tried to go too far back: he became dizzy and disorientated, was physically sick, and it took over a week to get over the bad effects. He was happy with the machine's limitations for the time being. He would leave further adventures to the developers of his invention. No doubt those brilliant innovators the Japanese would one day produce a pocket-sized time machine which would take travellers all the way to prehistory and the dinosaur age.

But they were a long way from that yet. Roger's time machine was at the same stage as the first jet engine, or the first hovercraft. It was simply a prototype, to be endlessly tested. On leaving the present, the rider needed to reach a speed of exactly 47.22 recurring mph and hold it for ten seconds. This was in order to create a personal time hole through which the bike could pass. Roger said this might explain the fact of disappearances. People vanished every day, without a trace. Maybe, he told his kids, they were in a vehicle that reached the right speed, held it by accident for too long, and were shot back into the past, never to return to the present day.

Arriving at the other end, or back from a trip, was different: the Matchless motorcycle could stop within a few metres.

For the moment it had to remain a secret: Roger felt the world was not yet ready for an invention like this.

1. A RUDE AWAKENING

The roar of the motorbike coming down the road outside the house woke Jack with a start. He sat up and rubbed his eyes and went to the window. Peering into the darkness, he yelled, 'Mum? Dad? Is that you?'

Jack was a no-nonsense fourteen. He'd been away at a school camp with his younger brother Davey and his sister Annie, both of whom were asleep in their own bedrooms. The coach had dropped them off outside the house, but when they opened the front door and went in, Dad and Mum were out. There was a note on the fridge that said, *Making a quick trip to 1903 Prague. Be back in a few minutes. If we're not in when you get home, help yourself to supper. Any problems, call Nanna and Grandpa.* The children were disappointed they hadn't been greeted with enthusiasm after a week away, but they knew Prague was important at the moment. As the evening wore on, though, and Mum and Dad still didn't arrive, they realised something more serious was going on.

At ten o'clock Annie had rung their grandparents, but there was no answer from them either. It was only when they'd all tramped up the stairs exhausted to bed that Jack remembered his grandparents were on a cruise. His parents must have forgotten that too. The other set lived in Australia. They'd have to call their Aunt Julia in the morning. He fell into a troubled sleep, only to be jerked awake by the revving of the 1947 Matchless 500cc motorcycle.

Jack wondered why his mother or father hadn't answered his call from the window, even though it was late at night. When he looked down into the street outside, though, he could see a large man climbing off the motorcycle. The man ambled towards the front door of the house, just as Jack remembered he'd forgotten to lock it. Jack crossed the dark room quickly and tripped over his drum kit in the dark. The cymbals dropped to the floor with a crash. A pair of drumsticks went flying across the carpet.

Now someone was coming up the stairs: a heavy-footed person by the sound of it.

'Who is that?' cried Jack, now thoroughly scared. 'What do you want?'

No one answered.

Jack's heart was racing as the footsteps paused outside his bedroom door – and then the door opened.

'Say something!' Jack ordered, terrified, as footsteps entered the blackness of his room. 'Anything!'

'*Guten abend*,' came back a husky voice. '*Wie ist das?*'

German. A strange accent too. Jack was a fluent German speaker, as were his sister and brother. Their mother Kate was of Austrian extraction and had taught them all from birth. Who was this? Jack broke into a cold sweat. Then the light went on and the immediate brilliance made him wince and close his eyes for a few seconds. When he opened them, Annie was standing in the doorway, staring at the stranger. She too looked a little frightened, but true to her nature was trying not to show it. It was like her to go on the attack when she was scared.

'Why are you wearing Dad's watch?' she said, in an accusing tone.

The man was indeed wearing the octagonal watch which doubled as the starter key to the motorcycle time machine. He was swarthy and bearded, and his eyes glittered in the light. He was dressed in odd clothes. But Jack got the impression the man was as frightened by this experience as Jack was himself.

'What were you doing on Dad's bike?' demanded Annie, with not a trace of fear. Her hands went to her hips. 'You stole it.'

'German,' Jack told her. 'He speaks German.'

Annie repeated her question in that tongue.

'No, no,' replied the man quickly in his own language. 'I am here to help . . .' He looked around wildly. 'Wherever this is. Your father showed me this infernal device. He gave me the watch so that I could use the machine. I am no thief.'

Jack and Annie knew that Roger did not always leave the machine ready for a quick getaway when he went back in time. He thought it was dangerous to leave the machine ready to shoot back to his own time and place, and did so only when he thoroughly trusted those who guarded it for him. This man must have simply sat in the saddle and turned the key.

'Where's Dad?' asked Annie in German, still firmly rooted but now with folded arms. 'What have you done with him?'

'I? If you are speaking of Roger Kettle, I have done nothing with him. I fear he is arrested. He was taken by the secret police for questioning and his wife went to find him . . .'

'Mum?' cried Annie. 'Mum was there too?'

The man hung his head. 'Your mother? Then you are my distant relatives, from Britain. My name is Blazek. I live in Prague.' He looked around him again. 'This does not look like a house in Prague. Any house. Where are we?'

'You're in London,' replied Jack. 'Er, what year is this?'

'Year?' Blazek looked startled. 'Why?'

'Can you just answer, please?' asked Annie in a much more conciliatory tone. 'It would help us.'

'Why, 1903. How did I get to Great Britain?' Blazek stared at the ceiling as if the answer might be there.

11

Jack looked at Annie and said, 'Nineteen-oh-three. Of course it is.'

Jack decided not to confuse Blazek with the time difference. Then the significance of Blazek's words sunk in. Their father and mother had been arrested in 1903 Prague. Heck! What were they going to do? Wait until they were freed and came back? But how could they return without the time machine? He'd have to send this Blazek bloke back to where he came from and tell him to watch over the bike like a hawk until Dad and Mum came for it. What a mess! What a terrible mess. What if they never let them go? Who knew what prison was like in those times in the Czech Republic? Was it even the Czech Republic then? Probably not. Probably . . . what?

He asked Annie, who was better at history than him.

'Probably Bohemia,' she said, looking as worried as he felt. 'Is that right, Blazek? Do you come from Bohemia?'

'Yes, this is true. This is Bohemia. Some call it Czechy.'

'Who rules it – Bohemia?'

'Why, it is part of the Austrian Empire,' replied Blazek, looking as if he were a schoolboy at an exam. 'We are ruled by Austria. I am of a mixed Austrian-Czech family myself, as is your mother, though we have lived here for two generations. Prague is the capital of Bohemia.'

'We know that,' sniffed Annie.

'Good. Well, your mother came looking for her relatives. It is a bad time to be looking. Prague is full of suspicion and intrigue at this time. There is an international meeting of alchemists and the government is very concerned by such a gathering of foreigners. They are worried it might be political.'

'Alchemists?' questioned Jack.

'A worldwide society of sorcerers – they seek the black art of turning base metal into gold. The authorities don't want them in Prague, simply because they gather in secret, which is in the nature of alchemists. The authorities fear plots and conspiracies. I think the alchemists are magicians, but their magic is harmless. It is their love of secrecy which makes them untrusted and suspicious.'

'Good old Mum,' muttered Jack, bitterly. 'She couldn't be satisfied with Ancestor Find on the internet, could she? She had to go back and shake hands with them all.'

'Never mind that now,' Annie said. 'What are we going to do?'

'Conference – in the kitchen.' Jack switched back and forth from English to German with ease. 'Blazek. Will you wait here, please?'

'Why does he have to wait here?' asked Annie.

'Because,' Jack explained, 'he'll freak out if he sees something that's way out of kilter with his time. Look how he's staring at my computer. If he sees the fridge and the microwave he's going to go bananas.'

'Didn't they have fridges in 1903? Ice boxes?'

Jack shrugged. 'I'm just saying the less he sees, the better. Come on.'

Out on the landing, Davey was standing rubbing his eyes. 'What's all the noise? What's up?'

'Nothing, Davey,' said Jack. 'Go back to bed.'

'Go back to bed yourself.' The ten-year-old glared belligerently at his siblings. 'Somethin's up. I want in.' His face brightened. 'Are we raidin' the fridge? I heard you say fridge.'

Annie was always honest. 'Mum and dad are trapped in 1903,' she said bluntly. 'We have to figure a way of getting them back again.'

'Where's Nineteenothree?'

'It's a year, not a place, dope,' said his brother. 'Come on, we'll talk it out in the kitchen.'

Annie looked back nervously at Jack's bedroom.

'He – he won't go back again on the bike without us, will he?' She nodded towards the doorway, indicating Blazek.

Jack replied, 'Nah, it's not set for anywhere yet. Come on, let's get a sandwich and some lemonade and discuss this properly.'

Once the sandwiches were in their hands and the drinks distributed amongst them, Jack spoke.

'There's only one thing for it. I have to go back and rescue them.'

Annie looked worried. 'That's crazy. You could get lost too. We must both go. If one of us always stays by the machine, ready for a quick getaway, it's much better.'

'I'm not stayin' here on my own!' stated Davey spraying crumbs all over the kitchen table. 'You can't make me.'

'He's right,' Annie said. 'We can't leave him on his own. And we can't send him anywhere either. He will have to come too.'

Jack set his jaw. 'I say I go alone. I don't want to be responsible for you two. I'll have enough to think about, looking after myself.'

'You're not the boss of the world,' shouted Davey, spilling his drink and soaking Jack's tomato sandwich. 'Who made you the boss?'

'I'm in charge when Mum and Dad are not here,' replied Jack stiffly. 'I'm the eldest.'

'Poooph! By one year,' said Annie. 'This situation has not arisen before now and Davey and I have an equal say. We live in a democracy here, not a dictatorship.'

'Yeah, flippin' dictator,' cried Davey.

Jack knew he was not going to win. He had been thinking hard, ever since leaving Blazek in the bedroom. There was no way they could give Blazek instructions to go back and seek out their parents because he wouldn't be able to get back to the present again. Jack could set the time machine to go back to 1903 Prague, but he wouldn't be there to set it to return home. If Blazek never managed to get their parents released he would not be able to get word back to Jack, Annie and Davey. Either Jack had to go with Blazek, or Annie, who could also work the machine – or all three of them. If the other two wouldn't let him go alone, then he'd have to take them.

'All right,' said Jack. 'We've all been on a short trip back with Dad so we know what to expect. But I want you two to promise me that once we get there you'll both stay by the machine and use it if you have to get away quick. I'm in charge here, don't forget. You have to do as you're told.'

They said nothing, simply staring at him with expressions of mild contempt.

'Look,' he continued desperately, 'someone's got to be the leader here. It's an expedition. Expeditions aren't democracies. That doesn't work. It's been proved. You have to have someone in charge. That's why the army has officers. That's why you get people like – like . . .'

'Scott of the Antarctic?' offered Annie.

'Yes – yes, that sort of bloke. Scott of the Antarctic. You understand, Annie. He was a leader of men.'

'No chance,' Davey announced, standing up. 'You're not leaving me behind. I'm going to get out of my jarmies. What shall we wear? Tracksuit?'

'Nineteen-oh-three,' Annie said, also getting up and automatically taking their plates to the draining board. 'Tracksuits are too modern. Wear trousers, shirt and jacket. School clothes. That's nearest, I think. We'll probably still be stared at, but school clothes won't be too weird.'

'You'll have to wear a skirt,' said Jack. He had lost the battle for sole supremacy and wanted to go away with some sort of victory. 'You hate wearing skirts.'

'I'll wear a skirt,' she replied, loftily.

Jack returned to the bedroom, where he found Blazek smoking a foul-smelling pipe. Jack waved the smoke away from his face and said, 'We're coming to Prague.'

'Who is *we*?' asked Blazek, with more confidence than he'd shown until now.

'Me and my sister – and my younger brother.'

Jack put on some slacks, a shirt and a jacket, and his school shoes.

'Do I look OK?' he asked.

'What is this "OK"?'

'All right. Normal. What I mean is, do these clothes look weird – I mean unusual to you?'

'They look a little strange – but if you are coming with me I can get you some clothes.'

'And my brother and sister?'

'Clothes for them too. What will you do? Seek your father and mother? Is that it?'

'That's the idea, yes.'

'It will be very dangerous. Prague is full of intrigue, full of suspicion. The secret police are everywhere. It is like . . .' Blazek seemed to search his mind before continuing with, 'like the Italian *sgraffito* on our buildings.'

The children looked puzzled.

'Ah well – *sgraffito* is two layers of plaster, one dark, the other light. The pale layer is etched to show the dark layer underneath. That is what my city is like: a beautiful city of light, with a dark underbelly.'

'I see,' said Jack, trying to look intelligent.

'The police believe there are conspirators and rebels who want to break from the Empire. And anarchists who want to blow up everybody, no matter what for. Really, it is only the alchemists, and also those who choose to follow a similar path. Thaumaturgists and theurgists.' Blazek paused as he was presented with Jack's blank expression after these long words. 'People who believe they can use the spirit world, or the world of angels, to make wonderful things happen. Prague festers with half-magic at the moment. Secrets prosper. Intrigue rules.'

'Sounds just the sort of place for a holiday,' said a voice from the doorway, and Annie stood there looking down at herself in disgust. 'Is this grey skirt *grey* enough?'

'Who cares?' muttered Jack, absorbed by worries. 'Yeah, looks all right. Where's Davey?'

'Here, boss!' cried the youngest sibling from behind Annie. 'And may the Force be with us.'

17

'This is no joke, Davey,' said Jack. 'It's going to be very dangerous.'

'That's why we need the Force with us,' replied his unsquashable brother.

'German, please,' Annie said to Davey. 'Otherwise it's impolite to our friend, who doesn't speak English.'

Davey shrugged and nodded, staring hard at the thickset man with his haggard looks and dark clothes.

When they were finally ready to leave, they went downstairs and wheeled the bike out into the road, lined by terraced houses. Fortunately this late at night there was no traffic. The black strip of tarmac stretched out before them like a long shiny runway. It was from here that they would take off into another time, another city. The time hole that would be created by their father's invention, the secret device he had installed in the motorbike, would carry them back to 27 November 1903, to the city of Prague in Bohemia: the city of a hundred towers.

Blazek sat on the rider's seat with Jack on the pillion behind him. Annie and Davey squeezed into the sidecar.

'Hold on to your wigs!' Jack cried. 'Here we go!'

When they reached 47.22 recurring mph, they were almost level with Mr Singh's corner shop at the end of the street, travelling through a blur of gritty light and darkness. Jack likened it to being in a sandstorm (although he'd never been in one), the visibility being almost zero. Travelling through time caused a sensation of whirring through dust and cobwebs, as if they had to pass through a thousand attics full of clocks before reaching their destination. This was accompanied by a slight difficulty in breathing, though nothing to be worried about. He decided to talk to his dad about wearing goggles in future. Those old-fashioned things they used to wear on motorbikes before helmets had clear visors. And earplugs too, to block out that whirring, whooshing sound.

When they came to rest they were at the end of the street – but not the street they had taken off from. The terraced houses were not so very different from the grand Victorian ones that lined the London street they had left behind, but the children could see horse dung on the road and in the gutters. At Blazek's insistence they wheeled the bike to the top of some basement stairs, then bumped it down those stairs to the well at the bottom. Blazek then used a large key to open the door to the basement beyond.

In the basement was a tiny window letting in grey light. Feet belonging to passers-by could be seen outside. There was junk scattered around the floor, a rack of what looked like bottles of beer in one corner, potatoes spilling out of a sack, and a pile of damp-smelling books. Here were cobwebs and spiders and probably rats. The place was dreary and messy, but obviously visited. A set of wooden stairs led up to a door above. The door was open. Someone stirred in a corner.

Jack peered. There was a man standing there. He had a lean and haunted look. In his right hand was a bottle, from which he had obviously been sipping. This now fell from his fingers and smashed on the flagstones, splashing his shoes with beer. Clearly he had been shocked by the sudden arrival of four people in his basement.

2. IN FRANZ KAFKA'S BASEMENT

In German the man said, 'You startled me.'

Jack replied in the same language. 'Sorry, we didn't mean to.' He felt he ought to explain about the time machine. 'This isn't magic, you know – this is science.'

The young man nodded slowly. 'I know about the motorcycle.'

Blazek explained. 'You are in the house of my employer – the Jewish merchant Hermann Kafka. This is his son, Franz. He will help us all he can.'

'Have you met my dad?' Jack asked Franz. 'What did he tell you about the, er, machine?'

Franz's voice had a sort of hollow tone to it. 'I know that it moves through time.'

Annie said, 'And that doesn't bother you?'

'It delights me,' he replied, sounding anything but delighted. 'It lifts my spirit.'

Blazek took a brush and began sweeping up the glass on the floor, saying, 'Franz, perhaps we should take our guests upstairs, to the house?'

Jack went to the time machine and set the controls for automatic return to the twenty-first century. Then he put the safety switch on. Once that was done, he announced himself ready to ascend the stairs. They followed Franz up to the ground floor of the house. Franz took them past a study or library room. Jack peeked in. There were papers scattered over a desk. Franz saw him looking and said, 'I write a little.'

Once in the living room, they all settled into chairs. Annie stared at their host. He was not exactly what she would call a great looker: he had awkward sticky-out ears, though the rest of his features were pleasant enough. What struck her most were his eyes. They were so dark they were almost black, and they were certainly strange. There was no malice in them, but somewhere behind them lay thoughts that she knew would be quite weird.

She knew who he was. Just three months ago a children's author had visited her school and given a talk to her class. She had said to them, 'Now any one of you can be a writer when you leave school. Really. You're probably writers now, some of you. You don't need to be published to call yourself a writer. There's a very famous author – famous now, but not when he was alive – called Franz Kafka, who hardly published during his lifetime. He wrote at least three really brilliant novels, which they found in his sock drawer after he died . . .'

Annie had not read any of the novels. She hadn't even tried them. She knew nothing about Franz Kafka except for that one mention of him by the visiting author. But she had not forgotten the reverence in the author's voice when she spoke his name. Clearly he was someone really important in the literature world. Or would be, once he was dead.

Funny, thought Annie, *I* know who he is, but *he* doesn't know who he is.

Suddenly, she realised that Franz was staring back at her and she looked away, embarrassed.

Jack was saying, '. . . what can you tell us about our father and mother.'

Franz said, 'Your mother was asking too many questions on the street – the secret police don't like foreigners, not at the moment. She was arrested in Old Town Square as a suspected alchemist. Your father went looking for her. We haven't seen him since. Tell me, though – you are from England?'

'Great Britain – yes,' replied Jack, cautiously.

'What is it like there?'

Jack shrugged. 'I dunno. Not sure how it's different from here. I haven't seen Prague yet.'

'You have cities, towns, villages?'

'Yep – we've got those all right.'

'Does every village have its own church?'

'Most of 'em, I suppose. Some have more than one. And pubs, where they sell beer.' Jack used the English word for 'pubs' and he saw Franz take out a little notebook and scribble in it.

There were more questions, about life in Britain, famous buildings, the countryside, the people, the royal family, until Jack began to get a bit exasperated. It was he who should be asking the questions, since he was here to find his parents. But Franz was quietly relentless, digging away at Jack and Annie for at least an hour. Both the children deliberately steered clear of really modern inventions, like the mobile phone and the iPod, knowing these would be deep water.

Franz continued to probe until he finally realised his guests were growing tired of the interrogation, and called a halt.

'Actually,' he said, 'questions that don't answer themselves at the moment of asking are never really answered.' A bit later on he said, 'God gives us nuts but leaves it to us to crack them open.'

'He's not really right in the head, is he?' Jack whispered to Annie.

Davey had fallen asleep on the overstuffed sofa, amongst the lace-covered cushions. Jack and Annie were also beginning to feel tired. Jack asked Franz, 'Are your parents coming home in the morning?'

'No, they've taken my sisters to the south – they're visiting cousins. You can stay here for the time being. You,' he nodded at Annie, 'can have Ottla's bedroom. Jack and Davey can use Valli's room. My sisters won't mind, especially if they never know. We'll talk some more in the morning.'

Jack realised Blazek was no longer around. He asked Franz if he would be back.

'Oh yes – in the morning.'

3. IN THE STREETS OF PRAGUE

Jack woke at about ten. He went to a window and looked out. There beneath and all around lay the magnificent city of Prague. It was truly impressive. Towers and spires rose from many many extraordinary buildings, some of them dark and spiky, others studded with stained-glass windows. In the distance was a river, sparkling in the early-morning winter sun. A wonderful bridge spanned this river, which he knew from his mother was called the Charles Bridge. There were statues along the parapet, and beyond the bridge were palaces with sprawling skirts of parks and gardens.

The city of a hundred towers!

Jack left the view to look for his brother and sister. He found Annie and Davey already up and eating breakfast. There were ducks' eggs and rye bread and butter. Like them, he was hungry and tucked into the food, most of which went down very well. Annie asked if there were any bananas, only to receive a blank look from Blazek.

'I've heard of them' he said, 'but I've never seen one.'

Franz hovered around the kitchen while they ate, staring at the children and taking in every word they said, but he didn't shower them with any more questions, for which Jack was thankful.

After breakfast was over, it was decided that Jack would go out with Blazek to seek information on Roger and Kate.

'We must be careful who we ask,' said Blazek. 'We'll try to find the Bureau of General Enquiries – this is the least dangerous place to ask questions, since the employees are quite stupid people on the whole, having got their jobs because they have an uncle or a cousin already working in the civil service – but government offices move location often and rarely say where they are going, so it may be difficult.'

Jack said, 'If they're stupid people, they might not know the answers to our questions.'

'This is true,' replied Blazek, 'but what choice do we have? Now, we have to get you some proper clothes. Franz, can you help?'

'He can have some of mine,' replied Franz, 'that I wore when I was his age. I keep them in a trunk.'

Jack was soon kitted out with a musty-smelling jacket, a waistcoat, a shirt with a stiff collar, trousers that came to just below his knees, and black boots with tops that came halfway up his shins. The suit's material was coarse and more uncomfortable than Jack was used to, but he put up with it uncomplaining. He was then given a topcoat, a scarf and a peaked cap, all of which went to transforming him into something that caused a great howl of laughter to erupt from his younger brother's mouth.

'What an anorak!' cried Davey. 'Wish I had a camera.'

'You'll get a thump in a minute,' growled Jack.

Annie smiled. 'I think you look the part, Jack,' she said. 'Are there some clothes for me too, Franz?'

'I'll look for some once Blazek and Jack leave,' he promised.

'Well I don't want any,' cried Davey. 'You can stuff *that*.'

'You'll do as you're told,' replied Annie.

'Who made you boss of the world?'

Davey's older brother and sister didn't even bother to answer this predictable retort.

Jack and Blazek left the house.

There were few people in the street outside. Those that had braved the cold wind wore many layers of clothes. Coat collars were high and hats pulled down low. Scarves covered mouths and noses. The passers-by were merely rough human shapes, dark figures showing only the occasional pair of wary-looking eyes. Jack was amazed at the lack of traffic, which consisted mostly of carts, drays and wagons drawn by horses, with the very occasional motor car. This was a residential street, however, and carried little commercial traffic.

'Do you have motorbikes here, Blazek?' Jack asked, as they hurried along.

'Oh yes.'

'Are they like my dad's bike?'

'Not so large. More in the way of an ordinary pedal cycle with an engine attached. But others are coming. I have seen pictures from America of a machine made by a company called Triumph.'

Jack was also vaguely aware of the buildings. Many of them were tall four-storey dwellings with a multiplicity of windows in the upper storeys, the ground floor having only large wooden doors, some of them arched, some squared. They were the sort of buildings which in Jack's time had crumbling old edifices, but some of these were newly built with glistening brickwork and beautifully painted window frames. Behind the windows, blinds hid the interiors from the prying eyes of the public in the street, as if the occupants either had something to hide or were fearful for their privacy.

'This way,' said Blazek, but as they rounded a corner they came face to face with two men in uniform. 'Police,' muttered Blazek.

What Blazek had not explained to the children was that the government had recently ordered the police to be more vigilant and tough in their duties. Whether rightly or wrongly it was believed that the police force had become lazy and sloppy in the last few years. The policemen on the beat were being watched closely by their superiors, and those who did not shape up were being sacked. So now they were tending to overreact to any situation, fearful for their jobs.

At first it seemed these two policemen were going to let them past without stopping them, but Jack made the mistake of looking into the eyes of one of them. There must have been something about Jack's face that betrayed his nervousness. The policeman stared back impassively enough, but then called to the pair.

'Just a minute!'

Blazek groaned audibly and turned.

One of the policemen said, 'Where are you going?'

'Only to the Bureau of General Enquiries.'

'In that direction?'

Blazek shrugged. 'It was this way last week.'

'No, no, I think not,' said the policeman sternly. 'Are you telling the truth? Where are your identification papers?'

Blazek reached into his coat pocket and pulled out a soiled manila envelope. He handed it to the policeman, who shook his head. 'You take them out.'

Blazek did as he was told, handing a card and a sheet of paper to the policeman who was doing all the talking. The other one was simply standing there, staring down hard at Jack. Jack did his best to ignore the scrutiny, but every so often, when he looked up, he found those penetrating eyes still on his face. It was very disconcerting and made him feel very uncomfortable. Had he been in his own country, in his own time, Jack might have asked what was wrong, why he was being glared at, but he was wise enough to remain silent for the moment.

27

The first policeman flicked through Blazek's papers with a bored look on his face, but then said, 'The stamped date is not clear – is this the seventh month? Or January?'

'January, I think.'

'You *think*?'

'It is difficult to remember – it was five years ago. Look, it is not my fault the date stamp is faint. It is the fault of the stamp. There was not enough ink on the rubber to make it clear.'

'Are you accusing the official?'

'No – I'm not accusing anyone. Perhaps the official was trying to conserve ink, thus saving government money. Perhaps he was a very diligent man. I don't know.'

'You two had better accompany us,' said the policeman, putting Blazek's papers in his pocket. 'Come! This can more easily be sorted out at the station.'

Blazek protested. 'There's nothing to sort out. The papers are in good order. They've been seen a hundred times before without any trouble.'

The second policeman spoke for the first time.

'Perhaps those who looked at them did not notice that the papers were out of date?'

'They're not out of date.'

'That's what we must determine,' said the first policeman. 'How can we tell if we cannot read them? You realise it is a grave offence to walk the streets without proper papers? You could go to prison for a long time for using a false identification card.'

Exasperation showed in Blazek's features.

'False? Who said anything about them being false? They

28

are genuine identification papers. Why are you doing this to me? I am a good citizen. I pay my taxes. I have nothing to hide.'

'So, what is a short walk to the police station? Nothing. Is your time so very precious? Who is the boy? Where are his papers?'

'A distant cousin, come from the country.'

The policeman was impassive. 'I repeat, where are his papers?'

'With his mother,' replied Blazek, gesturing weakly. 'We thought it safer to leave them at home. The boy loses everything that he touches.'

'You'd better come with us,' said the second policeman, as if they had not ordered this before.

While all this had been going on, Jack had been disconcerted to notice someone else in the street. It was a shadowy figure, lean and wasted, almost translucent. If it was a man, it was a man of dark mist, with a hat and a long coat that reached almost to his ankles. The shape of a tall thin person was there, certainly, but he was just too far away, and on the edge of the shade from the buildings, to be made out clearly. He seemed to be watching Jack rather intently.

Jack and Blazek were marched down the street. When Jack looked back, the shadow-man was gone. They were taken up the grey steps of a grim-looking building, through a doorway flanked by chipped statues of lions. Their footsteps echoed on the tiled floor of a large hallway. Huge marble pillars, also aged and chipped, shouldered the high ceiling. It was a cold and miserable place, with a wooden counter behind which sat a bulky police sergeant on a high stool. Jack and Blazek were presented to this man and then left to give their details, to be laboriously written in a huge ledger. The pen was dipped in a giant inkwell and words scratched onto a page with irritating slowness. Once Blazek had given his name however, he was asked for his papers.

'I don't have them. The constable took them from me,' he explained. 'They are in his left pocket.'

The sergeant looked up and frowned. 'You don't have your papers? That's a very serious business. You should never let your papers leave your person.'

'But he took them from me. I had no choice.'

'You expect me to believe that? Why would the constable do such a thing? Your papers are your property.'

Blazek almost shouted, 'Ask him! He has them now.'

'That particular constable has gone off duty,' replied the sergeant, 'and yelling at me will do you no good. I'm an officer of the law. I am entitled to respect. I'm afraid if you can't produce your papers I am going to have to put you in the cells . . .'

Jack panicked. If he was jailed he would never be able to find his mother and father. He turned on his heel and ran. Fortunately no one was between him and the outside world. He flew through the doorway and almost fell down the stone steps. He heard shouting behind him, but no one came after him. After running for a few minutes he reached the end of the street where Mr Kafka's house stood. With his heart pounding he raced up to it and knocked on the door. It seemed an age before it was opened by Franz.

'Why, Jack, what is it?' asked Franz. He looked down the street both ways. 'Where's Blazek?'

Jack asked to come inside, then once in the house explained breathlessly what had happened.

'Will the police come round here?' asked Annie. 'Will you get into trouble?'

Franz shook his head. 'Blazek will not give this address – he'll give his own. I don't know how he'll explain Jack, but he'll think of something. These are very trying times, but they can't last for ever. I myself am being taken to court for something soon – I don't know what it is yet. I've been attempting to find out.'

'You don't *know*?' said Annie. 'Won't they tell you?'

'I can't seem to find anyone who knows anything about it. I have received the summons through the post. But anybody I speak to has never heard of me.' He stared at Annie with those haunted eyes. 'It is best not to enquire too much, even about things that are important to one's future.'

Davey was behind Franz and out of his sight, and Jack caught his younger brother tapping the side of his head, as if to say, 'We've got a right nutcase here.' He frowned at Davey, whose face cleared and who then said brightly, 'Anyone for ping-pong?'

'What are you talking about, Davey?' asked Jack.

Annie explained. 'Davey and Franz have been playing table tennis on the living-room table, using books as a net. Franz is good at ping-pong.'

'I find it helps me to relax,' said Franz. 'I like the sound of the ball.'

The rest of the day was spent fretting and worrying, listening for a knock on the door, despite Franz's earlier assurance that Blazek would not reveal the address. No one came, however. Franz continued to quiz the children about the British Isles and constantly scribbled in a notebook. Jack and Annie tried to avoid any references to the twenty-first century, though Davey let slip one or two things that puzzled Franz.

The children were curious about the city in which they had landed, and asked their own questions.

Franz told them, 'Prague is the capital of Bohemia. We are ruled by the Austrian Empire. Some seek self-government, which makes Austria very nervous. And of course there are always the anarchists. I think the police confuse anarchists with alchemists, which is probably why they are jailing those seekers of the elixir of life.'

'What's an anarchist?' asked Davey.

Franz said, 'Someone who doesn't like goverment - any government.'

'Sounds a bit scary,' muttered Annie. 'The sooner we find Mum and Dad, the better.'

Franz seemed to realise he had worried the children, and he added, 'There are many things to love about my city too, though. The music, for example. We love music and you'll find it everywhere in Prague. The architecture is famed throughout the world - the Charles Bridge, the palaces, the churches. There are also many legends. Some say there is a creature of clay called the Golem, who stalks the narrow streets at night. Others say that Golden Lane, a cobbled passageway no wider than an alley, is where the alchemists still strive to unravel the secret of turning base metals into pure gold, and to discover the elixir of eternal life. However,' he added, 'in Golden Lane they are said to burn the philosopher's stone and poison the moonbeams.'

'Poison the moonbeams?' cried Annie. 'That sounds like occult magic! It could be the plot for a short story.'

'Ah – you think so?' murmured Franz. 'I think so too. Do you write short stories?'

'Yes,' said Annie, a little hesitantly. 'But tell us more about the alchemists. Do they just want gold?'

'No, as I said, they seek eternal life, free from disease. Their efforts at trying to discover the secret of turning ordinary metals into precious metals like gold and silver are merely sidelines to finding the secret of immortality. Alchemy originated, some say, in Egypt - which was called Khem by the Arabs - where the goldsmiths were among the most artistic metalworkers in the world. But there appears to be mysticism and magic in their chemistry. Even the most ordinary of chemical recipes is full of dark symbols and cryptic characters, which is why they are accused of being sorcerers. Anything that goes wrong in Prague while the alchemists are here - be it fire or flood - they will be blamed for it. They will be accused of creating chaos.'

'But they don't - create chaos, I mean?'

'Not, I think, on purpose. But who knows what dark incantations do to the minds of people? Perhaps a mantra is capable of turning a mild person into a mad one who runs amok with a bladed weapon. The mind is a strange and wonderful device, difficult to predict.'

'Oh.'

Jack asked, 'Who's this Golem?'

'The word *golem* means "shapeless mass". He is what

some might call a monster, created by Rabbi Judah Loew ben Bezalel in the fifteenth century, so that he could protect the Jewish population of Prague. They were much oppressed in those times, the Jews of Prague. The rabbi made the Golem of clay gathered from the banks of the river Vltava. He's supposed to be a silly creature, but with a good heart. I would not like to get on his bad side. Such a creature could crush your head like a walnut, had he a mind to.'

'You talk about him as if he was still alive,' said Annie.

'Perhaps he is, perhaps he isn't. It would make a good story one day. It is said that he has the letters *aleph, mem, tav* – meaning "truth" written on his forehead. If one rubs off the letter *aleph* then the Golem is left with *mem, tav* – meaning "death". This is the only way to stop him from crushing you. Interesting, eh?'

Annie shuddered. 'I suppose so.'

'But Annie – you too write stories?'

'I try,' replied Annie. 'I'm writing one at the moment – at home, that is – called "Lightning Rod".'

'And what is it about?'

Annie became animated. Few people had asked her about her stories before, apart from her parents. Her brothers treated her passion for writing fiction as something akin to smallpox and kept away from her while she was on her laptop in case they caught the same disease. Even now, after Franz's question, Jack was edging away from her.

'It's about a boy called Rodney who gets struck by lightning in a storm,' she told Franz. 'He becomes full of electricity.'

'How exciting,' breathed the young Bohemian. 'Then what happens?'

'Well, paper sticks to him and when he puts his hands on iron railings they crackle and spark.'

'Oh yes?'

'Yes, but Rod can secretly release thousands of volts if he wants to – when his dad's key fob gets locked in the car, the motor car that is, Rod puts his hands on the bonnet and lets go a thousand volts, and all the locks fly open.'

Franz's face showed puzzlement. 'Key fob?'

'Ah,' said Annie in disappointment, remembering that such things had not been invented by 1903. 'Well, anyway, the locks undo.'

'Yes, locks might react in that manner – electricity is a powerful force.' ·

'And after letting go so much electricity, small metal objects fly at Rod and stick to his body. The kids at school are fascinated by him – one girl in particular . . .'

'Ah, the romantic part of the story. A happy ending.' Franz sighed deeply. 'I like happy endings, though I cannot write them myself. All my own stories have quite melancholy endings.'

'Well, it's not a happy ending, you see; in fact it's quite tragic, because when she kisses Rod her hair stands on end and her whole body tingles like mad. She's spoiled for the rest of her life because no one else can ever kiss her like that again, or give her the same thrill. She will grow old and – and *melancholy* knowing she has experienced the ultimate kiss.' Annie added, 'I think sad endings are *deeper*, don't you? People don't take you seriously if you write a happy ending.'

'You could be right. Your story deserves to be taken seri-ously. Thank you for telling it to me.'

Annie felt something close to bliss. This Bohemian writer, Franz Kafka, had listened to one of her stories. Well, not all of it, but some of it, and he had listened intently. He was not yet famous himself, but he would be one day, and there would be those who would envy Annie were they to know she had captured the ear of this quiet man. He had not criticised her plot, nor had he offered his own version of what she *should* have written. Most people did both. Franz had simply listened and intimated his approval. That was the mark of a great man, Annie thought.

Just before they went to bed that night, Jack said to Annie, 'No matter what, we've got to look for Mum and Dad. We can't just sit here and wait for them to release Blazek. We've got to take matters into our own hands. Franz is OK, but there's not much action about him, is there? It's up to us. We've got to do it.'

'I agree, but what about Davey? Do we leave him here or take him with us?'

Jack frowned. 'That's a tricky one. If we leave him, he'll get bored and you know how antsy he can get if he's got nothing to do. He'll drive Franz up the wall. I suppose we'd better take him with us, but I hope he doesn't play up.'

'We'll warn him how dangerous it is – he'll surely take notice if he knows that,' said Annie, yawning. 'Oh, I hope we find Mum and Dad soon. I don't like all this.'

4.   WHERE'S DAVEY?

The following morning the children woke with a low winter sun streaming through the windows. It was very cold, though, especially the floor under their bare feet. Jack put some clothes on very quickly, telling himself that he would wash later. He had seen the great bath, of course. It was a huge metal job with dragon's feet that looked as if it could swallow an elephant whole. It would probably take a score of copper kettles to fill it full enough for a good wash. When he did use it, he knew he would be tempted to keep his overcoat on.

Jack told Davey to get dressed in the clothes he had been given by Franz and impressed on his young brother the need to keep his mouth closed when out in the street.

'I speak just as good German as you do,' argued Davey, through a mouthful of rye bread and dense cheese that Franz had given them for breakfast. 'Mum taught me just the same as you.'

'It's not whether you can do it or not, it's what you say, Davey. You might say the wrong thing and arouse suspicions. Listen, mate, this is important. Very important. We could end up in the salt mines if we're found out.'

'What salt mines?'

'I don't know, any salt mines. It's just a figure of speech. Prison. Jail. Whatever they have here. Dungeons by the look of the police station. Promise me you'll be good, Davey, or we can't take you with us and you'll have to play ping-pong all day with Franz.'

'He's a weirdo. He says weird things.'

'Well it's your choice, buddy.'

Davey heaved a sigh. 'I'll keep my trap shut.'

'Good man. OK, let's go and find your sister.'

Davey swallowed a lump of cheese whole, before asking, 'Don't they have any cornflakes or Coco Pops here? I'm fed up with this cheese. It smells rotten anyway. And the bread's stale.'

'We have to eat what's available,' Annie said, coming into the room. 'They don't have modern foods yet. It's not stale, it's rye bread. Rye bread is supposed to be hard. We'll try to get some fruit when we go out, some oranges, if Franz will lend us the money. I'll ask him.'

Franz gave them a little money, but he told them they would be lucky to find fruit, since it was winter. Someone might have a few shrivelled apples, but oranges? He doubted it. Some winter cabbage, perhaps, but that was not fruit. How about some nuts? There would be hot chestnuts for sale, he was sure.

When Franz saw them out of the door, he looked up at the sky and said, 'Golden sunlight! Yesterday it was grey sky. It must be the alchemists' doing,' and smiled at the children as if he had just revealed a secret.

Once they were out, Jack discovered there were more people in the streets today and Jack realised that the previous day had been Sunday. Franz had been worried about them leaving the house but agreed that their parents could never be found by sitting around doing nothing. The lean, shadowy-faced young man told them to be very careful and not to trust any strangers. Since everyone was a stranger it was difficult for Jack to know how to go about asking questions.

The children walked around Old Town Square without arousing any suspicions. Annie admired some of the buildings, especially Tyn Church, which had fairytale twin towers. There was a pie-seller on the corner and Davey tugged at Jack's coat, trying to tell him he wanted one. Jack bought three and they ate them within seconds. Rye bread and cheese did not do for them what it did for Bohemians.

They then began to walk towards the river and the Charles Bridge, peering at buildings on the way, hoping to find some sort of information bureau. Annie decided to take the bull by the horns and took out a photo of her parents. She began showing it to people, asking if they had seen the faces in the photograph. A woman looked surprised and asked how it was the picture was in colour. Annie, jolted into a quick reply, told the woman it had been 'painted'.

Jack was a little worried by his sister's boldness. He soon realised he was right to be, for he noticed they were being watched and followed by a man in a long dark coat and black hat. He thought the man might belong to the secret police, and when two other men joined him, he was certain. There was the possibility of the three children being taken for orphans and sent to work somewhere, either on the land, or in a factory.

'Quickly!' Jack cried, taking Davey's hand. 'Down this alley!'

The three of them ran down the alley, dodging people as they did so, with their pursuers close on their heels. They were in a part of the city that was a maze of streets. Ducking and diving down alleys and narrow lanes, they managed to stay ahead of their pursuers. When they emerged from a series of passageways and found themselves close to the river, Jack realised they had lost the men chasing them. He bent over, hands on his knees, gasping for breath. He could hear Annie wheezing a bit too, close by. Then came a cry of anguish.

'What is it?' said Jack, his head coming up sharply. 'Are they here?'

'It's Davey,' wailed Annie. 'He's not with us!'

Jack looked about him frantically. Annie was right. Davey was nowhere to be seen. Panicking, Jack ran back to the last alley and looked along it. Still no Davey. He retraced his steps. No Davey in sight. Had he been caught by the secret police? Or had he simply taken a different turning by accident? Maybe — Jack's conscience hit him hard here — maybe Davey had not been able to keep up with his two elder siblings? But he was normally electric on his feet. He was the fastest in his year at cross country. He could run like a rabbit being chased by a fox.

Jack trudged back to where Annie was waiting. When she looked at his face, she burst into tears. 'What are we going to do?' she cried.

'I dunno,' replied Jack wearily. 'It was my fault. I should've stayed with him.'

'It was both our faults. We should have both watched out for him.'

'Sorry, Annie.'

'But what are we going to do?'

Jack said, almost in despair, 'We've got *three* people to find now — the sooner we get started, the better. Let's go back as far as we dare. It we see those men again, we know we can outrun them.'

So they started back, wandering the alleys and byways again, not really knowing where they were going but trusting to providence that they would find their younger brother. It was a hopeless task, of course, more difficult than finding a needle in a haystack, since they did not know whether they were even looking in the right haystack.

At one point they found themselves in a darkened cul-de-sac. As they turned to leave, their way was blocked by a little horned creature about half the height of a human. It stared at them with yellow eyes as it raised two huge hands with long fingernails.

'Jack?' cried Annie. 'What is it?'

The strange little creature seemed about to spring at Annie when someone from behind it gave it an enormous kick and sent it flying through the air. It howled hellishly as it went, ending up on the gutter of a roof. It shook a gnarled fist at the children, but then it was gone, over the rooftops, amongst the forest of chimneys.

The two children turned to thank their rescuer, only to see a huge figure in a black cloak. It was impossible to tell whether his features were kind or hostile in the rapidly descending darkness, especially in that lightless alleyway. All they could make out was a big, brutish and bulky shape blocking their way.

41

'Oh heck,' muttered Jack, his heart racing.

He noticed that Annie had gone white with fear.

The giant figure spoke in a language Jack did not understand, so Jack said, '*Deutsch, bitte.*'

'Ah,' growled the giant, 'you speak German? I want to tell you not to be afraid of that *cert*. He is gone now.'

'*Cert*?' said Annie.

'That little devil. Ah – I see you are concerned about me, too? Because I am big? I mean you no harm. I am just on my way home, before I am seen by people.'

'We are people,' Jack pointed out.

'You are foreign children, which is not so important,' said the bulky giant in those rasping tones. 'If I am seen by local men, they will know who I am.'

'And who are you?' asked Annie, trying to look under the brim of the broad hat to see the eyes beneath.

'Ah – that I cannot tell you. If I did, you would know as much as I do myself.'

His words sounded rather silly to the two children and, despite his fear, Jack let out a loud laugh which startled the man.

'You make fun of me?' snarled the giant. 'Why do you do this?'

'No, no – really. It was a nervous laugh,' explained Jack, truthfully. 'I do that when I'm scared sometimes.'

'Scared? Why should you be afraid? I've said I will not harm you. And I can smell tears. One of you has been crying. The girl, I think. Why have you been sobbing? Who has made you sad?'

Jack studied the huge bulky figure, but it was impossible

to see his face beneath the many folds of that cape, or below the brim of the hat, especially in the early winter darkness that was now descending upon the city. The giant's hands were gloved too. Jack sensed a strangeness beyond normality in his bearing. There was a lumpiness about him, a leadenness that held him fast to the earth. If a car were to hit this big figure, Jack decided, it would crumple. The giant was an immovable object; rocks would bounce off him.

'We've lost our younger brother,' replied Annie, 'and we're strangers here.'

'Where have you been staying?'

Jack gave the man Franz's address, but the giant shook his head.

'I do not know where this house is situated.'

Annie then intervened and told the gigantic man their story, of losing their parents, then their little brother. Before too long his eyes were moist and he was shaking his head, murmuring that their troubles were many and difficult. 'Children should not be burdened with such things,' he maintained. 'They should be left free to do their schooling and to play their games.' He wiped his eyes with a huge handkerchief, then vowed he would do all he could for them, because, he said, he had been brought on the earth so that he could help those in need. 'Let me take you to a friend of mine. He will help you. You cannot stay with me – my house is far too small for just me, let alone visitors.'

Jack could imagine that there would be little space left in a normal-sized room once this man had entered. He was indeed a massive figure and looked to have great strength. Being so large and powerful, he need not be concerned by any other man, friend or foe. Yet, Jack thought, there seemed to be a soft core to him.

They followed the giant through the twilight and out of the alley. He led them down a long passageway at the end of which they found themselves in a very narrow street. A lamplighter with his pole was just leaving the other end, having lit the lamps all along the road. Halfway along this street, there was an even smaller alley, which the giant could barely squeeze along to reach another thin passageway that wove like a ribbon through a set of terraced houses barely wider than their own front doors.

'This is my little house,' he remarked as they passed a yellow mews house which was indeed quite small. He reached into a coat pocket and produced a large iron key. 'This is the key to my door, should you ever need my help again. Don't worry about finding this street, the key is a magnetic one that will lead you to its lock. It is like a compass, this key: you hold it lightly by its ring between two fingers – so – and you will see it will point the way you must go. Follow the direction of the key and you will find me. Ah, here we are at the house of Dvorak, the seeker of gold and everlasting life.'

Annie took the key from the giant's great fingers.

Jack and Annie were then led to a red door set deeply in a house very similar to that of the giant man. The giant bent down to lift the knocker, which was like a paperclip in his fingers. Soon there came the sound of footsteps and the grumbling of a low voice full of irritation. Finally the voice rose and asked, 'Who's there?'

'It's me,' growled Annie and Jack's companion.

'What do you want?'

'I have some children with me – they are lost.' He looked down as Annie shivered. 'And cold.'

'Well – let them find themselves.'

'Open the door, Dvorak, you old fool,' growled the giant, changing his tone, 'or I'll knock it down with my little finger. I have no patience with you.'

There was more grumbling and the sounds of bolts being drawn, then finally the door inched open and a chin poked out.

'Why do you bother me, you great lump?' snarled an old man with a bent frame and lank grey hair hanging to his shoulders. 'Don't you know I'm always busy?'

'Busy chasing rainbows,' replied the giant disparagingly.

'You won't say that when I uncover the great secret.'

'No, I won't, because you never will. Look, these children have nowhere to go tonight. I insist you take them in. At least they will be warm. See, the weather turns worse,' said the giant as soft flakes of snow began to drift down, glinting in the jaundiced glow of the gas lamps. He laid a massive hand on Annie's shoulder, but his touch was so light she hardly felt it. 'Also,' he said in that grating voice he could not seem to soften, 'they have lost a young brother. The boy is somewhere in the city and they do not know his where-abouts.'

'Is that my fault?' cried Dvorak. 'Do I have to become a home for lost souls because of that?'

'Yes,' came the simple reply.

'Oh, very well.' The door opened wider to let the chil-dren enter. 'But don't touch anything,' Dvorak warned them.

'If there's so much as an iron filing out of place, you'll be back on the street. What are your names?'

Annie said, 'Thank you – Jack and Annie.'

'Which one of you is Thankyou? No, don't answer that,' said Dvorak with a wave of his hand. 'It's a joke. I'm a man of cheerful disposition, as you can tell by my smiling face.' His face was actually hideously pitted. 'Off you go, big fellow. I'll see you in the morning.'

Jack said to the giant, 'We are very grateful for your help. What do we call you? Do you have a name?'

'You can call me Friend.'

'Well, thank you, Friend,' Annie said, 'for everything.'

'Think nothing of it,' growled the giant. 'Happy to be of service.'

Dvorak led the children down a hallway. When they entered the room at the end, they were truly amazed by what they saw. Not a sofa or a soft chair was there in sight. Instead, the place was cluttered with junk: metal objects that had once been useful, but were now broken or bent out of proper employment. Where the fireplace would be in a normal house was a red-hot furnace that filled the home with heat. It was more like a blacksmith's forge than a living room. Over the furnace itself was a cauldron in which something was bubbling.

'Is that beef soup simmering in the pot?' asked Annie, hopefully. 'Or mutton stew perhaps?'

'Neither,' replied Dvorak, cackling. 'It's molten metal.'

5.   FRIENDS OF FRIEND

'You'd burn your pretty little lips on *that* soup, girlie,' sniggered Dvorak. 'Oh yes indeed.'

'Please don't call me "girlie",' said Annie. 'You know my name.'

'Oh, very correct, aren't we?'

Annie said. 'I know you're being kind, letting us stay here the night, but we ought to get on better with one another, don't you think? Jack, tell him.'

'Don't mess my sister about, please, Mr Dvorak,' Jack said in the sternest voice he could muster. 'I realise you weren't happy about us coming in here, but we haven't got a lot of choice. We'd freeze to death out there in the streets. Why can't we just shake hands and make the best of it, and we'll be out of your hair in the morning.'

Dvorak extended a gnarled and bony hand which felt like cold greaseproof paper to Jack's touch. Jack tried not to wince, but failed to hide his revulsion as Dvorak gripped his fingers.

'Old skin,' said Dvorak, wearing a horrible lopsided smile on his scarred features. 'You'll have it one day. Well now, we're all friends, eh? You two sound like foreigners to me, with that strange German accent. Police after you, are they? Never mind, they're after everyone. They'd have the lot of us in jail if they had enough cells to hold us. As for me, I'm going to be as rich as Croesus one of these days.' He stared at the forge through slitted eyes. 'I'm close. Very close. Just a few more adjustments, a bit of this and a bit of that. I'm so close I can smell the gold in that liquid iron . . .'

Annie gasped. She could think more quickly than Jack. She said, 'You're an *alchemist*?'

Dvorak clapped, his eyes sparkling for the first time. 'Oh, you make it sound so devilishly clever. It is diabolical, my chosen profession. And worthy of a genius like myself. Gold, out of base metal. I am so very close. I'm not sure whether it's the incantations that are the problem, or the balance of the mix. But I'll find it. I'll find it. You can sleep on the rugs at the back of the room. No need for blankets. This place is like an oven at all times. Ah, you're looking at my face, boy. Is it the marks?'

Jack admitted that it was. 'Have you had a disease, sir?'

'No, it wasn't smallpox or anything like that,' replied Dvorak. Then, after a thoughtful pause, he added, 'Unless you count an obsession as a disease of the mind – I am obsessed with finding the secret of turning ordinary ore into precious metal. These pits were made by pots of molten metal spitting into my face. Nickel, copper, iron. I melt them down, mix them together, say the words over them. Tears of white-hot iron or copper have buried themselves into my features, like tiny meteors flung from the ether. I'm ugly, aren't I?'

Annie said politely, 'No, not ugly – you have an *interesting* face.'

'Ha! I like that. *Interesting*. You lie, of course. I am ugly. But I don't care. Rich people don't care how they look. And I shall be rich. Rich and famous. I will be the envy of all Europe.'

48

'Sir,' said Jack, 'can you tell us about this giant of a man who calls himself Friend.'

'That's what he calls himself, is it? Well then, that's what he must be. He's a gentle enough creature, unless roused – and always has been, since those far-off times. And climb? He can scale a vertical wall with his fingertips and make it look easy. He was made, you see, to protect the weak. Someone like that needs strength and agility. He's got both. But very little brain. A stupid fellow.'

'I didn't think he was stupid,' protested Annie.

'Well you wouldn't,' retorted Dvorak. 'You haven't a bad word to say about anyone, have you?'

'But *made*?' repeated Jack. 'Life isn't made – is it?'

'If you have the power it is,' replied Dvorak. 'Look at me! I'm trying to make the great elixir. That's making life, isn't it, to prolong it beyond its natural length? Yes, yes, I think so. To cheat death. But how does one know if it is working?' He reached up to a shelf on which there were rows of dusty bottles, filled with coloured potions. 'This one, see – I think this is the one. I have taken this, and as you see, am still alive after seventy long years. But would I still be alive if I had *not* taken the potion? There's the rub, children. It's a terrible puzzle. The sad thing is, if I die, I will not be around to adjust the potion by adding this or that to it. I shall be dead and this will be tossed away with the rubbish, considered to be yet another alchemist's failure, when it might be just a drop of bat's blood away from success. You see how frustrating it all is? There is no sure way to test my magic draught.'

Jack cleared his throat and said, 'You said *since those far-off times*. When was that?'

'Why, in the sixteenth century.' Dvorak cackled. 'Our Friend is very old – very old indeed. He wears well, doesn't he? He has the secret of everlasting life, but who would want to be *him*? A cold, clammy thing, not even human.'

'I don't believe he can be that old,' said Annie firmly. 'You shouldn't make fun of him like that.'

'Oh, shouldn't I?'

'No – just because he's big doesn't make him stupid. You should be more understanding of people who – who are not quite of normal stature. You're shrivelled and old, that's why you say these things. You're jealous of him because he's fit and sturdy. You're envious because he's young-looking, and you're not.'

'It's true,' murmured the alchemist, 'that the heat from the furnace has dried me to a crisp shell. It's true that my skin is like crumpled wax paper. But I am a *man*. No matter what I look like, no matter if I'm so dried up you can see through me like a threadbare sheet hanging on the line in the morning sun, I'm still a man.'

The hot room was becoming dim, with only the light from the forge to illuminate it, so Dvorak lit a brass oil lamp and hung it from a cord that dangled from the ceiling. Shadows sprang up and began to move around the walls of the room to the swinging of the lamp. Dvorak's small, deep-set eyes seemed to grow brighter along with the lantern's flame. In the jaundiced light his wrinkles were more heavily engraved in his thin face and he suddenly appeared more ancient than the years he professed to be.

'Never mock an alchemist in his own home,' Dvorak murmured, 'for we are surely powerful magicians, though we might seem merely philosophers and charlatans. I can make a three-legged wooden stool walk the room and cause teaspoons to dance in a saucer. Ah! Your face! You sneer, eh? You think I can't do these things. Watch . . .'

Jack and Annie were startled to see a corner stool take several halting steps towards the centre of the stone floor.

'Hey!' cried Jack, turning pale. 'How did you do that?'

'It's still in the same place,' Annie stated, more to convince herself than Jack. 'It's – it's hypnotism.'

Two teaspoons then stood on end in a dirty saucer and began a clinking dance around its rim.

'Hypnotism,' repeated Annie, as firmly as she could. 'Really, Jack, we shouldn't encourage him.'

The teaspoons fell over with a clatter.

'Can I make you hear things too?' cried Dvorak. 'Are your ears hypnotised along with your eyes?'

Jack decided to let Dvorak have his own way. Perhaps he really was a sorcerer. Jack felt both tired and hungry, and he knew his sister must feel the same. He asked Dvorak if there was anything to eat and was told there was, if he could be patient. Some time later, as Jack's head was lolling to one side, and Annie looked to be similarly drooping, they were given stew of lamb, potatoes and cabbage. It was the best thing Jack had ever tasted. He wolfed it down with a chunk of bread, and then tottered to the rugs in the corner of the room and fell fast asleep to the flaring of the furnace.

In the middle of the night, Jack woke to see that Dvorak was pouring bubbling, spitting molten metal from one iron tumbler into another. There was a piebald dog standing on its hind legs, tongue lolling out with concentration, holding some large black tongs that gripped the second iron tumbler. Dvorak's face was shining with an expression of triumph as he nodded to the dog. The white-hot fluid looked like liquid moonlight, it shone so yellow and bright. A drop missed the edge of the second tumbler and splashed on to the floor, solidifying when it hit the cold flagstones, making a small sun. He's poisoning the moonbeams, thought Jack in a muzzy-headed way. He's stealing the sun's rays and turning them into gold. But he fell asleep again almost immediately, and afterwards was not sure whether he had dreamed what he had seen, or whether the midnight scene had been real.

The next morning everything seemed to be quite normal: normal, that is, given that two children from the twenty-first century were visiting a foreign city in 1903. Dvorak gave the children a breakfast of buns and coffee. He had obviously been out early to get the buns, which Annie told him was very kind of him. Dvorak pretended he did not care for these expressions of gratitude, but the children could see he was pleased with the praise. After they had eaten and taken turns at washing from a bowl in front of the furnace, Jack and Annie set off again, to scour the streets for their brother and show the 'painted' photo of their parents. This time they kept a wary eye open for any sinister-looking characters, hoping to stay one step ahead of the secret police.

At the end of the day they were no closer to finding either Davey, Roger or Kate, and were on the verge of despair. They went back to Franz's house, but were upset when no one answered their knock. So Annie took out the giant's key and gave it to Jack because, he insisted, boys were more technical than girls.

'What a load of rubbish,' she said, but she knew he liked things like compasses and maps, which did not interest her at all.

Jack held the large iron key by the ring end, very lightly, and it behaved like a divining rod, wavering and turning in his fingers to point in a particular direction. The key also had a pull to it, as if it were indeed strangely drawn. But even as they followed its bidding, Jack was puzzled as to how it really worked. He knew about compasses: they pointed roughly towards the North Pole in line with the Earth's magnetic field. That was magical enough for him. But this key obeyed more than natural laws; there was something rather odd about a key that knew its way to its lock, like a boat heading for its harbour. It was no longer natural, but *preter*natural.

Their 'key compass' led them through streets and alleys until finally they came to the heart of the labyrinth and found Golden Lane, the narrow street where Dvorak lived. Several times during that walk, Jack saw the strange dark figure, the wasted-looking man, out of the corner of his eye. He did not seem to be following them as a policeman would, but simply stood and watched from a distance. This featureless creature hovered like a phantom on the edge of Jack's reason: black-hatted, black-coated, insubstantial. Jack had noticed him several times, usually when he was lost somewhere in the streets of Prague and was searching to find a way.

'Do you see him?' he whispered to his sister. 'That ghost thingy?'

'Yes,' murmured Annie. 'I thought you *hadn't*. I try to

ignore him. We've got enough to worry about already.'

'So do I,' replied Jack in a determined tone. 'I think that's best, don't you? You – you don't think we could be mad?'

'Not both of us,' his sister replied sensibly. 'Not both of us at once.'

Once in Golden Lane, they did not bother Friend, but instead went directly to the house of Dvorak, who did not seem at all pleased to see them.

'You two back again, eh?'

Nevertheless, he opened the door and they went in.

Jack and Annie were surprised to see a group of people in the room as they entered. They stared with hostile eyes at the two children and looked hard at Dvorak. Dvorak shrugged his shoulders, saying, 'What was I to do? Turn them out into the night?'

'I don't like it,' said a rugged-looking man. 'How do we know they aren't spies?'

A woman said, 'I think they *are* spies. I've seen them around Old Town Square, asking questions.'

Annie told them quickly, 'We're not spies – we're looking for our family. They've been arrested for some reason.'

'Arrested?' cried the woman. 'That's even worse. We have a pair of wanted criminals in the house. I say we simply throw this pair off the Charles Bridge into the river. She,' the woman pointed at Annie, 'has an outlander accent.'

'What's that got to do with anything?' said Jack. 'First you accuse us of being government spies, then of being criminals. We can't be both. Make up your mind.'

'I'll make my mind up for you,' cried the woman, rising from her seat. 'You insolent child . . .'

'These children are under the protection of my neighbour and friend,' Dvorak told the room. 'He has taken to them in a strong way. You know who I mean.'

The woman went pale and sat down, looking very shaken.

Jack and Annie went quietly to a corner, leaving this group, who appeared to be alchemists like Dvorak. After a while a young man with a sharp face came and sat with them. He seemed to be sympathetic to their plight, asking them about their parents and brother.

'It's very difficult,' he told them. 'People disappear every day. Of course, some of them want to.'

'I don't think our parents vanished on purpose,' said Annie. 'That would be very silly.'

'I suppose it would,' said the young man. 'My name is Kaspar. I'm a friend of Dvorak, not an alchemist like the rest of them – I'm a gazer – but I'm useful to them as a middleman. Where are you from, by the way? And how did you find your way into the mystical Golden Lane? The byways and alleys that lead here are a complex maze – even the authorities cannot find us, which is why we can hold these meetings without fear of disturbance.'

Jack told Kaspar their names and that they came from London. It seemed simpler than trying to explain that they were from the twenty-first century.

'We found this street by accident, running away from the police.'

Kaspar said, 'Ah, that's the *only* way to find it. And this little brother of yours. No doubt he simply got picked up by the police and put in an orphanage, or an institution of some kind.'

'You really think so?' said Annie.

'It's a strong possibility.'

The group of alchemists were now gathered around a large old oak table in a separate room. They had left the door ajar and Jack could see that the table's surface had been burned and pitted by stray spits from Dvorak's experiments. The group all wore intent expressions on their faces and whispered to each other. Jack noticed several obvious foreigners amongst them. One was an Arab in a green turban and a black-and-yellow gown. Another looked as if she came from the Indian subcontinent, in a beautiful blue sari trimmed with silver. A third, in a fur coat, might have been from Mongolia or the Russian steppes. Certainly there was an exotic mixture of races and cultures around that table.

Kaspar nodded towards the room saying, 'It's very difficult for them. They're here ostensibly to exchange ideas, but their work is by its very name and nature a deadly secret. "Alchemy" is from an Arabic word, *al-khimia*, which means "the secret art". They want to be told things, but they don't want to tell them. So they sit there trying to extract knowledge from each other without giving anything away themselves – never really getting down to the business of exchanging the cryptic information each of them knows will lead to the elixir of life, or the transmutation of common metals into gold. I'm sure all those alchemists around that table have the collective answer to their eternal questions, but each of them has only part of it – and they find it almost impossible to share that piece with the others. It's a real tragedy. I don't expect they'll get any further with this conference than they have with others.'

'Is this the only group in Prague?' asked Annie.

'Oh no, there'll be others in the houses along Golden Lane, just like this group, just as tongue-tied when it comes to sharing secrets.'

'Sounds a bit selfish to me,' sniffed Annie, 'to spend your life searching for something to make you rich. When you find it, it won't be worth anything.'

'How do you make that out?' asked Jack.

Kaspar said, 'I know what your sister means. One reason gold is so precious is because it's rare. If it becomes common, then it loses its value. But they don't really do it to make themselves wealthy. They are genuine enthusiasts, seeking knowledge. What they are all really after are two great achievements – freedom from disease, and everlasting life. Even the experiments with turning metals into gold and silver are part of this goal. As their search has gone on over the centuries, alchemists have contributed much to the world of science. It was they who invented gunpowder and who produced the first inks, dyes and paints. Their discoveries helped with leather-tanning, ceramics and glass manufacture.'

'Oh. Well, I don't think gunpowder was such a good thing, do you?' said Annie primly.

'Not what it was used for, but the power it has could have been used, perhaps *has* been used, for better purposes.'

'Ah – look, one of them has something the others would give their hearts for . . .'

Around the table there was high excitement, as the Arab gentleman suddenly took out a red silk handkerchief containing something heavy-looking. He placed it in the middle of the table and unfolded it, revealing what looked to the children like a small chunk of pumice, such as the one they had in their bathroom at home. All the heads around the table bent inwards, to stare at this object.

'A piece of the Philosopher's Stone,' murmured Kaspar to Jack and Annie. 'Or so our man from the east maintains.'

'I know what that is,' Annie said. 'It's a magic stone.'

'Well, it's supposed to be the key that will unlock the secrets of life, but if that was the real thing, why has he brought it here? Why would he show it to this crowd of secret-stealers? No, he's probably almost sure it's a fake, but wants confirmation of it from others of his kind. I'm glad my discipline is different from theirs. Their work seems so much harder, being caught up in a tangle of thorny uncertainties.'

'Your work?' asked Annie, then remembered. 'Oh, you said you were a *gazer*. What's that?'

'I can see far-off things, in my crystal.'

Jack was naturally sceptical. 'Really?'

Kaspar smiled. 'You don't believe me? Well, I'm not offended. Many people don't . . . Ah, look, the group is breaking up. Nothing done, as I said. They're all going back to their rooms in other parts of the city. They've probably booked into their hotels as carpet sellers, or commercial travellers, or oil magnates. Dvorak,' Kaspar called to their host as he turned from the door when the last person had gone, 'these children don't believe in my powers.'

'Huh!' muttered that gentleman. 'A frippery work – why don't you use your talents for something important?' He dimmed the light, and crossed the room to his forge, leaving the children and Kaspar almost in darkness.

Annie said, 'If you can see far-off things, do you think you could look for our father and mother?'

'Are you offering me work?' said Kaspar, then smiled. 'Of course, let's see what we can do. We'll look for your brother too, though I have to tell you, people are almost always disappointed with the results of these kinds of searches. They are hazy and unsatisfactory.'

Jack felt a stir of excitement in his chest and said, 'Let's try anyway.'

Kaspar reached under his chair and lifted out a small cardboard suitcase, placing it on his knees. When he opened it, there was no sphere, no crystal ball, as Jack had expected. Instead there was a block of wood that looked like a pencil case. When the lid was lifted it revealed a small, smooth-cornered block of crystal, about the size of a bar of soap. The container itself was of dark wood, with dragons and serpents around the base and sides, and Chinese characters inscribed on the rests.

Kaspar placed his hand gently on the block of crystal and began to mutter incantations in a strange tongue, his eyes rolling up into his head. Jack looked at Annie and shook his own head, as if to say, *What have we got here? A nutter?* But once these seeming theatricals were over, Kaspar asked Annie to place her own hand on the crystal, explaining that he needed her 'filial vibrations' to arouse the right 'inscapes' within his far-seeing jewel.

Annie did not quite understand what was going on, but she guessed it was something that was needed to connect her to her parents through the crystal. Indeed, just a few seconds after she had touched the crystal, a misty picture began to form within it.

Jack gasped and almost fell off his stool.

'That's Dad!' he hissed. 'Look, Annie – it's Dad.'

'Yes, yes,' she replied, excited. 'Where is he? What's he doing?'

Their father appeared to be sitting on the edge of some piece of furniture, staring into space. He looked gaunt and thin. All of a sudden he buried his face in his hands, as if in great despair. He was in a small room of some kind, but the details were obscure. It seemed to have stone walls and floor, with hardly any furniture. A few moments later, the back view of their mother appeared. She was looking out of a window, but what lay beyond was not visible in the blaze of light that came through it. Then she too was gone, lost with their father in the depths of the crystal.

'Oh, where *are* they?' cried Annie. 'You can't tell from that.'

'I knew you would be disappointed,' Kaspar said, sadly, 'but I can't help any further. That's the sort of thing the crystal does. It's never very clear. But at least you know your parents are alive, wherever they are. At a strong guess, I would say that they're where you thought they were, in a prison somewhere.'

'Yes,' replied Jack, 'that much we now know, which is more than we knew before. Now what about Davey . . .?'

They discovered Davey's image lying quite still, under a long bench, in a room cluttered with dark shapes that were either animals or toys. It was impossible to tell. After a few heart-wrenching minutes he stirred and they realised with much relief that he was merely asleep, yet alive and well, which again was something. So long as this remained the case, the two children would not give up the search. They would find their parents and brother if it took a lifetime.

'That thing is amazing,' Jack said, as Kaspar carefully put the crystal back in its box. 'It's magic.'

Kaspar shrugged. 'Magic or some kind of mystical science, who knows? Since we don't understand how it works, we can't say for certain.'

Annie agreed with Kaspar, thinking about computers and the internet, which would definitely seem like magic to those who did not undertand how they worked.

Kaspar then bade the children goodbye, saying he had to return to his own city in Moravia in the morning, but he shook their hands vigorously and wished them all the luck in the world, saying he was sure they would find their parents and brother eventually, so long as they did not give up the search. He was sure they would not. And when they did find them, there would be someone around to help them.

'I believe in angels,' he said, smiling, 'even if they might look like something completely different to our eyes.'

6. THE KEY TO THE TIME MACHINE

Jack and Annie felt it was not safe to remain at Dvorak's house while he entertained anarchists. Although Golden Lane was difficult to find, there was always the chance the police might do so and raid the houses there. All Jack and Annie wanted to do was find their brother and their parents as quickly as possible. Once outside in the street, they hurried off in the direction of the river. On its banks they headed towards Charles Bridge, and from there to Old Town Square, where at last they felt a little more comfortable in these familiar surroundings.

'Let's see if Franz is home yet,' said Annie. 'We know the way to his house from here.'

'Good idea,' agreed Jack.

They found Zeltnergasse Street in which Franz Kafka's house was located, and began walking along it looking for number 3, passing a shop on the way. By sheer chance Jack happened to glance in the window, and what he saw there made his hair stand on end. He stopped dead where he was and stared. Yes, it had to be, even down to the metal strap. His father's wristwatch, the key to the Matchless motorbike! The last time he had seen it was when he had given it back to Blazek.

'Dad's watch,' he said excitedly to Annie. 'Look! It is, isn't it?'

Annie replied, 'I think so – I'm sure it is.'

Jack stepped back into the road to get a good look at the place. He soon realised, by the sort of articles in the window, and from the steel bars behind the glass, that it was a pawn shop. There was a notice high up in the front that read: VALUABLES BOUGHT AND SOLD AT REASONABLE PRICES. There were necklaces, bracelets, brooches and other jewellery. The were also carriage and mantelpiece clocks: a dozen at least, leather wallets, handbags, spectacles, binoculars, monocles, brass barometers, chronometers, paperweights, birds' eggs, porcelain figurines, and many other articles, including ivory carvings.

Jack said, 'That policeman must have taken it from Blazek.'

He went up to the door of the shop, only to find it locked. The shop had closed for the day. A cold wind was cutting down the street now, and Jack hunched inside his coat. He was desperately eager to retrieve the watch, without which the time machine was useless, but he knew it would have to wait another day. He hoped his parents were being well treated, but it depended on whose hands they had fallen into. Not all policemen were honest; not all policemen were interested in justice. Here in the Austrian Empire, there was no telling what sort of treatment they were receiving.

Jack and Annie did not even know what they would do if they found their mum and dad, but it would be a start. If they knew where they were, they could then form some sort of plan for getting them released. They talked about this as they battled their way against the swirling wind down the street where Franz lived. Annie had suggested that one of them might go back to their own time and fetch an adult, but Jack reminded her that the ignition key to the motorcycle was in the hands of a pawnbroker.

'We're trapped in Prague,' he told her, grimly, 'in 1903.'

★

The first knock on the door simply echoed through the house beyond, and the children began to fear there was still no one home, but a second hammering on the knocker brought footsteps. The door opened and a harassed-looking Franz stood there. 'Oh, it's you two again – no luck?' he said. He opened the door wider to let them in.

'Didn't you hear the first knock?' said an ungrateful Jack, blowing on his frozen hands. 'I banged loudly enough.'

'I was busy writing,' Franz explained. 'I hear nothing when I'm concentrating.'

'What are you concentrating on?' asked Annie, eager to learn.

'Oh, I think I'll call it *The Great Struggle* or something like that. I'm not sure yet.'

Jack was still absently blowing on his cold fingers and had stopped listening. He was staring at a large piece of card propped on the hallway settle. On the card was a drawing of the time machine.

'Franz! If someone sees that . . .'

Franz turned and stared. 'Oh yes, I've been sketching your motorcycle. I think I've done it quite well.'

'You have, you have, but if anybody sees it . . .'

'Oh, there are already machines something like this one,' Franz said, airily. 'There is the Excelsior made by Bayless, Thomas and Company, a British manufacturer, not so very different. See?'

He showed Jack a magazine open at a certain page. The 147cc Excelsior looked very little like the 1947 Matchless, which was obviously much more powerful at 500cc. But obviously to Franz's eyes the two motorbikes had a lot in common. Jack decided to suppress his protests. Probably people in Prague, those most likely to see the drawing, would have very little idea about what was happening in Britain or America. The two machines were different, but did not seem forty-four years apart. The Matchless would not raise eyebrows to the point of incredulity.

'Well, all right,' he said, weakly. 'I suppose it's not a Yamaha 1000A or a Honda Goldwing 2000.'

'Pardon?' exclaimed Franz, blinking.

Jack was not going to explain about the phenomenal rise of the post-Second World War Japanese automobile industry 'Nothing,' he said.

Annie went on to tell Franz about the watch they had seen in the window of the pawnbroker's shop.

'We need to ask him some questions,' she said. 'Someone must have taken it from Blazek and sold it – one of the policemen who arrested him, probably.'

Jack added, 'And get the watch back. Can you lend us some money, Franz?'

'I think so. Yes, I do have some.'

'We'll see you get it back,' Annie explained earnestly. 'Once we find our father and mother.'

'Please don't worry. My family isn't poor.'

'No, but . . . well, anyway, thanks,' said Annie.

'Would you like some food now? I have a stew simmering.'

The children readily agreed to participating in a meal, though they were thoroughly fed up with meat stew. They had seen few vegetables since they had been in Prague, except pickled red cabbage, which neither of them really liked. There were some potatoes to be had, but there was always more meat than vegetables.

'We'll be getting scurvy very soon,' Annie warned.

'Don't you have to be on a ship to get that?' Jack argued, thinking vaguely of nineteenth-century sea stories. 'I thought that was something to do with eating too much hardtack biscuit?'

'It's nothing to do with the ocean,' stated Annie, who was more into such things than Jack. 'It's to do with vitamins. Lack of vitamin C, to be precise. We need to get some fruit or vegetables.'

'OK – I believe you,' Jack told her. 'I could do with something like that.'

The pair thanked Franz for the meal and politely declined a game of ping-pong, saying they were tired.

Annie said, 'Though I don't know whether we'll get to sleep. There's always a lot of noise outside, isn't there?'

'Ah, you haven't seen it at night, have you?' Franz said. 'There is an energy at work after dark. I don't mean anything sinister. I mean the entertainment. Theatres, the opera, café life, the puppet theatres, concerts – Prague is teeming with society balls at night. I suppose you know that the polka dance is Czech? Ha, you thought it was Polish, didn't you?'

Jack and Annie thought no such thing, since neither of them had stopped to think about the polka for a single second in their so far short lives. However, Franz took their silence to mean that he had caught them out, and he was pleased. 'We are famous for many things,' he continued, 'beer and dumplings being two of them. You will not find better beer or dumplings in any other city in the world.'

'Well, we've tried the dumplings, and they are pretty

good,' agreed Annie, who actually hated fattening foods but was too polite to say so, 'but we're not yet old enough for beer.'

'Though I wouldn't mind trying it,' said Jack. 'Dad's always promising me a taste.'

'You won't like it,' Franz said sadly. 'Beer is like coffee. The younger you are, the more terrible is the taste. But you keep drinking it because everyone else does, and at some point you find you are enjoying it, and in fact can't do without it. It is a great shame we don't take good notice of that first sip, and ignore beer and coffee ever after, for neither is good for the constitution.'

Annie's eyes were closing and she said, 'I'm sorry, I have to go to bed. Please excuse me. Good night.'

'And a good night to you too, Annie,' Franz told her.

Once she had gone, Jack and Franz talked some more.

'Do you know someone called Dvorak?' asked Jack.

Franz replied, 'That's a fairly common name here in Prague. My baker is called Dvorak.'

'Oh, well this one lives in Golden Lane.'

'I know very few people. I try to keep myself to myself.'

'This Dvorak is an alchemist.'

Franz's face brightened. 'Oh, really? That's interesting. They are like primitive chemists, you know. They invented gunpowder.'

'I know, we've been told. Well this one – he has this room full of bits of metal which he's melting down on a furnace. I didn't see any gold though.'

'It's not real science, you know,' explained Franz. 'It involves a little magic too. I don't believe in magic – not that sort.'

'Well, I'm not sure,' said Jack. 'I'm off to bed. Thanks again for having us here.'

'You're very welcome.'

The following morning a refreshed and hopeful Jack and Annie went to the pawn shop, but on passing the window they saw the watch had gone. They rushed inside the shop. 'There was a watch in the window yesterday,' Annie blurted out to the stooped, balding man behind the high counter.

'Yes,' came the reply. His face creased as if he were thinking very hard. 'A strange mechanism. I opened the back and there were no works inside. Yet the watch still told the time. Very strange. I didn't know what to think.'

Annie then remembered that her father's watch was of course a quartz timepiece and would have no clockwork. That must have thrown the pawnbroker somewhat, as he looked for wheels, springs and cogs. However, she had no time to be concerned over the problems they were causing with their time travels.

'We would like to buy the watch,' she said, taking out the money Franz had loaned them. 'If you please.'

The pawnbroker shook his head. 'I'm sorry, that particular item was reclaimed just a few moments ago, but I have others here.' He reached under his counter to take out a tray of timepieces.

'Who by?' demanded Jack, his voice high-pitched. 'Who claimed it?'

'Why, a perfectly respectable customer, I assure you,' replied the pawnbroker, going on the defensive. 'Despite the fact that he had a false left hand.'

Jack asked, 'How did you know it was false?'

The pawnbroker smiled and touched the side of his nose.

'He wore black leather gloves, but I heard it knock, as if it was made of wood, when he put his hands on my glass counter. I'm not silly. I notice these things.'

'Well, that's something,' Annie said, feeling very low. Everything seemed to be going against them. 'At least we know *something* about him.'

'If we ever see him,' cried Jack, 'which is most unlikely. Oh, why didn't we knock on the door last night? Listen, sir – was it the man with the false hand who actually pawned the watch in the first place? Can you remember?'

'No, it was a member of our local constabulary.'

They asked the pawnbroker to describe the man who had claimed the watch. The pawnbroker was very suspicious and reluctant to do so, but a little money from Jack soon got over that hurdle. He told them that it was a tall man, with dark hair, quite lean. In fact, said the pawnbroker, he was painfully thin. No, no, he did not know where the man lived, nor had he seen him before the business over the watch. So far as he was concerned, this was just another customer. Yes, for a little consideration he would look out for the man in future, and when the children came back he would report any progress to them.

'Listen,' he said, looking slyly at the doorway of his shop, presumably to make sure no one was coming in, 'I have some other watches here – gold watches, going cheap.'

He reached under his counter and brought out a tray of wristwatches wrapped in a piece of velveteen.

'Gold!' he whispered dramatically. 'Gold – but yesterday

they were all just steel-cased watches. The alchemists turned them. Go on, bite one. You'll see it's real gold all right. I have so many it's going to be difficult to sell them without arousing suspicion from the police.'

Annie said, 'You've just bought them?'

'Yes, from a man who called himself Kaspar — just that.'

'Thank you, but we only want one watch — the one claimed by the man with the false hand.'

The pawnbroker looked disappointed. He folded the velveteen over the gold watches and put them back under the counter.

The children left the shop and began to scour the streets, looking for a tall, dark, lean man wearing black leather gloves. They spent an hour looking, but failed to find the buyer of the watch. Then, just as they were becoming exhausted with their search, Jack saw someone else. Davey, gripped by the wrist, was being hurried along through the dense two-way flow of people in a walk called Narodni Avenue, just off Wenceslas Square.

Jack yelled at Annie, who was a few metres away.

'Annie! There's Davey. I've just seen Davey, with an old woman! Quickly. That way. After them!'

7. LOST IN BOHEMIA

At the time he had become separated from Jack and Annie, Davey had been upset and scared. On leaving Franz Kafka's house, he had taken no note of his surroundings. He did not even know the name of the street in which the house stood. Because he had been with his older brother and sister, he had been like a passenger in a car, not really bothering to remember landmarks or what directions were being taken. He had left his siblings to do that sort of thing for him, not realising he would soon have to rely on himself alone.

For a while, he had wandered around, looking for them. When he realised he was not going to find them, he sat down on the freezing steps of a church for a long while, feeling wretched and sniffling away to himself. No one appeared to take any real notice of him. No one seemed to care in the least. A priest who later came out of the church stopped to ask if he was all right and Davey nodded rather pathetically, expecting then to be asked, 'Are you sure?'

But the second question never came, giving Davey no chance to say how he really felt, for the priest simply took him at his word and continued on his way. This was a different culture to the one Davey was used to, one which did not dance around things for the sake of politeness, and he was going to have to learn to be more direct.

The light was fading now and street lamps were being lit. Only horse-drawn vehicles went past, some of them with glowing oil lamps on their carriages, others as dark as death. No one came down that particular road on foot again. Davey found a place out of the wind, behind the Greek pillars of the church's portico, and tried to sleep. The cold was deadly, finding its way into his small bones and causing such an ache it made his eyes sore from weeping. He had never been so cold in his life before. And being without food made him even more vulnerable to the harsh elements. Morning took a thousand years to come: grey and desolate, with no promise of change.

Davey sat up and groaned. He found he was intensely hungry. His stomach felt as if it was weighted down with gravel. Then came a smell on the wind that wrenched at his guts. He rose from the steps and followed his nose to the corner of the street where a man was toasting buns over a brazier and placing them on a hot sheet of metal prior to selling them. Hunger is a strong commander, overriding common sense.

Davey watched and waited until the vendor's attention was taken with an elderly woman customer dressed all in black, even up to the black half-veil attached to her black hat. Then he ran forward and snatched a bun from the hot plate.

Instantly, the vendor whirled and grabbed his collar with a triumphant yell of 'Ha! Got you at last, you little thief!'

'I'm hungry,' cried Davey, squirming in the strong grip of the bun-seller. 'I haven't had anything to eat.'

The man took no notice of him, but turned to his customer brandishing the stolen bun and saying, 'I've been try to catch this one for a week. This is the third bun he's stolen. Well, it's his last. It's the cells for this dirty tyke.'

Davey protested, 'I haven't seen you before – this is the first time I've done it.'

'What a story!' cried the vendor, looking up and down the street for a policeman. 'How old are you, ragamuffin?'

Davey gave his age.

'Very small for those years,' growled the man. 'Are you lying to me again?'

The woman spoke for the first time. 'He looks quite a bright lad,' she murmured, 'yet he's small enough for the task. All those I've had before have been poor dim creatures. Too many turnips, not enough fish or meat to feed the brain. This one looks intelligent.'

'Intelligent?' said the bun-seller, laughing caustically. 'How bright do you have to be to steal a bun? Have you had any schooling, boy?'

'Of course,' said Davey, close to tears again.

'Well then, I think we can forget the police,' said the woman. She reached into a handbag with a black-gloved hand. 'I'll pay you to give the child over to me. This will do, I think?' She produced a banknote.

'More,' said the bun-seller.

'More, for something you don't own?' cried the woman, clasping Davey's wrist in a strong claw-like grip. 'This isn't a slave market, you know. Take the money and don't be so stupid. What will the police give you for him?'

The vendor saw the point. It was her offer or nothing. He took the note and released Davey's collar. Then he said to Davey, 'And if I ever catch you around here again, I'll cut your throat, you hear?'

Davey nodded, allowing himself to be pulled away by the woman in black. When they had gone a few metres, he resisted the pull. The woman said, 'If I have to drag you, child, you'll be sorry.' Davey shrugged and relaxed again. 'Where are we going?' he asked.

'You'll find out soon enough,' said the woman. She stared down at him. 'You look like a sharp boy. Someone with a bit of spark about him.'

Davey was still very hungry. 'What will I get if I do come?'

The woman laughed as she clip-clopped along the pavement, almost in time with a horse and rider that was passing. 'Thinking about your stomach, eh? Are you an orphan?'

Davey thought for a moment, then replied, 'Yes.'

'Well, I can promise better fare than the orphanage. I keep a good table. You'll be well treated, if you don't misbehave. Try to escape and you'll be soundly whipped, but do as you're told and you'll have a bench to sleep on, and one good meal every day. Understood?'

'I know a man called Franz Kaftan,' said Davey. 'If you take me to his house, he'll probably reward you.'

'Never heard of him. Besides, I don't want any reward. I want a boy to work for me. That's reward enough.'

'But . . .'

She shook him, severely. 'Be quiet, or I'll fetch you one around the head.'

'You're not allowed to hit me,' cried Davey desperately. 'It's against the law.'

'Oh, and whose law is that?' she cried. 'Yours?'

'No, it's . . .' but of course it was not the law of the land in which he found himself. 'It's human rights,' he ended, tamely.

'I'll give you human rights,' snapped the woman, hurrying him along. 'Around the ears if you don't be quiet. Understood? Any more out of you and I'll give you to the *polednice.*'

'Who's them?'

'It, not *them* – it's the noon witch. She takes small boys

like you to a horrible place when they're not good children . . .'

Davey wondered whether to yell out to passers-by, that he was being kidnapped. Would they pay any attention, though? His intuition told him that the woman would talk her way out of things, probably tell any crowd that gathered that she was his grandmother and that he was simply being naughty. She might even tell them he was mad. Davey did not want to be thought crazy. He might end up for ever in a horrible madhouse in this barmy world full of lunatics. If people here were crazy on the outside, what were they like on the inside? Better to go along with things for the time being, and look for opportunities later.

'Understood,' he said. 'What's for breakfast?'

She laughed again, replying good-naturedly, 'Boiled potatoes and braised beef.'

That sounded good to Davey's ears – very, very good. In his own time he might have turned his nose up at such fare, demanding hamburger and chips instead. Now he was starving, he would have looked forward to stale bread if that had been offered, and would have eaten it with great gusto. And there was going to be a bench to sleep on. Luxury, when all else on offer were the cold stones of church steps, or a dirty alley. Food and shelter. These two were suddenly very important. Davey could no longer take such things for granted. They represented life in a place where the winter temperatures fell to below zero and any creature outside a dwelling froze to death.

They passed a wrought-iron fence that ringed a house. Some of the spear-headed railings were missing.

'Look at that,' muttered the old woman to Davey. 'That's the alchemists for you. Half the metal in Prague has gone missing in the last few days. They steal iron railings and turn them into precious metals. I'd like to get my hands on some of that gold and silver, I can tell you. Instead, what do I get? A guttersnipe with more insolence than a hurdygurdy-player's monkey. Still, I can turn you into a getter of gold, lad, I can indeed, once you've been trained up for it.'

Davey at once thought of the Artful Dodger in the film he had seen called *Oliver Twist*.

'I ain't stealin' nothin' for you, lady,' he said. 'You won't get me pinchin' purses, no matter what you do.'

She cackled. 'You don't need to steal, child. All you need to do is a little acting. You can do that, can't you? Playact?'

'That?' said Davey, relieved. 'I can do that standin' on me head.'

8. PRISONERS OF THE WEASEL

All Roger and Kate had been told was that they had been arrested as spies. Apparently it was believed they were 'assisting foreign powers and criminals' supposedly in an attempt to bring about the downfall of the Austrian Empire. Roger knew he was in a huge building of some kind, but what its purpose was, or had been, was unknown to him. He was inclined to think it was some kind of large mansion, palace or castle. The passageways were long and twisting, even maze-like. Most of the rooms were big, though the cell to which Roger had been confined was – along with others in the row – narrow, with a low ceiling. His dear wife Kate was in the next cell along, and they were communicating by tapping on the pipes. They both knew Morse code from their Scout and Girl Guide days and used it to reassure each other they were all right.

It at least helped Roger's state of mind to know that Kate was not in any great distress, though of course being in captivity, both of them were feeling quite low and wondering how they were going to get out of their horrible predicament. They were also both dreadfully worried about their children, Jack, Annie and Davey, not knowing if they were coping.

Roger was inclined to think that Jack and Annie *were* managing all right, and taking care of their little brother. They were fairly resourceful children and not inclined to hysterics when things went strange on them. Roger thought that they had probably by now contacted one of their uncles or aunts, or their grandparents, and no doubt the police had been called in to investigate the 'missing parents'. How he and Kate were going to resolve their current difficulties was not clear, but Roger was an upbeat person and hope burned in him like a beacon.

Roger had just finished his breakfast – a kind of sloppy porridge, not unpleasant, but not particularly filling – when the guards came to take him for another session of questioning. He found these interviews difficult. Not because they tortured him, but because he could not tell the truth. Roger had soon realised on being arrested that not telling the truth made him seem very suspicious. He could not reveal that he had come to Prague on a time machine, so he had to make up a story about travelling from London. Yet he could not name the ship on which he had crossed the Channel, or give any details about the train that had carried him to Prague. In fact, the more he spoke, the less believable his story became. And as Roger's parents knew, Roger had never been a good liar, even as a little boy. His face went more crimson with every false word he uttered, and he looked undeniably guilty.

When he was shown into the interrogation room, there was someone he knew sitting on the other side of the table.

It was Blazek.

Blazek gave him a look that said, 'Well, they've pulled me in too now.'

Roger's chief interrogator was a man with a narrow face and protruding eyes. Roger knew he had a false hand and always wore black leather gloves to disguise the fact. He was a very tall, thin man, persistent in his questions, and was no doubt very clever. Sometimes he took the friendly approach, offering things like cigarettes or snacks of some kind. On other occasions he was stern and forthright. He never shouted, though, or lost his temper. Roger had privately named him 'the Weasel', for he had that pointed look about him, and was fond of seeming to walk away then whirling suddenly like a weasel attacking its prey, and asking a very difficult question.

The weasel was standing in the corner of the room as Roger was led in, observing how the two men reacted to one another.

'Ah,' he said, 'you know one another?'

'Yes,' replied Roger. 'Blazek is a distant relative of my wife – a second cousin, I believe.'

'Your colour has changed, Mr Kettle,' snapped the Weasel. 'You're lying again!'

'No,' interrupted Blazek. 'He's merely a little mistaken – I think we are *third* cousins removed, that's all.'

'No one asked you to speak,' the Weasel remarked. 'I was talking to the English spy. Please remain silent until you are asked for an opinion.'

'Yes, sir,' muttered Blazek. 'Pray forgive me.'

The Weasel continued to question both men alternately, obviously hoping for a breakthrough in his quest for evidence of espionage. Roger suspected that the policeman had been holding the English couple for so long now he had to find *something* to justify his suspicions. With sinking heart, he realised it might be years before they were eventually released.

Then he noticed something on the Weasel's wrist, and his heart sank a little.

'Ah?' said the Weasel, noticing Roger's look. 'You like my new wristlet watch?' He drew back his coat sleeve to show Roger the ignition key to the time machine. 'It's smart, isn't it? It was owned of course by our friend here, your cousin, and was taken from him by some stupid street policeman who immediately pawned it for the money. Fortunately the policeman's partner was jealous and informed on him. When I was told that the hands on this strange timepiece moved without any clockwork, I retrieved it. It's all very inter-esting. Indeed, the watch does not seem to have any cogs, wheels or springs – yet the hands still move and it keeps perfect time. Don't you find that strange?'

'Yes, that is a little peculiar.'

'Very odd,' said the Weasel, fingering the wristwatch with his good hand. 'I'm sure you know *why* it has no clock-work inside its silver case, yet it functions on the outside as if it had?'

'Not really.'

'Not really? Is that a good enough answer, I wonder? I saw your expression a moment ago, when you noticed it on my wrist for the first time. Is this watch important to you, spy? Did you give it to your cousin here for some nefarious purpose? It is not, do you suppose, really a *key*?'

Roger's head went up sharply and he felt his breath go very tight and shallow. Did the policeman know about the time machine? Did he know this was an ignition key to start the motorcycle? Surely Blazek had not informed on them? Would he do that, this ancestor of his wife? A quick look at Blazek's face told Roger that such a thought was quite unjust. Blazek looked as shocked as Roger felt.

'Ah-ha!' cried the Weasel triumphantly, watching the change in their faces intently. 'I have struck a *golden* chord, or perhaps a *silver* one, have I not? This timepiece – this object disguised as a wristlet watch – is indeed an alchemist's key to the unlocking of the eternal secret of immortality, yes? You *are* an alchemist. I knew it from the first.' He moved his head closer to Roger's, so that Blazek could not hear his words, and hissed, 'We can forget this business about spying. I could tell from the moment I met you that you were not from this world. You were too different. I sensed a strangeness in you, an otherness that separated you and your wife from us in this year of 1903. You are not like us. You are not from around here, are you? Not even the London of now. Tell me, admit to me, you are from another time, are you not?'

Once again Roger's throat constricted and his breathing grew sharp, as he thought wildly, *He* must *know our secret.*

'I know your secret,' whispered the Weasel in his ear. 'You are from another time – you are from the distant *past*, are you not? You have discovered the secret of ever-lasting life. When were you born? In the eighteenth century? The seventeenth? Even earlier? Perhaps you are older even than Christianity? You have the sense of the ancient world about you. Give me the secret, and you shall go free in this world.'

Roger laughed out loud, relieved that the time machine was not threatened.

'You think I'm an *alchemist*?'

The Weasel looked puzzled, then anger took over his expression.

'You deny it? Even now, with this as proof?' He held up the watch. 'This is an alchemist's tool, an instrument of the devilish art that has kept you alive for so long. I will learn its secret, you know, eventually. Until then, it stays here, on my wrist . . .'

'I'm not a spy,' replied Roger wearily.

'No, of course you're not.'

'Nor an alchemist.'

'Ah, there we differ. You say not, and yet I feel there are secrets to discover. I wonder why I feel that? We must

81

continue this discussion about the watch again sometime – until then, let's go over your relationship with Blazek here.'

Roger was finally sent back to his cell, but he had concealed in his hand a note from Blazek passed to him secretly under the table. When he had unfolded it from a tiny square and read it, the contents astonished him. He did not know whether to be hopeful or full of fear for his beloved children. It seemed that Jack and Annie, with Davey, had come to 1903 Prague to rescue them!

While he had every faith in his children's initiative, Roger was afraid that the same fate that had landed him in jail might overcome his children too. He was in two minds whether to signal Kate and tell her of the development. He was sure she would be frantic with worry.

In the end, he decided that not to tell her would be wrong, so he tapped out a message on the pipes. Her reply eased his mind somewhat.

'*Annie-Jack-cleverkids-chinup-darling.*'

9. IN THE HANDS OF POLICE

Annie could have wept. Jack's disappointment was immediately translated into fury. Davey and his companion had been lost in knots of people impossible to untangle. Jack tried to follow them, with Annie close behind, but there was a danger of brother and sister losing each other in the bustling crowds, so in the end they gave up.

'Poor Davey,' said Annie through her tears. 'Do you think that woman is treating him badly?'

'Who knows?' Jack said, seething. 'This place — no, not this *place* — this *time* — it's so, well, unpredictable. There are nice people here, as there are everywhere. There are bad people here too — again, same as where we come from. But it's harder for us to tell the difference. We're strangers in another time and place. We don't know the culture of either. It's completely foreign to us. We have to learn, that's all. We have to keep our heads and find a way through all these strangenesses.'

Annie said, 'I don't think there's such a word as *strangenesses*. You should say something like *oddities*.'

Jack stared at his sister. 'It's lucky you're good-looking,' he said generously, 'or you could be taken for a nerd.'

'Just because I'm beautiful doesn't mean I'm not intelligent.'

'I didn't say you were beautiful — I wouldn't know, you're my sister. But you've got a lot of the nerd in you.' Jack stared around him at the flowing ropes of people. 'Come on. We're not going to find Davey in this. I've got a good idea. Let's try the hospitals. If Mum or Dad has been sick over the last few days, they might have been taken to a hospital and they would have records of them. We could ask, anyway.'

They stopped a tall man wearing a heavy overcoat and asked him the quickest way to the nearest hospital.

'What do you want a hospital for?' the man asked suspiciously. 'You don't look sick.'

'We're looking for our parents. We think they may have been taken ill,' Jack explained.

'What? Both of them at once?'

'It was an accident,' Annie said, realising they were going to get nowhere without fabricating. 'An accident with a tram.'

At that moment a tram rumbled past, which of course was why Annie had chosen that vehicle for her story. The man looked at her through narrowed eyes.

'An accident with a tram? I still don't see how that could happen to two people at once. Unless one was trying to save the other, and both were run over at the same time. Even then I would think if you were hit by a tram you wouldn't survive without terrible injury. They can't do a sudden stop, those iron monsters. I had a friend who was knocked off his bicycle and the left side of his body was mangled beyond repair. The doctors made it worse by cutting off his right leg by mistake . . .'

'Never mind,' Jack muttered, thoroughly frustrated. 'We'll find it on our own.'

'. . . and just look what they did to *me*,' finished the man, and he suddenly removed his head and tucked it under his armpit to reveal a neck that had been sawn right through. He bowed forward so the children could see the sliced-through veins and arteries, and all the other tubes that led from a head down into a body. 'Nasty, eh?' said the severed head from its new position on the man's torso.

Jack let out a cry of fright and both children ran away down the street, their faces a ghastly grey with terror.

'If I were you,' called the man after them, 'I wouldn't go near those butchers. They'll cut something off your body as quick as you like. If your parents are really in the hospital, you're virtually orphans already . . .'

When they had recovered their composure a little, a shaking Jack said, 'I wish we didn't keep running into these supernatural creatures – it's very offputting.'

The next person they asked was, to their relief, quite ordinary and gave them precise directions to a hospital. As Annie had observed, like most cities there were kind people and there were idiots, and it was pot luck which type you met. On the way, however, they passed a building with a notice above the door reading BUREAU OF INFORMATION. Jack was very excited and bounded up the steps. When he reached the top he found a card pinned to the door that read: *Moved to Another Address*.

'Well, what address?' he yelled at no one in particular.

He tried peering through a window, but all he could see were cardboard boxes scattered over a dusty floor amongst a small ocean of crumpled litter – screwed-up typewritten sheets of paper mostly.

He came down the steps feeling very angry.

'Useless,' he said. 'Absolutely useless.'

Eventually they found the hospital, but there had been an accident on the river Vltava, a ferry had overturned and spilled passengers into its freezing waters. The place seemed far too busy to answer the questions of two children. Victims were being stretchered in through the front entrance and nurses were clip-clopping back and forth on stone floors, hurrying from one patient to another. There were two young doctors looking harassed, and one matron-type figure who seemed to be the only calm person in the building, but too imperious to approach.

The children did not even try. They left feeling despondent.

Not far from the hospital they passed a police station, and ignoring Annie's warning not to go in, Jack climbed the broad steps. Annie reluctantly followed him.

There was a large uniformed man with a huge moustache behind the desk.

'Please, sir,' said Jack, taking off his hat, 'we're looking for our mother and father.'

'Name and address?' said the policeman, without looking up but with a pen poised over a ledger.

Jack faltered. 'What – *our* name and address?'

Now the policeman did look up. He was heavy-jowled with dark bags under his eyes. He squinted at Jack. 'Who else's address would I be asking for?'

'Well, my parents . . .'

'They live at a different address?' interrupted the policeman, his eyes widening. 'Do you live with someone else?' His face suddenly broke into the light of comprehension. 'Ah, you stay with your grandparents – or an aunt and uncle, is that it? Address, if you don't mind, of your guardians.'

Jack panicked. He was in a quandary. He could not give Franz's address, that would simply lead to trouble. He thought about giving Dvorak's address, but could not remember the number on the door. He could see Annie looking at him with some concern.

Annie said, 'We're visitors to the city. We've become separated from our parents in – in the busy streets. We're from London, actually.'

'And your accommodations?' asked the policeman. 'Where are you staying?'

'We – we haven't had time to get any yet.'

'They're lying,' came a gravelly voice from behind them. 'They've been here at least three days.'

Jack turned and his heart sank. There was the secret policeman who had chased them through the streets the day they had lost Davey. He thought about running again now – but the man in the dark civilian clothes was barring the doorway. Jack knew that even if he could get past, Annie could not, and he refused to leave his sister.

'Come,' said the secret policeman, 'into the back room.'

Jack's shoulders dropped. Annie held her head high but followed orders. They were taken into a room where there was just a table and one chair. The man came in after them and locked the door behind him. He took off his hat and sat behind the table. The children were left to stand. The room was a dreary place. The only decoration on the wall was a soiled map of the city. Jack could see the area name HRADCANY on one side of the river, and ZIZKOV on the other. There were other words of similar size, but these had been smudged almost to oblit-eration. Several areas had been ringed with red ink, one of these was where Golden Lane was situated, and also, inexplicably, the opera house.

'Now,' said the secret policeman, 'if I can have your full attention?'

Jack's head jerked round again. 'I wasn't . . .'

'No, of course you weren't. You're not a spy, are you? Your parents will testify to that.'

Annie said, 'We – we can't find our parents.'

'So I understand. What are their names?'

Jack saw no point in hiding anything now. After all, they had come to this police station to find their mother and father. At least they would learn which prison they were in, which would be a start. Once they knew that, they could visit them, and Roger and Kate could advise them what to do next. So Jack gave the man the names of his parents. The policeman looked up and stared at the children.

'That surname. It sounds very foreign. You are foreigners?'

'From London,' said Jack, 'but our mother is from Austria, which is why we are here – to visit relations.'

'Those relations being?'

Annie said, 'They didn't tell us – we're only children, after all.'

'Fairly grown-up children. What are you? Twelve? Thirteen? Yes, I would think around that age. Wait here a minute.'

The policeman left the room, locking the door behind him. He was gone more than an hour. When he returned, he had a file with him which he slapped on the desk.

'I am sorry to report to you,' he said, his eyes glinting in the grey light from the window, 'that your parents are dead.'

Annie immediately burst into tears with the shock. Jack's heart almost stopped beating. He too felt like crying, but something stopped him. Something about the look in the policeman's eyes. Jack was not usually very perceptive when it came to subtle changes in a man's demeanour such as the tone of his voice, or half-closed eyelids – that would normally be Annie's area – but his intuition had been sharpened by recent experiences. He was able quickly to assess the worth of the words that came out of the man's mouth, and he was pretty sure they were untrue. The man before them was lying, for whatever reason.

'Oh dear,' Jack said flatly, which made Annie choke on her tears and look up to stare at him in disbelief. 'What an awful thing.'

'Yes,' replied the policeman not picking up on Jack's dull tone. He shuffled the papers from the file. 'Which means you are both orphans. I'm not sure what to do with you. We can't hand you over to your relatives – you don't know who they are, do you? We could send you back to London, I suppose. Would you want that?'

'No,' Jack said firmly. 'There's no one there.'

'Well then, that leaves an orphanage. However, you are getting too old to be in such an establishment. They usually turn them out on to the streets at your age, to earn a living. I wonder, what can you do, either of you? Are you good at anything?'

'No, not really.'

'Then I suggest it's the army for you, my boy – and perhaps service for the girl. Yes, that's the best thing. That way,' the man leaned forward, 'we can keep an eye on both of you. I shall make sure you go to the regiment of a friend of mine, and you, missy, the household of a lady of standing. We don't want you running around our city creating havoc, do we? Where's the young one? You had a boy with you?'

'We lost him,' said Annie. 'We'd like to find him too.'

'Well, he'll probably turn up. Or not. It doesn't really

matter. He looked too young to cause trouble. If and when he's old enough to make a nuisance of himself, we'll pull him in too. Now, you'll spend the night in the cells here, and tomorrow – it's a new life for the pair of you.'

Jack and Annie looked at each other bleakly.

10. TWO KINDS OF SERVICE

The cells were soulless, windowless rooms two metres square, with huge heavy iron doors. Captivity turned out to be very, very cold. Everything was icy to the touch, from the stone walls to the window bars to the doors. Jack was sure that the winter inside the police station had survived the summer from the year before. It had never been able to escape confinement. Condensation had run down the stone blocks of the walls and frozen into a layer of permanent frost.

The children were each given a single rough blanket, a bed with wooden planks in place of springs, and what passed for a pillow stuffed with horsehair. Food came in the shape of thin gruel, bread and a piece of hard cheese. The hours were long, sleep coming only in snatches, and both flesh and bones ached with the chill. They shivered continuously and would have been terrified by a rat that had been attracted by the smell of the gruel, if they had not felt so wretched.

There was a woman in the cell with them who was nice to them at first, but when – in answer to a question from her – they said they were not alchemists, she seemed to lose all interest. 'I need to contact my fellow practitioners,' she murmured, to herself more than Jack and Annie. 'They will find a way.' She rattled the window bars, loose in their brick-and-mortar sockets. 'If these were pure gold we'd be able to bend them and make our escape. Alas, they're solid steel. Gold is soft and lovely, easy to work if you know how . . .'

It was the most miserable night either of them had ever spent, and both brother and sister were determined never to spend another one in the same circumstances.

In the morning they were let out of the cell but not released to freedom. Jack said goodbye to Annie, managing to whisper, 'We'll get out of this, don't worry. I'll come looking for you later.' Annie replied that she was grateful to Jack for those words. She would have appreciated *any* message of hope at that point. Then Jack was taken away by a large policeman, who transported him to a barracks on the edge of the city. There he was left in the charge of an army sergeant, who beamed at him kindly.

A man made of nothing but shadows watched the two children being parted, but if he felt any pity for them in their distress it did not register on his storm cloud features. Seeming to hover rather than stand under the arches of a cathedral close, he studied both Annie and Jack as they were led away to their separate fates. Passers-by did not start backwards at encountering this phantom creature, but though he was plain for all to see, they were oblivious of his presence. Once the children were gone, he seemed to vanish into the morning air.

'Sit on that bench over there, boy,' said the sergeant. 'I'll get to you later.'

Jack did as he was told, and waited, and waited, and waited.

Over the course of the morning, the bench, and other benches around the large room, filled with youths and men. There was a young man with yellowed teeth and a hollow chest who sat on Jack's left. They got to talking, in low voices while they waited. Jack asked the youth if he had spent the night in a prison cell. The boy looked at Jack askance.

'Why, no. I've travelled all the way from Moravia to join the army. My father is a farm labourer, but there is little employment where I come from, so I have to look for work here. I've been here a month and found nothing. My money has run out. This is the last resort, for there is nothing else.'

'Oh.' It was incomprehensible to Jack that a youth should be volunteering for the army. 'Will you make it a career, then?'

'I shall be happy for a good meal each day and some warm clothes – these are in threads.' He showed Jack the garments he was wearing, which indeed were so worn they were almost rags.

'My name is Jiri,' said the youth, extending a hand that had fingers like twigs. 'What is yours?'

'Jack.'

'You speak good German.'

'So do you,' said Jack, aware that this was not Jiri's native language. 'I suppose you have to, these days, if you want to get on?'

'Indeed, yes. What regiment are you asking for, Jack?'

The policeman had told Jack the name of a regiment, but he could not remember it now.

'I don't know.'

Jiri lowered his head. 'Take my advice,' he whispered, 'and stay clear of the cavalry. It might seem wonderful – to ride a charger and wear a sabre – and indeed it was, once. But my master at school told us that since the invention of rapid-firing guns they call machine guns, to be in the cavalry is certain death. The air is as full of bullets as a summer's afternoon is full of insects. You cannot escape their bites or stings. Those who join the hussars or dragoons, and wear what I cannot help but describe as a beautiful uniform, are the first to die in battle.'

Jack remembered reading about the First World War for a history lesson at school, and recalled that in the beginning Polish cavalry were slaughtered by machine guns. The day of the horse was over; the machine had arrived. Jiri was right. If there was a war, and Jack had to fight, it was best it was not on the back of a horse. Horses and riders were doomed to a very abrupt end in modern battles.

'What should I ask for, then?' whispered Jack.

'Why, a good infantry regiment. You will have to march a lot, but they give you good strong boots. And promotion is quicker, if you stay out of trouble, for many of those who reach the rank of corporal or sergeant fall into drinking ways – what with the extra pay – and are soon demoted again. Beware of that, Jack. Stay away from the schnapps. It is the most evil of masters and will rob you of any ambition.'

Jack had every intention of staying away from the

schnapps, even though his ambition was barely evident even to himself.

Eventually a sergeant started to call out names and youths began to step forward to a table that had been placed in the middle of the room. On the table were ledgers and books, which a harassed corporal either wrote in or consulted. Finally it was Jack's turn. He went up and stood in front of the table.

'Stand to attention, boy,' said the sergeant, without looking up, but not in an unkind voice. 'You're in the army now.'

Jack did not know what to do, but brought his feet together and stood up straighter than before. The sergeant's face showed approval.

'Your name is Jack Kettle?'

'Yes, sir,' replied Jack nervously.

'Not sir − *Sergeant*. See that lieutenant over there?' the sergeant pointed with a pencil at a very arrogant-looking man in gleaming brown riding boots. The officer's uniform looked as if it had been sprayed on, it fitted him so tightly. 'You call officers like him *sir*. Everyone else you will address by their rank. You will learn the ranks very quickly.'

'Yes, sir − Sergeant.'

'Good. Now, in future you will answer to the call of 7632 Private Kettle, do you understand? That is your number, rank and name. If you are ever captured by an enemy, that is all the information you are empowered to give them. Here is a slip of paper with your number on it − learn it very quickly. That shouldn't be difficult for the son of an alchemist, even if you are a foreigner.'

'My father's not an alchemist.'

'Listen, boy, *every* foreigner in Prague at the moment is deemed an alchemist, until he proves himself otherwise.'

'Yes, Sergeant.'

'Your regiment is the 14th Regiment of Foot, based here in Prague itself. You are very lucky, Private Kettle, to be so near the city. Some regiments are sent far away, often into another country.'

Jack was indeed relieved to find he was staying in Prague, though he had some idea it was so that they could keep an eye on him.

'Please, Sergeant? May I speak?'

The sergeant looked up, encouragingly.

'Well, Sergeant – can my friend Jiri be in the same regiment?'

Jack looked back at Jiri.

'Your friend Jiri? Well, you make comrades very quickly, Private Kettle. That's good. The army is your family now and comrades are very important, especially in a time of war.' The sergeant stared across the floor at Jiri. 'I see no reason why not. Go and sit down now and wait for someone to call you forward again. Send your friend Jiri up to the table.'

As Jack sat down, Jiri hissed at him angrily, 'I don't want a Prague regiment – I want to go abroad. You earn more money abroad . . .' He went up to the table, and the sergeant spoke to him in a low voice for quite a long time. When Jiri came back he was in a better mood.

'I'm sorry I was angry with you, Jack,' said Jiri, sitting down. 'The 14th is a good regiment. We shall be proud soldiers together.'

'What was he saying to you, Jiri? He seemed to have a lot more to say to you than the rest of us.'

'Oh – he knew my father when he was in the army many years ago. We spoke of family matters. It's because he knew my father that we are allowed to be in the same regiment. It doesn't often happen, you know – being allowed to stay together. We shall get on fine. Comrades must look to each other for support. That's what we'll do, Jack, you and I. We shall help each other through.'

Some time later, it seemed forever, various soldiers from various regiments arrived and began calling for those who were to join their particular battalion. Every time one or two youths were led away, Jack could hear the soldier who had come for them saying something like, 'You're very lucky. We are the best regiment in the army. You couldn't ask for better. We have many battle honours. The rest of them are rubbish, even the cavalry. Our colonel is recognised far and wide as the most competent in the field . . .'

But of course, since they all said similar things, Jack decided the words meant nothing, until he was assured most enthusiastically by the lance corporal who had come to collect him and Jiri that the 14th Foot was without a doubt the most magnificent regiment the Austrian army had ever trained. Examples were given of the regiment's glories, medals won by individuals, honours now displayed on the colours (which Jack learned was what they called the regimental flag), until he was finally convinced that the 14th Foot was indeed the best regiment the Austrian army had ever produced.

Jack and Jiri were taken to an army camp on the edge of Prague consisting of many long, low wooden huts with a huge parade square in the centre. In one of the huts they were issued with uniforms. The storeman seemed to take little account of their size except to look them both up and down once, yet miraculously the boots, the tunic, the trousers and the cap all fitted. They were extremely uncomfortable, especially the boots and the stock (which fitted tightly around Jack's neck inside the collar of his tunic), but they were actually round about the correct size. The two boys were then taken to a mess hall, where they were given stew with dumplings, then finally with a number of other new recruits to hut number 37.

Inside the hut the wooden floor was like polished glass. Jack guessed it had been buffed continuously since the time of the Romans. There was a pot-bellied stove in the middle of the hut, in which two of the recruits lit a fire and warmed the room. Down each side were twenty iron bedsteads with a neat pile of blankets resting on their planks, and between each a sort of tall locker for keeping one's personal items safe, on top of which sat a tin mug and knife, fork and spoon. There was a threadbare rag which Jack was told was his towel and a bar of carbolic soap with a surface like sandpaper as well as boot brushes, polishing rags, and some white paste called 'blanco' for his white belt and rifle sling.

And of course there was his rifle, which looked ancient and rattled loosely when he picked it up. Jiri told him this was so that when they were on parade and all the rifles were shouldered together they would make a magnificent-sounding single crash, designed to impress the colonel.

'Won't it stop them shooting straight in battle?' asked Jack.

'Battles are not so important,' replied Jiri, who seemed to have a lot of prior knowledge learned from his father, 'as parades. You might never go into battle, but you'll have hundreds of parades.'

Inside the locker hung a thick greatcoat which Jack was told to guard with his life because it was an expensive item, kindly supplied by the state, and should it be lost or mislaid the soldier responsible would be court-martialled. He soon learned that this precious item could also serve as a supplementary blanket, during the nights when temperatures were at zero.

And the floor! This was the most precious thing of all. The first order the lance corporal in charge gave them was to tear a thirty-centimetre strip from the bottom of their blankets and make this piece of cloth into two separate pads. Thereafter whenever they crossed the polished floor of the billet they skated softly on pads, so as not to scratch or injure the gleaming surface of their most astonishing floor. The floor would still have to be repolished at least twice a day, using a huge can of yellow polish, but anyone caught actually *walking* on it in either bare feet or boots would be beaten with wet towels by his comrades.

That floor was a mirror that reflected the honour of Hut 37.

When the lance corporal had retired to his own room at the end of the hut, and having settled them down to cleaning their kit, the boots of which had to shine at least as brilliantly as the billet floor, two large youths came over to Jack's bedside and said, 'You're a foreigner. We don't like foreigners, especially sorcerers' apprentices.' Jack realised this was a veiled suggestion that he was an alchemist's assistant. 'Find another hut, or come outside now.'

The two youths then skated across the floor and waited outside in the icy wind for Jack to emerge.

Jack went out to try to reason with the pair, to tell them that he had no choice in the matter. He told them he had nothing to do with magicians or sorcerers, and that his father was an inventor from London who had gone missing. They scoffed at him, calling him a wizard's brat.

Without any of the three youths realising it, Jiri had followed close behind, and as the two youths began to close on Jack with bunched fists, he stepped forward.

'You'll have to fight both of us,' he said to the bullies.

They shrugged, seeing this skinny boy before them. But though Jiri looked frail, he was anything but weak. His limbs were lean but they were woody-tough. He had helped his father on the land since he was an infant, and there was the hardness of a hawthorn tree about him. He struck one of the youths in the chest and knocked him flat on his back. The other one stared at his comrade, gasping for breath on the frozen ground, and decided he did not want any of the same. He left silently and went back into the hut.

'You leave us alone,' said Jiri to the struck youth, as Jack helped him to his feet, 'or you'll regret it sorely.'

Afterwards Jack thanked his new friend and said, 'I'm sorry, I'm not much of a fighter with my fists.'

'We all have our skills,' replied Jiri. 'One day you will help me with something.'

11.   FROM SCHOOLGIRL TO SCULLERY MAID

Annie was collected from the police station by a severe-looking woman with her hair in a bun. The woman was not unpleasant, but appeared to be a very worried and nervous person. She said she ran an agency for domestic staff, and she told Annie that rich and powerful people were often the hardest to please. She said, 'I give them reasonable and competent staff, yet they complain at everything. A maid never dusts as her mistress thinks she should, nor does a cook ever produce a meal to the satisfaction of the master. Aristocrats are exacting in their standards, yet never seem to be able to communicate their precise needs. They think their servants should be able to read their minds. You'll see. I doubt you'll last two days with the first family I put you with. They'll run you ragged and then complain to me that you're lazy.'

Annie did not like the sound of this and began to wish she were a boy so that she could join the army instead.

'Surely if I do a good job . . .' she said.

'Oh, you'll do a good job, and they may sniff and concede that the work is adequate, but as soon as they see a smeared spoon you'll be castigated. You'll start your career as a scullery maid, which is the lowest form of kitchen life. You'll be blamed for everything, whether it's your fault or not. If some infant breaks a cup, it'll be your fault. If the master comes home late from work, it'll be your fault. If the mistress feels a draught, or shivers from a fever, it'll be your fault.'

Annie was horrified. 'What does a scullery maid do?'

'You'll start your day at four-thirty by lighting all the fires in the house, but for the most part you'll do as the cook tells you, or the butler, or the parlourmaid, or anyone actually, except perhaps the family dog. Mostly it'll be blacking the range, or cleaning the grease from the ovens, scrubbing floors, that sort of thing. Not difficult to learn. You'll probably be one of the last to go to bed too, unless the cook's a kind person. I haven't met many kind cooks in my time, though I expect one or two must exist somewhere. One supposes they must have human feelings occasionally – don't you think?'

This sounded absolutely horrifying, but what was Annie to do about it? She had an idea, and said, 'But I'm an educated person – couldn't I be a governess?'

The agency woman laughed. 'A governess? My dear, you need to be gentry to be a governess – a poor cousin of the family, or some such relative. They won't let you near their children if you're a foreigner anyway. And would you want to be? The little brats will pinch and kick you, won't do as they're asked, and will then tell their parents that you slapped them. You'd be accused of all sorts of things by the little swines and probably end up in prison for assault. Personally, I think one should steer very clear of any child of the upper classes. They're far more deadly and have far less conscience than your average Indian cobra.'

Annie could not think what to say in reply to this. She had gathered romantic images of governesses in her head from watching costume dramas on TV. Now that this agency woman had explained the real situation to her, she did see things a little differently.

'Well what about a housekeeper, then? Couldn't I be a housekeeper? I could manage a household.'

Before the agency woman could pour scorn on such elevated ambitions coming from the mouth of an orphan from the streets – Annie had about as much chance of being a housekeeper as she had of becoming Queen of England – a large dowager had entered the room wearing a thick fur coat and a wide-brimmed hat. Annie was astonished by the size of the feather which swept from the crown of the hat and brushed away cobwebs from the ceiling. The importance of the lady was evident from the huge shelf-like bosom to the way she flourished her pince-nez. The agency woman immediately leapt to her feet and offered this grand personage a chair.

The great lady ignored the seat.

'I would like a new scullery girl,' she announced in strident tones. 'The last one ran off with a young man – an ostler from an inn, of all creatures.'

'Yes, your ladyship. We have several on our books. I could send some round this morning . . .'

'Oh, I haven't time to interview the creatures – a girl's a girl. What's this one here?' Her ladyship pointed with a velvet-gloved finger at Annie as if she were an item on a shop shelf. 'She'll do.'

The agency woman started to protest. 'She hasn't had any experience, your ladyship. For anyone else, yes – but for you . . .'

'Good heavens, what experience does cleaning out a grate require? Send her round – better still, I'll take her with me.'

'To walk beside your motor car?' suggested the agency woman.

'Has she got lice?' came the enquiry.

'No,' Annie said hotly, 'I certainly haven't. I'm as clean as you are – ma'am.'

The agency woman looked suitably horrified.

'Don't you answer her ladyship. You'll speak when you're spoken to, my girl. The very idea.'

Her ladyship raised her pince-nez and peered at Annie through the lenses. 'Got spirit, has she? Learned it on the streets, no doubt. I'm not sure I want an urchin who is insolent. The last one was a bit too impudent for my taste.'

'Quite so, your ladyship. I'll send another . . .'

She was interrupted by a very angry Annie.

'Who are you calling an *urchin*? I'm as good a person as you are, even if you are – well, what are you? A baroness or something?'

'A countess,' said her ladyship coldly.

'A countess. Well, I'm not sure I know the difference, but I do know that I'm as good as you are. I don't mean to be impolite or bad mannered or anything – but I am a person just the same as both of you. Not a creature, or an urchin. I've fallen on difficult times, it's true, and need employment, but that doesn't give you the right to insult me. I'm happy to work for you, Countess . . .'

'Countess Kinsky von Chinic und Tattau,' finished the countess in a faint voice. The agency woman had gone bright red and looked as if she wanted to crawl under her desk. 'I'll take the child. Send her out to the motor car, if you please. She can ride home.'

The countess then swept out of the room in a rustle of stiff clothing to rival the sound of Niagara Falls.

'Well – I have never . . .' began the agency woman.

'You have now,' interrupted Annie, still seething with the injustice of being called an urchin. 'Now, do you want to keep her ladyship waiting, or shall I go and join her? I'm sorry, I'm not going to be treated like a dog or something. I'm a human being. Shall I go? I'll take that as a yes.'

Annie followed the countess down the stairs and out of the doorway to find a magnificent but very antique-looking car parked at the edge of the road with a uniformed driver at the wheel. The rear door was still open, so Annie got into the back seat with the countess. The countess looked at her as if she were a garden slug. 'In the front, girl!'

Annie did as she was told, her indignation having faded away, and with it some of her courage. As she sat down, she glanced out of the window to see someone standing in the shadows of a doorway across the street. It was that mystical, misty figure that Jack and she had seen several times since they had arrived in Prague, usually at the point of some change in their fortunes. Annie could define no features on the ghostly figure, only that it resembled a man in shape.

'Can you see that shadowy man?' she asked the chauffeur. 'Over there in that doorway?'

But the driver hardly turned his head and did not seem inclined to answer.

The motor car pulled away on the noisy cobbles. It was

a very draughty vehicle in the icy wind. The driver was wearing a thick coat and scarf, as well as large leather gloves. Annie's coat was quite thin. Neither driver nor countess took much notice of her shivering though. They seemed quite oblivious to her discomfort.

As they drove through the streets of Prague, mostly on cobbled roads that made the vehicle bounce like mad, Annie thought to make conversation.

'This is a very nice car,' she said to the driver, whose uniform consisted of goggles, as well as a cape and a peaked cap. 'Does it go very fast?'

She had touched the right nerve. Now he seemed inclined to open up and talk. 'Built by Carl Benz,' he told her with some pride in his voice. 'I think they're better than the Daimler or Mercedes. This vehicle can reach a top speed of thirty-seven miles per hour!'

'Impressive,' said Annie, smiling to herself.

They seemed to be doing about ten miles an hour when the countess rapped on the glass with an umbrella handle. 'Too fast!' she shouted. 'Slow down!' The driver did as he was told, and they went down to a pace which equalled the walkers on the pavements. The countess seemed satisfied at this and was able to study the shop windows as they passed. Occasionally she ordered the car to stop and went into one of the dress shops or stores, emerging with a harassed-looking shop assistant carrying the goods she had purchased.

Once, when the car had stopped to let the countess enter a shop, a dark-skinned man with a familiar face passed by. His eyes glistened in his face like jewels. Annie had seen those eyes staring into a crystal, and now they they glanced down at her in the front of the car.

'Kaspar! It's really you?' hissed Annie. 'Help me. Help me escape.'

Kaspar stared up and down the street, then at the car's chauffeur, who was occupied with shouting at a rider whose horse looked as if it were about to defecate on the car bonnet.

'What are you doing here?' whispered Kaspar. 'This is the vehicle of an important person. Have you told her you can make her a fortune by turning her fire tongs to gold, or her coal scuttle to silver? You will not profit by faking the Ancient Science, you know. If you learned anything from Dvorak, it will not work without his guidance.'

Annie shook her head and told him what had happened.

'Ah. But what will you do if you escape the countess? I think you're better off with her for the moment. I will tell Dvorak I've seen you.'

With that Kaspar left her and joined three other people standing on the corner of the street, one of them dressed like an Indian prince. He spoke to them quickly, pointing at the car. They all looked back at Annie with sympathetic expressions. They were gone, in amongst the crowds, and Annie was left to rue her fate.

Eventually they reached the edge of town and drove into the countryside, still at the same snail's pace. Finally they came to a driveway lined by poplar trees, which led up to the doors of a vast mansion with scores of windows. There were green domes on its several roofs, one or two spires, and a cluster of towers on one corner. Annie could see a weathervane shaped like a startled hare, running straight into the wind from one of the spires.

Servants appeared on the broad curving steps, presumably brought there by the sound of the motor, and stood there with hands clasped, waiting to assist the countess. The countess was helped from the car and ascended the steps with an imperious air. There were servants at every side, back and front, standing ready to catch her with gloved hands in case she slipped on the icy surface.

No one took any notice of Annie until the driver spoke to a thin, reedy man dressed in a claret jacket with silver buttons.

The man came to the car, bent down and said, 'Round the back, child – present yourself to the cook.'

'Are you a footman?' asked a curious Annie.

'I am Pokorny, the butler,' he said, straightening with dignity. He tugged self-consciously at the hem of his jacket. 'You should be aware there has been a misfortune in the family . . . but why am I explaining this to a scullery girl? Off you go, child. Find the cook and give her Tomas Pokorny's compliments.'

'Oh, sorry.'

'Quite so.'

Feeling a little miserable now, Annie walked right round the building with its elaborate statues and high gargoyles. The gardens rolled away on every side, but in winter they were not as impressive as they might be in other seasons. Everything was coated with a hoar frost, and though it sparkled, it drained the gardens of all colour. Then she actually saw a fox, sneaking through the vegetable patch near the kitchen windows. This familiar creature with its rusty-red coat lifted Annie's spirits.

At the end of the gardens stood a set of low buildings which Annie assumed were the stables. A youth in shirt-sleeves was grooming a horse in the courtyard outside one of the buildings. He looked up, letting his arms fall by his sides. He stood with the grooming brush in his hand, staring at Annie over a distance. Annie stared back, frowning.

Finally she yelled, 'You'll get cold in just your shirt!'

The boy simply continued to stare.

'Rude,' murmured Annie to herself, and turned away to find the kitchen door.

When she entered the kitchen there were two women in there and a man lounging near the cooking range, taking advantage of its considerable heat. The man, in outdoor clothes, picked up a shotgun standing against the wall and said, 'Well, I'll be getting about my business.' He winked at Annie, adding, 'One in, one out,' and passed her in the doorway. A large woman Annie immediately took to be the cook looked up at these words and frowned. 'And you are?' she demanded.

'Annie Kettle. I'm the new scullery maid. Pokorny sends his best regards or something.'

The cook put her hands on her hips and studied Annie from top to toe. 'Scullery maid indeed,' she remarked. 'Quite a sturdy-looking lass, from the size of you. Nice clean skin. Good. Where've you come from? Another household, or straight from home?'

'Straight from home, I'm afraid.'

'Indeed. Straight from home. Hungry?'

'Yes, ma'am,' said Annie eagerly. The cook was the first

person to offer her food, and the 'ma'am' sort of slipped out naturally.

'Just call me Cook. There's some cabbage and potatoes over there, in that black pot, and hot thick gravy in the jug next to it. Help yourself. You won't starve in this house. The countess isn't one to stint on food, for herself or her staff. She's no tyrant neither, not like some of 'em. You did well to get into her service, girl. The last one didn't know what side her bread was buttered on, silly little cow. I'll give you a copper coin if she's not been abandoned by that ostler by now.'

'You don't think it was romantic?' Annie said, ladling some of the vegetable stew into a tin plate.

'I think it was dimwitted and hare-brained,' growled Cook. 'What're they going to live on? Hearts and flowers?'

Until now, the other person, a lean, anxious-looking girl, probably in her late teens, had said nothing. She suddenly burst into tears and hurried out of the room. Cook raised her eyebrows. Annie said, 'Did I say something awful?'

'Take no notice of Kitty,' said Cook. 'She was soft on the same boy. He was all dark molten eyes and curls, but no character, silly girls. Go on, eat up,' she encouraged, 'plenty more where that came from. Keeps out the cold. When you've finished, you can help me cut the meat for tonight's meal. Kitty should do it, but she'll be useless for the next hour now that *he's* been mentioned. You won't find it a heavy burden, service in this house. The count is dead. Went off riding one day last year and his horse brought him back with as much life in him as a log, still upright and with the reins in a death grip. When the horse came

109

to a halt he fell out of his saddle without so much as a farewell, crashing on to the courtyard in front of the stable hands.'

'How terrible,' Annie said. 'But doesn't the countess entertain a lot of guests?'

'Hardly ever.'

'She looks formidable,' said Annie.

'Looks, yes, but not so much.' Cook sighed. 'She's not been the same since he left for the other place. She mopes, though no one really sees it but me and her chambermaid. She doesn't sleep well. I hear her walking the passageways above our heads in the early hours of the morning. It's a sad thing when the other half goes. A lamp goes out in heart and mind and it's all darkness for a long while after.'

'Are you married, Cook?'

'Me?' Cook gave a hearty laugh. 'Not me, girl. I could've had any number – any number. Not that I'm a Helen of Troy, as you can well see, but good food is a powerful love potion to a certain sort of man. They'd kill each other for *one* of my venison pies, let alone a lifetime's supply. But I don't want any man to be telling me what to do or how to do it. I'm comfortable as I am, my girl. Let 'em come to me with their posies and chocolates, I don't mind, but they don't get very far with Cook. Now, you get one of them sharp knives out of the block there and we'll start with the Dutch carrots. Ever seen a carrot before?'

Annie replied that she had come across one or two.

Annie sat in front of the blazing kitchen range. The door to the range was open, and when she wasn't cutting up carrots, she found herself staring into the heart of the fire. The heat was quite strong and she drifted off into a dreamy state of mind. It was while she was sitting there, half awake, half asleep, that something suddenly leapt out of the burning coals and into her lap. Whatever it was, its dress flared with blue and green flames. It danced on her apron with glittering red eyes and fiery teeth, hissing coloured gases.

Annie shrieked and jumped up, flapping her apron to rid herself of the horrible object. She very soon realised it was not a live coal, but a strange fiery creature, which tried to cling to her with charcoal fingers. She felt it burning through her clothes to the skin beneath. Finally she managed to shake it off and it fell to the floor and scuttled away under the kitchen range. When she looked at her apron, there were burns on it like criss-cross marks. Cook, who had been out of the room, entered and instantly saw her distress. She asked Annie what the matter was.

'A thing came out of the fire,' Annie said, shuddering. 'It was a – a small fiery creature.'

Cook's eyes widened. 'Ah – that'd be an *ohnivec*. My grandma saw one o' them, but she's the only one in the family who has.'

'What's an *ohnivec*?'

'A fire fairy. That's how a lot of children get burned to death. You're very lucky not to have suffered that fate, young Annie. *Ohnivecs* usually live in red-hot coals, that've been burning for some time. If I was you, I'd stay away from fires like that . . .'

From the sound of her job, thought Annie, she should be quite safe from the *ohnivecs*, since she only had to clear out cold ashes from the grates in the early morning, and light the new fires.

12. YOU'RE IN THE ARMY NOW

Jack was woken in the middle of the night by someone blowing a bugle. He sat up, angry that his sleep had been so rudely and thoughtlessly interrupted. Before he could protest, however, a large, bulbous-nosed but smartly uniformed corporal began yelling from the middle of the room.

'Up, up, you lazy tykes! On your feet. Grab your towels and into the washrooms with you. Now! Now! Not next week!'

Jack swung his legs over the edge of the bed and stared, bleary-eyed at Jiri, who smiled at him in an understanding way.

'Come on, Jack. What did you expect? This is the army.'

It was freezing. When Jack's feet hit the floor, the shock of the cold wood travelled up through his legs. Then someone screamed at him to get his feet on to pads and he remembered about the polished surface and did as he was told. The queue outside the washrooms was long, but went down quickly. Jack waited, shivering in the nightshirt they had given him, until it became his turn to stick his head under a tap that gushed icy water, rub some carbolic soap on his neck and face, and then wipe it with the piece of rough cloth that passed for his towel.

Once back at his bed, he climbed into the coarse uniform, having to struggle with the stock – the stiff leather ring – that went round his neck and kept his collar straight. The boots he had polished and polished the night before felt bullet hard on his feet. He combed his hair with a steel comb before putting on his cap. Then he saw that others were folding their blankets into a square at the bottom of their beds, and displaying their other kit. The corporal was going from one bed to another, yelling instructions on how to lay out the kit.

'Don't we get fed?' Jack whispered to Jiri.

Jiri whispered back, 'First the inspection!'

The clock at the end of the billet said 5.30.

Jack had never seen the day at this time before, and he did not want to see it again. Ghastly. It was black, cold and evil-looking. What was the point in getting up so early? Jack thought he would have a word with the corporal later and tell him that people just did not function properly at such a disgusting hour of the morning.

Jack went back to the washroom to clean his teeth. The only other occupant, at the end of the long line of basins, was a pale, thin boy whose hair was a startling black and looked as stiff as the bristles on a yard broom. It stood up straight, a good three inches from the top of his head, and made the boy look quite strange and unapproachable. Jack watched this weird youth as the other cleaned his teeth vigorously. Then, just as Jack turned away and went to one of the middle washbasins, the boy disappeared from the far right end and reappeared at the far left.

Jack blinked and felt his brain spin.

113

'How did you do that?' he asked.

'What?' asked the boy, grinning though a mouthful of foam, his high spiky hair almost touching the low ceiling. 'This?'

Again he was gone, and now returned to the far right.

Jack shook his head and turned back to his washbasin. This other youth was obviously tricking him somehow. Was it hypnotism? It had to be, thought Jack. The boy was blanking out Jack's mind for a few seconds while he changed ends, leaving Jack mentally unaware that time had passed.

'Are you an alchemist?' asked Jack. 'Is that why you've been dragged in here – into the army?'

'Name's Thrum,' replied the boy. 'Pinscher Thrum. Yes, I came for the convention, but I'm no alchemist.' He spoke the word with some scorn, 'I'm a magus – a sort of magician. We magi don't deal in mundane things like metal, even if it be gold or silver. They grabbed me for the army because I was born in Austria, though I've spent most of my life in a mystical city on the Silk Road to Chinese Tartary, a city by the name of Samarkand, where things are and they aren't, and sometimes will be but often will not be, even if they were once.'

Jack ignored the fact that this speech made very little sense.

'If you're a magician, why haven't you magicked your way out of joining the army?'

'Maybe I don't want to. Maybe I want to experience the horrors of war. We are all merely skeletons waiting for the flesh to be torn from our bones, Jack Kettle. Perhaps I want to see the stripping of those bones, the marrow burning and bubbling in the heat, the whole skeleton shattering, being ripped asunder, thrown to the far corners of the Earth.'

'What a weird bloke you are,' laughed Jack. 'You've got a strange mind. And how do you know my name?'

'I would be a poor magus if I didn't – but I heard it called out during roll call, along with a hundred others I've memorised.'

Jack finished cleaning his teeth, and as they both prepared to leave, he said to Thrum, 'I don't believe that – what you did before, that whatchamacallit.' He recalled a school lesson about electrons in atoms jumping about without appearing to move through space. 'That quantum leap thing.'

Thrum smiled. He was still standing at the left end of the washbasins – then suddenly he was at the right. Jack blinked again, annoyed. 'It's just hypnotism,' he said. 'It's got to be.'

'Stand back,' said Thrum, 'and look into the mirror at the far end, where I was standing a moment ago.'

Jack's eyes travelled down the long line of mirrors and found the one on the far left. To his amazement, Thrum's image was still in this mirror. It was smiling at him. When he looked frantically back at where Thrum was actually standing, the mirror in front of this youthful magus was empty. There was no reflection of the boy who stood in front of it! Jack swallowed, a little frightened now by what he was witnessing. Still he clutched on to his theory of hypnotism, but he knew it would be useless to argue with Thrum, who might do something even stranger if he was challenged again.

'It's my only *real* illusion,' Thrum told him.

'You're just weird,' was all Jack could find to say, before he ran back to the billet.

The inspection was carried out by an officer who was in a foul mood (and no wonder, thought Jack, since he also had been dragged out of a warm bed). He took issue with everything any of the new recruits had tried to do, even criticising the immaculate state of the floor, saying it was the worst he had seen in a decade. Jack's bedpack (the folded blankets) was 'an offence to every soldier who ever served' and was immediately strewn all over the place. Jack was then told to refold it in a manner that did not bring the army into disrepute.

When the inspection was over, they were marched on the parade ground until they formed some sort of semblance of order. Arms had to be swung in unison. Legs had to move together. Boots had to be crashed down on the frozen ground in a single note. Eventually, the corporal told them, they would move like a centipede, as a single creature. Until that time they were to banish all individual thoughts and to think as one. With their rifles they were taught to shoulder arms, present arms, stand to attention, slow-march, quick-march, stand easy, march in file, march in columns of three.

By seven o'clock they were exhausted. Yet still they marched, saluted, did eyes-right, about-turned, left-wheeled, right-wheeled, and many other manoeuvres. Jack's eyes glazed over. He went into a kind of dream motion, simply following the others where they trod, doing what they did, copying their movements.

The corporal had several funny sayings; at least he considered them hilarious, even if the recruits did not.

'Fall out for a cigarette!' he bawled. 'If you don't smoke, go through the actions!'

'Am I hurting you, soldier? I should be, I'm standing on your hair. To the barber with you after breakfast.'

'Quiet! I want absolute silence! I'm not getting it. I can hear someone breathing. Who's breathing on my parade?'

Very funny, thought Jack, <u>not</u>.

At eight o'clock they collected their tin mugs from their billet and were marched to the mess hall. It was true they marched much better now that they had practised, even for just two hours. The best that could be said for the breakfast itself was that it was hot. What it consisted of was a state secret and never revealed. The coffee too was thick and hot, but Jack, being unused to such dark, acrid-tasting stuff, felt a little sick and giddy after he had drunk it.

When breakfast was over, they were all marched to the barber, who sheared their heads as one would a sheep, leaving just short bristles. Jack had difficulty in recognising anyone after that, for they all looked like skinheads. Now his cap flopped down over his ears and he had to pull the drawstrings tight to make it fit again.

He was tired and miserable but the day had only just started.

They were taken back to their billet and told to strip down to vest and shorts but keep their boots on. Each soldier was then given a backpack which felt as if it were full of bricks and they were taken on a road run that seemed to go on for miles, with the corporal yelling at them the whole way. They saw other columns of soldiers also running;

in fact, by the time the exercise was over, Jack had seen hundreds of men, some marching, some doing an assault course, some running. For the first time he became aware that he was part of a huge army. An army that ruled a vast European empire. For some reason it scared him.

When they got back to the barracks, Jack was more tired than he had ever been in his life. Consequently he forgot about the floor pads and walked on the polished floor in his big boots. The corporal almost went insane, screaming at him. Jack was sent to the cookhouse and there spent the rest of the day and most of the evening peeling vegetables and scraping the grease from cooking pans and trays. It was horrible, demeaning work, which sent Jack's spirits down to somewhere lower than the boots that had caused the trouble. He was finally sent back to his billet at ten o'clock and there he met with an angry reception. The rest of the recruits had been plotting against him for bringing the hut into disgrace. They had knotted wet towels ready to hit him with.

Jack simply stood there, too exhausted to move.

'We're going to beat you until you beg for mercy,' the biggest of the recruits told him. 'So you learn to follow orders.'

As they advanced on him, Jiri stepped in the way.

'If you fight him, you fight me too!' he said.

Jiri had already established he was a good fighter, and the two youths he had vanquished before now backed away.

Others came forward, though, arguing with him.

'You can see this foreigner has brought disgrace upon us,' said the biggest youth. 'Why do you protect him?'

Jiri replied, 'We are all new here. You – me – all of us, we have had no experience in battle, we have brought no honours to the regiment – not yet. Some of us will, some of us won't. Perhaps none of us ever will. But for the moment none of us has the right to judge another. Jack here might end up the hero of the regiment, a man of courage and conviction. Then what will you say? Hurrah for Jack? Or remember that you beat him for scratching a stupid floor? Forgetting to wear floor pads is not important. Wait until the first man runs from the battlefield. *That* might be a disgrace. We shall see. We shall see how we feel, for I think we will all be afraid of death, if and when the time comes. For the moment it's more important to stick together, to form a comradeship so that we know we can rely on one another. Why make enemies amongst your comrades, who might be protecting your back in battle?'

There were mutterings amongst many of the recruits. Some were saying that this made good sense. There was one recruit by the name of Svejk who was very patriotic. The sergeant had pronounced him to be the best soldier material in the barracks, and Svejk was therefore highly respected by many of the other recruits, though there were some who questioned his motives. Now he berated the bullies for picking on their comrades and praised Jiri's speech so enthusiastically and at such great length that all the heat went out of the moment.

The biggest bully still glowered at Jack darkly. Jack knew this boy's name was Martin Steiner. He could tell Martin was not swayed by Jiri's argument, or by Svejk's long tirade. Jack himself was all admiration for Jiri's speech. He knew

119

the farm boy had had a limited schooling, yet he had managed to move them all with his words.

Jack said, 'I thank Jiri and Svejk for their support – and I shall now work on the floor and remove the marks made by my boots.'

Tired and dispirited though he was, Jack removed his dirty clothes and in his underwear went down on his hands and knees with a polishing rag and began to buff the scratches. After a while he was aware that there were others down with him. When he looked up, he saw that Jiri and a number of other recruits were on their knees, polishing the tracks that led from the doorway. In just twenty minutes the floor shone as it should and Jack was allowed to go to bed at lights out. He fell instantly into a deep sleep, from which he did not stir until the bugle call.

Five-thirty a.m. Every muscle and bone in Jack's body ached with fatigue, but he rose with the others and formed a queue in the freezing cold, waiting for his turn under the icy tapwater. When he got back from the washrooms he found the corporal inspecting the floor. The corporal looked up at him approvingly.

'You're learning,' he said. Then he turned to the rest of the recruits and added, 'You're all learning.'

They took that to mean they had done the right thing, by helping their comrade instead of beating him. All now saw the sense in Jiri's words, even Martin Steiner. It made every recruit in the room feel good. They were learning. They were learning fast. Even the inspection was not as turbulent as the day before. The marching came easier, just a little easier, and the breakfast seemed more appetising.

Army ways were difficult but not insurmountable. There were six more weeks of this continual spit and polish, marching and running to get through before they could even think of taking a rest.

Jack fell asleep that night with Martin Steiner's name on his mind. He was sure he had heard that name before, but he could not place where. Perhaps he was wrong. But the name continued to flicker at the edge of his mind. He was not too worried. He knew it would come to him sometime. These little memory knots always did unravel eventually.

13. THE ASSAULT COURSE

Although Jack had escaped a beating from his fellow recruits in Hut 37, he was still far from popular. There are always those who need the comfort of having someone to pick on, sometimes because they have been bullied themselves in the past and have learned to do the same to others. Newcomers, foreigners like Jack, were an easy target for such youths. So Jack learned to ignore the insults and jibes. He was sniped at a great deal, but bore it all with the knowledge that it was all only temporary. He was *not* like these boys, actually. He was from the future and knew things they could never know unless they lived to be over one hundred years of age.

Jack felt he ought to put his much vaster knowledge to good use, but somehow coming from a world of mobile phones, laptop computers, aircraft, advances in medicine, and all the other wonders of the twenty-first century did not seem to help him. He knew how to email and text message, he had seen television, he had flown in a plane – but what good did these experiences do him in a world where the horse was the main form of transport? Things like marching and making bedpacks had not advanced in the least by the twenty-first century. They still did these things in Jack's time the way his great-grandfathers had done them.

Everything changed, though, on the day that they went to the assault course. Pinscher Thrum whispered to Jack as they marched to the course, 'This is your day, Jack Kettle. Not Svejk's, not mine, not Steiner's. I know these things. I have been to Asia Minor in the night, flying over the ancient cities of Sidon and Tyre. I have spoken there with a caliph's magician who said, "This is Jack Kettle's day."'

'You're nuts,' Jack replied.

There were many more soldiers going to the assault course than Jack had previously seen. There had been a total of one hundred new soldiers recruited. They were in five separate huts, twenty youths to a hut.

In most armies at that time a battalion consisted of around a thousand soldiers. A battalion was normally made up of ten companies, each consisting of one hundred men. In Jack's regiment, the 14th Foot, there were two battalions. His was the newest company to be formed for the 2nd Battalion. They were now being trained so that they could join the battalion as a fighting force.

The whole of Jack's company gathered on a bleak piece

of countryside beyond Prague. Obstacles had been erected and placed on the field, over or through which the recruits would have to climb, crawl or swim. There were walls, tunnels and, at the very end, a small lake. It was one of the warmer winter days, which was why it had been chosen as the assault course day, but still very cold.

Their corporal, along with other non-commissioned officers, instructed the recruits.

'You lot, listen up,' said the corporal. 'Me and the sergeant expect a lot of you today. We have to beat the other four huts over the assault course or be humiliated. The quickest recruit through that course *must* come from Hut 37 – you understand? One of you has to win. My pride is at stake as your training NCO. I shall be a very unhappy man if we do not win – and you know what that means? More inspections, more parade-ground practice, more bulling of kit, more of everything you hate about the army.'

Jiri, Jack and every recruit standing on that field swallowed hard. There was a big sweeping sky overhead, flurried with cirrus clouds. On the horizon was nothing but black leafless trees. In between the sky and the surrounding woodlands was mud. Mud in vast quantities. Mud that was deep in places and shallow in others. But mud it was: thick brown gooey mud, with some freezing surface water.

'We must do our best, Jack,' said Jiri.

Most of the recruits came from the city or town. They were hollow-chested youths, pale and thin, some of them stunted in their growth through poor living conditions and illnesses that came from bad sanitation and damp conditions. Many of them had suffered lung infections and diseases of the stomach.

Jiri was tall, though not as tall as Jack. Jack – surprisingly, for he was a town boy too, and younger than most – was probably the tallest of them all.

'I'll try too,' he told Jiri.

As it was, Hut 37 was the last to participate. They had to stand in the cold air, getting more chilled by the minute, while the boys and men from other huts tackled the assault course. Finally it was their turn. All twenty youths set off at once. There were NCOs strung along the length of the course looking at watches, timing the speed of the recruits through each section.

The first obstacle was a wall about two metres high. Jack was familiar with a climbing wall in his gym at school. He was up and over this one in a few seconds, followed by Jiri and two other farm boys. The rest, including the big bully boy of the hut, struggled and struggled to surmount this barrier, many of them having to give up without success.

The next section was a series of canvas tunnels lying on the mud, through which the boys had to wriggle and crawl. Jack and the other three found this particularly easy. Farm boys especially are used to mud, having to tend cattle and plough fields in driving rain.

Then there were logs to scramble over, hoops to jump through and ropes to climb.

Jack's lungs were bursting after the first two hundred metres, but he kept going, vaguely aware that the other three were around somewhere, though exactly where he was not sure. He jumped up on to a long greased pole along which he had to walk. His balance let him down twice, but he was allowed to climb back on and finish that section, as others had done before him.

It was a great struggle though the sucking mud. The further he ran, the more thick clay he collected on his boots. His legs got heavier and heavier, until he was clumping along quite slowly. But he was nearing the end. He could see the shining stretch of water through which he would have to wade up to his chest. It was going to be cold, he knew that – very cold. But the job had to be done. He wanted, above all things, to finish the course. His physical condition, as a fit youth of the twenty-first century, was superior to that of the youths from this era. He realised that now. His mother had never let him, Davey or Annie eat junk food, and though he hated her for it sometimes, it was now paying off.

He reached the edge of the water and saw his corporal waving to him from the far side. The corporal's eyes were shining, but there was a tinge of panic in that wave. Jack knew he was doing well, but it was going to be a close-run thing. Suddenly Jiri was beside him, but he looked done in.

'Jack,' he croaked, 'I can hardly breathe.'

But in the next second Jiri had leapt into the lake. Jack was all admiration. He watched his friend ploughing through the cold water, the slick mud at the bottom slowing his progress almost to a standstill. Two more youths came up alongside Jack and they too stumbled groggily into the water. One of them was Martin Steiner, who snarled at Jack for standing on the edge and not following Jiri. This pair battled for a few moments, trying to make some headway in the mud, getting nowhere.

From the corporal's frantic hand signals, Jack knew that time was now quite crucial. Jiri was not going to beat the record set by a boy from one of the other huts. The bottom mud was grasping at his ankles and he had sunk past his shins in the stuff. It was pulling and pulling at the farm boy's boots, dragging him to a halt.

Jiri was standing fighting for breath, his hands on his hips. He looked distressed and beaten. It seemed he could go no further and his eyes were full of frustrated tears. He had given his all. So had the other two youths, one of whom was being hauled out to prevent him from being drowned.

All this had only taken seconds.

Jack made a swift decision.

He thought he could beat the clock.

He pulled off his boots, tore away his tunic and ripped off his trousers. People were looking annoyed and bewildered as he plunged into the water in a shallow dive wearing just his underclothes. He was vaguely surprised to see a little old man amongst them, a pipe between his wrinkled lips, but then all Jack's thoughts were gone.

The shock of the cold water punched the air out of his lungs and cleared his mind. All he knew was that he had to keep moving. If he did not, he would freeze to a standstill. Doing the Australian crawl, he crossed the short stretch of water in a quarter of a minute, cutting the surface and never letting a foot even skim that terrible pond-bottom sludge that had destroyed the efforts of his comrades.

Jack felt a rough-skinned hand grasp his own at the other end, and he was wrenched from the water by his corporal who wore a look of triumph. Jack knew he had done it.

He had beaten all other contestants on this gruelling training ground. At last his twenty-first century expertise had come in use. He realised now that a great majority of these boys could not swim. It had not even occurred to those who could to cross the lake that way. They had all followed each other, plunging into the water and wading. Jack's initiative and his confidence in his ability had won through.

Someone gave him his clothes. He dressed quickly, shivering violently all the while, but soon his wet underclothes did not bother him so much. The recruits, all looking bedraggled and fatigued, were marched back to the barracks. In Hut 37 someone lit the stove, someone else got Jack a hot drink, and then they all came up to him one at a time to shake his hand. Martin Steiner was last, but he was magnanimous, saying, 'Well done, Jack – you did good. I salute you.'

Later, the corporal and sergeant came to the billet and slapped Jack on the back, congratulating him, the sergeant saying, 'I always knew you had it in you – a tall strapping lad like you.'

Jack had been accepted at last.

The only one who seemed a bit funny with him now was Jiri.

Later that evening Jack went to his friend and said, 'Are you all right, Jiri?'

The beefy farm boy blustered, 'I suppose so,' not looking at Jack, and busying himself with his kit.

'Come on,' Jack said, 'there's something the matter. What is it, Jiri? Is it something I've said or done?'

Jiri looked at him fiercely. 'You won, didn't you? Isn't that enough? Why are you bothering me?'

Jack was a bit hurt, but guessed Jiri was feeling put out because he had come so close to winning himself.

'It was only a trick, you know,' Jack told his friend. 'You had me beaten really.'

Jiri hung his head. 'I wanted to do my best – for all of us.'

'And you did. You were brilliant. Just because I can swim? Like I said, it was a trick. I wasn't better than you. I stopped on the bank. I was absolutely worn out. You plunged in without a second thought.'

Jiri's head came up and a grin began to spread over his features.

'Stupid, eh? Like an ox? That's what my dad would say. Follow the leading goose's tracks and never put a step outside. Not you, though. You stopped and thought about it. That's clever, like a fox. I'm sorry, Jack. You deserved to win. You deserve all the cheers. A good soldier uses his brains as well as his brawn.'

'You're not angry with me?'

Jiri looked shy. 'No – no. If I was, it doesn't last long with me. I get all het up, then it passes. Here, shake my hand.'

Jack took hold of his friend's hand and felt his own being squeezed hard by the strong fingers of the farm boy.

Jiri grinned at the face Jack was making and said, 'If we wrestled, I would beat you, Jack.'

'I wouldn't bet any other way,' Jack agreed. 'Those hands have done things these softies could never do.'

Jiri had ploughed fields, harnessed carthorses, dug ditches, sawn logs, chopped down trees, dragged boulders from the furrows. He was very, very strong. But what he did not realise was that feats like crossing obstacle courses took more than strength. They needed the stamina born of a good diet, fitness created by eating the right kind of food at the right time in life. A healthy lifestyle; exercise; sound sleep; a warm, dry home built in an area where the atmosphere was not polluted; constant medical attention for all his ailments. In the future, Jack had taken these benefits for granted, but not now – now he was very, very grateful.

At night, he lay in his iron bed, the snores and breathing of nineteen other youths around him, thinking of his mother, father, sister and brother. He had been robbed of his whole family in just a few short weeks. His first priority was to find out where Annie was working and to see if he could meet her somewhere. For the moment he felt they were both doing the right thing. Once he had graduated from initial training camp and joined the army proper, he would have a certain status that would allow him to ask questions. He felt sure that once he had the ear of a senior officer, he could discover where spies might be taken to be inter-rogated or whatever they did with them in 1903. He had come to realise that he had to proceed slowly, not rush into things. He had faith in himself and Annie to come through this adventure unscathed. Once found and released, Dad would know what to do to find Davey.

One evening someone brought the duty roster to Jack to sign. It meant standing out in the cold for two hours with his rifle, guarding the gate on the perimeter fence. He saw that he was sharing two a.m. guard duty with Martin Steiner. It was the first time he had seen the name written down, rather than heard it spoken. Jack felt a shock go through him. He now remembered where he had seen it before. It had been one of the many names on his mother's genealogy chart, when she had been tracing her ancestors using the internet. Jack had not instantly recognised the spoken name but he did the written version.

Martin Steiner was his great-great-grandfather.

14. DAVEY IN FANCY DRESS

If Jack could have seen his younger brother at that moment, he would have been completely bewildered. That very afternoon Davey had been taken out by the old woman to a bespoke tailor. There he was fitted with a white-trimmed black tri-cornered hat, two white shirts with lace collars and cuffs, and a blue coat with silver buttons. There were also tight-fitting pantaloons, black shoes with square silver buckles. In fact, once Davey was dressed in these clothes, he was the very essence of a gentleman of the 1700s – in miniature of course, for he was not very tall, even for his age.

Once they had been to the tailor's, he and the old woman rode to her home on a tram and prepared for the evening's performance. Though Davey had an important part to play, he was not the star of the show. He did have the consolation, however, of knowing he was the most intelligent of the actors, the most animated, and the most appreciated. The audience would applaud him with far more vigour than any of the other players, and unlike them Davey would bow and wave at will.

He went to sleep under his bench in the workshop at night surrounded by ghostly hanging wooden figures. Some of these pale effigies were without arms or legs, or even heads. Body parts were everywhere, lying freely on the bench or in boxes scattered about the floor. In the beginning they did not bother Davey and Davey did not bother them. They simply shared the same bedroom. However, the longer he was there, and the lonelier he became, the more he began to treat these figures as if they were real people.

Many of them had names, but it was the one called Leporello who spoke to him first. It was true Davey had asked a question of Leporello, but he hadn't expected an answer. Perhaps Leporello had been stung into his reply, which was more like a retort, by Davey's criticism of his performance earlier in the evening.

'What do you know?' Leporello muttered. 'You've only been in theatre for a short while. I've been treading the boards my whole life. Who are you to tell *me* I can't act?'

Davey was not normally the sort of boy to be worried by atmospheres. He usually slept soundly, and like Jack his dreams centred on his parents and his brother and sister. He was not thoroughly miserable, for he was having a rare adventure, one could even say the time of his life, but he missed his family like any boy would. And the need to speak to other children was getting to him.

But he was stunned by Leporello's reply and he trembled for a while, lying there in the darkness beneath the bench. Surely these puppets – for that was what they were – could

131

not talk? Yet this one had spoken to him, clearly and distinctly. He didn't know whether to be pleased or terrified. He felt both for a while, as he tried to get his head around this new turn of events. He was a small boy with a big imagination, however, and though still troubled by this supernatural change in his companions, he somehow felt safe.

After a long time, when he couldn't get to sleep, Davey spoke again to Leporello.

'Beg pardon,' he said.

'Accepted,' replied Leporello, speaking his German with an Italian accent. '*Grazie*. Please to think no more of it.'

Davey said nothing more that night, but after the matinee performance the next day, he was again closeted with the puppets. He decided to test one of the more leading players.

'Don Ottavio, you sang like a flippin' angel.'

'I am aware,' came the reply, for Don Ottavio was not known for his modesty. 'I have the golden voice.'

'And you, Donna Anna, you was like a nightingale.'

'*Grazie, grazie, mille grazie.*'

'You're welcome.'

Davey was able to fall soundly asleep that night, secure in the knowledge that he was no longer alone, but had a whole workshop full of puppets he could talk to.

15. ANNIE AKA SOPHIA

Annie was not having a good time. As a scullery maid she was rising even earlier in the cold morning than Jack. The first jobs of the morning – cleaning out the grates and the kitchen range – were miserable ones. Then she had to light the fires, so that when the rest of the household emerged from their rooms the house would be warm and the range ready for cooking on. But she was not then permitted to go back to bed. If there were no dishes or pans to clean from the night before, or stone floors to sweep and then scrub, she would help Cook prepare breakfast – for the countess, and of course for the many servants.

Annie was constantly tired throughout the rest of the day. She was at the beck and call of almost every other servant in the house and grounds, including footmen, grooms and gardeners. She helped to arrange flowers, gut rabbits, pluck geese, polish banister rails, fetch coal, chop wood, draw water, make tea, stoke stoves, oil bicycle chains and grease pans. Some of these jobs, like gutting the rabbits, made her want to scream. But to her credit she did not complain. She scraped black saucepans and made them shine. She scraped muddy boots and made them shine. She scraped burnt fat from baking tins and made them shine.

When evening came round she had to drag herself through the last few chores.

Cook was kind, but Annie had tasks to do and these had to be completed, however much Cook was sympathetic to her weariness.

The parlourmaid, Jeanette, was a spiteful woman in her forties. Annie was often told to assist her and underwent constant criticism.

'If it was up to me,' the parlourmaid, Jeanette, said, 'I'd have you whipped and sent home. You're a useless creature.

GARRY KILWORTH

I've never met a girl who spent so much time dreaming. You're here to work, missy, and work you will. I'll make sure of that. You may have sweet-talked the cook, but your sly ways won't work with me. I'm too long in the tooth for that . . .'

'Too true,' muttered Annie.

'What was that?' snapped Jeanette. 'Were you answering me back?'

'I wouldn't dare,' replied Annie sweetly.

'No, and don't you think of doing it!'

Several days after Annie had begun work as a scullery maid, she was given hope. It came as a surprise. She was helping Jeanette dust porcelain figures kept in a glass-fronted cabinet, and had suddenly reached for the figure of a shepherdess holding a crook and with a dog at her feet.

Jeanette screeched at her, 'Don't you touch that one, my girl – that's very precious. It comes from Meissen, near the famous city of Dresden. There's only one in the world, and my lady owns it.'

Annie stared at the figurine. 'You mean it's unique?'

Jeanette looked at her and frowned. 'Don't you try to belittle me with big words, missy. I'm telling you, there's only one. It's priceless, that is. It's not for the likes of a scullery maid to dust. I'll do that one . . .' Full of self-importance, Jeanette reached for the shepherdess – with a bit too much haste – and accidentally knocked it with the tips of her fingers before she could grasp it properly. As it teetered on the shelf, the parlourmaid panicked and grabbed at the delicate porcelain, just managing to stop it from falling to the floor.

Annie stared, wide-eyed.

Jeanette had gone very pale, and with trembling fingers put the figurine safely in her lap. After a few minutes the parlourmaid had managed to regain her composure. She dusted the little figure with a soft cloth and placed it very carefully back in the cabinet.

'There!' she said, as if nothing untoward had happened.

The incident was not of any great importance, except that Annie had recognised the object the moment she had seen it. There was another one, exactly the same, back home in her own house, in her own time. There was no doubting it. Annie had seen it many many times. It had been a wedding present to her mother and father from some Austrian relatives. Now, if the figure was unique, it meant that the shepherdess at home could not be *another* one. It had to be the *same* one.

When Jeanette left the room, Annie reached into the cabinet and took out the shepherdess, turning it over in her hands. While she did this, she was suddenly overcome by a strong urge to look out of the window. There on the lawn she saw that weird phantom figure, that tattered shadow of a man who seemed to appear at crucial moments. She stared at the ghostly black form, and as if in obedience to some command, she replaced the figurine. Once she had put the porcelain statuette back in its rightful place in the cabinet, the shadow man vanished like blown morning mist.

That night, alone in her small box room, Annie lay in her lumpy bed and, tired though she was, she went through various possibilities in her head. How had the countess's porcelain shepherdess ended up in her mother's china cabinet in the twenty-first century? She could come up with only one answer that made sense to her and it lifted her spirits enormously.

It was this: when Annie finally left the countess's employ, she would be given the figurine for services provided. Her father had told her that one should take nothing from one time period to another, or there might be serious consequences. This meant she herself could not return home with the figurine, but would have to pass it to someone. An ancestor was the obvious choice. That ancestor would in turn pass it on a younger family member, and thus eventually it would be given to her mother and father.

The only ancestor she knew was Blazek. This gave Annie great hope that she would finally meet him again. She was certain she would find Blazek, or he would find her, and all would be well. Annie would be reunited with her brothers and parents, and they would all go back to the twenty-first century and be safe and well. She finally fell asleep with this happy thought in her head, not realising that the incident with the figurine would have more immediate consequences.

The next morning, at around eleven o'clock, Cook and Jeanette together came to find her.

'The countess herself wants to see you,' said Cook, breathlessly. 'You're to report to the butler straight away.'

Jeanette was triumphant. 'Now you're for it, you slattern – her ladyship has heard about your laziness and she's going to give you what for . . .'

'Don't be stupid, Jeanette,' snapped Cook. 'The girl's worked hard since she's been here. If you've been spreading evil stories about her, it's more likely you'll be sent off without a reference, not her.'

Annie left them arguing and found the butler, who led her to the drawing room, where the countess was sitting on a settee reading a newspaper through her pince-nez spectacles. When Annie shyly presented herself, the countess looked up from her reading and studied her most recent scullery maid through narrowed eyes. Finally, when Annie was feeling uncomfortable under the scrutiny, the great lady spoke.

'How does a scullery maid know the meaning of *unique*?' she asked. 'Have you had schooling?'

'Yes, I have, ma'am. How – how did you hear about me using that word?'

The countess raised her eyebrows and fluttered a hand in the air. 'Oh, the parlourmaid told my dresser, my dresser told the butler, and the butler informed me. Not much goes on below stairs that I do not hear about, child. Goodness, one has to have one's spies, or how would I maintain discipline amongst the servants? So, you have been schooled? Can you read?'

'Of course. I mean, yes, ma'am, very well. I can read in English, German or French.'

'Good heavens!' the pince-nez came up again, to regard this multi-lingual highly literate orphan. 'And this was all learned before you went on the streets?'

'Er – yes, ma'am.'

'What sort of author or authoress do you read? Shabby penny-dreadfuls, no doubt.'

'Well, it's true I've read Dickens,' replied Annie, carefully picking writers from the nineteenth century, 'but I've also read Goethe and Shakespeare, and Victor Hugo.' It was true that she had not read a great deal of Goethe or Victor Hugo, but she felt there was no harm in impressing the countess, whose eyebrows flew up again.

'Good heavens!' said the great woman again. 'Are you some kind of child genius?'

'No, ma'am,' said Annie modestly. 'I'm just an ordinary child – but I have had a good education.'

'So it seems. Well, you shall read to me now. English poetry, I think.' She reached amongst some slim volumes on the shelf above her head. 'Lord Byron? No – no, far too risqué for a child of your age. Tennyson. Harmless enough and very melodic.'

Annie was given a book and was told to read from In Memoriam. The countess fell asleep halfway through the poem, but Annie kept reading until the end. Then she sat there until the butler entered and woke his mistress with the message that there was a visitor. The countess dismissed Annie and she returned to the kitchen, where Jeanette and Cook were waiting to hear what had happened. Annie told them and Cook clapped her hands. Jeanette scowled, saying it was just a one-off thing and Annie would not be called for again.

But she was. That very evening. Not only to read to the countess, but to discuss other things, like history, geography and – something she knew nothing about – politics. After two or three days the countess said to her, 'You are very entertaining, child. Very bright. Extremely knowledgeable. How you came to be so cultured is beyond me, but I'm pleased with you. Very pleased. Henceforth you will be my companion. Tomorrow we go to the shops. I'm going to dress you properly. Now, this is a wonderful opportunity for you. Don't let me down.'

Annie assured her new benefactor that she would not let her down.

'I shall do my best to serve you in my new capacity, ma'am,' she said prettily. 'I'm fully aware of the honour you do me.'

'Now that's the kind of thing I like to hear,' cried the countess, seemingly thrilled by the arrangement. 'That's the sort of language one seeks in a young companion. Well done, child. Well done indeed. You and I will do very nicely together. I've been so lonely since my husband died. You can't replace him, of course, I don't expect it. But you can lighten my dreary life a little. We shall do all sorts of things together, you and I. But what shall I call you? Annie? That won't do at all. Not a name to cast amongst gentility, is it? I shall call you Sophia! My companion Sophia. There, what do you think of that?'

'I should like it very much indeed,' replied Annie, slipping easily into the mode of speech used by her employer. 'Thank you, ma'am.'

16. THE CONCERNS OF A MOTHER

Kate in some ways had an even tougher mental attitude than her husband. She did not like captivity, of course, but she was not one to lie down and bewail her fate. She kept her spirits up with various mental exercises, such as reciting favourite poems, or the lyrics of songs, or re-running old memories through her fertile mind.

As the children's mother, she was naturally worried about them, but she constantly told herself they were safe and well.

Then came that devastating news tapped by Roger on the pipes. The children were here too, in 1903 Prague. Somehow they had managed to get to the time machine and use it. All Kate could hope for was that they were being looked after by Blazek's friends.

She could of course go and plead with the authorities, tell them her children were alone and defenceless in a foreign city. But if she did that, they might arrest Annie, Jack and Davey too. Then there would be no one on the outside, interested in getting them out of prison. She decided it was best to leave them where they were and hope that somehow they would all soon get out of this mess.

What she did do, continually, was to request a trial.

If she and Roger could somehow get themselves in front of a judge, she felt sure they could present themselves for what they were: innocent people abroad. They were not spies, they certainly weren't alchemists; they were just two ordinary people trying to trace lost relatives. The secret police were not known for their great intellects. They were simple men, sometimes not much more than brutes, who fixed on an idea and stuck with it. If they decided you were a spy, then you were a spy, even if the evidence pointed to you being innocent. Changing their minds would be admitting they were wrong in the first place, and that they could not do.

But a judge was a different matter. Judges were not always necessarily fair, but they usually worked within the legal system. Secret policemen wanted to catch spies: they got praised when they grabbed someone, anyone.

'When are we going to trial?' Kate kept asking the policeman they called 'the Weasel'. 'Let a judge decide.'

The answer was always the same. 'We are still gathering evidence – once we have it, you will be charged with the crime you are so obviously guilty of – spying against the government.'

'I demand a trial,' Kate would say. 'Give us a trial.'

'You do not *demand* here! You do as you are told!'

'I have rights as a citizen.'

'You are not a citizen of Bohemia – you are a foreign visitor.'

'I have relatives in Prague.'

The policeman would then thrust his face into Kate's and snarl, 'Tell me their names then!'

But of course she could not. Not because she did not know them, but because they would be dragged into prison too, and interrogated, and possibly tortured. So she would stare into the Weasel's baleful eyes and reply, 'I'll tell you their names – when we go before a judge. I'll give the names to a judge. So, when are we going to trial? Tomorrow, or the next day . . . ?'

17. BICYCLE COMPANY

'Who can ride a bicycle? Come on! Step forward anyone who can ride a bicycle.'

Despite all his dad's warnings never to volunteer for anything if asked by an official of any kind, Jack took one pace forward.

'So? Our foreign boy is the only one with a bicycle?' said the sergeant, smiling at Jack. 'You must have had rich parents.'

Jack was astonished to see that he was the only one out of the new recruits who could ride a bike. Perhaps the rest of them were lying? Maybe they knew something he did not? Perhaps this 'job' was so onerous no one wanted to do it. He began to feel a fool.

'Not so rich, Sergeant,' he said. 'Bicycles do not cost a great deal of money.'

'Ha! So any rich boy would say. Some here would give their eye teeth to own one. It says much about you. Now,' the sergeant began addressing the rest of the recruits, 'you are almost ready to join the regiment. The Fighting 14th! I am pleased with you, almost. Not proud – you are only average, as a company – but most of you try to be soldiers, and that must be enough for now.

'You are probably wondering why I asked for bicycle riders. Yes? The reason is, the regiment is forming a bicycle company. That is, a company of soldiers who can move from one place to another very quickly on bicycles. A hundred men who can astound the enemy by the speed of their movement. One moment on the left flank, the next on the right, and the very next fortifying the centre! A company of brave stalwarts on wheels. The rest of the regiment almost has enough bicyclers to form this company, but we need three more from you recruits. Who amongst you is willing to be in the Bicycle Company?'

Once more, to Jack's astonishment, dozens of hands flew up. They all wanted to be in the Bicycle Company. He could see the looks on their faces. They were desperate to be part of this new band of fast-moving infantry. Was it really infantry, if it was on wheels? Who knew. This was a highly innovative change in the army. Not horses, which required fodder and tender care, and were likely to get sick or injured and die on you. No, these were machines that required only minimal maintenance. Devices that sped the soldier to where the fighting was at its thickest and so turned the tide of the battle.

'So,' muttered the sergeant, 'many volunteers. We need only two more. Private Kettle, you shall choose. After all, it is you who will have to train them in the use of these infernal machines. So, choose carefully – pick those who you think will learn quickly.'

Jack turned and was bewildered by the intense looks, the waving hands. It was like being back at school. *Choose me! Choose me!* But who? Jack's eyes roamed along the line of eager volunteers. Jiri! Of course. He had to take his friend. But who else? Then he saw Martin Steiner, his great-great-grandfather, hand in the air, looking at him as if he knew he had made a great mistake by bullying this foreigner. It was a hopeless look. The look of a youth who realised that through his own stupid prejudices he had lost any chance whatsover of being picked for this great opportunity.

Jack pointed at Jiri, who stepped forward with an ecstatic look on his face. Then he walked along the line, stopping to stare into the face of Martin Steiner. Steiner's expression was stiff and proud. It said, 'I don't care if you do not choose me,' but his eyes, which he could not control, said, 'Please, please.'

'Private Steiner,' said Jack, pointing to the big boy. 'These two are my choices.'

Steiner's eyes opened wide. He stumbled forward as if he was hardly able to believe he had been picked. There was a general groan from the other recruits, but the sergeant assured them they would all get their chance in battle.

'Who knows, these three might be killed in the first wave of fighting, then others will be able to volunteer.'

Jack, Jiri and Martin were told to report to the captain of the Bicycle Company, in another part of the camp.

Pinscher Thrum saw them off with a sneer on his face. 'Kettle,' he said, 'I don't need a bicycle to leap from one place to another quickly, *you* know that.' He waved his hand airily in Jack's face. 'I might start a company of conjurers – a whole company that can jump from here to there without moving their legs. What about that, then? How will your slow bicycles fare against my brave, swift one hundred?'

'What's he talking about?' asked Jiri.

'Oh, it's all wind,' Jack replied. 'Wind and sleight of hand.'

Thrum laughed as they walked away. 'Sleight of foot, more like,' he called after them.

As they walked on, Martin said to Jack, 'Why did you choose me? You know I dislike you.'

'I know – but I don't care. You are a good soldier. Perhaps one day you will save my life.'

'I think not,' replied Martin, 'but I thank you anyway.'

Once they had reported to the lieutenant, they were issued with bicycles and Jack was given two whole days to teach his comrades how to stay upright in the saddle.

The bicycles themselves were quite different from the one Jack owned in the twenty-first century. It was a very basic machine, this army bicycle of the early twentieth century. It had a solid frame, sit-up-and-beg handlebars, no gears whatsover, a chain without a guard, and a saddle without springs. The other way in which it differed greatly from Jack's bicycle was in the wheels. It had no tyres, not even solid ones. Instead the wheels had an extra metal rim kept separate from the wheel rim by small springs. The corporal who had issued them with the bikes said this was because rubber was in great shortage and in any case was inclined to rot in the foul weather soldiers often endured.

Left with the machines, Jack chose one and jumped on. He rode down the road, grinning to himself. Who would have thought it? His expertise at riding a bike, something almost every kid in his street could do, had got him into a prestige, elite company of his regiment. He rode back to the others and could not help showing off by letting go of the handlebars and steering the bike with his knees the way boys of his era often did. He was not tempted to do a wheelie, though, which he guessed would rip the sprung-metal rim right off.

'Wow!' said Jiri. 'That was very good, Jack. Can you teach me now?'

Jack had never taught anyone to ride. However, he got both his charges on their saddles and the lessons began. It was hard work. These two were both farm boys, though, and had a good sense of balance. At first Jack did not ask them to pedal. He stood in front and held the bicycle upright with his hands and told them to get used to balancing the machine. Once he felt they would not fall off at the very first movement, he got Jiri on to his bike and he and Martin took one shoulder each, holding Jiri upright while he pedalled painstakingly slowly over the parade ground. Then Martin and Jiri swapped places. By the end of a long afternoon, Jack felt they were ready to go solo.

Jiri fell off straight away, into an ugly tangle of bicycle and legs, causing him to graze his knees savagely.

Martin fared a little better, staying on for at least twenty seconds, before he too took a tumble.

The youths were angrier with themselves than anyone else. They felt they ought to be better at it. If a weedy foreigner like Jack could do it, Martin said, then surely it was an easy thing. But he had to eat his words. It was not an easy thing. It was difficult. They went to supper that night with only partial success. Still, they had a whole day the next day in which to improve upon their small achievements.

The following morning it was as if the youths had learned

to ride in their sleep. Jack often found this. One could try and try, and leave a skill wanting. But take a rest, get the mind right, and wonders happened the next time. They were not proficient, of course, but they were much, much better. Over the course of the day they managed to learn the basic art of riding the bicycle without falling off too many times. Jack was praised by his sergeant, but this time there was no jealousy from Martin Steiner, who agreed with everything the NCO said.

One thing Jack had not remembered to teach them was road sense. Of course they had no idea, for cars were not common, even on army camps and there was very nearly a terrible tragedy, which might have had monstrous consequences for Jack. When he thought about it later, his head spun with the complexity of it all. In the end, he decided to leave it until he could talk to his father about it.

Here is what happened.

Jack, Jiri and Martin were fooling around on their bicycles just inside the camp gates, waiting for orders from their sergeant. An open-topped motor car suddenly came hurtling round the corner, going very fast for a vehicle of its time. Jack heard the car long before he saw it, but the other two were oblivious to the sound. Jiri had already crossed the road, but Martin was still doing circles in the centre of the street, crying, 'Look at me! I shall soon be riding no hands, like Jack . . .'

Jack shouted a warning and reached out to grab Martin by his left epaulette, pulling him off his bike towards the pavement. The epaulette ripped away from its button. Jack kept hold of the loose end and managed to wrench Martin off the street just as the car swept past. The bicycle went under the wheels of the vehicle with a loud crunching noise. The officer in the back seat shook his fist and yelled something at the boys, but was obviously in a great hurry and ordered his driver to continue. The bike suffered further mangling as the car's back wheels went over it, leaving it a twisted wreck in the road.

'Hell! I'll get slaughtered by the sarge,' muttered Martin. Then he turned to Jack. 'You saved my life, Kettle. How did you do it?'

'I – I heard the car. I'm used to hearing cars. In London, you know, we have a lot of cars. You get to react quickly when you hear one . . .' He burbled on for a sentence or two more, before he asked, 'Are you all right? I tore your uniform.'

'Never mind my uniform. It'll stitch. Thanks, Kettle, I won't forget this. But, damn, the sergeant's going to have my blood for this. A new bicycle! I'll be peeling spuds on jankers for a year . . .'

Indeed, the sergeant was not best pleased and Martin did indeed find himself working late in the cookhouse for a few days afterwards, as well as having a tidy sum docked from his pay over the next few months.

But what puzzled Jack was that he had saved the life of his great-great-grandfather before Martin had helped to conceive his great-grandmother. How could that be? If he had not saved Martin, Jack would never have been born. But originally Jack was not there to save Martin. So who actually did save him? Jiri? Or someone else? Who had taught the other two to ride bikes, if Jack was not there?

The whole thing whirled around Jack's brain with nothing in the way of an answer except madness.

18.   THE MAKING OF SOPHIA

Annie was now dressed in fine clothes and was the pet companion of the countess. When she felt she was able, she broached the matter of her lost parents.

'I wonder, ma'am, if you can help me discover the whereabouts of my parents? I would very much like to find them again.'

It was evening, dinner having come and gone, the house dimly lit by both electric light and candles in the darker corners. The countess was half snoozing in front of a huge log fire, her ankles blotched and reddened by the heat. She seemed to wake up with a start and stared at Annie. Clearly she had been dreaming, perhaps of her dead husband, recalling memories of him in happier times.

'Parents?' she repeated dreamily. 'What of them, child?'

'My mother and father,' Annie said. 'I should really be looking for them. Could you help me find them, ma'am?'

The countess raised herself to a full sitting position and began to adjust her crumpled gown.

'I'm a little at sea. I understood you to be an orphan.'

'No, not an orphan. My parents have been arrested by the secret police. They think they're spies, which they're not. We're just English people on – on holiday in Prague.'

The countess was now fully awake and seemed very disturbed by this turn of events.

'Arrested? Spies? Good heavens, child, what are you telling me? Why haven't you mentioned all this before now?'

'I – I haven't really had the opportunity, ma'am.'

'Tell me the whole story, so that I can grasp the problem. Wait just a moment. I must get a drink of something.' She rang a bell and the butler appeared. 'A glass of elderberry wine, if you please, Tomas. And something for the child.'

Tomas dipped his head sharply and left, returning a few moments later with two glasses on a tray.

Annie then sat on a cushion at the feet of the countess and proceeded to tell her the whole tale. She only deviated from the truth when it came to explaining how they had travelled to Prague, letting the countess think they came by ferry across the Channel. When she had finished her tale, she took a sip of cordial.

'So,' said the countess, 'your parents came on ahead and were arrested. Then this Blazek relation – what is he?'

'A cousin, ma'am.'

'Quite so. This cousin was also arrested when he began asking questions about his missing relations. So you were left on the street without adult supervision?'

'Then Davey got lost, and finally Jack and I were split up by the police, and Jack was made to join the army.'

'And you were sent into service?'

'Yes, ma'am.'

'What does your father do? He's not from the aristocracy of course – he must be in trade of some sort?'

'Oh no,' replied Annie. 'He's an inventor.'

'Really? What does he invent?'

'All sorts of things.' Annie was extremely proud of her father's profession, which even her friends thought really cool. 'Why, only the other week . . .' She stopped suddenly, realising she could not tell the countess that her father had invented a new chip for a cell phone.

'Yeeees?'

Annie panicked a little. 'He – he invented a new aeroplane engine.'

'Aeroplane?' The countess looked bewildered and Annie suddenly realised that planes were yet to come.

'That is, an engine for a hot air balloon.'

'Ah – those Frenchmen, the Montgolfier brothers – they made one of those. Or perhaps several? Well, well. But you should call your father a *scientist*, child. It's all the vogue at the moment, science. It's far more respectable than being a mere inventor.'

The countess went quiet for a very long while, staring into the burning logs, which hissed blue and green and red flames as the gases escaped the wood in which they were trapped. Finally she looked up and spoke again.

'These are dangerous times, child. People are fearful of being overgoverned. The empire must be strong to keep itself intact. There are anarchists everywhere. Do you know what an anarchist is?'

'Someone who doesn't like any form of government, no matter what sort it is?'

'Clever, Sophia. Clever. Yes, that's right. But anarchists these days do not just dislike the government – they try to blow it up. With bombs, child. Imagine that. Then there are opposition groups – opposing the government and the monarchy. They try to assassinate people – not just ordinary people, but princes and kings!'

Annie did not think princes and kings were any more valuable than ordinary people, but did not say so.

'In order to counter these threats, the government has created a police force that is ruthless in its methods. It is quite certain they have arrested your parents not because they are anarchists or assassins, but because they are foreigners. Foreigners are the first people to be suspected of crimes against the state. You can see how it is – if you don't know who the enemy is, you trawl wide and deep, sieve through what you find, throw away the dross and hope you are left with the criminals you seek.'

'Can you help me, ma'am? Please?'

'Of course I shall try to help you. I may be a rich old lady who lives in her memories, but I can see how distressed you are, Sophia. We shall have to ask questions very discreetly though. As I say, these are dangerous times. No one is safe. I have no desire to follow the example of your parents. What we must do is throw an entertainment of some kind, which will attract the right people. A card party, I think. Yes, that will be it. Whist, chemin-de-fer, games of that sort. I shall invite, amongst others, people who move in the right circles. The chief of prison Governors. The minister in charge of the secret police. That type of person. But we must not go charging in like rhinosceroses, Sophia. This has to be done with some delicacy. Yes, I'm getting quite excited by it all. Intrigue and adventure. I thought it had all gone when my husband died – he was very involved with these spy networks, you know; not one of them, but the general scene.'

'I'm very grateful, ma'am. Please don't get yourself into trouble.'

'Oh, I'm quite powerful in my own little way. I shall ask my brother to help, though. It's always best to have the assistance of a gentleman. Men are so eager to prove themselves superior to women, they will break their backs to reach the desired goal. We shall ask Albert tomorrow, when he comes to drink tea in the afternoon.'

Annie felt a rush of hope go through her. At last things were going in the right direction. She had trusted the countess and that lady had come through. Annie was still no nearer to finding the whereabouts of her parents, but she now had some powerful helpers.

★

'Are you mad?' cried Albert. 'Are you completely insane?'

The countess raised an eyebrow. 'If you insist on insulting me, Albert, you will have to leave. I won't be bullied in my own house. In *your* house you are no doubt the master, but here you are a guest. Do please remember that I am not your ten-year-old sister any longer, but a woman of – well, mature years, and a countess!'

Albert glared at Annie.

'This child is probably lying through her teeth.'

'I'm not a liar,' protested Annie, 'but if I was, I'm not sure how you can lie without doing it through your teeth.'

Albert was a tall, broad-shouldered, white-haired man of

about sixty-five years of age, which would make the countess – his *little* sister – a lot younger than she really seemed at first glance. Annie guessed it was the way she dressed, her gowns very full with lots of layers, and her head and hands covered with heavy jewels. She appeared about eighty, but she was probably around sixty years of age. Albert said he felt a need to protect his sister from the riff-raff of this world.

'For which I am very grateful, brother dear. But Sophia here is not a threat to me.'

'Who knows?' He glared at Annie again. 'She's a waif off the streets – you could be making a big mistake.'

'Does it matter, now that my darling Frederick has gone?' replied the countess with a glistening in the corner of her right eye. 'I lived only for him, you know. He was my joy and my delight.'

'Oh, come off it. You were fond of each other, I don't doubt, but it was no Romeo and Juliet match, now was it? Oh, all right,' he said exasperatedly, obviously fearful his sister was going to burst into a flood of tears. He stared at Annie. 'I'll go along with this farce, but listen to me, young woman. If you are setting some sort of web to catch my sister and me, let me tell you we'll pull you in too. What are the names of your parents?'

'Roger and Kate Kettle,' replied Annie eagerly. 'Oh, thank you, sir. Thank you. Um, I don't know what to call you properly. Are you a count?'

He humphed. 'No I'm not. I don't have any noble rank. My dear sister here married into all that. But I do own a bank. I think that's more important, don't you? I know many impoverished princes, but I don't know any poor bankers.'

'If money is important to you, sir – yes, I agree.'

He seemed a little rattled by this reply. 'Well, why wouldn't it be? What else is more important? I suppose you will say *land*.'

'No, nothing you can touch. Talent, I think. To be able to paint, or write well, or make things.'

'Oh, really? I can *buy* paintings, books and things.'

'But that won't give you the happiness of the soul that creating them can do – you only get the satisfaction of owning them.'

Albert turned to his sister.

'Where did you get this child?' he grumbled. 'I'm the most successful businessman I know, yet she treats me as if I'm worthless.'

The countess smiled. 'She can also make you feel very valuable – she does me, I know. Come, child, read to us . . .'

19. JACK FINDS ANNIE AGAIN

Jack, Jiri and Martin were sent with their kit to join the Bicycle Company. When they were assigned a billet, Company Sergeant Major Borsch asked them what they could do besides ride bicycles.

They looked at each other. Martin shrugged. 'I can march. I can shoot a rifle.'

'No, not those. I know about those. What skills do you bring from civilian life? Can you play the trumpet? What about mending boots – any cobblers' sons? Or a butcher's boy, who can cut meat properly? Are you, heaven knows, able to read and write? What? You must be able to do something. You look a big strong youth,' he said to Martin. 'Come, what else? I need to know how to make the best use of you, in my new company of bicycle riders.'

'I can cook,' said Jiri quickly. 'I used to make meals for my mother, father and brothers.'

'Good, good.' The sergeant major wrote this down on a piece of paper attached to a clipboard. 'You will help the cooks. Now – you, Private Steiner?'

'I – Sergeant – I – I . . .'

'Nothing, eh? No skills. Just a soldier.' He had begun writing on his board when Jack remembered something he had seen printed on his mother's genealogy chart under Martin's name.

'Didn't you used to help your father fix his farm tractor or something?'

'Tractor? What is that?'

Jack bit his lip. He had tried for something that might not exist yet. But then a light came to Martin's eyes. 'Oh – you mean my uncle? My uncle's steam traction engine? Yes, I did that, sure.'

The sergeant seemed impressed. 'Engines? Well then, we know what to do with you. You shall join our small band of sappers. They are the company engineers.'

'An engineer?' cried Martin. 'Me?' His chest puffed out.

Jack had remembered seeing 'civil engineer' listed as his

great-great-grandfather's occupation. Clearly once he left the army Martin would follow up on his sapper skills. Both Jack's friends now had good jobs within the company. But Jack knew he had a skill that would ensure him an even better one.

'So now, Kettle? What can you do?'

Jack reached into his kit and took out his knife and fork. He held one in each hand and stepped over to a dustbin. Standing over it, he beat a rhythm on the lid, first slowly, then building up in speed, until he was rat-a-tat-tatting in the way he knew how. Jack had been playing the drums since he had been eight years of age. He and his pals had a band called Sunset Stampede, a name the lead guitarist, Alex, had thought up. They had played once at a gig at their school, with some success.

'Oh yes, we know what to do with you,' said the company sergeant major, smiling, and writing on his sheet. 'We need another drummer boy.'

'That was fantastic,' said Jiri, after Sergeant Major Borsch had gone. 'Where did you learn to do that?'

'I just picked it up,' Jack replied, smiling.

Martin's eyes had narrowed, though.

'How,' he asked, 'did you know about the steam traction engine?'

'That?' said Jack, thinking quickly. 'Why, truth is, I didn't, but I guessed you might have something to do with farm machinery, so I took a chance. Hey, don't you want to be a sapper? That's a very respected job, so I understand. It can get you special privileges.'

'Yes – but I wonder why everything you touch seems to

turn to gold, Jack. It puzzles me. Sometimes I think you are not from this world – you seem different from us. You move like a ghost amongst us. And you know things you shouldn't know, couldn't know. I am beginning to think you are one of those alchemist fellows who are tarnishing our wonderful city of Prague at this present time. My father says the place is crawling with riff-raff – conjurors, magicians and necromancers – all hanging on to the coat tails of these alchemists. Why, the very air we breathe at the moment is polluted with foul magic.'

'Martin, I have nothing to do with things like magic. I'm different because I was raised in another country, with different customs, different education, different everything. I'm going to seem strange to someone like you, a boy from a rural area.'

'What is wrong with coming from a rural area?' argued Martin belligerently, but Jiri interrupted with, 'Please, Martin. Why are you attacking our friend here? He does nothing but help us and you keep having these suspicions. Jack is all right. Leave him alone.'

Martin set his face, but then said, 'All right – we'll drop it for now. But I just find it strange, that's all.'

A short time later they were called out on parade. Jack grabbed his rifle and joined the others. They were sorted out into squads and stood to attention. In charge of the Bicycle Company was a captain, with two lieutenants under him. Then there was Company Sergeant Major Borsch, with a few sergeants and several corporals under his command. They were all marched in formation to join the rest of the battalion, another nine companies, waiting for them on the parade ground. There Jack saw the colonel of the regiment for the first time. He was a tall man with a hawk's-beak nose, dark hair and piercing blue eyes. But what Jack noticed most about this very imposing figure made him lose his step in the march.

The colonel only had one hand!

In place of his left hand was a two-pronged steel hook, which flashed in the low winter sun.

'Kettle,' snarled one of the corporals under his breath, 'pick up the step or you'll be on fatigues for a week.'

'Yes, Corporal,' whispered Jack. 'Sorry.'

After the parade, Jack sat down on the edge of his bed. His heart was racing. Was this colonel the man who had retrieved his father's watch from the pawnbroker? Perhaps the pawnbroker had mistaken an army officer's uniform for that of a policeman. And if it was the same man, why had he done it? Was it just the wristwatch itself that had attracted him? Or did he know something about it, learned from Jack's father? Had he discovered that the watch was the key to a strange and fabulous machine?

The reason Jack's heart was racing was because he knew he had to search the colonel's quarters. If he was caught, he would definitely go to prison. Probably an army stockade, somewhere far out in the mountains or forests. He had to be very, very . . .

'Jack?' cried a voice in his ear, making him jump. 'Where are you?'

'What?' asked Jack.

It was Jiri. 'You are a thousand kilometres away – on the moon, I expect.'

159

Jack rose and picked up his towel, intending to go for a bath.

'The moon is much further than that, Jiri,' he said absently. 'It's three hundred and eighty four thousand kilometres from the Earth.'

Martin was there, by Jiri's elbow. 'There, you see! Strange. He just comes out with these things. How does he know them? Have you measured the distance to the moon, Kettle? With a length of string?'

'Oh, everyone knows such facts,' replied Jack. 'You find them in books. I never said I couldn't read, Martin. I read very well – in two different languages.'

Before Martin could reply to this, Jiri brought his hand from behind his back and showed Jack three pieces of yellow paper with printing on them.

'Passes!' he cried in delighted tones. 'Weekend passes, Jack. We are soldiers now. We can go into Prague and have a good time. What do you think of that?'

Jack grinned. 'Sounds good.'

Martin grabbed his pass and shook his head. 'Not me. Not with you two. I shall go alone.'

'But Martin,' cried Jiri, 'we could have a really good time together. The Three Musketeers!'

When they got to the city, Jack told the other two, 'I need to do something. I'll see you two later. Five p.m. – by the mechanical clock in Old Town Square.'

Jiri looked upset, but it was Martin who said, 'What – you're going off on your own?'

'I have to go somewhere.'

'No, no – we should all stay together.'

'I'm going alone.'

Jack strode off.

On street corners and in alleyways and doorways were groups of strange-looking men and women. Were these more alchemists and their kind? They whispered to each other, or turned down their heads so the brims of their hats hid their faces. Perhaps there *was* a conspiracy abroad? Perhaps because of their profession the alchemists were a stateless people, looking for a place to settle, having been expelled from their homelands? In which case the authorities would be right to be concerned. Prague would be a good city for such as they to practise their dark chemistry. Jack had been told by Franz that Prague had never been razed by an enemy; that its buildings had never been put to the fire or come under the cannon, like most ancient European cities. A safe haven for magicians? Were the alchemists working to make Prague a city under their influence, under their direct power? It could be.

It was a time of change, a time when secrets were the only defence – against other secrets. Knowledge was power, and men gathered as much of it as they could, like birds collecting bits and pieces for their nests. Gradually, moving from one shadowy group to another, they could get enough knowledge to learn which side to take, to know who to trust and who not to trust. It was important to find out where to be at what time and by whose direction they could claim to be there.

Jack looked smart in his uniform. Yes, he knew he looked very young, but the army had always had young drummer boys. Not so long ago they were only ten to twelve years of age. Jack was fourteen, and though he was not a man, he was a soldier, and he looked every centimetre of one. He sought out home domestic service agencies, strode into the offices, and requested information regarding Annie's whereabouts. Some of the people in the agencies were a little taken aback, but he spoke with authority and said he was enquiring on behalf of his colonel, who was seeking a runaway cook from the army kitchen.

Finally he found the woman who had placed Annie.

'I thought it was the police who wanted her put into service?'

'Ah, they must have picked her up, with that no-good brother of hers.'

'Yes, yes – that's it,' said the woman. 'There was a brother.'

'I wouldn't give you tuppence for the pair of them,' Jack said. 'Always causing trouble. Bad family.'

'Yes, I guessed so.' She went to a slim drawer in a filing cabinet and opened it, flicking through the cards. 'Are yes, here it is – oh dear, the Countess Kinsky von Chinic and Tattau. That's who hired the girl, as a scullery maid.'

'That's a very big name.'

'The countess is a very important person.'

'Where does she live?'

The agency woman looked at Jack through narrowed eyes.

'I think your colonel will know that – it's not my place to hand out her address, which is confidential between the client and the agency.'

'Of course,' said Jack, retreating, smiling as he did so. 'I would not wish you to break confidentiality. As you say, the colonel will know the address. Good day to you, madam.'

'Good day.'

Next, Jack threaded himself through the grey streets to the pawnbroker's shop. There he confronted the pawnbroker, describing the colonel and asking if this was the man who had redeemed the 'wristlet watch', as he knew they called it in 1903 Prague.

The pawnbroker shrugged. 'Who can tell? I have customers every day. After a week has gone by I would not recognise one from another.'

Leaving the pawnshop Jack came nose to nose with Martin Steiner.

'I've been following you. What are you up to, Kettle?' demanded Martin. He glanced at the shop window. 'Run out of money, have we?'

'No,' replied Jack, somewhat incensed by being spied on, 'but that's no business of yours, Martin.'

Martin put his hands on his hips.

'It might be my business – if you were dealing in stolen goods. These places are notorious as fences for the proceeds of a burglar's swagbag. I would hate to think we have a thief in the billet.'

'I am not a thief,' snarled Jack hotly. 'And I don't go sneaking around prying into other people's business either.'

'Oh? You seem to know quite a bit about me, though. About my uncle's traction engine and such. There's something not quite right about you, Kettle. I can't put my finger on it yet, but I will get to the bottom of it one day. You can't hide secrets for ever, not in the army. Your comrades will find you out.'

At that moment, Jiri arrived, out of breath.

'Martin, why did you run away like that? Ah, Jack. He's found you. Come on, let's find a coffee shop and sit down for a cake and coffee or something. I'm famished.' He paused, glancing from one to the other of his two friends. 'And stop looking daggers at each other. I don't understand why you two can't get on. You're so much alike it's unbelievable, yet you are always at each other's throats. Why, you even *look* alike. Jack could be your brother, Martin. Stop baiting one another and just accept that you come from different birth-places. I swear I never met two boys who were so much alike yet so different.'

'My brother?' muttered Martin. 'God save me.'

But there were no more recriminations until after the coffee, which Jack hated because it was so bitter-tasting.

Martin then stared at him and said, 'And the employment agency?'

'My sister,' replied Jack, honestly. 'She was put into service with a countess – Countess Kinsky von something-or-other. I need to know where she is, so that I can send her money when they pay us.'

'The Countess Kinsky von Chinic und Tattau,' said a dark-faced man at the next table. 'I have the address on the tip of my tongue.'

Jack whirled round to find Kaspar smiling at him.

'You?' Jack said quietly. 'Are you still around?'

Kaspar was dressed in a suit of black silk. His penetrating eyes surveyed the three young recruits with amusement.

'Tinker, tailor, soldier . . . Ah, you look well, Jack. Dvorak sends his regards, if I was to see you again. And the big man, you remember, he lives in Golden Lane? He asks after you and your sister. I shall tell him you are now a soldier of the empire, and your sister a scullery maid. Oh yes, Jack, I have seen her in my crystal. She works from dusk until dawn. No – *after* dusk and *before* dawn. But all will be well. Even your little brother . . .'

Jack jumped up. 'Davey? Where's Davey?'

'He is amongst wooden friends. I can't tell you where, because there are many such places. But he is safe, Jack. He is safe and better left where he is for the time being, until you find your parents.'

'Wooden friends?' Jiri repeated. 'Does he mean scare-crows, Martin, do you think? Is Jack's little brother in the fields?'

'It's not crop-picking time,' muttered Martin, who seemed fascinated by the appearance of Kaspar, for he could not take his eyes off the man. 'It's winter, Jiri. What would he be doing in the fields?'

Kaspar rose in a shimmer of whispering silk.

'I must be going. They scour the cafés at this time of day.'

Jack said, 'The address, Kaspar.'

Kaspar gave a little flick of his fingers and a small white card seemed to float down from the ceiling. Jack caught it and quickly read it.

'Thank you, Kaspar.'

'Most welcome,' said that seer. 'Don't let the *trpasliks* get you.'

'*Trpasliks?*'

'Dwarfs!'

Jack put the card in his pocket.

Before Kaspar left, Jack mentioned the gold watches in the pawnbroker's shop.

'I'm not so sure that such sudden gold is not destined for the same fate as fairy gold. They might turn to leaves and bark before the year is out . . .' Then he was gone.

Jack was worried about Martin now. What would he make of Kaspar?

Martin made no comment, but sipped his coffee. However, a little later he said, 'I don't know who that Kaspar fellow was, or how you know him, but he had very strange eyes.'

'I met him at the house of a friend,' Jack replied. 'Other than that, I know nothing about him.'

Martin shrugged. 'He seemed harmless enough, under those silly clothes. He looked like a gypsy on a Sunday outing. Some sort of conjuror, is he, with that card trick? Anyway, I approve of what you are doing, Kettle – if my family was missing, I would do anything to find them. One must always look after one's family.'

When Jack got back to camp, he knew he had some hard decisions to make. He needed to get into the colonel's quarters so that he could search for clues. It was a dangerous enterprise, but necessary. The very next weekend pass he got, he intended to go and see Annie, to make sure she was all right. Being a scullery maid did not sound all that exciting: in fact it sounded awful. Jack hoped Annie was not going through a horrible time under the countess's roof. He could imagine what it would be like, being at the beck and call of employer and servants. Certainly he had not had a soft time of it in the army, but he had to admit it was exciting.

20. A PONY CALLED CLOUD

Unknown to Jack, Annie was not having a terrible time of it. She had been taken into the fashion shops of Prague and bought dresses, shoes, hats (Annie had never worn a hat in her life before), nightgowns and all sorts of accessories like reticules and evening gloves. She had been treated like a princess, and indeed looked like one. The countess, who was very rich, spared no expense in outfitting her new companion, for after all, how Annie looked reflected on the countess herself.

It was true that the clothes did not excite Annie a great deal. They were hardly boutique fashion, being gowns and dresses that enveloped her like bedclothes. They were made of metres of material, some of it very thick. A multitude of folds, creases, bows, buttons, pieces of lace and stitching inhabited those dresses. Annie felt as if she were carrying around the week's washing on her shoulders. Still, she did not complain. Her school friends could not see her, and that was all that mattered. Any other girl of the time was similarly dressed.

Annie was also introduced to all sorts of other rich and aristocratic people. These introductions were chaperoned, of course, for Annie was still not 'out of the schoolroom'.

Indeed, the countess hired a tutor for her and Annie had

lessons every morning from eight o'clock until half-past twelve.

She surprised her tutor with some things, but was chastised for her lack of knowledge in others. Her teacher, a severe woman in her fifties, seemed more interested in ensuring that Annie wrote in neat copperplate handwriting, rather than encouraging her creative abilities. Surprisingly, spelling was not one of the most important aspects. Good grammar was essential, though. Mathematics consisted mostly of copying figures so that they were legible. Annie's question as to when they were going to do some quadratic equations was met with a blank stare.

She was also expected to learn embroidery, how to play the harpsichord, how to sit, stand and walk in various situations. For instance, there was a mode of walking for a turn around the living room and a different mode for strolling in public in the park. She was expected to learn to paint with watercolours and reach an acceptable standard. The art of proper conversation was high on the list, and pretty manners were of the utmost importance.

'Would you like a pony?' asked the countess one day, as the thought obviously occurred to her. 'I had one at your age, I remember. Her name was Cloud.'

'Would I?' answered Annie breathlessly. 'Oh, yes please.'

The pony, a pretty piebald, was purchased and duly named Cloud after her predecessor, which pleased the countess beyond measure.

'Pleasant child,' the countess murmured, when speaking of Annie. 'Such a comfort to me.'

In her turn, Annie was always attentive to the countess's

needs, fetching things for her before the other servants even heard the end of the sentence, which infuriated them. Annie made no friends except Cook. This did not worry her unduly, since she knew her stay there would be temporary. Life was becoming far too comfortable for her, though – she was being spoilt beyond anything she had ever known before. It would be a wrench for anyone to leave all that behind, especially Cloud. Not surprisingly, she quickly became very attached to her pony and spent a great deal of time helping to groom her, which did not endear her to her tutor, who felt such things were best left to stable boys.

Annie had ridden horses before, mostly on holidays with the family, but was by no means a regular visitor to the stables back in her own time. However, under the tuition of the stable boys, it wasn't long before she became a good rider, able to handle Cloud on her own. Cloud was not a difficult young mare by any means; she was affable and happy to be out and about and using her stocky little legs. A strong, affectionate bond soon developed between rider and pony. Annie's rides out on Cloud were essential 'thinking' times. She had the peace, quietude and space to ponder on her problems and try to work out resolutions.

The countess had told Annie she must not ride out beyond the estate boundaries without a stable boy for an escort. However, the boys were often very busy and Annie was reluctant to bother them, so she tried to stay within the grounds as much as possible. Inevitably, though, there came a day when she found herself riding beyond the woods and meadows of the countess's land, and into the fields of a neighbouring estate. It was a day that started out fine, with a low sparkling winter sun picking out the early frost and dewdrops, but that clouded over with dark climbing nimbus towers in the late morning.

'I don't like the look of that sky, Cloud,' Annie told her pony, who was always a good listener. 'It looks a bit black up there.'

Cloud was inclined to agree, but somehow could never come back with any good advice. A pat on the neck told her that her owner was sympathetic to this character fault.

In her anxiousness to return to the house before the rain came down, Annie somehow lost her way on a woodland path. When she and Cloud emerged from the treeline, they were faced with a wide brook, almost a river, downstream of which stood a strange-looking mansion with at least two dozen pointed turrets, twenty tall twisted-brick chimneys, and many, many glinting, narrow leaded windows. It was indeed a sinister-looking building.

'What do you think, Cloud? Shall we try to cross the stream? I don't like the look of that spooky old house, do you?'

Just then Annie noticed a little elderly man in baggy clothes standing by a weathered post. He had his elbow on the stump and was smoking a corncob pipe. On his head was a battered shapeless hat and on his feet were large unshined boots. He gave Annie a ghost of a smile through the veil of pipe smoke that wafted around his features. Then he beckoned with his free hand, inviting her to talk.

'Yes?' said Annie, trotting over to him. 'What is it?'

'Ah, a German speaker,' murmured the little old man. 'Is

it that you want to cross the water, eh?' His head hardly reached Annie's stirrup as he shifted from one foot to another. 'Here's a good place to cross,' he said, pointing with his pipe. 'This is the right area to ford the stream, for it's too deep where you were, just back there.'

Annie studied the distance across the water. It was about five metres from bank to bank. But it did look quite deep, not shallow as the little man had suggested. She studied his face. It was pale and very lined. Why would he tell her a lie? What did he have to gain by doing that?

'Are you sure it's shallow here?' she asked. 'The water looks a bit deep – and fast.'

'The rate of flow can be deceivin',' replied the little man quickly. 'It looks fast, but it ain't really. It's quite slow. And with a hard bottom not far down. I'll show you . . .' and without further ado he strode in and crossed the stream to the other side, the water not coming above his ankles. Once there, he nodded and beckoned Annie to follow. 'On you come,' he encouraged. 'Nothin' to it really, girl.'

He seemed to be somewhat anxious in his bidding and took off his hat to wipe his brow with the back of his sleeve. To Annie's astonishment, hair dropped like bunches of string from under his hat and fell all the way down to the ground, grey and straight, with raggedy ends that curled in the mud. 'Come on, girlie,' he called. 'It's but a step or two, no more. Just kick that horse forrard. That's it.'

Annie was still unsure, but the alternative was to go through the garden of that horrible eerie-looking mansion. She did not want to do that. So having no other choice she nudged a reluctant Cloud into the stream. Almost immediately the water went up to Cloud's belly and the pony gave a whinny to show her disapproval of the bitterly cold bath she was getting. Not only was it deep, but the current was swift and twisting, threatening to take Cloud's legs from under her. Annie fought with the reins to keep the pony on a stable footing, while the little old man cried, 'Come on, come on! Further in. It's not that deep. You must have hit a hole. Get on with you. Further, further. Don't be scared. Look, I'll help you. I'll help you across. I've done this before for other children.'

With that the old man threw himself into the racing waters. The stream now came up to his shoulders. He reached out and grabbed Cloud's bridle, tugging on it, trying to force the pony out into the wide brook. The old man's hair stretched out on the surface, floating like long grey pondweed in the stream's rapid flow. Annie suddenly noticed with horror that his corncob pipe was dipping rapidly in and out of the icy water, yet still remained glowing, still alight, the smoke billowing from the bowl. The old man's grey eyes were feverishly bright as he yanked on the leather bridle, while Annie tried to back Cloud out on to the bank. It was a tug of war between the old man and the pony. Cloud wanted to obey Annie's instructions, but the little old man seemed to have immense strength, belied by his size and age.

'You will come into my house,' he screamed. 'I will have you for my very own, you obstinate child.'

Only now did Annie recall, with a terrible chilling feeling, a story told to her by one of the stable boys.

'There are watermen out there,' the boy had said with

round fearful eyes. 'Water ghouls what steals the life and souls of drowned children. They look like old men, but they come from under the ponds and lakes, and they holds you under with their hard hands. They holds you under till the breath bursts from your body, then they skewer your soul out of your dead body and hang it on a butcher's hook, down below the water, along with all the others they've got over the centuries . . .'

Annie had not paid a great deal of attention to what she had considered to be a fairy story, but now realised she was in a great battle with one of those very creatures. She could not doubt it. The little old man, his head now under the water, was trying to pull her from her pony by her ankles. His icy grip was like steel. Several times he managed to wrench her foot from the stirrup, but she kicked his hand away while urging Cloud gradually backwards. Once she lashed out hard and her kick took the pipe out of his mouth. It floated to the surface, still smoking, and would have been swept away by the speeding current had not the waterman scrambled after it.

This was their chance to escape. Cloud was no shirker when it came to emergencies. With a final struggle, she managed to get her rear legs onto the slippery bank. Once there, she dug her hooves into the mud and eased herself out of the water. Pipe in mouth again, the water ghoul returned, snarling, spitting and flailing, attempting to get another grip on Annie's ankle. Failing to do so, he slipped back down into the swirling waters, his face twisted in anger and frustration.

Annie let out a yell of triumph as Cloud finally got

out on to the bank, free of the racing flood tide. The little old man surfaced further downstream, beating the water with his arms and screaming in rage. He thrashed his way back to the other side of the racing torrent, letting out horrible curses in many languages, calling Annie foul names known only to demons. If she doubted he was a supernatural creature before this point, she did so no longer, for on the far bank he looked as dry as a bone. His baggy old clothes fluttered in the breeze and his pipe was back in his mouth. He took his hat and flayed himself in the face, neck and shoulders with it, crying out for justice, crying out for revenge, crying for the souls of drowned children.

At that moment the heavens let forth a deluge. It came down so heavily Annie could only discern the waterman as a dark silhouette through the curtains of rain. Realising she had only one alternative to crossing the dangerous water, she trotted Cloud towards the nearby mansion.

When she entered the gardens a little while later, Annie dismounted and took shelter in a gazebo that stood not far from the main house. She eased Cloud's head inside, but there was no room for the rest of the mare's body, which had to stand out in the rain. They were both quite shaken by the encounter with the waterman and were pleased to pause to gather their breath. While doing so, some French doors flew open at the back of the main house, and a large figure in a frock stepped forth into the hissing rain bearing a huge black umbrella.

The figure strode towards the gazebo with a determined tread. When it was within a metre or so, Annie realised that it was not a woman wearing a dress, but a large man in a purple cassock.

'Bring the horse this way,' he boomed, 'and put her in the stable – that's right, come under the umbrella.'

Annie, bedraggled and miserable, did as she was told.

Once Cloud was under cover, Annie was taken to the house, and there her host introduced himself.

'I am Stephen the Seventh of Krenz, the Viscount-Bishop. What is your name, child?'

'Annie – that is, Sophia.'

'Which is it? Or both? Perhaps you are like me, unable to relinquish either of your titles?'

'I prefer to be called Annie.'

'Annie it is then. Now, child, you have been caught out in the rain. Where are you from?'

'The neighbouring estate. The countess . . .'

'Ah, quite so. Then I will send a boy to tell her you are here. In the meantime, perhaps you would like to dry yourself and change? One of my maids will assist you. Then you must join me in my library while we wait for someone to fetch you. Is that to your way of thinking?'

Annie said it was. She was collected by an unsmiling parlourmaid, who took her along gloomy passageways and up dusty stairways to a room with a creaking floor. There she was given some clothes which she was told had belonged to a scullery maid, 'beggin' your pardon, miss,' who did not want them returned because 'She died at the turn o' the year of typhus or somesuch disease. The clothes has bin washed thorough and won't be carryin' nothin' nasty, that's certain, so you can wear 'em without concern or worrisome thoughts.'

Annie did have 'worrisome thoughts' but felt there was no option but to do as the parlourmaid said. She changed gingerly into the threadbare dress, which fitted her remarkably well. Then, gathering up her clothes, she assessed her situation. She was still in a strange house – a *very* strange house – but one with several people around. Had the viscount-bishop been completely alone, Annie might have declined his offer of shelter and warm dry clothes. But there were servants all over the place, as well as gardeners and stable people within short calling distance. She did not feel there could be a serious problem if there were so many others who would surely come to her aid.

So it was with a certain confidence that she entered the library, after she was shown the way by the dour parlourmaid. Her host stood by a huge roaring fire, his back to the flaming logs, his big-boned face set with small eyes. Hands behind his back, he indicated with a nod that she should join him at the fireplace. The pair of them stood, allowing the heat from behind to warm their backs, while Annie stared around the room at the same sort of paraphernalia owned by the countess. There were white marble busts of Roman generals, gold clocks, lace covers on small round walnut tables, a suit of armour in one corner, bookcases full of leatherbound volumes, worn Persian rugs on the floor, and a grand piano gathering dust in another corner.

The only real difference between the two houses was a set of display cabinets along one wall. Annie wondered if her host was a sort of Victorian gentleman who collected things, like butterflies or seashells, or perhaps geological samples of rocks and minerals? Though of course, she reminded herself, there were no Victorians here, for they were not British.

'Well, Annie,' said the viscount-bishop after a while, 'you speak German with an accent. You are not Czech or Austrian?'

'I have ancestors who are,' she explained, 'but I come from London.'

'Ah, London! Wonderful city, I'm told. Never been there, but always wanted to go. I see you looking at my cabinets. I am an avid collector. Would you like to view my precious religious relics?'

Annie felt she ought to be polite and said, oh, was that what they were, and yes, she would like to see them.

The viscount-bishop led her to the display cabinets and removed the covers. He said nothing, but allowed her to peruse the items sealed in glass cases without any comment. Annie stared for a moment, expecting to be bored by a load of fusty-dusty communion cups and brass crucifixes, then suddenly she recoiled in horror and stepped back from the cabinet with a gasp.

'Oh. Oh dear. You don't like my hobby?'

What Annie had been staring at was clearly a human finger, severed at the joint nearest the hand, trapped in a glass tube.

'I – I don't understand.'

'Relics! They're relics, child. Most precious and unique religious relics. I have several hands and feet – and fingers of course. That one you seem to dislike so much belonged to St Francis. Did he not beckon the birds of the air with it? Did they not rest on that very finger? Hair – plenty of hair. The saints all seemed to have lovely hair, even those who were monks. Several boxes of fingernails and toenails. Even some internal organs – the dried, shrivelled heart of a medieval priest is the pride of that group – and one or two tongues. Tongues that once spilled wise and wonderful rhetoric upon the followers of holy men. There are the eyelids of an elderly sage, pasted to the cover of his black book. And bones – bones beyond number. Knee bones, thigh bones, backbones, scapulas, mandibles. Jaws full of teeth that chewed blessed bread. Skulls over which halos hovered.'

Annie said, 'I think I feel sick.'

'Ah,' said a relieved-sounding viscount-bishop, covering his showcases, 'so *that* is the problem. It must be that you caught a chill out in the rain. I thought it could not be my collection, which is the delight of everyone permitted to view it. Never mind, child. I shall call one of the servants to bring a bowl. Then you may vomit if you wish.'

However, at that moment a footman came into the room and announced that someone had called at the door for the young lady.

Annie almost ran from the room to find a youth of about seventeen standing there. His right hand held two sets of reins; one belonging to Cloud, the other attached to a large bay. In his left hand was an oilskin cape, which he offered to Annie. He himself was wearing hooded oilskins.

'I'm from the countess's stables,' said the youth. 'She sent me to get you, miss. Here, put this on . . .'

Annie took the oilskin and pulled it over her head, handing her wet clothes to the youth and saying, 'I haven't seen you at the stables.'

'Tag. Name's Tag. I'm new.'

So much had happened to Annie within the last few hours that she trusted no one. But the youth did have a horse with him that she had seen before. And once again, she appeared to have little choice in the matter. It was either staying with the viscount-bishop and his grisly collection of body bits, or going with this unknown boy. Anything to get out of the weird house she was in, even if it meant some new unpleasant adventure. So, thanking her host civilly, she mounted Cloud, and soon she and the stable boy were on their way back to the countess.

On the way back Tag said, 'So, Miss Sophia, did the old boy frighten you with his bits of holy men's bodies?'

'I wouldn't say *frighten*,' argued Annie. 'It wasn't a very nice experience, though.'

'He's harmless enough,' replied Tag, 'but you shouldn't go accepting invitations from strangers. Riding out like that is dangerous. Keep to the estate in future is my advice.'

Annie said stiffly, 'Thank you, but I'm sure I know my own mind. I can take care of myself.'

'What, you mean like with that water ghoul?'

She whirled in her saddle to face him alongside her.

'You know about that? How?'

'Oh – I know a few things.'

'You were spying on me? Why didn't you help me, if you could see I was in trouble? I don't think I like you, Tag or whatever your name is.'

'Well, Tag is definitely my name, and I couldn't help you 'cause I was too far away. I saw the old devil later, when I came up alongside the stream. He and I exchanged a few uncommon pleasantries, you might say, when I saw he'd been thwarted of a catch. That catch could've only been you, 'cause no Czech would have fallen for a waterman's talk. He nearly had you, didn't he? Nearly got the soul of a pretty London girl.'

For some reason his use of the word 'pretty' infuriated Annie, but she did not let her passion rule her reply.

'What pleasantries?' she managed to ask in an even tone.

'Oh, I told him what I thought of his ugly profession and he told me to go to hell, or somesuch place.'

'Weren't you scared of him?' asked Annie, impressed in spite of her negative feelings.

'Naw,' replied Tag carelessly. 'I've been encountering his kind since I was a nipper. So long as he doesn't get you in the water, you ain't got nothing to worry about. I told him he was more or less useless as a soul-catcher, and that made him as mad as fire.' Tag laughed, recalling the waterman's reaction. 'He threw his pipe at me, but I caught it with my free hand and tossed it far out on the meadow. He won't dare to venture that far from water. He's got to give up his smokin' now. They're not very good without their pipes, water ghouls ain't. They lose what's called their potency. I did for him all right.'

Annie laughed along with the stable boy at the image of the furious waterman, lost without his corncob pipe.

'That was very brave of you,' she said.

When they reached the gates of the countess's mansion, Tag took Cloud and promised to give her a good rub down. Annie carried her wet clothes to the house, shrugging off the oilskins in the hall. When she appeared before the countess, she was moderately tidy, having changed again in her room. The scullery maid's dress from the viscount-bishop's house went into the rubbish basket. The wet items were given to one of the maids. Then Annie went straight to the drawing room to see the countess and give an account of her adventures. She did, however, leave out the story of the waterman, not being sure of the countess's reaction to such a tale.

'So you went to that ghastly man's house?' cried the countess, appalled. 'My dear Sophia, it must have been a terrible experience for you. He is a madman, you know. He would have been put away many years ago, if it were not for his rank.'

'He was kind, though, to let me in.'

'I suppose so. But he should have let me know you were there the instant you arrived at his house.'

Annie was puzzled. 'Didn't – didn't a boy come?'

'No one came, child. The first thing I knew of it was when you told me just now.'

'But – but what about the stable boy? Tag. You sent him to fetch me home.'

'Tag?' The countess screwed up her face in concentration. 'I know of no stable boy of that name.' She sighed. 'But then of course, I don't know them all. They're just boys, after all. And that sounds like a name given him by his companions. Tag. Yes, a nickname, definitely, and one I wouldn't be privy to, being the mistress of the house.'

The countess cleared her throat before adding, 'But I sent no one. I did not know where you were. I thought you were in the house.'

'Then – then he must have followed me or something

like that. Oh, I don't know. I'm so mixed up now . . .'

'It's been a long day for you, Sophia. You must take a powder and go to bed. Try to get some sleep. You look tired out, child.'

Annie did as she was told, wondering if the day had actually been the night, and she was indeed suffering from a nightmare.

★

One Sunday Annie was busy learning needlecraft in the schoolroom when Jeanette the parlourmaid came to summon her to the countess.

'You're wanted in the drawing room,' sniffed Jeanette. 'I expect you're in some sort of trouble.'

'I expect not, since I haven't done anything wrong,' replied Annie curtly. But her heart began beating faster, and her mind started running over all the things she had been doing lately, wondering if there was something there that the countess could find fault with. It was true that since Annie was out of her own time, there were rules that she did not know or understand. She occasionally said something that made the countess wince, and it was not difficult to offend her delicate sense of decorum. Until now the countess had put Annie's ignorance down to being young and from a lower-class background, and had simply corrected her.

Annie was astute enough not to make the same mistakes twice, and left the countess feeling that she was managing to turn her companion into a Bohemian lady.

Entering the room, Annie saw the countess standing

facing a young man in uniform, a soldier of some kind. He had his back to Annie, but she admired the way he stood straight and tall. His cap was in his right hand while his left hand was straightening a seam on his trousers.

The countess was looking her most imperious, staring the young man in the face with the superior expression she could muster for visitors.

'Yes, Countess?' Annie said. 'You sent for me.'

'Yes, my dear. This young person seems to be your brother.'

The soldier turned and Annie's eyes widened.

'Jack?' she cried. 'It is you.'

Jack smiled. He looked very grown-up and smart in his uniform. He stepped forward and hugged her briefly.

'Well – look at you!' Annie cried. 'A soldier!'

'Private Kettle, drummer in the Bicycle Company of the 14th Regiment of Foot,' he intoned. 'And look at you, in your flounces and ribbons and stuff. Can you breathe in that lot?'

Annie glanced at the countess, who was working up to her most severe wince.

'I can see you young people have something to talk about, Sophia. It's too cold to take a walk around the garden, so I'll leave you in here.'

'Oh, thank you, ma'am.'

'Would you like some lemonade and cakes, young man?'

'Lemonade would be great, thanks.'

This familiarity made the countess raise her eyebrows, but she left the pair together to discuss their adventures.

Once she had gone, Jack turned on Annie.

'What the heck is all this "Sophia" business? And look

at you, Annie. You look like a birthday cake. I came here expecting to find you in rags and tatters, and scraping out pans. They told me you were a scullery maid. Quick promotion, eh? I though I'd done well, but I wouldn't have beaten you unless I made it to colonel.'

Annie quickly explained what had happened to her since she had left Jack, telling him about Jeanette and Cook.

'Oh yes, it was the cook who told me you'd become the companion to the countess. She seemed proud of you, the cook.'

'Oh, she's lovely. Not Jeanette, though – and some of the others. They're very jealous. I don't know why. None of them can read German and English, and that's what got me the job. So, what's happened to you? You're a drummer boy. Is that exciting?'

'Could be. Dunno yet. I've only just finished training. But I don't plan to stay around long enough to fight any battles. I think I've found the man who claimed Dad's watch from the pawnbroker . . .' Jack stopped talking as a footman came in with a tray of cakes and lemonade. He waited until the man left, then continued. 'He's the colonel of our regiment, and he's only got one hand! I'm waiting my chance to search his quarters.'

'Isn't that very dangerous, Jack?' said Annie, worried. 'What do you hope to find anyway?'

'I don't know, do I? Anything. Any clue as to Dad's whereabouts. You've got to remember that was a quartz watch, and they haven't been invented yet. I've been reading the newspapers and there's been nothing about an amazing watch being discovered.'

'I don't know, Jack. Perhaps whoever has the watch hasn't opened up the back yet? Perhaps he doesn't know it's quartz?'

'I still think the person who bought that watch knows Dad.'

'Well, I'm hoping to get to someone who does too. The countess is going to help us. I've told her we're a family on holiday from England and Dad and Mum were arrested because they looked suspicious. The countess is throwing a card party for important people and will ask a few discreet questions. I don't know whether it will come to anything, but it might. We've got to be patient, Jack.'

'I know – slowly, slowly, catchee monkey.' Jack frowned. 'I hope she's careful. Even countesses aren't safe these days. It's very good of her.'

'She's a very nice lady, and actually it's *softly, softly,* catchee monkey – but it means the same thing.'

'You and your reading. OK, let's hope she finds something. Oh, by the way, there's someone we both should know, serving with me in the regiment.'

'Who's that?'

Jack grinned. 'Our great-great-grandfather – on Mum's side, of course. His name's Martin.'

Annie's eyes widened. Does he know who you are?'

Jack snorted. 'No, of course not. You think I'm barmy? How would I tell him?'

'No, of course you couldn't – and shouldn't. Is he a friend of yours?'

'He is now. Wasn't at first. Hated me for some reason.'

'Maybe he sort of felt the close *relationship* – you know?

Wondered what it meant. They probably confused him, those feelings, and he didn't know how to deal with them. I expect he sort of reacted to them by attacking you.'

'What a load of rubbish,' scoffed Jack. 'You girls and your flippin' *feelings*. He didn't like me because I'm foreign.'

'Well, you might think that, but I think blood's thicker than water, and I'm sure he felt an indefinable filial attraction of some sort.'

'Where the heck do you get these words from, sis?' Jack was genuinely alarmed. 'You'll get slaughtered by your mates when we get home.'

'I've been reading novels. There's not a lot else to do here. I left my iPod at home, remember? By the way, have you seen anything of that ghost – you know the dark tattered figure we kept seeing when we first arrived?'

'Yes.' Jack frowned. 'In Prague the other day, when I was with Martin and Jiri. Does he come out here as well?'

'Only once, that's why I asked. But I just get the feeling,' Annie gave a little shiver, 'that he's watching me still. Trouble is, in a big old mansion like this, it would give me a heart attack to see him in the passageway one night.'

'He doesn't usually come that close. I've only seen him at a distance. I had a thought that maybe he's someone from our own time. Why should Dad be the only man on the planet to invent a time machine? Maybe it's some jealous inventor, looking for a chance to make sure we don't make it back to the twenty-first century?'

'But he looks so – so misty and unreal. Like a phantom. He doesn't look like a solid person at all.'

Jack shrugged. 'I dunno, sis. Look, we've got enough to worry about as it is. Maybe it is a ghost thing, to do with being in a different time? Some poor soul trapped halfway between time worlds and looking at us helplessly, thinking we can save him with the motorbike? We've got enough to do without that, I think, what with Mum and Dad in prison and Davey trapped among people made of wood.'

Annie squealed, 'What?'

'Oh yes – I ran into Kaspar, or he ran into me. He told me Davey was safe but with some wooden people. Jiri and Martin were with me, so I couldn't question him too hard. Wouldn't have done any good anyway, since he seemed to have only a vague idea about where Davey actually was. Jiri thought he was talking about scarecrows, but Martin reckoned it was more likely mannequins, so we looked in a few shop windows, but not with much hope. That's the trouble with these alchemists and magicians – they don't seem to know any details, only things in general. Bit like horoscopes in the newspapers back in our time. You can read anything into them if you want to.'

'Jack,' said Annie, 'something happened to me to the other day – a very weird experience . . .' and she told him what had occurred with the waterman. 'Why are we seeing these weird creatures? It's gruesome.'

'Yeah, like Pinscher Thrum, back at the barracks. He can do this thing where he's standing here one second and he's way over there the next, without him even moving a muscle. I've got a theory about that. Look, we've travelled back through time, right? Well, maybe when we did that, we sort

187

of crossed another dimension – the fourth dimension, something like that. Now we can see into both worlds – the real world, and the imaginary one we knew as little kids. You know, the world of fairies and giants? Except here we see the weird creatures of Bohemia, like your water ghoul. I think I saw one of them myself, when I was on the obstacle course.'

At that moment the countess returned, to find the lemonade and cakes had disappeared.

'You'd better be getting back to your unit, young man,' she said. 'They will be blowing the Last Post soon.'

Jack seemed impressed. 'You know army bugle calls, ma'am?'

The countess laughed. 'I know the two most important ones – Reveille, to start the day, and the Last Post to end it. My husband was in the army when I married him. A captain. He looked very dashing in his uniform, and of course I went everywhere with him in those days. Even to the battlefields. I've seen many battles, young man. I hope you have no need to do the same.'

After Jack had left, the countess said to Annie, 'Sophia, your brother is a very handsome young man.'

Annie replied, 'Oh, I wouldn't tell him that, ma'am – his head will swell like a balloon.'

The countess laughed at this. Those servants who heard the strange sound coming from their mistress's mouth simply stood and wondered.

21. DAVEY THE ACTOR

The theatre was full and the audience seemed to be thoroughly enjoying the performance. Davey sat in the front row of the stalls, dressed in his eighteenth century costume, complete with tri-cornered hat. He was munching biscuits. Next to him was the old woman who had taken him from the streets. Every so often, when there was a lull in the singing, Davey picked up a wine glass next to his seat and turned to the audience, waving and crying, 'I am so talented! I am so brilliant!'

The audience laughed and cheered him, then turned their eyes back to the stage on which the opera was still taking place.

When the opera was over and the last note died, Davey jumped on to his seat and stood looking at the rows and rows of faces that stretched to the back of the stalls, and those above on the balconies. He smirked and bowed. They stood up and clapped and whistled, while Davey cried, 'Please, please, no flowers. Just throw money.'

They laughed at this too, and though they did not shower him with notes, one or two people in the seats next to him pressed coins into his hands. Then they gathered their coats and hats, and filed out of the theatre, chattering excitedly. Davey whispered urgently to one man as he passed him by, 'Can you help me? I don't belong here really. They won't let me go . . .'

The man looked puzzled, but then the old woman took Davey's wrist and cried, 'Now, my dear, dear grandson, don't you go bothering the gentleman! You and your jokes.'

'I ain't your grandson,' growled Davey. 'You won't let me go.'

'Is this true?' asked the gentleman.

The old woman shook her head solemnly. 'The poor child is a little touched in the head, sir. That's why his mother made me his guardian. This – what he does here – he does like a parrot, repeating what we've told him to say. But he's not right, sir. Not right at all.'

'What a load of old rubbish,' said Davey.

'You see, sir? He comes out with these strange sayings, which mean very little in themselves. But we do what we can with him. We do what we can.'

The gentleman's wife was calling him from the doorway and finally, with one last pitying glance at Davey, he joined her.

The old woman immediately glared into Davey's face.

'I warned you. Stop your tricks, my lad, or I'll hand you over to the police. You know what they do with boys like you? They put them in the coal mines. Is that what you want? To work in the dark sixteen hours a day? A miserable existence that would be, wouldn't it? Dragging trucks of coal along a rail in the pitch black. It would either be that or the insane asylum. You babble, child, such strange things. Look – I'm trying to help you, you know that. It's best you stay here with us until you find your relatives. We're doing what we can. Now, give me the money.' She held out her hand.

Davey handed her the coins.

'Well, how did I do tonight?' he asked. 'Not bad, eh?'

'Not bad for a novice,' cackled the old woman. 'Not bad at all. You're becoming quite a performer.'

'Get an Oscar next,' Davey said.

'Eh?' came back the old woman.

Davey stared at her. 'Never mind, you wouldn't understand. What's for supper?'

'Chopped liver and dumplings.'

'Again?'

'You like chopped liver and dumplings.'

'Yeah, but not every day. What's happening about my brother and sister, then?'

'What? Oh, I'm still wondering where to look.'

Davey frowned. 'I told you – they're staying with a bloke called France. France Kaftan or something.'

'This is a big city, Davey. He could live anywhere.'

Davey's brow remained furrowed. 'I wish I could remember where the house was, but I was just following Jack and Annie. You don't worry about where you're going when you're with someone, do you? France Kaftan, that's a pretty weird name, ain't it? Surely be easy to find that person. Just look in the phone book.'

'Phone book?'

'Telephone book. Oh yeah, maybe there's no phone book yet. Dunno why, some people've got phones, yeah? Well *somebody* must have a list of numbers and addresses somewhere. France Kaftan. I *think* it was Kaftan . . .'

'Stop babbling and come and get your supper.'

'I can't stay here for ever, you know. There's my mum

and dad to find, as well as Jack and Annie. Liver and dumplings, eh? All right . . .'

But later, when he was lying under his blankets, Davey's misery came upon him like a flood, and he cried real tears, with Masetto calling softly to him from the shelf above, saying, 'Davey, Davey, your sorrow is too hard for us to bear,' and Zerlina moaning, 'Our bodies are wood, but our hearts can be injured by sadness.' Don Pedro was made of sterner oak, murmuring, 'Pull yourself together, lad!' but there was sympathy in his voice. Afterwards, Masetto climbed down from his shelf, which was quite an effort for a dummy. He sat down beside Davey and put a wooden arm around the little boy's shoulders.

'Never mind, Davey,' he said. 'We will look after you – you are one of *us* now. You are a man of the stage!'

They were all a comfort to him, his wooden actor friends. Without them, Davey would have abandoned all hope.

22. A BATTLE IN THE STREETS

Jack was roused from his bed at midnight by the harsh sound of a bugler blowing his horn. At first he was annoyed, thinking it was a prank. Then he realised the lights were on and there was movement around him. Bleary-eyed solders were sitting up.

When he was fully awake, he saw that everyone was getting dressed and grabbing their rifles. Some soldiers – the less efficient ones – were hurriedly seeking bits of kit from their lockers and putting them on. There were NCOs there in the doorway, and in the room, striding about. Something important was happening, but Jack had no idea what it was. Was the city under attack?

The hut corporal bawled, 'Come on! Come on! Look lively. Fall in outside, three deep – that's one behind the other twice. That's it. Let's be having you. *Now*, Kettle, not next week. Boots and braces. Don't forget your rifle and drum, boy. Snap to it.'

Jack snapped to it, getting dressed very quickly. Unlike some of his careless roommates he had laid out his clothes on a chair in preparation for the morning. Very soon he had everything on, including his greatcoat and gloves. He would need those. It was wintry outside. He jammed his forage cap on his head, picked his rifle up with his right hand and his drum with his left, and went through the doorway. Others followed, while in the background the corporal still bellowed.

Once outside in files of three, Jack could see the whole regiment was up and ready to march. There were officers and NCOs everywhere, getting their companies together. His own captain shouted an order for the Bicycle Company to fetch their machines.

Jack slung his rifle over his back. The bicycles in their shed had white numbers painted on them. His was 10. He took it and clipped his drum to the handlebars, putting his drumsticks into the top pocket of his jacket. Someone was issuing bicycle lamps. He was given one then was left wondering where he was going to fit it, because the drum was in the way. Finally he put it in his greatcoat pocket, thinking there would be enough light from the lamps of the others to guide him.

Soon they were on the road outside the camp, cycling through the darkness, the beams of the lamps cutting swathes of light through the blackness. It was very, very cold, but at least the surface of the road was not too icy. There were patches of snow on the verges, which glistened in the lamp-light. Occasionally eyes lit up in front of them: deer that had been caught crossing the road, dashing from one side of the forest to the other. The black trees swallowed them up.

Jack's stomach was churning as he pedalled. For one thing, he needed a hot drink of some kind. For another, he was bewildered and frightened by what was happening. He tried talking to his friends, asking them where they were going, but they were just as ignorant.

'I've no idea,' Jiri said, coming up alongside him. 'There's the whole regiment behind us, marching in our wake. We're going to be the first there, that's for sure.'

'What do you think it is? A battle?'

'We're not at war with anyone, not that I know of,' replied Jiri. 'Wars don't start just like that, overnight. They build up.'

'That's true. What could it be then?'

Jiri did not bother to answer this, having answered the same question a few seconds earlier. As the houses began to increase in number, Jack realised they were not heading out into the countryside, as he had first thought. They were going deep into the suburbs of the city. But everything seemed quite peaceful. There was no distant sound of artillery, nor even gunfire. But when they turned the next corner, there came the faint sounds of people shouting. Soon, a final corner was turned, and they were in a square. In the middle was a monument crowned by a stone statue. On the far side was a huge mob of people with several police confronting them.

The statue – some military man, one hand on his sword pommel, the other holding a cockaded hat – had been attacked and its head knocked off. The head itself was resting on the ice of a frozen horse trough that stood by the monument. It seemed to be glaring at Jack as he was ordered to dismount from his bike. Jack would not have been surprised if the head had asked him for help.

The mob were mocking a thin line of policemen who it seemed had rounded them up.

'Alchemists,' one of the policeman told the boys. 'We've been raiding and rooting them out of the houses in the district, but they've turned nasty. Too many of them for us to handle now. Didn't realise there would be so many. We should have brought in the army earlier . . .'

The noise the alchemists were making was not so much loud as very threatening. Some of the ringleaders carried sticks and clubs. Others were throwing stones at the police. It was a very ugly scene, with malcontents other than alchemists joining the fray. There were plenty of street people in Prague. People with grievances against the government and the police. With more rioters arriving by the minute, there would soon be several hundred. The police looked scared and were backing away as the mob advanced.

The captain of the company cried, 'Drummer! Sound formation!'

Jack had hardly got his drum on when this order came, but soon he was rat-a-tat-tatting. The company formed up in two lines, one line kneeling in front of a standing file. Right in the centre of the front line, looking the very model of courage and determination, was the best soldier in the regiment, Private Svejk. The company sergeant major went down the lines handing out ammunition and nodded his approval of Svejk, whose shoulder companion, looking equally brave and determined, was Pinscher Thrum. At this point the police retreated from the mob and melted through the ranks of the army into the background. The soldiers were ordered to aim their rifles at the rioters.

The mob was still advancing, yelling threats at the soldiers now, waving their clubs. Suddenly Pinscher Thrum did that illusionist trick of his and was instantly far in the rear, out of harm's way. Jack blinked. He was probably the only one who had seen Thrum first in the front rank, then, as the crowd got closer, immediately at the back.

Jack stood rock still on the right flank of the two lines. He was glad he had not got a rifle in his hands. It was still slung over his back. The last thing he wanted to do was shoot someone.

'Take aim,' ordered the captain. 'Ready! Fire one round!'

There was a tremendous rattling crash that echoed round the cobbled square. Flashes came from the muzzles of the rifles. Jack's stomach flipped. It was a horrible experience. He stared at the mob, expecting to see some of them fall writhing to the ground, wounded or dead. None of them did. They had all stopped stock still in their tracks, though. Many of the pale faces had gone a lot paler. They stared at one another as if wondering why they had not been hit.

'That volley was blanks,' called the captain to the mob. 'The next will be live rounds. Disperse immediately, or I will be forced to order my men to use live ammunition.'

A muttering went through the alchemists and their hangers-on. They remained where they were. They did not do as the captain had ordered, but they did not advance either. Jack's heart was pounding. There were more rioters than there were soldiers, but at the same time the rioters were not heavily armed. One or two had shotguns, but for the most part they carried sticks and clubs. Jack was hoping and praying that the rest of the regiment got there before the mob decided to charge.

'Drummer, sound the advance,' said the captain.

Jack's head was spinning. Could he remember the tattoo? Yes, as soon as his sticks began hitting the taut skin of the drum, the rhythm came to him.

The company began to march towards the rioters, Svejk in the vanguard but Thrum still safely at the rear. It was a very slow advance. The mob seemed unsure and lost its leadership. Some stumbled backwards, some stood their ground. Jack could see it was a horrible decision for them to make. Facing a long line of levelled rifles was not an easy thing to do. If Jack had been on the other side, he was sure he would have turned and run away before now.

This was exactly what happened next. The mob began filtering away into side alleys and passageways beyond the square. They had no taste for confrontation and Jack did not blame them. By the time the rest of the regiment marched into the square, their boots crashing on the cobbles, the rioters had dispersed. It seemed foolish to follow them through the dark narrow alleys, where the soldiers would be at a disadvantage. The rifles of the 14th Foot were long, awkward firearms that would get entangled with bodies and limbs in enclosed spaces.

'Bicycle Company may now withdraw,' ordered the colonel, once he was appraised of the situation by Jack's captain. 'Well done, lads! A bloodless end to the night.' He went and placed his hands on the shoulders of two of the recruits. 'This man,' – Svejk – 'was dauntless in his encouragement to his fellows, as was this man also.' – Pinscher Thrum, once more magically returned to the front. 'They are to be commended, perhaps even promoted. Well done. Well done, all.'

As they marched away to where their bicycles were stacked, guarded by some of their comrades, Jack heard one or two silly soldiers say they would like to have seen some proper action. Jack was sure that if someone had been shot they would all have gone home with a horrible feeling in their stomachs. Violence was not a thing Jack could take as lightly as some of these young men seemed to. He guessed it was mostly bravado, and that they had been as frightened as he had been.

Later, he was pleased to hear Martin say, 'I'm glad we didn't have to shoot – those were people out there, even if they were alchemists and conjurors.'

'They were breaking the law,' another soldier answered. 'They deserved to be shot.'

'Don't be stupid, man,' Jiri said, backing Martin. 'You'll be shooting someone for dropping litter next.'

It was left at that. The experience was one that Jack had not enjoyed. He had discovered that being a soldier was not just marching and parades. It also meant going out to face violence.

Pinscher Thrum grinned at him from across the room. How had he worked that trick? It could not be hypnotism this time. Jack had no idea, but it had gained Thrum respect that was unjustified. Thrum had managed to be in the front ranks when threatening, but in the rear ranks when the action took place. A very neat trick. Private Svejk was a genuine and sincere soldier, but Thrum was a chancer.

Jack fell asleep that night wondering whether it was worse to be shot by someone or to shoot them. He could not make up his mind which he thought the more terrible.

23. ANNIE MEETS A BOY NAMED BOOTS

The countess was exceedingly slow to arrange the gathering of people that Annie hoped would help find her parents and her brother Albert proved to be next to useless. It was not so much that the countess did not want to do things, but she was somewhat scatty and kept forgetting to set a date.

One day Annie was chatting to the cook, with whom she still had a strong friendship. Unknown to the countess, she would slip away and go to the kitchen, where Cook was usually to be found. Sometimes others would be there too, for the kitchen was often a gathering place for the servants. One of these was a small, quiet boy who polished the boots and shoes for the whole household. He was called 'Boots' by the rest of the staff and treated as a nonentity.

Boots remained unnoticed by the rest of the staff, though Annie often glanced up to see him watching everyone from a corner in the kitchen, his dark eyes glittering. She had never seen him without his hands and much of his face covered in brown or black shoe polish. Boots was often part of the shadow from which he viewed the world, as he quietly polished the footwear of both servants and aristocracy. Annie somehow formed the idea that he did not want to be noticed and that the polish he wore was his camouflage.

One day Annie decided to speak to Boots, and entered his shadowy world in the far corner of the kitchen.

'Hello,' she said, offering him her hand to shake. 'My name's Annie.'

He stared at her hand without taking it, saying nothing. Annie stood there awkwardly for a few moments, realising she had made a mistake in approaching the boy. But as she turned to walk away, he spoke to her in a low voice.

'I thought you was Sophia?'

Annie turned back to him.

'That's just what the countess calls me – my real name is Annie.'

'Oh. You was lucky. Scullery maid to countess's girl, all in one day.'

'Yes – very lucky.'

The boy stared at her with those black-pebble eyes.

'You're not like us, are you? You're different. You talk different, you walk different. You're not from around here.'

'No, I'm not. I come from England.'

'Where's that?'

Annie nodded. 'Over the sea. It's another country.'

'Oh. I'll remember that. Do they do things different there?'

'Yes they do – some things are very different.'

'Is England ruled by the Austrians?'

'No, it isn't.'

'When you go back there, can you take me with you?'

Annie suddenly felt very sad for the boy.

'No, I don't think so. I'm sorry.'

'Do you like it here?'

'Not especially. They've put my mum and dad in prison. I'm here to find them and try to help them get out.'

'I haven't got any parents. My ma's dead and I don't know who my da is. If I had parents, though, I would want to get 'em free too.' Boots looked across the kitchen and saw that Cook was busy at the oven. The gamekeeper was just leaving through the back doorway, a pie in his hand. No one else was around. 'I could probably help you.'

Annie smiled. 'How could you help me, Boots? I mean, thank you for offering, but . . .'

'I'm not what I seem,' he said, with another quick glance at Cook. 'There's many of us.'

'Many of you what?'

He licked his lips, seemed about to tell her, then changed his mind.

'Nothin',' he said, looking down and beginning to polish a boot vigorously. 'I'm just talking. It's nothing.'

After that he seemed to be swallowed up by the darkness again.

Annie thought about Boots quite often over the next few days, but did not get the opportunity to speak to him until she met him coming through the hedge on his way to work. Boots lived in the village and used a short cut across the countess's vegetable plots to reach the kitchen. Annie happened to be in the rose gardens nearby when she saw him. She immediately called to him and ran to his side. Boots looked a bit disturbed by this encounter and tried to leave.

'Wait. Wait a minute, Boots. I need to talk to you,' said Annie.

'I – I got nothin' to say,' muttered the boy, looking anxiously towards the house. 'Leave me alone.'

'I will leave you alone,' replied Annie determinedly, 'once we've cleared something up. You said you could help me. What did you mean?'

'I didn't mean nothin'.'

'Yes you did. I could tell.'

Boots looked miserable. She knew now that he was regretting ever saying anything at all. But he had said quite a lot really. He had implied that there were others who shared his views. What those views were, Annie had no idea, but she was determined to find out.

She continued, 'You told me there are others. Who are they? How can they help me with my parents? Listen Boots, I'll be sworn to secrecy. I won't tell a soul, I promise you. I'd be in as much trouble as you, I'm sure.'

Again that nervous glance towards the house, then back at the stables, and finally he said, 'The Sewer Rats.'

'What?' Annie was naturally perplexed. 'What rats?'

'That's us. That's what we call ourselves. The Sewer Rats. That's our secret society.' He seemed eager to let it all spill out now. 'There's twelve of us, see? We're all Bohemians – none of us Austrian. We want our country to be ruled by our own people, not by foreigners . . .'

Annie felt inclined to argue. 'But many so-called Austrians were born here, Boots.' But then she bit her lip. Clearly Boots was not going to be turned from his line of thought.

'So you say.'

Annie asked again, 'How can you – the Sewer Rats, I mean – help me find my parents?'

'We can ask other secret societies – there's connections, see.'

Annie did see. She suddenly realised the potential of what Boots was telling her. There must have been dozens of secret societies in Prague and the surrounding countryside of Bohemia, all linked in some way, even if just by one person in each group. A huge network of spies! Someone surely knew something. Such a network would surely be aware of most of what was going on in the land. Boots himself was just a boy who shined the shoes of a big household, but Boots the Sewer Rat could be the carrier of a great deal of information.

'Could you find out about my parents? Their name is Kettle – Roger and Kate Kettle. We came from London and they were arrested by the police. No one seems to know where they were taken. Do you think you could ask around, Boots? It's very important to me.'

'I s'pose I could. I could try.' He looked intently at Annie. 'I like you,' he added hoarsely. 'I think you're very pretty.'

'That's nice of you to say so,' replied Annie, looking down

at herself, 'but I expect it's these fine clothes that make me look pretty. I'm very ordinary really.'

'No you're not. You're beautiful.'

Annie laughed. 'Beautiful? Now you're going too far, Boots.' But then she saw she had offended him. He looked embarrassed and turned away. Annie sought to repair the damage. 'Anyway, I think you're very good-looking too.'

He turned back again and grinned, wiping a hand across his black-and-brown face.

'You mean, under all this muck?'

'Well, boot polish must be very difficult to remove, I expect.'

He nodded. 'We only have cold water from the pump.'

'Freezing cold, I expect. Not the best stuff to get greasy polish from your skin. I hope it doesn't stay for ever.'

'I 'spect it probably will, but that's no matter. It's what's in your heart that counts, isn't it? I think so anyway.'

'I think you have a good heart, Boots, or you wouldn't be helping a foreign girl who you owe nothing at all. I'm very grateful that you and the Sewer Rats have agreed to help me. That shows great generosity, I think. Now don't get into trouble on my behalf, will you, Boots. I don't want you to end up in prison too, like my parents.'

'If I do, it'll be worth it,' he told her fiercely, his eyes flashing with zeal. 'I'll find out somethin' – just you wait and see.'

With that he was gone, running in his ragged jacket and short leather trousers towards the kitchen of the house, probably late for work and due to get a scolding. She watched until his tousled dark head disappeared through the doorway, then finished cutting the roses she had been sent to get and carried them in the basket towards the house.

Help was now coming from an unexpected quarter.

Annie wished the countess would get on with arranging the gathering of important people she had promised, but now the underclass of the city was assisting in her quest to find her parents. If anything, they probably knew more than the important people.

Things were beginning to move at last.

24. JACK MAKES A TERRIBLE MISTAKE

Following the quelling of the riot, Jack was very shaky. He suddenly started feeling extremely homesick. He wanted to be back in London again, where there was relative safety. Things seemed so unpredictable here, in 1903 Bohemia. It was all very well finding excitement in being in the army as a drummer boy, but there was attached to this excitement a great deal of danger. Jack did not want to die so far away from his home in a century that was not really his. He wanted to be back at school with his mates, laughing and joking about the music teacher, looking forward to a game of soccer once the school day was over.

'I've got to get out of here,' he said to himself. 'This is going on far too long.'

He was determined to investigate the one-handed colonel, and planned a raid on the colonel's quarters for the following day. He knew the officers of the regiment were having a grand dinner in their mess that evening. All were obliged to attend, and certainly the colonel would have to be there. Those dinners – Jack had observed one as a kitchen hand – went on until the early hours. There would be plenty of time to look through the colonel's rooms.

So at the end of that day, when all the rest of the soldiers in the billet were fast asleep, Jack crept out of bed and dressed. Then he sneaked from the hut and made his way across the parade square to the officers' quarters on the far side. In his pocket was his bike lamp.

The colonel was unmarried and lived in a large block that served as accommodation for single officers of the regiment. The colonel, of course, had more spacious rooms than his subordinates and Jack had observed that these were luckily on the ground floor of the two-storey building.

When he came to the moonlit officers' block he found the main doors shut and locked, so he went round the side to look for a window left ajar. He found one unlatched but too high for him to reach. A quick search of the area in the moonlight revealed a dustbin, which he was able to move and stand on to reach the window. He opened it carefully, stood on the sill, and squeezed himself through. His hips became stuck for a moment or two and panic ensued as he struggled. The front half of his body was dangling inside the building, while his legs from the hips downwards were outside. He wriggled and wriggled and finally his hip bones went through the opening.

He fell head first, arms outstretched, on to a toilet. Luckily the lid was in the closed position or he would have fallen straight in. Not a pleasant thought, plunging head first into a toilet! However, instead, he merely tumbled on to the tiled floor beyond. After a quick inspection of limbs, he found he was unhurt and got to his feet. Switching on the light, he realised he was in a communal toilet. Then he switched the light off very swiftly, remembering he was not supposed to be there. For a few minutes his heart beat fast in his chest. If a guard had seen the light go on and off, in a block where there were supposed to be no occupants – well!

No one came, however. Jack left the toilet and found himself in a passageway which was almost pitch black, there being no windows to let in the moonlight. He turned on his bike lamp and went along the doors until he came to one marked with the colonel's name. Trying the handle, he found, miraculously, that it was unlocked. He entered the room quickly and closed the door behind him, then went to the windows and closed the curtains before anyone noticed the light.

Jack found himself in one of two rooms. The door between them was open and he could see a bed in the next room, which was furnished quite luxuriously for a soldier's quarters. The room in which he was standing, however, had a desk against one wall with an old wooden armchair in front of it. The desktop was covered in papers, held fast under paperweights, with pens and coloured inkpots visible. There were other soft furnishings in the room, along with cupboards and a chest of drawers. A working uniform was draped over another wooden chair, with the rank of colonel displayed on the epaulettes.

'So far, so good,' muttered Jack.

He went straight to the desk and began rifling through the drawers, looking for his father's watch. When he did not find it, he started wading through the papers, hoping against hope that he would find his father or mother's name listed there. Nothing. Then he searched other cupboards and drawers in the room, hoping, hoping, hoping – but with the sure realisation that he was going to find nothing. He was in despair. Now that he was in the colonel's room, he wondered what he had ever hoped to achieve by such a desperate enterprise. So what if he did find his father's watch? What would that tell him? Probably nothing. But without it, they'd never be able to return to their own time.

It was a case, he decided, of what his mother would call 'magical thinking'. He had done this thing hoping for a miracle. And miracles did not happen. Not to people like Jack. The best thing now would be to get out and return to his bed, before he was caught.

It was at that moment that the door opened and the light was switched on. Jack was suddenly faced by an elderly corporal who strode into the room. He was small and lean, with a face like a rodent. He had a pair of shiny boots in one claw-like hand.

The corporal's eyes widened. He took a quick step backwards as if he expected to be attacked, then seemed to gather his courage.

'What are you doing here, Private?' he asked.

Jack felt his heart racing and he immediately went on the offensive. 'Who the heck are you then?'

'I'm the colonel's batman, and I repeat – what are you doing in his quarters?'

Jack's heart sank. Of course. The officers might all be at their dinner, but they had servants. This was the colonel's servant – the man who cleaned his boots and generally looked after his needs. The colonel's batman. It was no good making a run for it. The batman was blocking the doorway and Jack would not get very far anyway, not if there were other servants around.

'I – er – I came to see the colonel.'

'At this time of night? In any case, no soldier ever comes to the colonel's quarters; he has an office, but you'll be aware of that. You came here to steal, didn't you?'

'No – really, I – please, please let me go. I'll give you my pay. Can't you let me go?'

The elderly corporal's mouth tightened and Jack knew he was going to get nowhere.

'You will follow me, soldier, to the guardroom. Don't try to run. I know your face now and you can't hide. I can see your insignia. You're in the Bicycle Company, a drummer boy. It's all up with you, my lad. You're in deep trouble. Come on!'

Jack followed the batman miserably, out of the room then out of the building. He was led up a path towards the entrance to the camp, where the guardroom stood. The corporal was right. There was little point in running. He would be caught easily and then the charge would be desertion: a much more serious crime even than stealing. At least he had not been caught with goods on him. He could continue to plead that he had wanted to see the colonel.

At the guardroom, he was pushed into a stone cell by a disgruntled military policeman whose nap had been interrupted. There he spent a horrible night, having to urinate in a bucket in the corner and drink from a battered tin mug that had been grudgingly thrust through the bars by the same policeman. The bed consisted of rough planks of wood on an iron frame that jutted from the wall. There was only one blanket and no pillow. It was so cold that by morning his drinking water had frozen solid in the mug. If he slept at all, it was in fits and starts. He spent most of the time shivering violently. By morning his bones ached all over, he had a headache, and his spirits were at zero.

A replacement military policeman came into the cell area to look Jack up and down.

'So here's our little thief, eh? Coming it a bit strong? The colonel's quarters? Starting at the top, are we?'

'No, you don't understand. I wasn't stealing.'

'Look at the state of you, man!' The policeman's tone was contemptuous. 'You look like a rag bag.'

'Can I have something to eat?'

'You'll get it when I'm ready.'

However, the policeman went away and came back with a tin plate on which was a hunk of stale cheese and two pieces of bread.

'Anything hot to drink?' asked Jack wistfully.

'This is not a hotel, Private. You get what you're given here. Think yourself lucky it's me on duty today. If it had been anyone else they'd have given you a beating by now. It's one of the privileges of being an MP. There's not much in favour of it, that's for sure. But knocking the prisoners about is one thing.'

Jack did not know whether this man was speaking the

truth, but he guessed he might be. He ate the miserable cheese and bread then sat on the edge of his bed and waited. They came for him at about noon. He was led back to his billet and told to smarten himself up. The other soldiers were nowhere around, and Jack was grateful for that. He would not have wanted to be humiliated in front of them.

Once he had washed and changed his underclothes, he was led by the guards to his captain's office. There, hat in hand, a guard on each side of him to prevent him from attacking his superior officer, he was questioned about being in the colonel's quarters. He insisted vehemently that he had gone to see the colonel and was innocent of any intention to steal.

'I got confused,' said Jack. 'I woke up feeling very homesick and I thought if I went to see the colonel he might grant me some leave to go home to London. I got really confused. You know what it's like, sir, when you wake up out of a deep sleep, a dream, and you hardly know where you are? It was like that. I sort of went looking for the colonel with a fuzzy head . . .'

'Why not me?' asked the captain, looking up from studying his desktop, his eyes penetrating Jack's. 'Why not ask me for leave? I can grant it as well as the colonel. I'm your superior officer. Why didn't you come to me?'

'I – I don't know, sir.'

'Private Kettle, do you know how much we hate thieves in the army? And for good reason. You are in a billet with many other men – and other billets, and quarters, are wide open to you. It is too easy to steal. We must be able to trust our soldiers implicitly.'

'Sir, I would never, never, steal from my comrades.'

'But the colonel is exempt from this code of honour?'

'No, no really, sir. I did not go to the colonel's rooms to steal anything. Look, I was there quite a while before the batman came in. I could have taken anything in that time.'

'You went through his papers. The batman said they had been disturbed.'

'No – yes, yes, I did, but that was just curiosity. I – I wanted to know what the colonel thought of me. I simply looked for my name on those papers . . .' This was partly true, Jack having looked for his father's name, which was the same. 'I looked for Kettle.'

The captain smirked. 'And did you find it?'

'No, sir, I didn't. I'm very, very sorry. I stole nothing. I didn't go there to steal. I just got confused.'

'So you keep saying, lad – but it won't do, you know. You were in the colonel's quarters. You tried to bribe his batman – another charge against you which will be taken into consideration at the appropriate time. The colonel is quite rightly furious, of course. He wants to make an example of you. I'm going to have to send you to the stockade – the army prison – to await a court martial. I'm afraid you'll find it rather a rough place. The guards there have a regime that they rigorously enforce.' The captain gave a little shudder. 'I wouldn't want to be in your boots, Private. Perhaps, though, you'll learn to respect other people's property. I imagine the court martial will give you at least two years when you eventually come before them, so I wouldn't count on getting out of the stockade for quite a long while. Dismissed.'

Jack was led in a daze from the captain's office. As he was marched back to the guardroom, Jiri and Martin rushed over to him. The guards told them to go away, but Martin grabbed Jack's sleeve.

'Did you do it? Did you steal?'

'No,' replied Jack emphatically. 'I was looking for something belonging to my father.'

To Jack's great surprise, Martin nodded.

'I believe you,' he said. 'What can we do?'

'Get word to my sister,' Jack hissed. 'Her name's Annie – no, wait, she's called Sophia there. She lives with the Countess Kinsky von Chinic und Tattau. Tell her I'm in the stockade.'

'Will do,' said Jiri, pulling Martin away. 'You just keep your chin up, Jack. We'll find a way.'

Then the guards pushed him away from his friends and onward to the guardroom, to await transport to the terrible stockade.

25.   ANNIE HAS A VISIT FROM THE ARMY

Annie was sitting with the countess in one of that lady's favourite rooms. The countess was asleep, draped over a red-satin-upholstered settee. Her mouth hung open in a most undignified way and her pince-nez was askew on the bridge of her large nose. Annie was used to this happening. The countess often succumbed to slumber in rooms where the coal fires puffed out smoke and made her eyes sore. Annie herself had difficulty in staying awake.

Annie had suggested to the housekeeper that a chimney sweep be called in. The housekeeper had agreed with her but said that the countess resisted the idea, being concerned for the state of her furniture, decor and carpets. Apparently chimney sweeps caused the place to billow with soot, even though they put sacks over the fireplace entrances.

Annie continued to read the Tennyson poem she had been halfway through when she heard the first snore. If anyone had told her six months ago that she would enjoy reading the melodic verse of some dead poet, Annie would have laughed at them. But take away television, and the other entertainments of the twenty-first century, and girls like her found themselves searching for things to fill the time. It was frankly quite boring having long hours with nothing to do.

When she had finished the poem – Ulysses – she placed the book carefully on the floor and strolled around the room, idly picking up ornaments and putting them down. There were dozens to look at, mostly Dresden china like the shepherdess. Annie was not much interested in them, but she did not want to wake the countess. When she was on her second circuit of the room, the butler came in. Seeing the countess was asleep, he tiptoed over the carpet and whispered in Annie's ear.

'Miss Sophia, there are two soldiers at Cook's door, asking to see you. They say they have news of your brother.' He nodded. Tomas quite liked Annie, who always tried to be polite to everyone in the household, servant or otherwise.

Annie followed him out of the room and went to the

kitchen. There she found Cook pushing cakes into the hands of two youths in uniform. They were not resisting the food very hard. One of them already had crumbs all down the front of his tunic.

'You wanted to speak to me?' asked Annie.

The shorter, darker one of the two, the one covered in cake crumbs, said, 'Are you Jack's sister? The one they call Sophia?'

'Yes, I am.' Her heart began beating faster. 'Jack's all right, isn't he? He's not hurt or anything?' The alarm was building in her breast. 'Why are you here?'

'He's not hurt – not physically,' the other one replied. His protruding teeth had jam smeared on them and he licked it off self-consciously. 'My name's Jiri, by the way. This is Martin. We're good friends of Jack.'

'Oh yes, Jack's spoken about you.'

Annie studied Martin, seeing her not-so-distant ancestor for the first time. There were one or two family likenesses in his features. She felt herself reaching out to him emotionally. However, Martin simply returned her look with puzzlement in his expression.

'Look,' he said, peering into Annie's eyes, 'Jack's in deep trouble. He's been sent to the stockade – that's the army prison – for stealing. He said he didn't steal anything and I believe him, but they don't, and the stockade – well, it's pretty rough in there. They have a really tough programme . . .'

'Stealing? Oh dear. I expect he was looking for Dad's watch.'

Jiri blinked. 'Watch?'

215

Annie explained. 'We had our father's wristwatch when we arrived. Someone took it and pawned it. The only thing we know about the man who has it now is that he has a false hand.'

Martin snapped his fingers. 'The colonel!'

'Yes, Jack said he only had one hand and he thought that this colonel might be the one with the watch.'

'So he *was* stealing,' muttered Martin.

Annie stared at her great-great-grandfather until he looked away, unnerved by her scrutiny of him.

'Martin,' said Annie at last, 'you have to trust Jack. He's not a common thief. He was simply looking for our father's property, which is very important to us. You don't know it, because I know Jack hasn't told you, but you're related to us. We're — we're cousins. Not first cousins, but we are quite close. Jack was going to tell you one day.'

'What?' cried Martin. 'You're crazy.'

But Jiri came in here. 'Martin, you do look a bit like Jack — and Miss Sophia here. I always wondered about that.'

Martin shook his head, furiously.

'This is stupid. I don't know you. I only just met you.'

'Nevertheless,' Annie murmured, 'we are cousins. Jack and I are certain of it. Jack is not a thief. We're both searching for our parents who've been imprisoned by the secret police, and our little brother, who's lost somewhere in Prague. Once we all find each other, we're going back to London. The wristwatch is an important part of it all. I can't tell you how — it wouldn't mean anything to you. But please trust Jack.'

'Well,' replied Martin, 'whether we trust him or not doesn't really matter. We can't help him in the stockade. Then there's the court martial when they get around to it. We can speak up for him at that, but we'll only be character witnesses.'

'Where is the stockade?' asked Annie. 'Do you know?'

The soldiers did know. They told her where it was, up in the forested mountains, and how to get there. Then they ate two more cakes each, drank some milk, and went on their way. Martin, Annie suspected, was thinking about their relationship. She believed that eventually he would come round to believing in it.

That evening, Annie went to find Boots. He was in his usual place in the corner of the kitchen, working by lamp-light. Cook was busy at the stoves, making dinner.

'Boots,' Annie said in a low voice, 'have you found anything out?'

He looked up, his bright eyes shining through the dark polish that surrounded them.

'No – sorry. We've tried.'

'I believe you, but I have a favour to ask. A very big favour.'

'What is it? More information you need?'

'No – my brother has been put in prison. I wondered – I wondered if you and your friends, the Sewer Rats, could get him out?'

His face fell and he stopped shining the boot he had on his hand.

'The city jail?'

'No – it's an army prison. They call it the stockade.'

His eyes narrowed. 'Oh, that? I know that place. It's like a wooden fort in the woods, surrounded by a wire fence. What did your brother do?'

'They think he's a thief.'

'Oh.'

'Does that bother you, Boots?'

'Me?' He seemed surprised. 'Course not. I know hundreds of thieves. That's what most of the Sewer Rats do. If you ain't got a job, then you got to get your food somewhere, ain't you? Only thing is to nick it. He's not a bank robber, is he? Your brother. No, they wouldn't put him in the stockade for that. He's probably stolen someone's money or something.'

'He didn't actually take anything at all – but they found him in his colonel's quarters.'

'Ah, burglary. Same thing. Leave this to me. If it's just the stockade I think we can get him out.'

'Won't it be guarded? I don't want you to get shot or anything.'

'Oh, don't you worry about me,' said Boots airily. 'I've been shot at before now. When I poach game with my uncle, we get shot at all the time. Nobody's managed to hit me yet.'

Annie's eyes widened. 'You – you don't poach on the countess's estate, do you?'

'Course we do. That's why we never get shot. We know the gamekeeper, don't we? We know where he's likely to be and at what time. And that gun of his, it's only buck-shot. It wouldn't kill us. Uncle has got a few pellets in his thigh from that gun. They don't hurt him much, 'cept in the cold weather. What's your brother's name?'

'Oh – yes. It's Jack – Jack Kettle. He's a drummer boy in the 14th Foot Regiment. He's one of the Bicycle Company.'

'Was, not is. He's a prisoner now.'

'Will you be able to find him?'

'We'll find him. We've got friends on the inside. If it'd been the state prison, well that would've been difficult. Not impossible, mind, but not easy. Stone walls and iron doors and all that. But wooden walls and a fence. Huh! We'll get him out. Then he'll have to hide somewhere, for a while anyway. The army's not that worried, though. They'll stop looking for him after a while. S'not like he's a hardened criminal, is it? Just a rotten old thievin' drummer boy.'

Annie said defensively, 'He's a very *good* drummer boy.'

Boots sighed. 'I wish I had a sister,' he said.

26.   UNDER THE STREETS OF PRAGUE

They were in one of the big sewers, under the south side of the city. It was like a long winding cavern, the walls tiled with slate, with a brown-and-yellow stream running down the middle. There were walkways on both edges, which the sewer maintenance workers used when they came down to clear blockages. It smelled down there, and their voices echoed along the tunnels, but it was very safe. No fussy secret policeman would ever think of going down into the sewers. In fact, it was probable that they never thought of them at all. It was a stinking city beneath the streets, which few people knew existed.

All the Sewer Rats used their working names, rather than their real names, again for safety reasons. They were all orphans and knew each other from the orphanage. Some of them actually did not know their real names.

'So what you're sayin', Boots, is we got to get this English brat out of the army stockade,' said Sweepy, a lean girl with a pointed nose, who cleaned the streets for a living. 'What I want to know is why?'

'Look,' Boots replied, 'are we rebels or not? That's what I want to know. We made an oath against the Austrian Empire, didn't we? Here's somethin' we can do to get at 'em. This English boy is a spy for the British government, so I've been told, against the empire.'

Boots did not want to bring Sophia into this, for reasons he did not quite understand himself. One of them was he liked Sophia and did not want to have to defend her position, which he knew would happen when he told the Rats she was a companion to a countess. But there were other, more complicated reasons, to do with his feelings.

Cheesy, a youth who worked as a grocer's boy, nodded a dome-shaped head. 'If he's aginst the empire, then he's one of us.'

A pinched-faced lad called Dung-fly, who shovelled horse droppings off the streets, argued against this.

'I dunno about that. He might be aginst the Empire, but he might also be aginst Bohemia and Moravia – aginst us Czechs, eh? Anyway, ain't this dangerous? I mean, what if we get caught? They'll chuck us in jail, won't they?'

Boots sneered at Dung-fly, cleverly ignoring the first question.

'Are we scared Rats, then? Is that why we're a secret society? What are we goin' to do? Just meet down here an' *talk*? What good's that? We got to do some *action*. Here's our chance at last. Something we *can* do. Strike a blow for freedom!'

Several other Rats cheered this statement.

'So, let's take a vote,' Boots cried, jumping to his feet. 'I vote we get him out. If you lot won't come with me, I'll do it alone. Who's with me? Who's for freedom and gettin' rid of the Austrians.'

Another cheer, and several hands went up. The vote went for the proposal. They would attempt a prison break. Boots was glad of that, because he knew it would have been impossible for him to do it on his own. He needed his comrades to work with him.

Sweepy was a very bright girl, uneducated but naturally clever. They turned to her and asked her to make a plan for them. How were they going to do it? Sweepy threw back her head and sniffed all the dust and phlegm out of her narrow nose. She spat a thick gobbet of grey–green snot very accurately into the putrid stream below.

Having cleared any blockage that might have prevented her thoughts from travelling through her sinuses, she creased her brow. The other children stared at her dirty face, marvelling one and all at the wonder of someone who could actually think up plans. Her expression was one of intense and deep concentration.

'We need someone inside,' she said at last. 'Anybody work at the stockade?'

Another girl, Copper, put up her hand. Copper worked for a laundry. She was the one who stirred the dirty washing as it soaked in boiling water in the huge ceramic tub known as a copper, which was heated by a coke fire underneath. 'My sister goes there, to get the laundry.'

Boots asked, 'Will your sister help us?'

Copper shook her head. 'No, she'd be too scared – but I could take her place for one day. We could swap jobs.'

'Excellent,' said Sweepy. 'Boots, do you know what this drummer boy looks like?'

Boots felt a sinking feeling in his stomach.

'No.'

Copper saved him. 'It don't matter,' she said. 'They have name tags on their shirts. We could get a message to him that way.'

'Excellent!' said Sweepy. 'Now, does anyone know what the stockade looks like inside? Which is the cookhouse? Which is the livin' huts? Anyone know anythin'?'

No one did. Boots's stomach sank again.

'Don't matter,' Sweepy said. 'The Austrians build every-thing in squares – they like things neat. You can bet the stockade is a square. Give him a message – to be in the corner left of the main gate at midnight on Friday. All right?'

Boots coughed and then said, 'The message – it'll have to be in German. He don't speak Czech.'

The other Rats stared at him.

'It don't mean anything,' said Boots. 'His mother's Austrian, but she's not a imper – imper . . .'

'Imperialist,' finished Sweepy for him.

'Yeah – she's with us. She's in prison too.'

Swab, a little boy with a snub nose, asked, 'Do we have to get her out too? This *mother*?'

There was a short, peaceful moment as this bunch of

ragged orphans all pondered on this mother person, a figure none of them knew very much about.

'No,' replied Boots, finally breaking the silence, 'just him. His name's Private Jack Kettle, of the 14th Regiment of Foot. He's the only one we've got to get free.'

A sigh of relief swept through the rest of the Sewer Rats, and Sweepy took the opportunity of a break in the conversation to clear her blocked nasal passages again.

But mentioning the regiment gave Boots another idea. He would have to speak to Sophia about it, but it was a good idea. After all, the Sewer Rats were mostly only young children. To get a couple of older people involved would be to ensure the plan would work much better.

27. PRISON BREAK!

Jack had found the message scrawled on the folded tails of his army shirt. It had been badly misspelled and only with careful rereading did it make any sense whatsoever. But now he thought he had the gist of it.

Be in the left-hand corner of the stockade at midnight on Friday.

Today was Friday.

Could he be sure the message had come from people who wanted to help him? What if it had been written by one of the soldiers in here, in the stockade, who wanted to get him into trouble? Or worse still, someone from the authorities? Maybe it was a trap? He had plenty of enemies, he knew that, on both sides. There were prisoners who disliked him simply because he was a foreigner. People were people, and those who were in miserable circumstances liked to make life miserable for others, because they believed it would make them feel better in themselves. It never did, but they thought it would, and so some tormented Jack. The guards tormented *everyone,* regardless of class, country or creed. It was their job to make life unbearable in the stockade, and that they did.

The stockade was everything the sergeant had promised him.

There was a strict regime.

Jack rose at 4.30 and was taken straight out on a road run in boots, shorts and vest, within the stockade. An hour later he was back in his hut, polishing his kit ready for inspection at 6.30. This was a much more rigorous inspection than those he used to get at his regiment's camp. A speck of dust would be rewarded by two hours in the canteen kitchens, cleaning pans thick with black grease. The days were filled with exercise of some sort, interspersed with bawled lectures on the state of prisoners' souls. They were bad soldiers, but they would be good soldiers when they left the stockade, or die in the process. Only after an evening of more cleaning – toilets, showers, washrooms – was Jack allowed to rest his head on the horsehair-stuffed mattress and try to sleep. He could hear some of the men sobbing in the dark. He cried himself sometimes, wondering if things would ever be back to normal again.

Yet here was a light in the darkness. Could he afford to risk that it was genuine? Could things actually *be* any worse? Short of executing him, Jack wondered what prison could do to him that it had not done already. Then there were those curious spelling mistakes, as if the message came from an illiterate hand. Some poor uneducated person? If there was anyone you could trust in places like this, it was the poor people who had nothing to lose.

So at ten to midnight that night, Jack crept quietly from his bed, dressing in the dark. Boots in hand, he sneaked the length of the hut in his sock-covered feet, only to find the door locked. That was actually to be expected, he told himself. He then went the whole length of the room again, bodies stirring restlessly on either side. At the far end were the toilets. He entered these and tried the windows. One of them was loose. With a bit of heaving and pushing, the catch finally gave.

Jack went still for a minute, listening to see if he had disturbed anyone, especially the corporal of the guard, who slept in a single room right at the far end of the hut.

When no one appeared, he pushed the window open wider and climbed through, dropping down into the yard below. There was a fresh light fall of snow on the ground, which upset him. He knew that he would leave prints in the snow that the guards might follow. However, they prob-ably would not be able to use their tracking dogs, which was a good thing.

With the snow crunching underfoot, he made his way to the left-hand corner of the stockade. He dodged from one piece of cover to the next: sometimes a wood store, sometimes a water tank, sometimes an outbuilding. Even-tually he reached the edge of the buildings, which left a short stretch of white ground to the corner of the fence.

Looking back and forth to make sure there were no guards patrolling that part of the fence at that moment in time, he made a quick dash.

He had no watch on, but he had looked at the time on the billet clock before leaving. He had allowed himself ten minutes to cross the stockade and by his reckoning it was around midnight. Halfway across the ground to the fence a small figure popped up in front of him and tried to trip him over. Although he didn't know the name of this creature he was aware that it was a Czech fairy of some kind. He was getting used to these strange creatures and he took it by the hair and tossed it away. It yelled something at him, but its voice was small.

Finally Jack reached the high chain-link fence and crouching in the corner he called softly. 'Are you there? Jack Kettle here!'

There was no answer.

The moon came out from behind a cloud, illuminating the courtyard of the prison. Jack crouched down, trying to blend in with the fence posts. Should he climb over? He looked up and saw that the fence curved upwards and inwards and was wrapped around at the top with coils of barbed wire. He could never get over that lot.

The moon slipped out of sight again.

'Is anyone there?' he whispered. 'Please answer.'

On the other side of the fence was a stretch of about twenty metres, then a dark forest. If his rescuers had remained within the trees, they would never hear him from there. Where were they? Jack had followed his instructions to the letter. They should be here.

'Hello! Answer me. Jack Kettle here.'

Nothing. Jack felt like weeping. All this risk for nothing. He would have to retrace his steps back to the billet and climb back in through the window. Then there would be those telltale footprints for the guards to find. They would rouse the whole hut, make sure no one was missing, then interrogate everyone. Jack was not going to be popular with the other members of his billet. Already he had been bullied since arriving in the stockade. Now it would get much worse.

I don't understand it, he told himself. Everything seems to go wrong. Why can't something go right for a change?

Then he chastised himself for feeling sorry for himself. That was not going to get him anywhere. He needed to be strong for his sister and younger brother. If this attempt had failed, he would look for the next opportunity. Well, best get back to the billet, he thought. No sense in staying out here in the cold.

'Jack Kettle!'

The voice came out of the darkness.

His spirits lifted. But was this a trick? He hoped not.

'That's me,' he whispered.

'Stand back, we're going to clip the wire . . .'

Snick. Snick. Snick.

The sounds were just in front of him.

At that moment a searchlight went on in the watchtower above the gate. Jack expected it to swing his way and light up the whole corner of the stockade. This did indeed happen, but the light illuminated the *other* corner, on the right side of the gate. He could hear guards shouting, asking who was out there. It came to him then that his rescuers were creating a diversion on the opposite side of the stockade, so that he and those with the wire-clippers would be free to work.

'Quickly! Come through the hole.'

Jack bent down and felt in front of him. He touched the cold wire of the fence and groped around. Finally he found the hole and got down on his hands and knees to crawl through. But it was smaller than expected, and his great-coat caught on the open prongs of wire. They hooked into his coat and held it fast. Jack struggled blindly, hoping to wrench away from these snares, but the thick woollen over-coat was well and truly snagged.

'Cut me away!' he pleaded. 'I'm stuck.'

A girl's voice said, 'I can't see properly.'

'Haven't you got a torch?' asked Jack. When no answer came, he changed it to 'An electric lamp?'

'No. Never heard of one.'

There was some attempt to cut him free, but the primi-tive wire-clippers were very inadequate for the task. Finally, Jack said, 'Wait. Get back.' Then he undid the buttons on his coat, struggled for a while until he had shed it like an unwanted shell, and scrambled free. Just at that moment the searchlight swung in his direction. With his companions he began to race for the treeline.

'Hey! I see you there. Stop!' cried a guard. 'Halt, or I shoot.'

But the searchlight was not on Jack, it was on another soldier, a stranger ten metres to Jack's right. The soldier was waving his arms as if he *wanted* to be seen by the guards. Then he was gone, in the blink of an eye and reappeared several metres away, but this time to Jack's left. The search-light swung again, it seemed frantically, and again picked out the same soldier in its dazzling light. But instantly there was nothing in the beam. The soldier had vanished once more. He reappeared in a completely different spot, fluttering a pale hand to attract the attention of the guards in the watch-tower, who were by this time swinging their rifles back and forth, confused by these strange events. They were unable to shoot because just as they got the target in their sights it vanished and reappeared somewhere else.

All the while, Jack and the others were running for the woods.

Once inside the forest someone grabbed his sleeve and held on to it, acting as his guide and tugging him along. The moon had suddenly appeared again and cut through the trees, creating dark lanes of shadow and bright strips between. Jack could see his own breath coming out of his mouth in plumes. He knew he should feel cold, having only his tunic on now, but he was too excited to be uncomfortable. The pace they kept up was warming too, as they ran through the crisp snow, which flew up like dust around them. Someone tripped over a root or branch and went sprawling, but they were up again within a moment, running, running, running. Jack noticed they were all kids.

All of sudden they emerged from the woods and seemed to join up with two or three other figures.

'On to the road,' yelled one of the newcomers. 'There'll be motor vehicles and carts along the road – they'll churn up our prints.'

'Good thinking!' snapped Jack. 'You should've been a soldier.'

'Huh! You think? I bloody well am!'

It was then that Jack recognised Jiri's voice.

'Jiri? Are you here? You'll get court-martialled.'

'So will I, if we're caught.'

Jiri was of course accompanied by Martin, and another soldier was running alongside his great-great-grand-father.

'Pinscher Thrum?' cried Jack, astonished. 'Was that you back there, messing around in the searchlight? I thought it was another prisoner escaping, but I should have guessed. There's only one person who can do that trick of quantum leaping.'

'Actually,' replied Pinscher, 'there's three – one is an Arab who lives in the Yemen, one is a German from Munich, and then of course there is me. But we're all here in Prague for the convention.'

'You're crazy. You could have been shot.'

Pinscher replied carelessly, 'Oh, I would have seen the bullet coming and taken avoiding action as necessary.'

'Well, thank you anyway.'

'You're welcome.'

Jack said no more until he had been taken past an iron grid that seemed to be a sort of gate and into a tunnel in the bank of the river. The air in there was foul and Jack coughed in distaste. Candles were lit and faces came into the light. He found himself on a ledge with a stream of what appeared to be sewage flowing just below his feet. It was then he guessed he was in the city sewer system.

Martin was there, and Jiri, and a bunch of dirty-faced

urchins who stared at Jack with curiosity in their eyes.

One of them – Jack guessed she might be a girl – then spoke to him.

'Why wasn't you where you was supposed to be?' she challenged.

'What – up there? I was in the right place. Left of the gate.'

'You was right of the gate.'

Jiri interrupted, saying, 'Just a minute. Just a minute. *Whose* left? Those inside the camp or those outside?'

'Of course,' cried Jack, answering the girl. 'You were looking at it facing the gate – I thought you meant *my* left.'

The girl's brow furrowed, then some of her comrades started muttering, 'We didn't that of that,' and other such phrases.

'And that diversion,' said Jack, 'wasn't really a diversion – it was just the rest of you, still in the wrong place.'

'The *right* place,' insisted the girl. 'You was in the wrong one.'

'Never mind. You got me out. That was brilliant. Though you and Jiri, Martin – you'd both better get back to camp. If they were to guess you helped to spring me, you'd be in deep trouble. I don't want that on my conscience. I just want to thank you both, for arranging all this . . .'

'We didn't arrange it. We *helped*,' replied Martin. 'He's the one who put it all together.' And he pointed to a young boy with a brown-and-black complexion.

Jiri, Martin and Pinscher Thrum shook hands with Jack, said they would see him soon, then began to leave the sewer. Jack called his thanks to them again, for their selfless assistance. Pinscher, the last one to leave, turned and said, 'Jack Kettle – now you see me, now you don't,' then promptly vanished in the wake of the other two soldiers.

Jack turned to the boy.

'Who are you?' he asked. 'Why did you put yourself – and these other kids – at risk to help me? I don't know you, do I?'

'I'm Boots,' said the boy. 'I work at the house where your sister lives – with the countess. Sophia asked me to get you free.'

'Sophia? Oh, you mean Annie.'

'Annie, yes. I keep forgetting. Anyway, she said to get you free. And I did.'

There were a few coughs from others in the vicinity.

'Oh, yes – and this lot, they helped. That's Sweepy, that's Swab . . .' and he went through all the names, pointing out Jack's saviours one by one. Jack thanked them all individually, shaking a hand here and there, patting the odd head or shoulder of the littler ones, saying he was extremely grateful.

'I owe you a lot,' he murmured. 'I'm sure a court martial would've found me guilty and I'd have had to spent years in that place. You have no idea how bad it is in there.' He stared at them, realising he had said the wrong thing, for their lives were far worse than his, being as they were impoverished orphans without any real homes, having to work twelve to sixteen hours every day. 'That is, I'm sure you do know, even if you've never been inside the fence.'

'Oh, we can guess,' said Boots. 'Now, thing is – what do we do with you now?'

Jack sniffed and nearly threw up on the spot with the smell.

'Well, I can't stay down here. Are there any other hiding places?'

'This is the only one we know. There's the cathedral crypt, but they turn us out of there if they catch us. Under the steps behind the opera house? It'll get really cold, though.'

Jack knew he could not live outdoors. He would freeze to death in the kind of temperatures they had in Prague. He did not want to go back to Franz Kafka's house either, in case Franz's father was back. It was best they stayed away from there until they were ready to use the motorcycle to go home to their own place and time. Jack looked down at himself.

'I'll need a disguise,' he said. 'Some new clothes.'

'Ah,' said Sweepy, smiling at him for the first time, 'we've thought of that, Jack my lad.'

They made him change his uniform for some ragged clothes. Then Sweepy took great pleasure in hacking his hair about a bit with a broken dinner knife that had been sharpened on a stone. Finally Boots stepped in and gave him a makeover – with brown and black shoe polish. When they had finished with him, they all stepped back to admire him in the candlelight.

'You look just like me,' said Boots, grinning, his white teeth showing behind the dark polish. 'You're a proper boot-black, now.'

'I can't thank you all enough,' said Jack as they parted. 'And Boots, give my love to my sister – tell her I'll get word to her soon.'

'I can do that,' said Boots. 'Yes, Jack.'

Jack left them as the dawn was splashing grey light over the palaces on the other side of the river. Boots had given him a cloth bag to carry, which was supposed to hold his brushes and polishes but which contained sods of earth instead. If they insisted on searching him, Jack would be lost, but there was no reason why they would want to look in the grotty bag of a bootblack on his way to work.

Indeed, there were army police in the streets, but they walked past Jack without a second glance. His disguise was perfect, especially since there were others ragamuffins like him, all hurrying over the cobbles to get to their places of work. As the sun crept through the narrow alleys and passageways that reached out like the arms of an octopus from open areas like Old Town Square, Jack weaved in and out of the thronging streets. Eventually he reached the tiny alley using the giant man's key which he knew would lead him to Golden Lane.

The first house he tried was Dvorak's, but the alchemist only opened a small shutter in the middle of the door, peering through it with dark, chaotic-looking eyes.

'What?' hissed Dvorak. 'What do you want, boy? Aren't you supposed to be in the army? Kaspar said you were a soldier now. Get back to your barracks.'

'I've deserted,' said Jack. 'They put me in prison and I escaped.'

There was panic in Dvorak's tone. 'Then you can't come in here! It's getting too dangerous, after those raids. I've even had to turn away foreign alchemist friends. No, no, you must find somewhere else to hide. Not here. Not here.

234

They would shoot me for harbouring a deserter and criminal. All they need is an excuse . . . Go and see the other one. The one who brought you to me. He might help you.'

With that, the little shutter slammed shut.

'Dvorak?'

'Go away. Go away.'

Jack stepped from the doorway. The big man, that great lumbering ogre of a man who had taken him and Annie to Dvorak's house. Jack remembered where he lived. He decided to take Dvorak's advice and go and find the house along Golden Lane.

He wondered whether the big man would mind harbouring a criminal and guessed it would depend upon what *kind* of crime had been committed. A deserter from the army? He hoped the giant would have no real love for the army of the Austrian Empire.

Jack found the giant's door and lifted the large brass knocker.

The sound of it falling echoed through the little house behind the door.

Several times Jack had to knock, until neighbours were calling out, 'Who's there?' 'Is that my door?' 'Who's at my door?'

Finally the door opened and the big creature stood there, bleary eyed, glaring at Jack.

'What?' he bellowed.

'It's me,' said Jack, swallowing hard. 'You remember?'

'I don't know you. Are you off a ship from some foreign land? Who are you?'

Jack then remembered his face was covered in shoe polish.

'Jack. Of Jack and Annie. You met me and my sister some time ago. I − I need your help. I'm being chased.'

'Help? You need help? Why didn't you say so? The huge man − Jack had forgotten just how large he was − peered down the lane. 'Who's chasing you? Demons?'

'No . . .'

'Bad fairies, then? They can be quite vicious. Or vampires − vampires, yes, up the river from Transylvania, eh? Come in, come in. They won't get past my door. A witch has cursed that door. It's been painted with the blood of an albino wolf. Anyone who touches it will shrivel up and vanish in a cloud of yellow steam.'

Jack did not like to point out that he had touched it just a few moments ago and was still hale and healthy.

He was soon inside the house, which was incredibly small. Even Jack had to stoop to avoid banging his head on doorways and ceilings. It looked as if there were just two rooms, one downstairs, and one up. A living-room-cum-kitchen and a bedroom. The toilet, Jack guessed, would be outside in the back yard. The giant man was almost bent double in these cramped circumstances, and had to sit on the floor, before he could feel comfortable enough to talk.

'So,' he said, 'Jack. I remember you now. You were here last night, weren't you? I sent you along to that fool Dvorak.'

'Not last night. Some weeks ago.'

'No, no,' said the other, shaking his head, 'it was last night − late last night. Now, what do you think of my house, Jack? Spacious, eh? It was given to me by my master. We lived here with his wife, all three together just like a real family, until they both died within twelve short hours of each other. It was me who had to bury them, on the banks of the river – deep, deep into the clay that . . .'

A large, trembling tear formed in the corner of the giant's eye as Jack tried to imagine three people in such a small space.

'It's – it's very nice,' he said, politely, as the big man's legs shot out and almost took Jack's from under him. 'Very – *cosy*.'

'Oh, it's cosy all right,' said the giant, rubbing his huge hands together with a rasping sound. 'But sit. Sit, boy. Don't stand on ceremony. There's no spiders on this floor, and it's quite comfortable for a boy of your years, eh? Now tell me, what have you and your sister been up to now? Frightening the water ghouls, eh? They don't like that, you know, the water ghouls. What they like is stealing children's souls, not being the butt of their jokes. Still, who's to say they don't deserve it? They cause of lot of grief, the water ghouls, with their soul-stealing ways.'

'Could I stay here?' asked Jack quickly. 'Just for a short while?'

'Of course, my lad,' boomed the giant. 'Plenty of room for two – plenty. You just squat in the corner there while I make you some breakfast. One pancake or two? Two, I think, for a growing boy. Now, tell me about your sister. How is she? Well and happy?'

'She's – she's fine, er – look, what do I call you? What's your name? You've never said.'

The giant turned round and fixed Jack with large round eyes buried deep in a vast brow below a huge bald dome of a head.

'Me? You don't know me? I am the Golem, boy. Protector of the weak but good, scourge of the evil strong. The Golem. Surely you've heard of *me*?'

28. DAVEY ON THE FARM

There were rumours that conspirators were meeting at the theatre where Davey was being held by the old woman, so the police shut it down for a while. It was only a temporary closure while they investigated the rumours, and it had happened many times before. The old woman took Davey to a friend's farmhouse outside Prague, where he was put to work as a farm boy. He did not mind the work so much – in fact he enjoyed collecting the eggs the chickens had laid, and feeding the cows with whom he slept at night in soft warm hay – but he was missing his family sorely. Even the optimistic Davey began to think he would never see his mum, dad, brother and sister again.

Out in the country, too, when Davey was alone he found himself bothered by some very strange creatures. One time he had been told to watch the goats grazing, to see they didn't stray too far, and suddenly he was confronted by one of those small magical beings that had plagued him while he was away from Prague. Suddenly there was a foul, horrible smell in the air. Davey coughed and pinched his nose with his fingers, trying not to let the stench get to him.

'Pooh!' he said to the small creature standing near the

stump of a tree. 'You smell worser than a fresh cowpat. What are you?'

'I am *meluzina*,' Davey heard in his head. 'What are *you*?'

'I'm a boy, of course. And you're a stink fairy, ain't you? Go and blow off somewhere else.'

The *meluzina* hissed at him and let out a long, loud, incredibly vile fart. It was all Davey could do not to throw up. A sort of greenish gas settled on the bushes around him. The *meluzina* seemed proud of this and let out a coarse, bitter laugh. Davey, whose humour was just as coarse as any fairy's, laughed too, even though the smell was unbelievably disgusting.

'I did one of them in class, and got lines.'

Later, he tried to tell the old woman and the farmer's wife about the stink fairy, but they hushed him and made some sort of sign in the air to protect themselves against the supernatural world.

'How long are you staying?' asked the farmer's wife of her city friend.

The old woman replied, 'A week. Maybe two. They've closed the theatre before now – they never leave it closed for long.'

Davey was eating his breakfast of cheese and milk.

'I'm the most important person in the show,' he announced grandly, waving a piece of bread. 'The other actors are lumps of wood next to me. Even Donna Elvira's not got what I've got. Crisma, that's what I've got. Loads of it. I could win an Oscar back home.'

'You be quiet,' snapped the old woman. 'What drivel you talk sometimes. Who is this Oscar, anyway?'

The farmer's wife had taken to Davey.

'Oh, Beth, leave the boy alone. He's no harm, is he? What are you doing about his parents? Are they still missing?'

'They're in prison, so I'm told,' replied the old woman, looking at Davey through narrowed eyes. 'I've enquired twice now. You know what the authorities are like. If you ask *too* many questions, they start to suspect you're up to something, so I'm not asking again. I'm doing the boy a favour, looking after him at my own expense.'

'Your own expense?' Davey crowed. 'I earn my keep, I do. I'm the best actor you've ever had. You should be paying me billions.'

The old woman ignored him. 'It's either me or the orphanage. He's better off with me, I think.'

Davey made no comment. He thought so too.

The farmer's wife, however, felt sorry for him.

'Why don't you leave him here, Beth? He seems to like farm life. He'll be well fed and looked after, you know that. You can soon get another boy to take his place in the show. Think about it.'

The old woman considered this offer. After all, Davey was a lively child, a bit too full of himself. A more compliant young person would suit everyone at the theatre much better. When she put it to the boy though, he cried, 'What? Stuck out here in the middle of nowhere? No one would ever see me again. I'd rather be in the city, where they can find me.'

'Who're you talking about?' asked the old woman.

'Old Nick,' replied Davey cheekily.

29. SOPHIA AND THE STABLE BOY

Boots was pleased to be able to report to Annie that her brother was out of military prison. The pair were meeting behind the garden sheds, out of sight of the main house. The gardeners, busy getting the beds ready for the coming spring, ignored the young pair.

'He's stayin' with a friend of his – Lem, I think he called him.'

Annie frowned. 'Lem? We don't know any Lem.'

'No – wait,' said Boots. 'It was Go-*lem*. That's it. I remember now.'

'The Golem?'

'Yes, he said that too – *the* Golem. I thought it was a funny way to say somebody's name. Using *the*.'

'What does this Golem look like?'

Jack had described the giant he was staying with to Boots, who now told Annie. She immediately recognised the description as that of the figure who had shown her and Jack to the door of Dvorak's house. Annie also remembered Franz Kafka's explanation of the Golem, and realised he was one of those supernatural creatures who were visible and real to Jack and herself in this out-of-time Bohemia.

She nodded. 'Good!' she said. 'I think he'll be safe there. The Golem was made to protect Jewish people from harm, but I'm sure he'll be just as kind to kids who aren't Jewish.' She thought for a bit, then added with a note of satisfaction in her tone, 'People have enough trouble finding Golden Lane, without actually knowing about the Golem.'

'Who's the Golem anyway?'

'Well, traditionally he's a monster made out of river clay. He's as big as a house. He'll be able to protect Jack, I'm sure. Oh, you've done ever so well, Boots. I can't thank you enough.' And Annie leaned forward and kissed him on the cheek.

Boots blushed from his neck upwards, grateful that the polish engrained in his complexion hid his embarrassment.

That morning Annie looked like a Russian princess. She had on a pale blue coat, trimmed with ermine, which swept down to her ankles. On her head she wore a matching hat, also trimmed with fur. Her hands were both tucked into a white fur muff, her feet into fur-lined black boots. The outfit brought out the blue of her eyes, enhanced by a wisp of blonde hair that had escaped from the hat.

Boots swallowed hard, wondering if he would ever know anyone quite so beautiful as the girl who had just kissed his cheek. He did not think so. She smelled of heaven too. He wondered if the angels had lent her their fragrance. Boots knew he would remember this moment for the rest of his life, which would probably be a short one. Then, as he stared at this princess, he felt a bolt of consternation go through him.

'Oh, Sophia,' he said, 'you've got boot polish on your lips.'

Annie laughed, taking a hand out of her muff and wiping her mouth. Then she went all serious again. 'I don't know how to thank you, Boots – or all the other Sewer Rats. I should probably try to help you, but I don't know how. I could speak to the countess . . .'

'No – don't do that,' said Boots in a panic. 'Best you don't, Sophia.'

Boots did not like attention from those in authority. It might be pleasant in the short run, but the rich and powerful soon became bored of projects that involved the poor. Anyway, what could they do for him? Stick him in the army, like Jack? Boots would rather just keep cleaning shoes for a living. It was not a terrible existence, after all. A simple one, but it put food in his mouth and a blanket over his sleeping body. Orphans like him expected little more from life. At least if you were a boot black they did not shoot at you or expect you to kill someone – just to clean shoes. He said as much to this girl, Sophia.

Annie shrugged. 'Well, if you think of anything, let me know, Boots, because one day I'll find my parents and they can probably help you in some way.'

'I'll remember. Thank you, Sophia.'

'No – thank you. Now I must get back. The countess will be wondering where I am. She's having guests to a dinner party tonight and it's all for me. I'm hoping someone will know where my mum and dad are.'

'Good luck!'

'You too, Boots. We'll talk again, don't worry.'

Boots's heart lifted. This wonderful princess actually *liked* him. How was that for a cleaner of other people's shoes?

Annie went back to the house to find the countess pacing the rooms, giving orders via the housekeeper for the evening dinner. Cook was sitting at a table, busy writing a menu as the countess thought of things she would like her guests to eat.

'Oh, partridges for hors d'oeuvres, Cook, and . . . Ah, Sophia, where have you been? I can't look after you this morning. You'll have to make your own fun, child,' said the countess, as if she and Annie played games every day. 'This dinner requires my whole attention, I'm afraid. I'm sure you'll find something to do.'

'I could ride Cloud.'

The countess stared anxiously out of the large windows at the lawn beyond.

'It's still very frosty out there, Sophia. The ground of the paddock will be as hard as stone. If you should fall . . .'

'I'll be all right, honestly, ma'am. I'll be very careful – and Cloud is such a wonderful pony. She hasn't thrown me yet. She has such a lovely temperament. Why, I think she actually understands every word I say, ma'am. Only the other day . . .'

'Yes, yes, child. All right. Make sure the stable boy stays with you all the time, though. You dismissed him the other day, didn't you? That's not fair to him, Sophia. The stable boy is responsible for you when you're riding. And don't gallop. It will cause damage to the pony's legs and then we'll have to shoot the poor creature.'

'Really?' cried Annie. 'Shoot Cloud?'

The countess raised her eyes to heaven. 'I'm just warning you, child – trot by all means, but no cantering or galloping. Do I make myself clear?'

'Yes, ma'am.'

Annie went up to her room and changed into her proper

riding clothes. The rich and famous had clothes for every occasion and it was considered very bad form to wear just anything. A young man who had called on the countess had even apologised because he was on his way to a quarry to look for fossils and was wearing his 'fossicking clothes' and not his 'visiting clothes'.

When she was suitably attired, Annie went to the stables. There she found the stable boy, Tag, the same youth who had rescued her from the viscount-bishop's house. Tag always seemed to be around. He stared at her quite a lot.

Now he grinned and winked, saying, 'Who'd have thought it – you an' Boots, eh? I saw yer, down by the rhubarb patch.'

Annie looked at the stable boy coldly. 'I'm going to saddle up Cloud and ride her in the paddock,' she said, 'and if you make any more remarks like that, I shall have the countess dismiss you from her service.'

The stable boy went a little pale, but whether from anger or fear, Annie did not know.

'Sorry, miss – just joshing.' Then he frowned and seemed to retrieve some of his fire. 'You was just a scullery girl yerself, only shortly ago.'

'And now I am companion to the countess, and unfortunately for you I have a lot of power.' She came down off her high horse for a moment, aware of how snooty she sounded. 'Look, Tag, I wouldn't say anything to the countess. I'm not like that. But you mustn't make fun of me. I wouldn't let anyone do that, even if I was still a scullery maid. Boots is a friend of mine, nothing more.'

'I saw you kiss him!'

There was a little acid in his tone and Annie suddenly realised that this young man was jealous of Boots.

'Boots has done me a very great favour.'

'If I do you a great favour, will you kiss me too?'

'I'm talking about something quite extraordinarily brave. Something I would only want doing once in my life. You'll have to settle for a smile, Tag, and leave it at that. I can't go around kissing all the handsome young men I meet. They would think I was . . .'

After a long pause Tag offered, 'A trollop?'

'Something like that. Anyway, you're too old for me. When I'm eighteen, you'll be – oh, twenty-two. That's ancient.'

Tag grinned at this, helping her with the bridle while Cloud stamped her hooves impatiently, wanting to be out in the cold fresh air.

'So you think I'm handsome, eh?'

'You're not bad looking – but here's an end to this talk. If the countess caught us saying such stuff, she'd have a fit.'

'I suppose.' But Tag seemed to have grown a few centimetres in stature after this compliment. He patted Cloud on the shoulder and then breathed into her nostrils. The pony stared at him. 'You'll be my girl though, won't you, eh, sweetheart?'

Annie, now up in the saddle, looked down sharply at Tag, but was relieved to see that he was talking to her pony.

30. JACK IN THE HOUSE OF THE GOLEM

Being in the Golem's downstairs room was like living in a shoe box with an elephant. Anywhere Jack wanted to be, he found a foot, or a leg, or an arm belonging to the Golem. Happily the Golem had not been upstairs for a long while, due to the narrow, twisty staircase, which even Jack had trouble negotiating. There was an old ship's rope nailed to the wall to help one ascend and descend the stairs, but the sharp turn halfway up took some squeezing to get Jack's body through.

Once up there, the amount of dust was amazing. Centimetres thick, in places. And there were dead flies and spiders covering the bed, the chest of drawers and of course the floor. The bedclothes seemed to have rotted away to dusty fibres and the floor mats disintegrated under Jack's firm tread. In the wardrobe, he found some old woollen cardigans belonging to the Golem, who asked him to bring them down. However, they had so many moth holes in them that they just fell to pieces in Jack's hands when he tried to remove them from their hangers.

'Sorry,' yelled Jack down the stairway. 'Nothing's any good up here. It's all gone to pot.'

'Gone to pot? But I distinctly remember everything was fine when I left it there last week.'

The Golem had been in this room *last week*? Surely not, thought Jack. No one had been here for years. And the

Golem could not have been any slimmer a week ago. Did he have another way of getting up there, apart from the stairs? He would have to. The stairs were too narrow. It was all very puzzling to Jack.

'I've found a domino set in the chest of drawers but the spots have gone mouldy. There's also a war medal, but the ribbon has rotted.'

'My master's medal,' cried the Golem. 'Throw it down.'

Jack did so. Then the Golem called out, 'Look under the bed, will you? My cat went missing.'

Jack wrinkled his nose. 'What?'

'My cat — oh, and the woman who used to clean for me. They might be under the bed. They both went missing on me.'

Jack stared at the bed, very reluctant to peek underneath in case he found a pile of bones. Or to be precise, two piles. Then suddenly an idea came to him.

'Was the cat valuable, Golem?'

'Yes, very. It was an Egyptian Mau, a very rare breed.'

Jack was satisfied that the bodies of neither the cat nor the cleaning lady were under the bed. The cleaning lady had obviously stolen the Egyptian Mau and run off with it. He stooped and stared under the bed. There was a small carcass there that had long since been eaten to a dry shell by maggots. White bones poked through cracked hide that had once been soft fur. Jack straightened quickly, the sight of the corpse making him feel a little queasy.

There was of course a second explanation. The cleaning lady had accidentally killed the cat, hidden it under the bed, then never returned to the Golem's employ, fearful of his anger.

'The cat's here,' he called.

'Well send her down – I've missed her. *Here, kitty-kitty.*'

Jack had now got an insight into the Golem's strange concept of time. Clearly the cat had been missing for a least a year, if not more, but the Golem believed her to be still alive. Why? Jack guessed that time passing meant very little to the Golem. A year, a day, an hour; they were all one to him. That was why, when Jack appeared, the Golem had mistaken his period of absence for a short one. In his own mind he had seen Jack just a day ago.

'Um – I'm afraid it's dead, Golem,' called Jack.

'Dead? Poor kitty. How?'

No sense in getting the Golem worked up about the cleaning lady. It was only a theory, after all.

'Don't know. Just died, I suppose. Old age?'

'Well, well.' Jack could hear the Golem muttering downstairs. 'It wasn't supposed to be an *old* cat. I only bought it the day before yesterday. I shall have to see the man I got it from. Obviously it was on its last legs. I've been cheated.'

'What shall I do with the corpse?' yelled Jack.

'Oh, I'll give you a bag to put it in.'

When Jack had fetched the bag from downstairs, he started putting all the rubbish in it, until it was full of shreds of clothing, buttons and lots of other stuff. Then he got a broom and swept up. This exercise took him quite a long time, but eventually the dust, dirt and dead bugs were gathered up. He gave the bag to the Golem, who simply opened a back window and threw it out into the yard. There were other rubbish bags out there. A great number of them, built into a kind of mountain. There were rats out there too.

'Er, don't you think you'd better put it out for the dustman?'

'Dustman? What dustman?'

'The man who comes to collect the rubbish.'

The Golem's eyebrows rose a full three centimetres.

'They have a man to do that? I never knew.'

'Most places do – otherwise the world would be one big rubbish tip.'

'Very true. I just never thought.'

Jack helped the Golem gather up some of the bags and put them outside his front door on Golden Lane. The rest would have to wait: there were too many. Jack certainly hoped there would be a dustman coming to collect these few, or they would remain a bit conspicuous, though there was no reason to suspect that whoever the house belonged to it, harboured a criminal. It was just that Jack preferred that people did not knock on the Golem's door under any pretext at all.

That night Jack slept on a pile of newspapers spread on the springs of the old bed. It was the best night's sleep he had had in a long time. The Golem snored fit to bring down the walls of Jericho, but Jack was so tired he heard nothing. When the winter sun came through the dirty windows the following morning, he woke feeling refreshed and able to start tackling his problems. He went downstairs to the sink to wash and found the Golem had gone out, which gave him space to do so.

The Golem returned a short while later with bread, milk and cheese, and some very red, delicious-looking plum jam.

31. THE WEASEL'S GAMES

The Weasel seemed to have changed his mind about Roger. He had given him an overcoat and allowed him outside the walls of the prison. There were gardens there, through which Roger was allowed to walk, accompanied by only the Weasel. The Weasel had linked arms with him as they strolled through the shrubbery together, looking for all the world like old friends out for their morning exercise. Roger actually might have fallen if it were not for that arm. He had been severely weakened by his time in prison and was not as sure footed as he had once been.

'I think, Roger, there has been a ghastly mistake.'

Roger quite naturally was taken aback by this abrupt change, but remained very wary.

'Oh yes?'

'Yes, I really do. A gross error has been committed. I shall have the people responsible disciplined, of course. It seems they had you confused with another man, another Englishman. This man has caused us a lot of problems in the past.'

'And what will happen to me?'

The gravel of the path crunched under their feet. The walk was lined by roses that had not been dead-headed since the spring. The old hips were covered with frost. In the distance, on the far side of the gardens, Roger could see two guards each holding the leash of a large black

251

dog. They were not looking at the pair of strollers, but pointedly staring away from them, at the surrounding walls.

'What do you mean, Roger?'

'I mean, can I go now? Can I leave?'

The Weasel laughed. 'Why of course. Why not? We have to clear up some administration, of course. We must get the paperwork right. You will have realised by now what a bureaucratic people we are. Much like you British, I think. Look at India! But anyway, once that's done, by all means. No hard feelings, I hope?'

Roger could have happily strangled his erstwhile tormentor.

'No – no, of course not. Mistakes will happen.'

'Oh, look at that! A hare in the grounds!'

Roger stared. There was indeed a hare, bolting from a vegetable patch at the back of the gardens. How free it looked. How exuberant its racing form as it flashed across the frosty lawns. Roger had always admired hares. They had been sacred to the early Celts who inhabited England before the Romans arrived – and indeed, after. Such a strong, swift runner. It could never be caught by a fox, that was for sure.

'If only I had my gun with me,' said the Weasel.

Such a statement was only to be expected from the man.

'So when do you think the release papers will be ready?' asked Roger.

'Oh, a few days. Perhaps a week. We must check a few more details with you. We shall need the addresses of any of your friends here in Bohemia – people who might provide references for you. Alchemists, people like that . . .'

'I've told you, I don't know any alchemists,' replied the exasperated Roger.

The Weasel smiled. 'Oh, I'm sure you can dig some up, can't you?'

'I came looking for relatives of my wife, who don't even know me.'

'Ah, yes. Now, as to your wife, she is a different matter.'

Roger stopped walking. 'What?'

'Well, she is of course of Austrian blood.'

'Austrian descent, yes – but only partly.'

The Weasel smiled as if talking to a three-year-old child. 'Once an Austrian, always an Austrian.'

'She was born and bred in Britain. She is a British subject.'

The Weasel shook his head. 'We of the Austrian Empire do not recognise any divorce of our citizens from their original homeland. There are no papers here stating that your wife is no longer an Austrian, even if you have papers stating she is a British subject. To us it is as if she has never left the fold.'

'My wife was never *part* of the fold. She has always been British. As I said, born and bred in England.'

'Well, we have to yet to establish that. You may go, once we have all the relevant paperwork, Roger. But she must remain.'

Roger was in despair at these games the Weasel played. He should have guessed much earlier what was going on. His mind was being worked on again, to turn it upside-down, inside-out.

'Surely,' he said, 'if as you say my wife has never ceased

to be an Austrian, she would hardly be spying against the empire. If she were a native Bohemian, she might.'

The Weasel sighed. 'You are so naïve, Roger. I like you for that. A gullible Englishman. Roger, Roger – people will do anything for money. Do you think there have been no collaborators in history, no turncoats, no traitors?'

'My wife is not a traitor.'

'I believe you think so – but I need hard proof of that.'

'Surely you mean you need proof she *is* a traitor – not that she is *not* a traitor?'

The weasel smiled again. 'Ah, this wonderful British idea that one is innocent until proven guilty. You have it completely the wrong way around. This, Roger, is a witch hunt. Witches have to prove they are not witches, otherwise they are drowned or burned. You understand the concept?'

'Catch 22.'

'What is that?' asked the Weasel, his curiosity clearly aroused. 'Catch 22?'

'Meaning I can't win either way.'

'It sounds more American. The British have stiff lips.'

'Stiff *upper* lips.'

'Quite. Now, I'm taking you back to your cell, Roger. I shall need those names and addresses very soon, if you are to be released. I especially want the name of the alchemist who made the silver fish – you can provide me with that, I'm sure.'

Once more Roger was bewildered.

'What alchemist? What fish?'

'Ah, you know, I'm sure. There is an alchemist some-where in Prague who has discovered the secret of changing iron into silver. I am told he makes freshwater fish out of the silver, which by some means he brings to life. He then puts the living silver fish into backwater ponds, the locations known only to him, thus hiding his wealth from people like me. I want those silver fish, Roger. I will have them by one means or another. Be sure of that.'

Roger went back to his cell, his upper lip anything but stiff.

32.   A GUEST UNHANDED

When Annie came back, in the late afternoon, Tag was waiting to give Cloud a rub-down, having completed his other duties.

'Was she good?' he asked.

'Yes, very,' replied Annie. 'There was a rabbit hole and she stumbled, but still kept her footing.'

As Tag wiped down the tired pony he said quietly, 'What will you do when you have to leave here?'

Annie stared at the stable boy. 'Who said I was leaving?'

'Oh, you will one day. Soon I think. You don't belong here, anyone can see that. You'll go back to where you came from.' He stared into her eyes. 'I always knew, when I first saw you, that you weren't quite real. You didn't look real. I thought, "She's like a fairy – she'll be here and gone." You'll go back to where you came from and you'll grow into a beautiful woman and marry someone rich.' His tone held a mixture of wistfulness and sadness.

Annie saw it was no use keeping up any pretence.

'You're right about some things, wrong about others, Tag,' she told him. 'I do have to go back where I came from, but as to marrying someone rich – well, I'm not sure yet whether I'll marry anyone at all. Where I come from, a woman can have a career of her own. I may fall in love with someone – or I may not. But I will have to earn my own living, after university and I'm looking forward to it.'

'After university? Girls can do that – there?'

'Yes – and they can become anything they want, if they want it badly enough. Doctor, company director, engineer – anything.'

Tag shook his head. 'It sounds like a fairytale to me.'

'I'm not telling untruths, Tag.'

'I know that. But there's a lot I don't understand about you and where you come from. It's what I said, you don't seem real. Will – will you be able to remember me, in that place?'

'Of course, Tag. I'll never forget you.'

He looked up quickly. 'You won't?'

'Never. And I hope you won't forget me, either.'

He laughed scornfully. 'As if I could.'

'You sound as if you want to.'

'It wouldn't be a bad idea.' But then he shook his head. 'No, I don't mean that. You look after yourself, won't you. And don't you worry about Cloud. She'll be in good hands. I'll make sure the countess sells her to a good home.'

Annie reached up and stroked Cloud's neck. The pony looked at her.

'Of course, I'll have to leave her behind too, won't I?'

Annie sighed. 'Oh, it's all so hard – but there'll be some lovely memories, amongst the horrible ones.'

With that she walked away from the stables, knowing that Tag was staring at her back and wondering about it all.

When evening came around, Annie began to get very excited. Here was a real chance to discover the whereabouts of Roger and Kate. Some of the most important people in Prague were coming to the dinner. Surely one of them would know something? The countess had told Annie not to go around questioning people openly, but to leave it to her to have a quiet word with each of the guests. Annie was happy to leave it to the countess, being a little over-awed by the company. The countess had told everyone on the invitations that her niece Sophia would be at the dinner, and so Annie was a little on show that evening.

Soon the carriages began to roll up on the driveway and guests emerged in their finery. Some of the women's gowns were magnificent, and the men looked immaculate in dinner dress and black ties. Most were ancient souls with white hair, the men with white beards, but one or two were Annie's parents' age. The main language of the evening was German, though Annie heard English and French spoken too. They sat down to dinner with silver cutlery and crystal glasses, the meal served on porcelain plates. In the centre of the long table was a magnificent silver salt cellar, a work of art as large as a coal scuttle, in the shape of a knight killing a dragon with a long lance.

'That's the patron saint of England, you know,' Annie

remarked to a large portly gentleman across the table. 'St George.'

'Also the patron saint of Moscow and Madrid,' replied the man, who was covered in gingery white whiskers (Annie suspected the ginger came from the tobacco he smoked). 'Did you know that?'

'No – but they're only cities, not countries.'

The gentleman laughed. 'This is true, of course. Do you know the countries of which they are the capitals?'

'Why, Russia and Spain, of course.'

The gentleman laughed again, saying, 'Quite correct, young lady,' while Annie's answer seemed to bring her to the attention of the woman on her right, who peered disapprovingly down at her through her pince-nez and remarked, 'The child is a bluestocking! I'm sure we were not required to know such things at her age. Geography indeed! Are you a bluestocking, girl?'

'What's that?' asked Annie

'A young woman with too much learning.'

'Oh, I don't think you can have *too* much education,' Annie said. 'Surely we should try to know as much as we can about everything?'

The woman looked startled by this. 'Dreadful!' she said. 'I must speak to the countess about you. Your tutor is obviously highly unsuited to his work if he puts ideas like that into your head. Indeed you can have too much knowledge. How does a child like you retain her innocence if you are exposed to worldly knowledge?'

Annie thought this woman would have a fit if she was suddenly transported to the twenty-first century.

After dinner the women retired to another room while the men smoked cigars and drank brandy. Later the men drifted into the same room as the women. Annie noticed the countess speaking quietly with her guests in turn, and she hoped the conversation concerned the whereabouts of her parents. Indeed, one or two of the guests looked her way as the countess had words with them. Annie smiled sadly at them and tried to look as unhappy as she actually felt.

There was one tall, lean man with a narrow nose who stared at her rather too keenly for comfort. This man had been wearing black silk gloves all evening, even for dinner, which Annie thought strange. No one remarked on his affectation, which made Annie think they were used to seeing him in the gloves.

Card games were started at various green felt tables, and one man began to play the piano. After two pieces of music he asked if Annie could sing for the guests. Annie's heart plummeted. She had never done anything like entertaining house guests, but the countess said it would be very nice if she could. So she sang a song her mother had taught her and actually sang quite prettily. At least the guests thought so, because they clapped her when she finished.

One person did not clap: the man in the black silk gloves. It seemed to Annie that he was sneering at her, as if he held her in great contempt. Once she had finished, she stepped quickly away from the grand piano, only to bump into this man. Unfortunately she caught his arm with her elbow with some force. To her horror, his gloved hand flew off and went spinning and sliding across the polished floor.

'Oh! Oh, I'm so sorry, sir,' cried Annie, running after the

hand. She reached it and picked it up before anyone else did and held it out for him. 'Here, sir.'

'Clumsy girl!' barked the man. 'Look where you're going!'

The countess stepped in here.

'Herr Spitzen, it was an accident. Sophia did not mean to be awkward. She has apologised.'

Herr Spitzen ignored the countess and reached out to snatch back his false hand. As he screwed it back into its base, Annie saw something silver attached to the wooden wrist. It was her father's watch!

Herr Spitzen glared at Annie. 'Why is your niece staring at my hand in that gaping fashion, Countess. I find the child most rude. Has she not seen anyone with a disability before now? By God, if she were my child I should teach her some manners . . .'

'But she is not, sir,' said the countess in her most imperious way, 'and I shall thank you, Herr Spitzen, not to utter profanities in my house in front of my niece. It is most unseemly for a gentleman of your standing to blaspheme at such a time. I'm sure you use language of this sort with your comrades, but this is a dinner party with ladies and a child present.'

Herr Spitzen did not look at all remorseful and simply bowed curtly to the countess, before saying it was time he left. He requested his overcoat of one of the servants.

Annie fled from the room on the pretence of being upset, and ran down to the kitchen hoping to find Boots. But the boy was not there. Eating at the kitchen table, however, was Tag. The stable boy was round-eyed, staring at her party dress, and said, 'Look at you, standing there like a birthday cake!' Then he saw that Annie was looking distressed and instantly asked if he could help.

'I don't know,' said Annie, glad that Cook was busy elsewhere. 'I need someone followed.'

'What?' Tag said, looking surprised.

'There's this man, Herr Spitzen – he's leaving the dinner party at this minute. I need to know where he lives.'

Tag rose from the table and wiped his mouth on a tea towel.

'Tell me what he looks like.'

'I'll show you.'

Annie took Tag out of the back door and round the corner of the mansion, to where a coach with a single horse was drawn up in front of the big main doors. Herr Spitzen was just stepping up into the coach, barking orders at his coachman above him. The coach then began to pull away, around the first curve of the driveway.

'At least it's not a car,' muttered Annie. She asked doubtfully, 'Can you keep up with that horse, Tag?'

'I can do better than that,' muttered the youth. 'Watch.'

She saw him run through the shrubbery, then leap on to the rear of the coach without being seen. The last she saw of him that night, he was clinging like a crab to the back of the vehicle as the horse trotted out through the main gates. She was filled with fear for Tag, knowing that in the present climate of Bohemia he would surely go to prison if he was caught.

'Oh, he's so brave,' cried Annie. 'I hope he's all right!'

33. TAG MAKES A VISIT TO JACK

The Golem was still fast asleep at eight o'clock in the morning when there was a thundering knock on the door. Jack was already awake and dressed, having washed in cold water from the plain white jug and china bowl that stood upon the ancient chest of drawers. He was just thinking of emptying the chamber pot he kept underneath the bed when the banging startled him. Who could that be? No neighbour would bother the Golem at this time in the morning. A creditor, perhaps? Some bill that needed paying? Or – a chill went through Jack – the military police, come to arrest a deserter? The Golem's snores continued to reverberate through the house. Jack knew the big fellow would not wake up to a simple knocking on the door, no matter how loud.

Should I go down? he thought. After all, it might be Annie or someone sent by her.

Sensibly enough, he went to the window and looked down into the street. Below him was an old cap perched on a tousled head of brown hair. These belonged to a youth perhaps two or three years older than Jack. He was not an army man, that much was certain: his hair was too long and badly cut. Also he was wearing a threadbare jacket over a collarless shirt. Both items of clothing were too small for him, and bare arms stuck a good six centimetres out of the ends of his sleeves. His trousers were also too short, revealing a lot of ankle and worn socks. Suddenly the boy looked up to see Jack staring down at him.

'Hi!' Jack said. 'What do you want?'

The youth stepped backwards and put his hands on his hips.

'Your name Jack?'

'It might be.'

The youth snorted. 'It either is or it ain't. I'm Tag. I know your sister. I work at the stables of the countess.'

'Oh,' Jack said. 'Is she all right? Annie, I mean.'

'We call her Sophia, and yes, she be very well, Jack. She told me where to find you.'

Jack glanced up and down the street. 'Look, stay there, Tag – I'll come down and let you in. The owner is still asleep, but he won't mind, so long as we don't wake him up.'

Jack took his chamber pot and went down the steep angled stairway, reaching a point where he had to negotiate the Golem's feet, which were poking up the stairwell. Climbing over these, Jack then ducked under the left leg, which formed a pointed arch over the table. Then he had to squeeze past the heaving chest, with just a few centimetres to spare between the ribcage and the downstairs room wall. Finally he found an arm draped right across the front doorway. He had to lift this, carefully, and slide underneath. Happily he had spilled nothing from the pot, which was a miracle.

Finally, he opened the door just wide enough to struggle through and into the street.

The youth stepped forward, but Jack held up a hand and said, 'Wait a minute – got to empty my guzunda . . .' and proceeded to walk to the sewer hole a few metres away.

There he lifted the iron lid and poured away the contents of the chamber pot. The youth Tag wrinkled his nose, and Jack, on seeing this, said defensively, 'It's only natural. There's no loo in the house.'

'Of course,' replied Tag. 'We all do the same.'

'All right,' said Jack, 'you have some news for me, from my sister? I suppose she told you where to find me?'

'She's found the man who took your father's watch!' cried Tag dramatically. 'I followed him to his home.'

'What?' Jack was ecstatic. 'How did she do that?'

'She accidentally knocked his hand from his wrist at a dinner party held by the countess. The watch was on the wrist of the false hand.'

'She did what? That's terrific. I mean, it's great that she's found the man. What does he look like?'

Tag described the man he had followed. 'But as I said, I know where he lives.'

'Can you show me?'

'Of course – that's what I came to do.'

Jack went back indoors and found one of the Golem's big woollen scarves, which he wound around his head and neck, as much to hide his identity as to keep himself warm. Then he rejoined Tag in Golden Lane. The pair of them wove through the alleys and narrow streets, past small groups of grey-and-black men with their hats pulled down low and their coat collars high. Jack was aware of how closely he was being scrutinised. So long as there were no army police amongst them, or secret policemen, he felt he was not in any real danger.

They went through an open market and out the other

side, to enter a wide boulevard with trees lining the pavements. There were no sinister gatherings here, only a
single elderly woman taking a poodle for a walk on its
leash. At the tops of the stoops, all the doors appeared
tightly shut, and the windows even tighter. Tag stopped
about halfway along this road and pointed to a house
with half-pillars supporting the portal. It was a large
terraced house but it looked anonymously important, its
windows blacked-out by shades and the door having three
different deadlocks at various vertical points.

'You go back now,' said Jack. 'I'll wait here, in the shadows.'

'You be careful, boy. That man is a member of the secret
police. I think he's the chief of it.'

Jack shuddered. 'I'll be very careful, don't you worry.'

Tag waved a hand as he walked away, saying, 'I ain't
worried, but your sister be concerned for you.'

While he stood there, shivering in the cold shadows, Jack
decided on his plan. But one thing made him a little anxious:
he could not remember whether it was the right or left
hand that was supposed to be false. Before he could make
up his mind, the door to the house opened and the very
man Tag had described stepped out onto the street and
began to stride down the street.

Jack realised that this man wasn't the colonel from his
regiment whose rooms he'd broken into! But there was no
time to dwell on that. Fortunately, Jack now knew which
hand was the false one: in his right hand the man gripped
a brass-knobbed cane.

Jack reasoned he would be carrying his stick in his good
hand.

Jack walked behind the man, gathering speed all the while, until finally he broke into a run. The man half-turned in surprise as Jack came up behind him. Jack whacked the man's left hand, sending it flying through the air. It landed on the pavement ahead. Jack picked up the appendage on the run, hearing an angry shout behind him. The brass-knobbed cane whizzed by his ear, almost taking his head off. It clattered against some iron railings, breaking in half.

Jack kept running as fast as his legs would carry him.

When he was amongst the crowds in the marketplace, he inspected the hand. To his great relief, the watch was on the wooden wrist. He stripped it off and tossed away the false hand, still wearing its black glove, on to a stall full of bric-a-brac. Then, with the watch safely in his pocket, Jack hurried through the market and out the far side, back to Golden Lane and the house of the Golem.

The giant was still asleep.

Back in his room, Jack inspected the watch again. It was indeed his father's timepiece. Now that he had the key to the time machine in his possession, he felt a little more positive. The motorbike was hopefully still in the basement of Franz's house. Franz had said he was the only one who went down to the basement. His father's knees did not allow him to descend the steep steps, and the women in the house had no reason to go down there. So the machine would not have been disturbed unless something drastic had happened, such as the house being sold, or an earthquake. Jack had not felt any earth tremors.

Yet the main problem was still there: he and Annie had to find Roger and Kate. There was only one way. Jack would have to follow the man. Perhaps he would lead him to where his parents were imprisoned. It was a huge risk, though. There were others out in the streets looking for Jack, wanting to capture him. The military would not have given up hope of putting him back in the stockade.

34.   THE WEASEL ENRAGED

Jack's parents were dragged from their sleep in the middle of the night and found themselves before an enraged Weasel. The secret police chief was highly incensed. A white-hot temper had consumed him and he hardly made any sense at all. He was so angry he choked on his words, and spittle flew into the faces of Roger and Kate.

'So, you have accomplices out there! Filthy spies who are trying to destroy the empire. Well let me tell you, it won't work. It will never work. We have police combing the streets for them. They will find your comrades and we will have you here all together. Then we will see how clever you are ...' The Weasel continued to rage, his arms flying around his head.

Roger noticed that his false hand was gone.

'What are you laughing at?' shrieked the Weasel, slapping Roger hard around the face. 'Why are you smiling?'

Roger's face smarted under the stinging slap.

'Was I? I wasn't aware of it. I'm sorry, we don't know what you're talking about. I have no accomplices.'

'LIAR!'

'If you say so, of course you're right, but then I have no idea who or what they are, or where they come from.'

Kate said calmly to the Weasel, 'Look at you! You've lost your reason. I hate you, of course, for what you've done to my husband and myself, imprisoning us in this detestable place – but one thing I always did rather admire you for was your ability to remain cool. Now even that's gone. You should be ashamed of yourself.'

For one moment Roger thought Kate was going to get one of the weasel's violent slaps across the face. He knew that if that happened that he would – despite the presence of two burly guards – leap on the Weasel and hit him as hard as he could. This would ensure even greater punish-ment for both him and Kate, but he would be unable to help himself. However, Kate's words must have got through and had some effect, for the Weasel suddenly did calm down.

He smirked with long chisel-like teeth into Kate's face.

'You're right, of course. You have had training in this sort of thing, haven't you, you spies? Well, we have all night to discuss this.'

With that he left the room. It was one of his tricks to leave them for an indefinite period and then return later. All the while they would be waiting, wondering when their tormentor would come back through the door and begin the interminable questioning again. It was wearisome on the mind and soul, that waiting. There was nothing worse than the misery of uncertainty. And on top of all his other worries, Roger realised that someone, probably an oppor-tunist thief, had stolen the key to the time machine from the Weasel. If and when the time came to go back to their own time, they would not be able to start the motorcycle engine.

35. JACK FINDS HIS FATHER

'What you are doing, Jack, is very dangerous,' said the Golem. 'These secret policemen can be vicious if they think they're being tricked. I've heard of prisoners going through terrible tortures in the hands of those people.'

Jack was muffling himself up in a rather itchy scarf, an overcoat with the collar turned up, thick socks, stout shoes and woollen gloves. Finally a woollen hat went on his head and was pulled down over his ears. All that could be seen of his flesh was a band across his face where his eyes were. *Brussened*, his grandmother would have called it. That was her word for being buttoned up to the neck in heavy outdoor clothes. But Jack did not want to get cold. He did not know how long he would be out there, and in what circumstances. He also needed to be covered up for disguise purposes. The policeman had seen him once, though it had been only a passing glimpse as Jack ran away. Policemen were by the nature of their work observant people. Jack had to be very careful.

'I'll watch it,' he assured the Golem. 'I might need your assistance later, when we come to getting my parents out of prison.'

The Golem blinked. 'How can I help?'

'I don't know yet. I'm not even sure you can. But I do know I need all the friends I can get.'

The Golem's body was twisted sideways in the small room as he cooked on his little stove.

'Well, you'll need some food inside you before you go out into the deep dark night,' he said. 'Here – I've made you some buttered toast with a lightly boiled egg. And there's a nice cup of tea.'

'You sound like my mum,' said Jack, grinning. Then he recalled where he was going that night and added, 'My poor old mum, locked up in a damp prison cell.'

'We'll soon have her out,' said the Golem, turning to hand Jack two thick pieces of toast, swimming in butter, and his boiled egg. 'Come on, no miseries tonight.'

Jack scoffed the food, then solemnly shook the Golem's huge hand, before opening the front door and slipping out into the shadowy Prague streets. After leaving Golden Lane, which was deserted, he entered the wider streets of the city. Here there were contrasts. People were either moving quickly from one place to another, or they were standing, lurking in doorways and hallways, peering out. When Jack reached the opera house, however, the audience was just being disgorged from the satin interior. Groups of men and women in evening dress descended the steps of the building, hailing horse-drawn cabs or saying good night to one another under the statues of generals and politicians. Jack shouldered his way through this crowd, most of them chirruping about the performance they had just been to, and Jack joined in with the flow heading in the direction in which he wanted to go. In amongst them he was safe from discovery by the police or the military, or indeed from attack by foot-pads. Safety in numbers.

When he reached the street where the secret policeman lived, he slipped out of the throng and down some basement steps, to hide below street level. There was a light on in the basement flat itself, but the curtains were drawn so the occupants could not see Jack.

There he set himself to wait, while the remnants of the opera-goers found their keys and let themselves into their grand homes. The policeman's house was directly opposite, and Jack could keep an eye on it without showing too much of himself. He did not know whether the policeman worked a night shift, or what time he left home in the morning, but he was determined to be there when the man opened his front door and came down his steps.

It was three a.m. when Jack woke suddenly. His bones ached with the coldness of the stone steps and wall. He shivered violently, wondering if he should go home and climb into a warm bed. It would be nice, he thought. Then he wondered what had actually woken him. Not the cold, that was for sure; he had been cold for hours.

There was a noise by his head. He looked up and round to find a stray cat staring directly into his face from six centimetres away. The scruffy-looking beast was peering through the railings above the basement steps. Its eyes were almost level with Jack's and it was a shock to find the creature so close. Jack hissed at the moggy, to make it go away, but it simply narrowed those green eyes and stared more intently into Jack's own. At that moment Jack heard shoes tripping down the stone steps on the opposite side of the street. His enemy was descending, as nimble as a dancer, to the pavement below.

The man crossed the street, walking straight towards where Jack was hiding. Jack's vision was limited, since he did not want to poke his head above the level of the pavement. He could see a pair of long, lean legs encased in narrow, neatly pressed black trousers. Those trousers had creases you could cut bread with, they were so sharp. The legs ended in a pair of highly polished black shoes that gleamed in the lamplight.

Jack held his breath. Had he been seen? Thank God for the cat. If that stray moggy had not woken him, he would have missed his prey. Yet was this his prey, or was he the quarry now? Then he heard a scratch and light filled the basement stairwell. But the light was momentary, coming and going within seconds. Jack smelled cigarette smoke. The policeman had been lighting up. Jack stole a glance upwards and saw that the man was staring into the middle distance, obviously thinking very hard about something. He drew on his cigarette, the end glowing bright red, then he was off, striding out alongside the road, heading east.

The cat, who was still sitting there staring indignantly at Jack, suddenly changed shape. It became a lumpy little creature with a malicious face, standing no higher from the ground than Jack's knee. It wore an expression of deep annoyance.

'What . . . ?' Jack was startled into jumping backwards. 'Who are you? What are you doing here?'

'This is *my* patch,' said the *trpaslik*. He was one of those creatures that lived in the basement stairwells, there being few woods and fields in the streets of Prague. 'More to the point, what are *you* doing on my property? Get out! Get out!'

'Not yet,' muttered Jack. 'I can't go yet. That man will see me.'

'Not interested,' cried the *trpaslik*, kicking Jack's foot. 'Couldn't care less.'

Jack saw now that the policeman was at least a hundred metres along the street. Throwing a grimace at the *trpaslik*, he slipped out of the stairwell and followed his target. The *trpaslik*, yelled an oath after him, but the curse was lost on the wind.

From the back, Jack could see that the man was wearing an expensive-looking dark overcoat. There was a white silk scarf around his neck and on his head was a black top hat. With a chill Jack suddenly realised that the policeman must have been one of the opera crowd! He had not recognised him amongst all those other people, all dressed alike. Of course there was no reason why – just because he was evil – the policeman should not like opera as much as any other lover of such music. Perhaps while he listened to Mozart or Wagner he planned his tortures for the next day? Who knew what went on inside the head of such a man?

Clearly he had not been to bed.

At the end of the road, the man turned left. Once he had disappeared, Jack raced for the corner and peered round, only to find his quarry had vanished. He had been afraid of that. There were so many alleys and side streets for the policeman to disappear into. Jack stepped out boldly towards a junction just a few metres ahead. There he saw a sign that said in both German and Czech: RAILWAY STATION.

Was that where his man had gone? Jack spun round, staring at the other streets down which the policeman could have disappeared. He could see to the end of two of them, and they contained no human figures.

'Must be the station,' muttered Jack to himself.

He followed the signs.

When he reached the railway station, he found it almost deserted. There was freight being loaded on to rail trucks, and another train stood against Platform 1. Milk churns were being loaded into its guard's van. There were no potential passengers on the platform. The guard appeared about to wave his flag and blow his whistle. Jack hurried up to the squat figure in his seedy-looking uniform.

'Sir, please could you tell me where this train is going?'

The guard took his whistle from his mouth.

'Where do you *want* to go?'

At that moment Jack had to look away, quickly. His prey had just come out of the waiting room and now strode past Jack and the guard, saying, 'Don't blow that thing yet. I'm not aboard. And by the way, tomorrow I would like to see a better fire in that room. A few glowing coals was all it had. See to it.' He had not studied Jack in any way, probably thinking him to be something to do with the station staff.

'Yes, sir,' said the guard, touching his greasy cap. Then, under his breath, 'Not my job, waiting room fires. That comes under the station manager and his staff, not my responsibility.'

'Who is that?' whispered Jack. 'You seem scared of him.'

'Important man,' replied the guard. 'Best not to cross him.'

Then he seemed to realise he was talking to a youth. 'Anyways, are you going to get aboard, or what? You *have* got a ticket?'

'Yes, sir,' snapped Jack. 'Bought it yesterday.'

It was safe to assume that at this time of the morning, no one would be around checking tickets.

Jack trotted away from the guard and climbed into an empty carriage. The guard blew his whistle, waved his flag, and then jumped into his van as the train pulled slowly out of the station. Jack could hear the steam engine hissing and puffing as the carriages creaked forward, some banging into the one in front, their ironwork clanging. Soon the train gathered speed and was chuffing out into the night, with the city streets and buildings swishing by on both sides.

A little while later the train pulled into its first station, but it was just the depot on the edge of the city. No one alighted or came aboard. The guard exchanged something with another railway man and they were soon on their way again.

Jack let the window in the door down by slipping the leather sash off its holder. It fell down into its slot in the door with a noisy crash. Then he stuck his head out into the night, to try and see where they were going. It was black as tar outside and he could see nothing – but he did choke on the smoke. When he looked at his face in the oval mirror above the long seat, he got a shock. He was smutty from hairline to chin with black flecks, presumably from the smoke that belched from the stack.

They began to stop regularly at stations. Each time they did so, Jack cautiously poked his head out of the open window to see who got off the train. Hardly anyone did. A man alighted at one stop, but he was dressed in a collarless shirt and threadbare jacket. Not Jack's man.

There was then a long stretch of track with no stations and nothing much for Jack to do but wait and hope. He was feeling very tired. The train had a soporific effect on him, with its gentle heat and the *over-the-points, over-the-points* rhythmic clacking of its wheels on the track. It was inevitable that he should fall asleep.

He woke as a carriage door slammed further down the train. Jumping up, he looked out of the window to see that they were just pulling out of a station. Frantically he searched the platform for the one-handed policeman and saw him disappearing into a sort of café in the middle of the station. Jack reached outside and fumbled with the door handle, managing to turn it as the train gathered speed. He opened the door and leapt from the carriage, landing on the end of the platform and jarring his ankle. He picked himself up and tested his leg. Nothing seemed to be broken, though it felt a bit sore. He hobbled along the platform and made his way cautiously towards the café.

The sign over the door was a broken piece of plank. In hand-written painted letters it said simply: LOLA'S BAR. Jack could hear the murmur of voices within, and the clink of glasses, but he did not go near the doorway. He simply waited in the shadows until the policeman emerged again, which he did after about half an hour. The smell of schnapps wafted out through the doorway with him.

Jack followed him up a winding track leading through some houses and up a shallow hill. On the top of this hill

– it could almost be called a mound – stood a Gothic-looking castle. It had one main high, square tower and one or two smaller ones. Unlike with English castles, these towers had steep little roofs on them, some with tiny windows. One was crowned with a great spike that pierced the sky. Below were castle buildings, tightly clustered, like great shoulders dropping away down the steep incline. The walls looked high and strong, with crenellations meandering here, there and everywhere, as if there were no real symmetry to the shape of this magnificent chateau.

Jack saw the policeman disappear inside the large gateway. He was not going to follow him in there. Instead he went back to Lola's Bar and this time went inside. There were two elderly men drinking at a rickety table. Behind the bar itself stood a large muscular woman polishing glasses with a rag.

'Excuse me,' said Jack, aware that all three were listening, 'but could you tell me the name of that castle outside?'

There was silence for a while, as the woman kept polishing the glasses and the men stared at Jack. Then one of them growled, 'Don't you know where you are, boy?'

'I've been on army manoeuvres,' explained Jack, 'and I got lost on the way back.'

The other man narrowed his eyes. 'Why are you in civilian clothes, if you're an army man?'

'I'm supposed to be a spy,' said Jack, laughing with convincing authority and confidence. 'On the exercise, I was the enemy.' He looked down at himself. 'I dressed all in black so that I shouldn't be seen. It's very effective, don't you think?'

Their expressions did not change and they were clearly having trouble believing him.

Jack elaborated on his story. 'I'm actually a drummer boy, in the 14th Foot. Hey, let me liven the atmosphere in here a bit.' He picked out two knives from a cutlery box and proceeded to beat a tattoo on the bar top. 'That's Reveille,' he said to his audience. 'This is Retreat,' and he drummed a rhythm so fast and furious it had the barmaid tapping her feet.

'Makes you want to dance,' she said, speaking for the first time. 'Makes your toes tingle in your shoes.'

'I'm afraid it'd make your blood tingle in your veins if you were on the battlefield, madam,' said Jack gravely. 'I hope I never have to play that one – the tattoo all brave soldiers like to hear is Advance. That's what I joined the army for, anyway – to serve my country in war.'

'Of course, of course. But listen,' her voice sounded friendly, 'you don't want to talk about spies round here, young man. That's Karlstein Castle up there on the hill. That's where they take the real spies they catch. You go saying you're a spy and you'll find yourself inside those walls quicker than that.'

Jack let out a false laugh. 'Oh my gosh. Really? Oh, heck. Good job none of the guards were in here for a drink, or I might have been in trouble. Karlstein. Yes, I know where that is on the map, all right. I'll be able to find my way now.'

'Why don't you just catch a train?' offered one of the men, a little more amiable now he believed he was talking to an army man. 'There'll be one through here in twenty minutes.'

'Or thirty,' said the other man.

'Or even forty,' added the woman.

They all laughed.

'Not running to timetable, eh?' said Jack, joining in the laughter. 'What's the country coming to?'

'It was always the same,' replied the older of the two men, the one with a white wispy beard. 'Never any different. Mail coach was always late. So was the wagon that took you to market. O' course, when I was a lad there weren't no train in these parts. You had to go by horse – or shanks's pony if you didn't own an animal. Youth of today don't know how good they've got it. No gas lighting then. No 'lectric neither. Pitch black at night and candles at a farthin' a dozen. Why, I remember walkin' thirty mile just on the hint of a farming job . . .'

The woman groaned and rolled her eyes at Jack, as the old man continued to illustrate how soft the world had become since his own youth, back in the age before machines had taken over.

Jack stayed in the warmth of Lola's Bar. He failed to ask if the lady behind the bar was Lola – she did not look like a Lola; she looked more like a Gertrude or a Brunhilda. Eventually the train did come. 'Only seventeen minutes late – a miracle!' said the older man.

Jack jumped on board.

This time he purchased a ticket, for morning was rapidly approaching and people such as ticket inspectors might have left their beds and be on the prowl. By seven o'clock he was back in the little house in Golden Lane, climbing over the Golem's feet to get at the stairs that led to his lovely feather bed and a morning's sleep.

36. THE TRAIN TO KARLSTEIN CASTLE

When Jack woke again, from a very refreshing sleep, he lay there planning his parents' escape. Once he got them inside the wandering, melancholic passageways and vaulted arcades of Prague, it would be difficult for the police to find them. The Golem had promised to help. They had talked about how the rescue might take place and how the Golem's skills might best be put to use.

'And you could protect us, if we get in trouble,' said Jack. 'You're good at that too.'

'Yes,' said the Golem, his large, flat face devoid of expression. 'This is the thing I do best. To serve. To protect the traveller in the night, the weak and the vulnerable. I can be your bodyguard. I will crush the life from any man who attacks you. I will squeeze his body till his bones break and the splintered ends poke through his skin. I will hug him so hard the blood will gush from his mouth. His eyes will shoot from his skull like bullets from the barrel of a gun. His heart will burst as easily as a balloon full of water.'

'I think I get the idea,' said Jack, a little squeamishly, 'but it won't come to that, will it?'

The Golem shrugged. 'It depends on our luck.'

'My plan is this,' said Jack. 'I will . . .'

The Golem waved his arms. 'No, no, don't tell me. If I get caught, they may torture me. You must always keep your plans to yourself. Never tell others what you intend, or they may let you down.'

'I'm sure you'd never let me down, Golem.'

'Who can tell? I'm flesh and blood, after all.'

'Are you? I thought you were clay.'

Jack was joking, of course, intending to lighten the mood, but the Golem took him seriously. A look of sadness came over the monster's features as he inspected his pale yellowy hands and he sighed deeply, as if he had just discovered an unwelcome secret about himself.

'Clay? Clay. You have reminded me I am not like others. I am a *thing* of dirt. Sometimes I believe myself to be human, to be like you. But my brain fools itself. I am soil, earth, loam. I am the walking land. I was moulded from meadow. Fashioned from field. You – you are a real person. You were born and you will die. But I will just remain.'

Jack knew the Golem was indeed made from clay. He did not try to argue with him; he simply told him all men were made from dust, and that they returned to dust when they died, so a man of clay was not really that much different. After that, the Golem cheered up – as much as he was ever cheerful, which meant his face went from utter misery to merely mournful – and they were able to chat about other things for a while.

That evening Jack visited Annie at the countess's home.

'I think I've found out where Mum and Dad are being held,' he said. 'I'm going to do my best to get them out.'

'I'm coming with you,' said Annie quickly.

'No – I think it best you stay here,' Jack told her.

'You're not the boss of me – I'm coming with you.'

'I knew you'd be awkward, but I thought I had to tell you to stop you worrying, even if just for another night.' Jack sighed. 'All right then. Can you be at the railway station in Prague at eleven o'clock. That's when we're catching the train to Karlstein Castle.'

'We?'

'The Golem's coming too.'

Annie grinned. 'Oh, quite a gathering. Listen,' she flicked the hem of her flouncy dress, 'I'm not coming in this. I'll borrow trousers and jumper.'

'Good thinking. How will you get there? To the station, I mean.'

'Tag will take me. I'll ask him.'

After Jack had gone, Annie was in two minds whether to consult the countess or not. She was afraid the countess would prove to be an adult of her time and be horrified at the thought of a young woman charging about the countryside at night. But equally if she found Annie missing without an explanation, she would be beside herself with worry and would probably call out the police to form search parties. Under the circumstances that would prove disastrous for both Jack and their parents. So she went to the drawing room where she knew the countess was sitting doing needle point and told her what was happening.

'How exciting!' cried the countess, throwing her work aside. 'How I wish I could come with you!'

Annie was so astonished by this response she almost fell over.

'I shall take great care,' she said.

'Of course you will,' replied the countess, 'and you'll have your brother and this Gorgon person to protect you.' Her brow furrowed in puzzlement. 'Pray don't mistake me for a blue stocking,' she added, 'but I always thought the Gorgon was female.'

'I think she is, but I'm going with the *Golem*.'

The countess brightened. 'Ah, that accounts for it then. No, no. You go off and have your adventures.' She sighed. 'I wish I had done so at your age – now I'm far too old. I would like to try, but I know I'd probably be out of breath before I'm at the end of the driveway. Be very, very careful, though, my child. Do as the men tell you!'

'Oh, of course,' replied Annie, who had no intention of being told what to do by her brother or the Golem, just because they were males.

When the countess turned to Annie, she saw that the elderly woman's eyes were wet. 'I shall miss you, child,' she said. 'Give me a hug goodbye.'

Annie did as she was bid. Then the countess reached into a cabinet and took out a statuette. 'I want you to have this, to remember me by,' she said. Annie took the object, then realised with a start that it was the shepherdess. She looked at the countess, who smiled through her glistening tears.

'Jeanette once told me you almost broke it – well, you can do what you like with it now. It's yours.'

'I shall treasure it for ever,' mumured Annie, overcome. 'You know I will.'

When she left the room, Annie almost bumped into Jeanette, who seemed to be drifting past the doorway. She opened her mouth to question the parlourmaid, but Jeanette was on her way down the stairs to the kitchen before she

could get the words out of her mouth. Annie shrugged and
went straight to see Tag.

'You want to borrow my trousers and jumper?' he cried.
'You can't.'

'Why not?' asked Annie reasonably. 'Oh yes – and that
greasy old flat cap you wear.'

'You can't.' he repeated.

'One good reason?'

'Well – because they're for – for . . .'

'Only for boys to wear? Huh. Look, are you going to
lend them to me or not? I'll be in horrible danger if you
don't. I've got to travel on a train with my brother tonight,
and if I'm seen in this thing,' she indicated her dress with
its lace, ribbons and sashes, 'I'll be reported for sure. You
don't want me to be in dire straits, do you, Tag?' She was
rather pleased with her efforts at drama. She could see Tag
was affected by them.

He squirmed in his shoes. 'The clothes . . . they're not
as clean as you'd wish 'em, Miss Annie.'

'I'll survive.'

The stable boy's clothes did indeed smell somewhat of
horse sweat and other odours of yard and tack room, and
even though Annie was not a fussy girl, she did let out a
little shudder as she pulled on the youth's stiff ancient
trousers. The jumper was full of holes. Finally, she put on
the unsavoury cap. Tag had also given her a sheepskin coat,
which smelled as if it had just been on the sheep. She
inspected her reflection in the bedroom mirror and said to
herself, 'You'll never make a model, Annie Kettle!' Coming
out of her room, she ran smack into Jeanette, the parlour-

maid. The older woman's eyes went wide with disbelief as she stared at Annie.

'It's a sort of joke,' Annie told her carelessly from under the flat cap. 'I'm going to pretend to be Tag, the stable boy, and fool someone.'

Jeanette continued to stare at her for a moment, her waspish features appearing more pointed and severe than usual. Then the woman left without a word, walking swiftly along the landing carpet with short, quick steps.

Annie did not know what to make of this encounter, but she decided Jeanette would probably tell the countess, and the countess would thank her gravely for her information and giggle to herself once the parlourmaid was out of sight.

Annie had the shepherdess, of course, and did not know what to do with it. If she took it with her on this escapade there was a good chance it would get broken. And in any case, she could not take it back with her on the time machine – her father would not take that particular risk so she did the only sensible thing left to her.

'Tag, will you give this to a Franz Kafka, who lives at 3 Zeltnergasse Strasse, Prague. Ask him if he will pass it on to the relatives of the English family. Can you do that?'

Tag frowned. 'I think so.'

'Thank you, Tag – you've been very kind to me.'

Tag seemed upset. 'I'll see you outside.'

When she went to join him, he was waiting at the stables with Cloud and another saddled horse. They rode out over the dark fields towards the city, arriving on the outskirts with enough time to walk to the railway station. They left their mounts hitched to an old oak in the corner of a meadow and continued on foot.

When they arrived at their destination, Annie went to the courtyard to the side of the station, where she was to meet with Jack and the Golem. There was no one there. She waited with Tag at her side, anxiously staring down the cobbled road that led to the heart of the city. One or two people came along that road, but not her brother.

'Oh, where is he?' she said aloud to Tag. 'He's always late!'

Tag had gone very quiet and thoughtful. Now he said, 'Never mind your brother for a moment. We must say goodbye.' He looked extremely sad. 'We must say goodbye for ever.'

Annie stared into the misty eyes of the handsome youth and caught his feelings, and a sadness came over her too.

'Yes, we must.'

'Before we part, I have to tell you what I am, Sophia. I'm not a stable boy. This is my disguise.'

Annie nodded. 'I guessed as much – the countess had never heard of you when I spoke about you. Who are you then?'

'*What* am I is the real question. You know that you and Jack saw strange shadowy figures when you first arrived in Prague? Well,' Tag confessed, 'I was one of those – *am* one of them. We – we are time guardians, here to make sure that time travellers like you don't alter history in any way. Think of the terrible consequences! What if you changed the future? That's why you are not permitted to carry things from this time to your own – like the porcelain shepherdess. I saw you were tempted, which is why I appeared to you in the garden.'

'Oh, that was you?'

'It was indeed me, until for convenience I changed my form and took on the guise of a human, a stable boy. It was easier to watch you. But from watching you, I went on to watching out for you, looking after you, seeing you came to no harm. I wasn't supposed to do this. I was ordered not to interfere, but you see, when one takes on human form . . .' he hesitated, but then continued, '. . . one takes on human *feelings*, human emotions. Sophia, I grew very fond of you, and – and now you must go away. We shall never meet again. You see standing before you a youth of only seventeen summers. That is how I feel. A young man from whom a life will soon be stolen. This youth, this young man, Sophia, will miss you very badly when you are gone.'

Annie's eyes welled up at these words, but she had no time to answer him properly, for someone was coming their way. All she could do was touch his cheek with her fingertips and murmur, 'Goodbye, Tag.'

A few seconds later two figures stepped out of the shadows, one much smaller than the other, who was immense.

'Annie? Is that you?' Jack's laugh rang out. 'I didn't recognise you. We've been standing here watching the pair of you, hoping you'd go away. Then I heard your voice.'

Jack was brussoned to the neck in a black overcoat, while the Golem was wearing a thick necklace of coiled hemp rope.

'Oh Jack, thank goodness you're here.' Annie gave her brother a hug, then Jack said, 'Hi, Tag!'

'Hello, Jack. Here's your sister, safely brought.'

'Right.' Jack took the stableboy's hand and shook it vigorously. 'Well done, Tag. Thanks for looking after her.'

'She's quite well able to look after herself,' Tag replied, 'which you probably know, bein' her brother.'

'That's true,' Jack said, laughing again. 'Look, we've got to get going now. We've got to slip down the sidings and climb on to one of the freight wagons. We can't ride in a carriage with passengers, it's too dangerous.'

'An' he's too big!' said Tag, impressed, indicating the Golem. 'He's a blamed oversized giant, he is.'

The Golem stared down at Tag and then put a huge meaty hand on his shoulder. It felt to Tag as if someone had dumped a side of lamb on his collar bone. The side of lamb suddenly opened and then closed over his shoulder in a strong grip, making him wince with pain.

'You did good,' growled the giant in a gravelly voice. 'This time I probably won't kill you.'

Jack said, 'He's having fun with you, Tag.'

The Golem released his grip, and Tag gave him a grimace.

Annie said they ought to get going. Jack bade a swift goodbye to the stable boy, and the three then used the darkness to cover their movements to a freight train standing on the tracks. As they slunk along the edge of the train, Annie asked her brother if he was sure it went to Karlstein. He assured her he had done his homework. The train stopped at every station along the line to pick up milk churns.

The found an empty wagon and got on board.

The train left Prague fifteen minutes late, but they were on their way at last to rescue their parents from prison.

37. JACK IN THE WEASEL'S DEN

The train pulled into the station below the forbidding castle just after midnight. Jack, Annie and the Golem leapt from the freight car and crept across the tracks to the fence. The Golem took hold of a post and ripped it from the ground, the fence coming with it. They stepped through the gap.

Annie stared up at the formidable-looking castle, visible in the moonlight.

'Mum and Dad are in that horrible place?'

'Well,' said Jack, following her gaze, 'it's only horrible *because* they're there. It's really quite a beautiful castle.'

'With dungeons, probably.'

'Probably.'

Jack turned to the other two. 'You have to wait here,' he said. 'I need to find out where they are.' With that he removed his overcoat. Underneath he had on his army uniform, neatly pressed. From his pocket he took his forage cap and put it on his head. He looked every centimetre the soldier. Crisp and smart, ready for duty.

'Oh, Jack,' said Annie, 'what are you going to do?'

'It's the only way to get inside,' her brother replied. 'Now – listen. If I'm not back in, say, half an hour, you must leave. You understand? It'll mean I've failed and it'll do no good to get us all caught. You must catch the next freight train back to Prague and try to figure something else out. Promise me you'll leave, Annie.'

'Oh, Jack!' Her eyes welled up with tears.

'Now, Annie – none of that. It'll be all right. But we must have these contingency plans.'

She rallied. 'Where did you learn such words? Contingency plans?'

'In the army. I'm an army man, didn't you know?' Jack said, smiling. 'I'm in one of the most famous infantry regiments. You'd be proud to see me march, Annie, beating my drum.'

'I'm proud of you anyway.'

Jack turned to the Golem, who was unwinding the length of rope he had brought with him, then coiling it neatly on the ground like the ropes one sees on the decks of ships. 'Look after her, Golem.'

The giant looked up from his task and nodded his huge head.

'I will.'

Jack started off along the winding track that led up to the castle gates. The moon was skidding back and forth, sliding behind clouds and out again. Along the track were cottages and empty stretches lined with trees.

Just as Jack was congratulating himself on nearing the castle without incident, he saw two army officers coming towards him. They had their arms linked and Jack could smell the schnapps on the downward breeze. They had obviously been drinking.

There was no time to duck away into the bushes. Jack straightened his back and snapped up a smart salute as he came alongside them. His heart was beating fast. He could not afford to have a long conversation with these two. The officers stopped and looked at him.

'Soldier,' said one in a slurred voice. 'You're drunk!'

'Beg pardon, sir, but I haven't been drinking. I'm on duty.'

'Oh, then it must be me who's had one too many,' the officer said, and giggled loudly. ''Sme who's the drunk one.'

'An' me,' cried his companion, as if it was the funniest thing he had ever heard.

They both laughed uproariously and one of them stamped his foot in mirth. They wandered on, still arm in arm, the shorter one calling back, 'Is Lola's still open?'

'Yes, sir, I believe so, sir.'

'Jolly good.'

'Jolly, jolly good.'

Jack sighed deeply, then continued up the path. The incident with the officers had rattled him. He was still shaking a little. Could he go through with his plan? When he was lying in his bed at the Golem's house, it had seemed strong, if not infallible. But now? Now it felt flimsy. It needed an iron nerve to go through with it. Jack had to bluff his way through, which meant he had to look and sound the part completely. Once those gates opened there could be no faltering. He needed to convince people absolutely. He paused for a minute to strengthen his resolve. Then, once he felt able, he continued towards the gates and pulled a bell rope.

It seemed an age before a small door in the gateway was opened and a face appeared in it.

'Yes?'

Jack said in a firm voice, 'Private Schell, sent by Major Borsaw to see the foreigners.'

A frown appeared on the face. 'Foreigners? What foreigners?'

'The English prisoners.'

'Ah, those . . .' The gates opened to reveal three guards, who stared curiously at Jack. One of them was a sergeant. It was he whose face had been framed by the opening in the gate. He studied Jack from head to toe. 'What regiment?' he snapped.

'Fourteenth Foot, Sergeant,' replied Jack, coming to attention. 'Major Borsaw would like me to see the prisoners, to – to *ascertain*,' he spoke the word as if he were remembering an exact message from his commanding officer, 'whether they are who he thinks they are. If I can just get sight of the man? My major thinks he has information on these spies.'

The sergeant looked at one of the other guards, as if to say, *What's this young soldier talking about?* The guard rolled his eyes.

The sergeant turned to Jack. 'We were told nothing about this.'

'No, I know. My major hasn't had time to contact anyone before tonight. He's – he's just back from a long convalescence. He broke his leg playing polo. While he was in hospital, he heard about the prisoners from one of your people. One of your guards or officers, I think, but I'm not sure. The major didn't say.'

The sergeant again turned to his men. 'Who would that be? Who's gone into hospital lately? They shouldn't talk. This is supposed to be a secret establishment. The chief won't like it.' He turned back to Jack. 'My superior isn't here at the moment. He sometimes comes in at night, to interrogate the prisoners but I don't know whether . . .'

Jack decide to take a huge gamble. His heart thudding

in his chest, he said, 'Oh – is that the gentleman with only one hand?'

The sergeant stiffened and stared hard at Jack, who felt he ought to continue. 'Only, he was with the major tonight, at the officers' mess.'

'I don't understand,' said the sergeant. 'If my superior was there, with your major, why didn't *he* speak to you?'

'Perhaps the gentleman did not wish to talk to an inferior private in the army?' said Jack, shrugging. 'I don't know. He looked – well, forgive me if I'm overstepping the mark – he looked a bit snooty to me. I suppose he and the major had talked about it before I was sent for. I don't know.' Jack began to sound annoyed. 'I get dragged from my warm bed on a bloody cold night. I'm sent out here with a half-baked message. How am I supposed to know? I'm just a drummer boy. Everybody puts on me. I think my corporal was supposed to come, but oh no, send Private Schell instead. He won't complain. He can't complain. He's just a boy.'

The sergeant grinned. 'Snooty, eh?'

'Seemed like. Maybe you'll report me for these remarks, Sergeant, but he did seem more snobby than the usual officer.'

The guards laughed, and the sergeant said, 'You're dead right, lad, snooty as hell. But don't tell him I said so. Come on then. A quick look at the prisoners. What do you hope to learn?'

'Well, I want to know whether one of them has a white scar on the back of his right hand – the man. It's about a centimetre long.'

The sergeant frowned. 'I never noticed one. Let's go and

see. Would that mean something to your major?'

'I suppose so. That's what I've been asked to check. Perhaps Major Borsaw has come across this spy before?'

'Maybe he gave him the wound?' said the sergeant.

Jack knew that scar had come from his dad falling off his bike on to their gravel path at home, but he said, 'Could be.'

The sergeant told the guards to stay where they were and led Jack along a maze of passageways, up several flights of stone stairs, and finally to some cells high up in the castle. A guard sat at a desk with a huge ring of keys. He raised his eyebrows on seeing Jack and the sergeant.

'What's to do?' he asked.

'Just hand 'em over, Novacek,' said the sergeant, his hand outstretched. 'You don't have to know everything that goes on around here.'

The guard shrugged and handed over the jangling ring of keys, saying, 'You're the sergeant, Sarge.'

There were only eyeholes in the doors through which to view the prisoners, so the sergeant opened the cell door with a large key and took Jack inside. It was pitch black. The sergeant switched on a torch and highlighted a figure on an iron bed. It was a man, covered by a single blanket. The man woke up suddenly, trying to shield his eyes from the light with his hands.

'Not another damn cross-examination?' muttered Roger's irritated voice. 'Can't you leave me in peace for one night?'

Dad! Jack almost shouted out with joy – but fortunately managed to restrain himself. Roger, with the torchlight directed at him, could not see his son standing there, and probably would not have recognised him anyway. Jack looked quite different from his old self in his army uniform.

'Put out your right hand palm downwards,' the sergeant ordered his prisoner. 'Then you can have all the peace you want.'

After a few seconds, Roger did as he was told. The sergeant shone the torch on the skin. The white puckered scar was clearly visible.

'Well, I'll be . . .' murmured the sergeant. 'There it is, Private – you can report back in the affirmative to your major.'

'Aren't you going to chop it off?' snarled Roger, his arm still at full stretch. 'You bloody barbarians are capable of anything.'

'Go back to sleep,' said the sergeant. 'We're finished with you.'

'What was that all about?' argued Roger. 'Waking me up to look at my blasted hand? More subtle torture, eh?'

'I must repeat my order! Go back to your bed!'

'You're the one who disturbed me, not the other way around. I'm wide awake now. I can stand here all night.'

While this exchange was going on, Jack peered through the barred window and looked out and down. He could see a shed far below in the moonlight, just to the right of the castle wall. He judged it was about twenty metres to the ground. Having fixed his position, Jack walked quickly back to the doorway and stood waiting while the sergeant lambasted his dad for having the effrontery to question why he had been disturbed in the middle of the night just to see his hand.

'Well,' said the sergeant, as he led Jack down the steps

back to the gate, 'you can see what trouble he is. So, the scar is there. You'll report to your major? That's good. I'm glad you've got what you came for.'

They opened the gates to let Jack out. A figure was coming up the track as Jack walked away from the castle and he froze in fear. What if this were the one-handed man, coming to interrogate his parents? The alarm would be raised and there could be no escape after that. But the figure was weaving badly and Jack realised it was one of the drunken officers, returning to the castle. Probably one had been meant to relieve the other, but someone had produced a bottle and they had indulged.

'Night, sir,' said Jack, saluting as he passed.

The officer grunted, his earlier merry mood obviously gone now. He flicked a return salute and continued to meander his way up the dirt track. Jack hoped there would not be too many questions asked when he saw his sergeant. The officer seemed really very inebriated, so it was hopeful he would just flop in a chair and go to sleep.

Annie and the Golem were waiting in agitated silence for Jack's return. Annie was so delighted and relieved to see her brother she hugged him hard, until Jack peeled her away and said, 'Come on, we've got to move fast.'

He led the pair around the castle walls until he found the shed he had seen from Roger's cell. It was in some vegetable gardens, which probably served the castle kitchens. Then he looked up and pointed to a row of windows near the top of the wall.

'That's where Mum and Dad are – and Blazek probably. Golem, can you do your bit?'

The Golem, brilliant climber that he was, began to scale the wall of the castle, crabbing up the rough stone blocks towards the windows. Over his right shoulder was the long coil of rope.

38.   ESCAPE FROM KARLSTEIN!

When the Golem reached the cell windows, he tried wrenching one of the bars out of the mortar. Bits of old mortar drifted like snow down on to Jack's head, but the bar seemed to remain fast in its setting. After a while the Golem descended again.

'Too hard,' he grunted. 'New cement's been used.'

'They've reinforced it, have they?' muttered Jack. 'Well, we'll try something else.' He pointed upwards. 'It's not far from that row of windows to the roof of the castle. There's an ordinary window in the roof, one without bars. Could you reach that and force an entry, without too much noise?'

'I could try,' the Golem answered.

'Then attach the rope to the central pillar of that window and let it hang down the castle walls. Once you're inside, there's only one guard on the floor where the cells are located. He's got the keys. If you could get them from him, you could let Mum and Dad out, and they could climb down the rope to the ground.'

'Better still,' interrupted Annie, 'we could attach the other end of the rope to that telegraph pole,' she pointed, 'and they could use it like a zip-wire. You know, use a belt or a piece of clothing and slide down the rope to the ground. Much quicker and safer for Mum. She might not be able to do hand-over-hand down a dangling rope.'

'Good thinking, sis,' said Jack.

'Only one thing.' Annie took a deep breath. 'You won't have to hurt the guard, will you, Golem?'

'I break his neck.'

'No, no – please don't do anything like that,' Annie pleaded. 'Can't you sort of threaten him?'

The Golem nodded thoughtfully. 'I pick him up, shake him hard, and take the keys.'

Annie said, 'Well, that's better than breaking his neck.'

Once more the Golem ascended the wall, his large, sure hands finding the deep cracks between the stones. The pair on the ground held their breath as he reached the roof and scrambled up the incline. On finding the window, it was but a moment before he had wrenched it open. They watched as he climbed awkwardly inside, his great bulk difficult to force through the opening. Finally he was in. After another minute the rope came sailing out and the free end hit the ground. Jack tied it to the tele-graph pole, making sure it was taut. The angle was about thirty degrees, so it was not too steep – though steep enough.

They waited and waited, their hearts beating fast. While they were standing there, not far from the track that led up to the gates, a car arrived out of the night, its lights winding their way up to the castle.

'Oh heck,' muttered Jack. 'What if that's the sergeant's chief – the man with one hand?'

'Jeanette!' cried Annie softly. 'I bet she followed us. She's split on us.'

'Maybe. Or it could just be the guard changing.'

Fortunately, out in the darkness Jack and Annie could not be seen from the track. The gates opened and the car entered the castle. Just then, someone appeared at the window on the roof above. A few seconds later they had slung something around the zip-rope and were hurtling down towards the two children. The pair stood on either side of the rope with Jack's overcoat stretched between them. This would act as a sling to break the speed of the person descending from the roof.

It worked like a dream, and the person jerked safely to a stop before they reached the pole. They tumbled forward and rolled on to the grass, got up immediately and grabbed Annie in a bear hug, sqeezing her hard.

'Oh Annie! Jack! My children. How wonderful!'

It was their mother. But there was no time for a reunion now. The second person to arrive was their father. He was harder to stop and three people went for a tumble this time. Then another came, and another, Jack and Roger holding the sling, stopping the slider from crashing into the telegraph pole. Soon there were a dozen other freed prisoners on the ground. Many of them started running off into the darkness as soon as they hit terra firma. The last person down the zip-rope was grabbed and held by two of the other men. He struggled a little, and protested, but was hauled off into the night fields by his captors.

'We'll take care of him,' said one of the men. Jack and

Annie realised the speaker was Blazek. 'Don't worry about him.'

'The jailor,' explained Roger to the children. 'The man with the keys. We can't let him go yet. He'll rouse the rest of the castle. Blazek will release him when they're far enough away for it not to matter. Come on, let's get out of here quickly. What have you got planned, Jack?'

'A freight train?' suggested Jack. 'That's how we got here.'

'Good idea. Where's that big fellah – who is he, anyway?'

'The Golem. He's coming now.'

The Golem was just finishing his climb down the walls and the five of them ran off, down the track to the railway station, just as alarm sirens began whining in the castle.

Annie caught her breath as they ran, and said, 'We think the man with one hand is here – a car went through the gates a little while ago.'

'The Weasel?' cried Mum. She was shivering with the cold, having only thin clothes. 'We must get away quickly then – he has a brain as sharp as a razor. Roger, do you think he'll guess we're taking the train?'

'I don't know, but what choice do we have? They'll be out with the dogs soon, scouring the fields. Those others we let out, I think some of them will be caught.'

Mum said, 'I hope Blazek makes it all right.'

Jack gave his mother his coat and she thanked him for it. Dad was scantily clad too, but he seemed not to mind. The heady feeling of freedom was keeping him warm for the time being. They scrambled down the embankment that led to the railway tracks and skipped across the rails to the far side. Luck was still with them. A train pulled into the station a few minutes later, just as a group of men with dogs on long leads came hurrying down the track. It was not a freight train, but Dad told everyone to get into a carriage.

As the train pulled out of the station, a car skidded to a halt outside. Dad saw the Weasel jump out and run into the ticket office. After some shouting, he came out again and stared at the steam train gathering speed. Then he jumped back into his car and began to follow the train, the roadway running parallel to the tracks most of the time, occasionally bending away, but always coming back alongside again.

Jack was watching through the window with his father.

'How are we going to shake him off, Dad?' he asked.

Annie said, 'I've got an idea. Listen, we get out at the next station, on the far side from the platform, and slip off into the darkness. Then we catch the next freight train that comes along. I'm sure whatsisname, the Weasel, will wait to see if anyone gets off, then follow the train as it pulls out again.'

Mum said, 'What if he keeps the train there and searches it?'

'No, no,' Dad murmured, nodding. 'He's on his own. He can't search the train by himself. He'll wait until it gets to Prague, where there's people to call on to assist him. Good thinking, Annie. You two kids are amazing. Where's Davey, by the way? Did you leave him with someone?'

Jack looked down at the carriage floor, as did Annie.

'What is it?' cried mum. 'Davey's all right, isn't he?'

'We don't know,' replied Annie in a quiet voice. 'We tried to find him. We even saw him once, near Wenceslas Square, but some woman had hold of him. We had to concentrate on getting you and Dad out. Now we have to find Davey too.'

'Oh my,' cried Mum, and she started to cry for the first time since she had been imprisoned. 'My poor little boy.'

Roger put his arm around his wife. 'Don't fret, love. We'll find him. You know what a resilient little beggar he is. Whoever's got him will be going through a hard time. Davey's a tough boy. There's not much gets that kid down for long.'

'Dad's right, Mum,' confirmed Jack. 'He's probably driving them round the twist. I'm pretty sure he's still in Prague, or why would we have seen him in Wenceslas Square so long after he was lost? We'll find him, don't you worry.'

Annie hugged her mother and started to weep a little too, and Kate allowed herself to be consoled. She told herself it was no time to break down and put an extra burden on the others. She had to be strong still for a while longer. Everyone's liberty was as stake. The forces of the empire were still ranged against them. Others were going through just as much hardship and injustice as they were themselves. There would be help available from the good citizens of Prague. Corruption had not reached all corners of Bohemia; far from it.

The train hissed and slowed, the wheels coming to a halt. Everyone except the Golem left the carriage.

'I'll be all right,' he told them. 'I'll just hold you up. My bigness makes me too – big,' he finished lamely. 'No one saw me at the castle. I'll be home safe in my little house before you can say Jack Kettle.'

So they left him and went into the dark streets of a little hamlet, hiding in an alley until the train pulled out again. They could hear the Weasel's car crashing through the gears as it went by the end of the alley. It must have been very difficult for the Weasel to drive with one hand, but somehow his fury was assisting him in the task. Perhaps he could work the gears with his false hand, but was making a bad job of it? It certainly sounded like it. Dad said the car would be a wreck before it got to Prague, grinding through the gear box like that.

'Hopefully it'll break down,' Jack said, 'and we'll have a clear run.'

'Oh, he'll have phoned through to the Prague station,' said Dad grimly. 'He's not that daft. There'll be a reception committee waiting for us there, have no doubt about that.'

They caught the next freight train out. It would probably have been sensible to catch one going the other way, but Prague was where they believed Davey to be and Prague was where the time machine was sitting waiting. They needed to be in the city to stand any chance at all.

In the freight car the family caught up with each other's adventures. Mum and Dad were now doubly astonished by their children. One had been a drummer boy in a famous regiment. The other had been the companion of a countess. Jack had lived with the giant who called himself the Golem. Annie had a pony called Cloud and was the idol of two young men, one called Boots and the other named Tag: a shoeshine boy and a stable lad, both of them smitten by this girl from the future.

The children were just warm with happiness at having their parents back safe and sound again.

'They sound very nice boys,' Mum said. 'We'll have to do something for them before we leave for home.'

She said it in such a firm and convincing voice that they were all absolutely sure they *were* going home. That is, until they started shunting into the freight yard close to Prague railway station. Then they heard and saw that there were a great many soldiers and police combing the area, no doubt searching for the family who had finally outwitted the Weasel.

'Stay here,' said Dad quietly. 'They'll expect us to leave the train and make a run for it. If we go out there, we'll be caught for sure. There's straw in here to lie on. Try to get some sleep.'

'Won't they search the train, Dad?' asked Jack.

'If they do, we're stumped. But look how many freight wagons there are in this yard! Hundreds. It would take an age. Remember, they don't know we're here. They'll have caught one or two of the others by now and will think we all did the same thing. Even if they half guess that we took a train, there are sheds and warehouses all about, that any person on the run would try to hide in. My guess is they'll patrol the area, watching for signs of us. My first inclination was to try to run for it – but I've learned never to do the obvious. They won't expect us to stay and wait it out. They'll think we haven't the nerve for that. No, the more I consider it, the more it seems the most sensible option.'

And so they remained in the wagon, waiting for morning.

39. THE CAMERA OBSCURA

They were woken by the sound of the freight wagon door being opened. Then there was a *clunk*. They soon realised that the clunking sound was a ramp being placed on the edge of the wagon: some cattle were soon afterwards herded up this ramp and clattered inside. Jack, his parents and his sister were crammed along one side wall until all the beasts were aboard, then the doors were closed.

Jack whispered, 'Oh heck, Dad – I hope they haven't locked it.'

'Locked it,' repeated Dad, but clearly he was thinking of something else. Something he thought far more important. His voice dropped to a note of despair. 'Listen, you lot, I've just remembered something. We haven't got the starter key to the time machine.'

'Yes we have,' said Jack in a smug voice. 'The watch is in my pocket. I pinched it off that secret policeman.'

Both Mum and Dad let out a sigh of relief.

'Well done, Jack – and Annie.' said Mum. 'It was very brave of you to take on the man dad calls the Weasel.'

Annie said in an exasperated tone, 'His name's Spitzen, but never mind weasels, I've got a bull's bum in my face. We've got to get out of here, Dad. I'm worried it's going to do something in a minute.'

They waited for a little while longer, while uninquisitive bullocks shuffled around the wooden floor, moaning about their change of environment. Then one of them did indeed loosen its bowels, splattering the wagon floor and filling the confined space with a terrible stink. This forced Kate to try the door.

Luckily it was open.

'They haven't bothered to lock it because bullocks can't open doors, thank the Lord,' said Roger. 'Come on, you three. Let's get out of here. I think I'm going to choke.'

They jumped down from the wagon, Kate closing the door behind them. Then they crossed through the rail yard, which was still cluttered with other wagons and carriages that hid their escape. No doubt there were police and army people still looking for them, somewhere around, but Jack decided they had to be getting frustrated by now. They found an empty shed on the far side of the yards and Dad made a decision.

'Annie, you're the one least likely to be stopped. You're disguised as a boy for a start. You have to get to Franz Kafka's house and ask him to do something. You know where it is?'

'Shouldn't I go to the countess? She'll help.'

'It's too far away. We need somewhere nearby to hide – and quickly.'

Annie looked worried. 'All right.'

'Not scared, are you, sis?' asked Jack, genuinely concerned for her. 'I'll go if you are.'

''Course I'm not. After all we've been through? I was just thinking, that's all. OK, Dad. I'll go.'

Annie slipped out of the hut, into the daylight. The others waited anxiously for her to return. Although they found a rusty old tap from which to drink, they were all as hungry as gannets. Jack started to talk about food – something he did when he was hungry – and his mother snapped at him to please be quiet.

'I haven't eaten properly in weeks,' she said. 'Sorry to bite your head off, Jack.'

Jack shrugged, a little miffed, thinking that he deserved better for saving his parents from a life in prison, perhaps even execution. Mum read his mind and begged his pardon again.

'I s'pose we're all a bit testy,' said Jack. 'Listen, Mum – Dad. You know when I was in the army – well, I still am, technically. I'm an army deserter and a prisoner to boot . . .'

'Shame on you,' said Dad, kidding him.

'No, listen, Dad, this is important. One of my best pals was a boy named Martin Steiner.'

Mum let out a little shriek, then stifled her mouth with her hand, realising they could be heard outside.

'But that's one of our family names,' she said after removing her hand. 'That's the name of one of my great-grandfathers!'

'And my great-great-grandfather,' confirmed Jack. 'Well – it was him, I'm sure of it. Martin Steiner. He bullied me at first, but after a while we got to be pals. Weird, eh?'

Dad frowned. 'Did you tell him? Did he know you were his descendant?'

'As if,' snorted Jack. 'Do you think he would have believed me if I'd told him I was his great-great-grandson, traveller through time? I think Annie sort of hinted we might be related – cousins or something – but didn't go any further.

But Dad, I've been waiting to ask you. Look, I saved Martin's life – I pulled him out of the way of a speeding car – before Martin had even met my great-great-grandmother. How can . . .'

Dad held up his hand. 'If you're going to ask me to solve one of the many paradoxes of time travel, forget it. I have no answers. There *are* no answers. Maybe Martin wouldn't have been killed. Just terribly injured. Maybe he wouldn't have been in that place, at that time, if you hadn't taken him there. Who knows? Just be thankful this is not 1999 and there's not a younger version of you lurking around the corner who you might run into at any time. How would you like to come face to face with yourself? Not a scenario I would wish on any sane person.'

'Weird.'

'It's all weird, son – it's time travel . . .'

At that moment Annie arrived back, her face flushed with both the cold wind outside the hut and her success.

'I knocked on the door and Franz's dad answered. I just said I had a message for Franz from one of his friends. Franz came to the door then. He couldn't come here himself, but he gave me a key to an empty flat. It's in Old Town Square.'

'Excellent!' murmured Dad. 'Whereabouts is it?'

'Next to the church. Lefthand side. A timber framed building, Franz said. Flat 4b.'

'Which church?' asked Dad. There's two. The St Nicholas Church and the . . .'

'It's the one with the towers with all the points,' said Annie. 'The one that looks like something out of a Walt Disney film.'

'Ah! The Church of Our Lady Before Tyn.'

'Let's go,' said Mum. 'I'll go first, with Annie. Then Jack at a reasonable distance. Roger, you bring up the rear. Don't get too close and don't look as if you're following us.'

When Mum spoke in that tone, everyone obeyed, even Dad.

Fortunately, the streets were fairly busy. Mum and Annie weaved through the crowds, walking quickly but not running, passing the Old Town Hall Tower and the astronomical clock. Jack followed at a distance, as did Dad behind Jack. There were police about, but no army men were to be seen. By the time Jack and dad reached the flat, Annie had unlocked the door and soon they were safely inside. Annie was sent out again. She had money that had been given her by the countess, and she bought bread and cold meats, along with cheese and milk. Soon the family had feasted and drunk, and were able to start thinking straight.

The was furniture in the flat, but not a great deal. The only bedroom overlooked Old Town Square. When Jack and Annie had last seen Davey with the old woman, they had been hurrying towards this place. Mum wandered over to the window of this room and looked down on the square.

'You think Davey is probably in this area?'

'Pretty sure of it,' said Jack. 'Like I told you, mum, he was walking from Wenceslas Square in this direction. Oh, and Kaspar – he's someone we met – said Davey is with wooden people.'

'Wooden people?' said Mum. 'What on earth does that mean?'

'Search me,' replied Jack. 'Maybe mannequins or something?' he shrugged again. 'Anyway, this is Old Town Square – everyone comes through here, sooner or later.'

'Then I'll sit at this window until I see him.'

She took a wooden straight-backed chair and looked determined to stay where she was until she either saw her son or Doomsday arrived.

'You can't do that,' Dad argued. 'Kate, come away from the window.'

'Why?' she said, her mouth set.

'Because you'll be seen. Especially if you sit there day after day, waiting and watching. You'll arouse suspicion in no time.'

'You, Jack and Annie go home – I'll stay here and take my chances,' replied Mum. 'I'm not leaving my youngest son.'

'Nor am I. Nor are any of us,' Dad said. 'We'll all stay together. We made the mistake of splitting up before. It's not going to happen again. If we have to remain in 1903, then we'll all stay, as a family. Agreed?'

'Agreed,' murmured Annie and Jack together.

'But I hope we don't have to,' said Annie, 'because I want to go home.'

'We all do, and we *are* going home,' continued Dad. 'Once we find Davey, we're on our way. Now, Kate, come away from that window, please. I've got a better idea. We can all watch for Davey. Four pairs of eyes are better than two. But we can do it without anyone seeing us, without anyone even knowing we are up here.'

'How?' said Mum suspiciously, obviously refusing to accept

Dad's word until he had explained it to her. 'Look through a chink in the curtains?'

'Something like that,' said Dad. He pointed to the white walls of the bedroom. 'I'll make a camera obscura. That way we can sit here like a cinema audience and watch all that goes on in Old Town Square while the windows remain blacked out.'

Mum's eyes opened wide. 'Of course!' she said. 'Brilliant, darling.'

'I know,' murmured Dad, never one for false modesty.

Jack did not want to be the one to ask, but when Annie kept quiet he knew he would have to reveal his ignorance.

'OK,' he said, 'what's a camera obscura? Some kind of film projector? Did you invent it, Dad? Where is it?'

Dad laughed, even though the business was serious.

'No – it was invented long before my time. I believe it was first discovered by Mo-Ti, a fifth-century BC Chinese philosopher. Just think of that.' Dad's eyes glazed over a little. 'Five centuries before Christ! Remarkable. Aristotle understood it too – but that was later. Mo-Ti was the first in a long line of inventors who came to the device independently. The Islamic scholar Alhacen. Then Leonardo da Vinci, of course. The Dutchman, now what was his name? Oh yes, Gemma Frisius. He discovered it just before Giambattista della Porta. Then Kepler . . .'

'Dad!' shouted Annie. 'What *is* it?'

Dad's eyes unglazed. 'Oh – oh yes. Well, it's a device . . . Look, what we do is black out that window with some dark material and put a tiny hole in the centre. What happens is the world outside will be projected on to that back wall

– upside-down. But we can recognise Davey upside-down, sideways or backwards, can't we? Our Davey. Full colour too – not black-and-white. You see, Annie, light travels in a straight line, and when the rays pass through the small hole we make in the dark material, they don't just dart off everywhere, they cross each other and form again as an image – an upside-down image – on a flat white surface.'

He paused and stared at his children.

'I can see I'm boring you.'

'No, no, very interesting, Dad, but look – Mum's already in the process of making one.'

'Ah yes,' murmured Dad, as Mum pulled the thick heavy curtains tautly across the window. 'The teachers and the doers . . . In the meantime, I'll be first in the bathroom. I must stink. Everyone else does.'

40. HERE'S OUR DAVEY

Just as they were adding the last few touches to their camera obscura, Blazek arrived at the flat. He had been to Franz Kafka's house first, and Franz had told him where to find the family.

'You made it!' cried Mum, and hugged the big man.

Dad hugged him too. 'Thank God you're safe,' he said, while the children looked on, embarrassed by this unusual show of affection. They were glad Blazek had not been caught, but they had never seen their father hug another man before.

Blazek looked harrowed and worn. He sat in a chair and ran his thick fingers through a mop of tangled, greasy, grey hair.

'By the skin of my teeth,' he told them. 'One or two of the others were not so lucky – well, they took their chances, didn't they? Some of them *are* guilty of crimes, of course. Political crimes. But there . . . he spread his hands wide and managed a smile, 'we are all safe.'

'All except our Davey,' said Annie with a catch in her voice. 'We have to find Davey.'

'Ah yes. And when we do, you will all be on your way back to your own time.' Blazek looked up with a frown on his broad brow. 'I wonder – no, it is too much to ask.' He shook his head.

'Nothing is too much for you to ask, Cousin,' Mum said. 'You have sacrificed your safety for ours. What is it?'

'I would like to come with you.'

Dad looked at Mum. Mum looked at Dad.

Dad said, 'I'm afraid we can't take the chance. You might upset all the laws of the universe by going into the future and staying there.' He sighed. 'It sounds very ungrateful, when one looks at all the help you've given us, but I have no idea what damage it might do.'

Blazek nodded. 'I understand.' He looked sad. 'So this is goodbye, eh?'

'I'm afraid so,' Dad replied. 'But we are concerned for you. What will happen to you if they catch you?'

Blazek laughed. 'They won't catch me. Once you have gone I shall go to a farm in Moravia, to our cousins there. I have been promising them for years that I will visit. Now

313

I shall go and stay. It will be no problem, I assure you.'

Mum said, 'I hope so. We really are sorry.'

Blazek said, 'Please, I have said I understand. Now,' he rubbed his hands together with a rasping sound and looked more cheerful, 'let us find this wayward brother of yours, Jack, Annie.' He looked around him. 'What is this infernal contraption you have here, Roger? Another of your devious inventions, eh?'

'Not mine,' Dad replied. 'It's been around a few thousand years. It's a device often used by painters. Vermeer, Canaletto, Guardi – they all used it . . .'

'Don't get him started, Blazek,' groaned Jack. 'He goes on and on if you do.'

'Now don't be rude about your father,' Mum said warningly. 'Annie, can you go out and get some more groceries, please? Blazek looks starved and we could all do with something else.'

'All right.'

'And buy some stationery – notepaper, envelopes, pencils.'

Jack was puzzled. 'What for?'

'Never mind,' Mum said. 'You'll find out soon enough.'

Annie did as she was asked, while Jack sat and watched her in the camera obscura. On the wall at the back of the room the whole square was displayed in colour – upside-down. He saw his sister emerge from the bottom of the picture and into the square. She crossed over to a stall on the far side and Jack watched her buying eggs. He followed her into a small baker's shop, then out amongst the crowd, mingling with men on horseback, pedestrians, the odd motor car. The whole panorama of Old Town Square, with its bustling, hustling citizens, was there to view. It was like watching a film or TV with the sound turned off. There they all were, the shoppers, the vendors, the message-carriers, the dogs slinking in and out of human legs, children playing with hoops or balls, grave-looking policemen searching for runaways, and the runaways themselves.

Thankfully Annie was soon back.

'Right,' announced Dad, 'we're splitting up into shifts. Mum and Jack, Annie and me. Hour about. You must watch and study intently and it'll be a tiring business, so one hour and then the new shift goes on.'

'I'll help too,' said Blazek, 'after a sleep.'

And so they began the watch for Davey.

Hour after hour they sat in front of the camera obscura, staring into the crowds, looking for the small boy they knew so well. There were fears, of course, in all their breasts that Davey was no longer in Prague. If that were true he might be lost for ever. At first no one wanted to even think about the possibility. Their fears were instinctive, not a matter for reflection. Mum especially would have sunk into despair if she did not believe that Davey was nearby and could be found. So no one spoke about these dark feelings. They simply kept them to themselves and each time they sat down to watch for their brother and son, they did so with a prayer on their lips and a positive and confident attitude.

The days went by slowly. The police and army presence decreased as time went on, until they were no longer to be seen in the square, not in any numbers. Of course the occasional lone policeman did his rounds, but that was to

315

be expected. The search for the escaped London family had either ceased or had gone elsewhere.

One or two of the family began to develop eyestrain. It was not easy studying a moving picture for days on end, even if one was being relieved every hour. Gradually, too, the positive feelings were displaced by a gnawing horror of what might be. It was inevitable that as time went by the worst view overshadowed the best. Davey. Davey. Where was that boy? Like the others, Jack occasionally felt anger towards his little brother, saying to himself, 'Where is the little twerp?' as if Davey were hiding on purpose, or had gone out and carelessly strayed too far from home. It was sometimes difficult not to blame Davey, wrongly thinking that it was his own fault that he could not be found. A prankster, a trickster, a thoughtless little twit who could not care less whether his parents or siblings were worried to death about him.

Then of course there were moments when Mum's eyes filled with tears and she began crying, and they would all crowd round her and silently curse the people who were making them so unhappy. Who was it out there who had captured Davey and held him prisoner all this time? Of course it was not Davey's fault. He would never stay away so long on purpose. Jack imagined his brother in terrible misery, locked up somewhere damp and dark, a slave to a master or mistress without feelings or compassion of any kind. Perhaps they beat him – or worse – and he was now a broken child without the possibility of being mended. There were ugly people like that in the world. Few and far between, but if Davey had been unfortunate enough to fall in the hands of evil men, he might never again be that happy-go-lucky boy they knew so well.

The pictures on the wall became dream like. Annie began to hate them with venom. All those stupid people, scurrying around, doing their stupid shopping, meeting their stupid friends at pavement cafes, chattering, frittering their lives away like the sparrows that scattered under their feet. Did not they realise there was a young boy out there, lost in despair, wanting to be found? What idiots they were. And what a stupid device Dad was making them watch, hour after hour, day after day! Only a woolly-minded inventor could think of such a waste of time. Dad's head was full of fluff. What possibility was there that they would see Davey on that screen in front of them? Hardly any. None at all.

'How are we all faring?' asked Dad on the afternoon of the seventh day. 'Not giving up, are we?'

A dispirited chorus of no-of-course-nots came back to him.

'It's only been a week,' he told them. 'Look at Blazek – he sits there all the time. He's not given up.'

'There!' cried Blazek.

'Yes,' confirmed Dad, 'I just said, you sit *there* . . .'

'No, no,' cried Blazek, pointing into the camera obscura's picture. 'I see the boy. He's there. By the statue of Jan Hus.'

Instantly all those tired eyes were wide awake. They rushed to stare at the screen. Yes, there was Davey, with an elderly woman. Suddenly this person took him by the hand and led him back across the square.

'Quick!' cried Dad. 'I'll go out and get him.'

'No, wait,' Blazek said. 'I see where they're going. Yes, they've gone in. I know where they are. What time is it?'

'Er,' Dad was caught off guard, but Mum replied, 'Three o'clock – mid-afternoon.'

Blazek nodded. 'The first performance will be starting. Let's all go down there now.'

'Is it safe?' asked Mum.

'There are no police around. I think we might need all of us to cover the exits in that building, if it becomes necessary.'

'Well, what is it?' asked Dad. 'What goes on there?'

Blazek smiled. 'It's a puppet theatre,' he said. 'Prague is famous for them, and that's the most well known of them all. They always do the Mozart opera *Don Giovanni*. It's renowned throughout Europe. Come on. I think I know what Davey is doing.'

Mum raised her eyebrows. 'He's a puppeteer?'

'No,' laughed Blazek. 'He's a puppet.'

With the strange vision before them of little Davey Kettle as a puppet, the family followed Blazek down the stairs, out of the flat and into the puppet theatre ten doors down.

All that time Davey had been just ten doors away!

Blazek purchased the tickets.

There was not a large audience inside, probably because it was a matinee performance. It was dark. The family fumbled around and found empty seats. Jack's heart was beating fast as he stared about him, the only light coming from the stage. The performance had indeed begun. On the stage itself the stringed puppets, just a third life-size, were

318

performing *Don Giovanni*. Music and singing came from the direction of the wooden characters treading the boards. A quick glance at Blazek reassured Jack. He did not seem in any great hurry to show them where Davey might be; he seemed relaxed and happy enough to enjoy the show. Jack and the others awaited his move.

The performance continued. Eventually a trapdoor suddenly flew open on the stage, the terrible figure of the Devil leapt up out of the depths of hell to claim the soul of Don Giovanni. It was a shocking moment, for Satan was played by a live person, who towered over the puppets like a giant. He was lithe and swift in comparison to the jerky wooden movements of Don Giovanni and the contrast was quite startling if one was not ready for it. Jack and Annie actually jumped at the sight, as they were supposed to do. The puppet master of this theatre knew his business and he knew the value of jolting his audience.

But that Devil figure was not Davey. Had Blazek been expecting it to be? It was clearly a grown man. Jack glanced at Blazek, who still seemed unperturbed. He nodded gravely at Jack.

The performance ended. The lights came on.

Jack and the others were suddenly aware that Mozart was there, in the front row of seats, watching the performance of his own opera. On his head he was wearing a tri-cornered hat, on his back a frock coat, and a lace collar at his chin. In his right hand was a wine glass, while in his left was a half-filled bottle. He turned, stood on his seat, and faced the audience, waving his wine glass as if a little tipsy. Then he tossed the contents of the glass over the people in front of him. It was filled with confetti but of course the victims ducked and laughed as if it were real wine. Bits of red paper floated down upon the heads of the watchers.

'Ha! Ha!' cried Mozart. 'How did you like my show, folks? Brilliant, eh? Can I write 'em, or can I write 'em? I'm the coolest composer the world's ever seen. Like, I'm the snazziest musician on the flippin' planet, whatever. Did you see old Giovanni, tryin' to get out of the clutches of the Devil? No chance. He's a goner. His soul'll have to chill out in hell for eternity and get tortured to bits, poor old bugger . . .'

'Davey,' cried Dad, 'what have I told you about swearing? Cut it out or you'll be grounded for a week!'

Mozart stopped in mid-sentence and stared.

'Dad! Mum!' he yelled. He threw away his bottle and glass and scrambled over the backs of the seats to reach his grinning family. 'Bruv! Sis! Where've you bin?'

In front of a puzzled audience, Davey was soundly hugged then hustled out of the theatre. Outside, the group spread out and made their way back to the flat in ones and twos. Blazek was the last to arrive, having remained to speak to the woman who ran the puppet theatre. She assured him she meant Davey no harm, saying she usually got her Mozarts from the local orphanage. Davey, she said, did not seem to know where the rest of his family was and she had tried to trace them.

Blazek said he doubted she had tried very hard and warned her he would inform the police if she ever thought of doing the same thing again. The woman did not seem overly concerned by his threats, but there was not a lot else that could be done with her, considering the police were the last people Blazek wanted to see.

The reunited family were in happy mood when Blazek walked into the flat. Davey had been passed around for more hugs, despite the boy's vehement objections. Dad ruffled his hair, Mum kissed him several times, Jack got him in a headlock and Annie kept pinching both cheeks at once.

'I'm squeezed to death, you lot!' Davey yelled. 'Leave me alone. I'm not really a tactile person.'

'Wow, he's learned some big words while he's been in captivity,' cried Dad. 'Tactile?'

'I bin reading a lot,' admitted Davey, shamefaced by the betrayal of his former principles. 'They got me books in English out of the library. There wasn't nothin' else to do.'

'No TV, eh?' said Jack, grinning, 'or Nintendo.'

'And though you read heaps,' murmured Annie, 'your spoken grammar hasn't improved a jot.'

Blazek let the family rejoice, listening to Davey's account of what had happened to him.

'They weren't exactly *cruel* to me,' Davey said. 'Din't treat me bad or nothing. But they wouldn't let me go, neither. There wasn't anywhere to go anyway, so in the end I just said what the heck and stayed. I knew somebody would come in the end – an' you did.' He grinned. Then he looked back wistfully at the theatre. 'I din't get a chance to say goodbye to the others. They can't escape, can they?'

'Others?' said Mum, looking puzzled. 'What others? Are there more boys like you back there?'

'Not *boys*. My mates, the puppets. There's Don Giovanni, o' course, an' Leporello, an' Masetto, an' Zerlina . . .'

Mum interrupted with, 'But they *are* only wooden puppets, Davey – not real people.'

'You don't know nothin', Mum,' argued her youngest child. 'They *talked* to me. They kep' me company.'

Mum said something about a child's imagination.

'No, they was real – really real.'

Annie came in here on her younger brother's side. 'There are things that have happened to us,' she said, 'that wouldn't have happened to you. You were locked up all the time. We've seen things – very strange things, Mum. Jack thinks we crossed some sort of fourth dimension.'

'Only the other day,' Jack said, 'I met a troll.'

'A *what*?' laughed Dad.

Even Blazek looked amused.

'But the Golem?' argued Annie.

'Ah yes – a big man who calls himself the Golem,' said Dad. 'I grant you he *looked* a bit strange – but he is, after all, only a man.'

The three children looked at each other. Almost as a single entity they suddenly realised this was not the time or the place to enlighten their parents. Let the adults believe that kids had overactive imaginations. What did it matter? Let them think what they liked. They, the kids, knew the real truth, and that was the important thing.

'Never mind,' said Davey, 'they was my friends.'

'Of course they were,' murmured Mum, ruffling his hair. 'You spent a lot of time together.'

Dad said, 'Well, I suppose if you had to be lost, a puppet theatre was as good as anywhere. Now, what's that commotion going on down in the street. Oh damn – look who's back!'

When they looked at the picture thrown on the white

wall by the camera obscura, they could see the one-handed Weasel down in the square, directing the operations of police and army personnel. Obviously their presence at the theatre had not gone unnoticed by the authorities. Pamphlets with their descriptions had been circulated amongst the population of Prague over the past week and some civic-minded citizen had reported them. Probably the proprietor of the puppet theatre or a member of the audience.

41. HOMEWARD BOUND

'The time has come,' Mum said, 'to put to use the notepaper and envelopes. Just imagine it's Boxing Day. There are thank-you notes to write. I want you all to quickly write some letters. Annie, you will need to thank the countess for all she's done for you . . .'

Annie cried, 'Can't I go and see her?'

Mum continued. 'There isn't time. We're in great danger every minute we remain in Prague. You must tell her that we, your parents, appreciate her generosity and help. Ask her if she would be so kind as to make sure Boots and the Sewer Rats are taken care of somehow.'

'I'll write to Tag separately.'

'If you like. Now, Jack, you must write to the Golem. Tell him he has been of great service and was there when we needed him most. Also you will want to write to Jiri and Martin. Don't mention time travel — say we were whisked back to London and had no time to say goodbye, but thank them for their friendship and – well, you'll know what to say.'

'Yes, Mum.'

The two older children set to work straight away, while Roger and Kate also had one or two people they needed to thank.

'We'll give the letters to Franz Kafka – he'll make sure they're delivered,' said Mum, licking the gummed edge of an envelope. 'You never know, one of them might write back. There's nothing to say we can't receive a reply in the twenty-first century, is there? It might have to wait a long time, until it finds us in the future, perhaps stuffed in some chimney niche or nailed to an old attic rafter? Who knows?'

'Oh yes,' sighed Annie, staring dreamily into the middle distance, 'a faded letter on yellowed paper, full of hopes and dreams impossible to fulfil!'

'How literate!' Dad said.

'How romantic,' Mum added, smiling.

'How yukky!' cried Davey.

Blazek went to the window, then called back softly, 'There's a house-to-house search on. Quickly.'

Having finished their letters, they followed the Bohemian out of the room and down to the ground floor.

'We have to get to the Church of Our Lady Before Tyn, next door,' Blazek explained. 'There's a secret tunnel there that leads from the crypt to a small chapel in the street next to Franz's road.'

One by one the family left the building by a tradesmen's entrance, dashed across the dark alley and entered the old Gothic church by a side door. Once they were gathered together in the darkness of the aisle Blazek took some candles from the altar. He lit them and handed them round. Instantly the baroque interior of the church leapt up around them. Marble images, icons of dead saints, carved wooden pews and choir stalls, soaring organ pipes, all suddenly appeared.

'Votive candles,' Blazek explained. 'You light them when you need a prayer answered.'

'Well we certainly need one of those,' murmured Roger.

Jack was not sure whether his dad meant they needed a candle or a prayer – perhaps they needed both?

Blazek led them down some worn stone steps to the crypt below the church. The Czech then went ahead, leaving the family to follow. Davey, still in his Mozart costume, shivered. He found it very spooky down there. There were dozens of stone oblong tombs, some of them with a statue of a reclining knight or lady on the lid. Shadows jumped back and forth as the family moved through this gloomy atmospheric place with its musty smells. There was an air of dampness and death in the crumbling limestone, which penetrated Davey's bones and sent pictures into his mind of rotting corpses.

'We're leaving here soon, right?' he said to Jack. 'I mean, we don't have to stay here for long.'

Jack put an arm around his brother's shoulders to comfort him.

At that moment an oblong stone tomb spoke a single word.

'Jack?'

The whole family went rigid in their tracks. Shadows

trembled in the flickering candlelight. Faces were suddenly very pale and drained of any expression except that of naked horror.

'Jack Kettle?' groaned the tomb, in a hollow tone. 'Is that you out there?'

''Sa dead man speakin'!' shrieked Davey, clutching at his sister's hand.

Annie had trouble not screaming herself.

The heavy tomb lid began to scrape open. Gradually, under the aghast eyes of the Kettles, a grey hand appeared to grip it and push it aside. Next the top half of a body emerged, as if the corpse within had come to life and were sitting bolt upright. The figure then stood up and a grin spread across its gaunt, shadowy features.

'Hello, Jack, how are you? I bet you thought I was the begging skeleton, that poor boney creature who sold his body to the anatomy professor for a few pence and now walks the streets of Prague with his begging bowl. You did, didn't you? Come on, confess it!'

'Kaspar?' cried Jack. 'Is it you? Yes, it is. Mum, Dad, this is Kaspar, he's an alchemist or something.'

Kaspar shook his head. 'I'm a crystal gazer, not an alchemist – though there are plenty of those around here . . .'

Just then a great many of the lids of the tombs began to shake and scrape, and figures started to emerge from every part of the crypt. It was like Salvation Day, when the dead are supposed to rise up and go to judgement. But these were not corpses, they were live people. Some of them Jack recognised as the alchemists who had met in Dvorak's furnace room. It seemed they had gathered down in the crypt after being hounded by the police. This was their hiding place, Kaspar told the family, following the raids on friendly houses.

'We can leave at night, in ones and twos, to visit the homes of Prague alchemists, then return here before dawn. There are small stoves and provisions hidden in these hollow tombs, which we gratefully share with our hosts, the long-dead knights and bishops of yesteryear. I lie beside someone else's ancestor, and though we are not of the same culture or religion, we get along very nicely in our tight stone box.'

'Isn't it smelly?' asked Kate. 'I mean — corpses?'

Kaspar smiled again. 'Our hosts have been dead for many centuries. Their bones are dry, their clothes and flesh are dust. Their small houses are a little musty, it's true, but no more than that, and harassed alchemists and magicians can't be choosers. Are you leaving, then? On your way back to London, England, Jack and Annie?'

'Yes,' replied Jack. 'Nice to have met you, though.'

'And you too.' There was a murmur of approval from the other residents of the tombs. 'May you have a safe journey.'

'Thank you,' Annie said. 'Goodbye.'

'Farewell to you, and God speed, Kettles!'

At that moment Blazek came back, took an astonished look at the crowd within the crypt, shook his head in disbelief, then herded the family further into the maze of resting places beyond. Weaving their way amongst the tombs, they eventually came to a largish one with no statue on the lid, only a name and date.

'An old Hussite,' murmured Blazek. 'They were rebels too.'

He asked Roger to help him move the lid, which the pair of them did. Shining his candle inside the tomb, Jack saw there were steps leading downwards. He helped his mum over the edge of the tomb, then Davey. Annie scorned his outstretched hand and climbed over the obstacle herself, without his assistance. Jack shrugged and smiled at his sister's strong streak of self-reliance. Soon all of them were hunched, creeping along a narrow tunnel. Blazek and Roger had pulled the lid of the tomb back into place, to keep the secret passage hidden.

Halfway along, Davey yelled loudly, startling them all, as hot wax from his candle dripped on his fingers.

'Sorry,' he whispered, sucking the burn.

Blazek stared at Davey and said, 'I think my heart has stopped.'

The tunnel came out, as Blazek had said, in a small chapel located at the far end of a road running parallel to Zelt-nergasse Strasse, the street where Franz Kafka lived. Blazek left the chapel alone. He was gone quite a long time, leaving the family all feeling anxious about their precarious position. No doubt the Weasel was desperately seeking their where-abouts. He was a determined man who hated to be thwarted. It was only a matter of time, thought Jack, before they were caught – if they did not move from the chapel.

Time. This whole adventure had been about time. And it was time it ended. They were all weary and wanting normality. Adventures were not supposed to go on for ever. The best adventures were brief affairs that came and went, leaving one with memories of exciting times, but no lasting scars. Jack certainly did not want to stay in this time and place, interesting though the time was, beautiful though the place.

There were shouts somewhere at the end of the road.

'Where is he?' asked Annie. 'What's Blazek doing?'

'We need the motorbike to be ready,' said Dad. 'He's arranging our getaway.'

Mum said, 'You sound like a bank robber.'

More shouts from the distance, but nearer.

Dad replied, 'I feel like one. I'm being hunted.'

Then Blazek was back.

'Quickly,' he said. 'We've got the machine. Franz and I manhandled it up the basement steps and it's now standing in the street, ready. You will need to change your clothes, back into your old ones. Roger, you said you can take nothing from this time home with you?'

'That's true,' Dad said.

Blazek told him, 'I have them here . . .' and dumped a bundle on to the floor of the chapel.

The family quickly changed into their twenty-first century clothes, then followed Blazek out of the chapel and into the dimly lit streets of Prague, through another of those miraculous alleyways, to Zeltnergasse Street.

The lean, pale Franz Kafka was standing outside number 3, by the motorcycle and sidecar, the time machine from the twenty-first century. The young man waved to them briefly, then descended the basement steps to his house. He did not want to be caught with renegades outside his own home. His father knew nothing of this escapade and would be horrified to learn his son was aiding political criminals, no matter how much they protested they were innocent of the crimes.

'Does he have the letters?' asked Mum.

'Yes,' replied Blazek. 'He'll see they're delivered.'

The machine stood in the middle of road. Mum climbed into the sidecar. Davey sat on her lap. Dad was in the driver's seat with Annie behind him. Jack perched on the back mudguard, holding on to Annie's shoulders. It was a heavy load for the old Matchless motorbike. Everyone could see that Blazek could not add to the weight. As it was, Dad was going to have a hard time controlling the machine. Blazek looked on helplessly. Everyone felt a wrenching in their hearts.

'Goodbye, friend,' said Dad, shaking Blazek's hand.

'Goodbye cousin,' chorused Mum and the children.

Blazek smiled shyly. 'Goodbye, everyone. Safe journey. Don't worry about me. I'm like a wildcat – they won't catch me again.'

With a last lingering look at the motorbike, Blazek slipped back down the alley.

Dad took the octagonal-shaped wristwatch from Jack and fitted it into the recessed shape on the dash, then turned it sharply to the right. The Matchless coughed, spluttered, and the engine burst into life. Dad gave the engine some revs and tested the bike's ability to cope with the heavy load. It rolled forward in an ungainly fashion as he cautiously turned the handle-grip accelerator. At least it had moved! The tyres looked alarmingly flat, having not been pumped up with air for some time, and now having to bear the weight of a whole family.

Shouts came from the end of the street, and the sound of steel-toed boots on cobblestones.

'Dad!'

'All right, Jack – I see them.'

Mum said, 'Roger – it's the Weasel.'

'Yes, I can see.'

Roger gunned the engine, but the Matchless hadn't been started for a long time. It was cold and clunky. Then suddenly it did the worst thing it could do – it stalled.

'Roger!' cried Kate. 'He's coming!'

Dad stared along the road as he tried to start the engine again.

It was indeed the Weasel, Spitzen, running towards them in the lamplight. The hated Weasel who had tortured him and Kate without mercy. Who had refused to listen to their pleas of innocence and had denied them the right of justice before a court of the land. This figure of malevolence was running towards them now, the glint of victory and revenge in his eyes. His raincoat was flapping wide, giving the appearance of a bat trying to take off. A long way behind him were his thugs, those men he had nurtured in the culture of hate. Spitzen's zeal and fury had put wings on his feet and he had raced far ahead of his minions. Unfit though they were, they were his hounds of hell and he would unleash them on this troublesome family when they caught up.

The Weasel reached the motorbike well ahead of his men. He took hold of Roger and dragged him from the motorbike. For a thin man, the police chief was very strong. But Roger was strong too, having wielded many spanners in his time. Spitzen caught the inventor off balance, but Roger was soon on his feet and grappling with his assailant. Indeed, he had the strength of a man fighting for his life and freedom, which counted for a great deal. They remained locked together, arms gripping each other, neither willing to let the other go.

Of course, the policeman had the upper hand, since all he had to do was hold on until his men caught up with him.

'All those weeks in that prison,' snarled Roger, twisting the man's collar at his throat. 'I ought to break your neck.'

More police came swarming out of the alleys and passageways. Roger felt his chances of escape slipping away from him.

Spitzen snarled, 'Try it, Englishman – you'll find my neck harder to break than you think.'

All the while, Spitzen's henchmen were getting closer and closer, running along the dimly-lit street. For Roger, everything seemed to slow down almost to a stop. He felt drained and useless. So close. He had been so close to getting home again. Now his arch enemy of had the upper hand again. Spitzen had *time* on his side.

'You will never get away!' hissed Spitzen, into Roger's face, tightening his grip. 'I shall have you back in Karlstein.'

Roger couldn't let go of the struggling man. If he did, Spitzen might do something nasty, like kick him with those steel-toed boots he wore, and perhaps badly injure him. Once the policeman had disposed of Roger, he would go for Kate and the children. That could not be allowed to happen. So Roger held on to his opponent and yelled, 'Jack, start the engine. Get your mother, brother and sister out of here – now!'

Jack looked upset, but after a second firm order from his father, he did as he was told, leaping from the mudguard onto the rider's seat and turning the key. Happily the engine had had time to settle down again and it started after the second attempt. Jack turned the machine round and headed away from the police. He cruised along gently, warming up the engine.

A distressed Kate cried, 'Your father!'

'Don't worry, Mum,' Jack said grimly, 'I'm not going to leave Dad behind, no matter what he says.'

Jack turned the motorbike again, slowly, aware of the weight of all its passengers.

His father and Spitzen were like statues, standing in the middle of the road just a hundred yards away now. Each had a hold of the other's clothing, gripping it hard. It seemed they would be fused together like that for all eternity. Jack had other ideas, though. He knew his father's courage and he thought he knew what men like Spitzen were made of, which wasn't a great deal.

Jack gunned the engine.

'Here we go, Mum – hold on tight, everyone.'

With that he roared down the street, heading straight for the two men locked together in the centre of the road.

Spitzen's eyes widened as he saw the motorbike bearing down on him and his captive.

'He – he wouldn't kill his own father,' cried the policeman, 'even to save his mother and her children.'

'Oh yes he would,' laughed Roger in a crazy way. 'Oh yes he would – he inherits my fortune when I die.'

This rather feeble lie was not obvious to Spitzen, a man who probably *would* have killed his own father for a fortune, if it had been necessary. The motorcycle got closer and closer, until Spitzen could stand there no longer. He let go of Roger and leapt aside, convinced he was going to be run down by the boy in the rider's seat. His headlong attempt at getting out of the motorbike's way caused him to trip against the kerbstones and he fell heavily into the gutter.

At the last moment Jack had decelerated and swerved, cruising past his dad easily. The many uniformed policemen were almost on them now, but Jack managed to do a U-turn right in front of them, narrowly missing being clutched by the foremost man.

He headed back to his dad again, slowing down as he passed. Annie slid to the rear mudguard position, allowing Roger to leap into the saddle of the pillion like a cowboy mounting a moving horse in a Hollywood Western film.

'Take it away, Jack,' cried Dad exultantly into his ear. 'Let's see you drive into the future!'

Dad's goggles were hanging on the handlebars.

Jack picked them up and pulled them over his head as his dad gripped him round the waist.

'Hold on tight, everyone,' Jack shouted. 'Here we go.'

The faces of his mother and brother in the sidecar looked pale. There were some tight lips and even tighter knuckles in there. Jack tried to smile at them, but he knew he could only manage a grimace.

It seemed they would make it easily, but as they approached the far end of the street, they found it blocked by two long police vehicles. Jack could not reach 47.22 (recurring) mph without running into those cars. They had to U-turn yet again and head back towards Spitzen, who was now on his feet. Did they have enough road to reach their required speed? Jack wasn't sure, but there was nothing else for it. They had to keep going – and hope.

The motorbike sped forward, gaining speed, but ever so gradually under the great weight on its shoulders.

Faster, faster, faster.

'STOP!' cried the Weasel, standing astride in the middle of the road, his arms wide. 'Stop, I tell you!' It seemed he was not going to jump aside a second time. If they hit him, however, it would not only kill the policeman but end their attempt at escape.

Jack grimly gunned the engine, going up through the gears. The bike gathered more speed: 28 mph, 33, 45.

'Stop, I order you to stop!' yelled the Weasel, now statue-like in the centre of their path. 'You can't escape. You're trapped.'

His cruel pinched features were visible in the light of the Zeltnergasse Street lamps.

Forty-seven mph.

Hair was streaming from the heads of those in the machine. They gulped down the passing air. Surely they were going to hit this terrible man, who seemed intent on committing suicide. What would that do to their time travel? They would probably crash. They needed to be travelling at a constant speed of 47.22 (recurring) mph for at least ten seconds in order to go through the time hole and return to the twenty-first century. If they hit an obstruction, even such a thing as a human body, the motorcycle would lose speed and they would fail.

The Weasel's eyes went wide with fear as the motorbike

was almost upon him. Clearly he thought he was going to die, for such a weighty machine would mangle his weasely body at that speed. The last thing they saw him do was throw up his arms in horror . . .

. . . then they were through the buffeting winds of time until they found themselves speeding down the street towards their own home, in their own town, but more importantly *in their own time.*

★

Everyone cheered as Jack brought the motorbike to a halt outside their house. It was clearly night-time and it had been raining. Street lamps brighter than the ones they had left behind lit the wet, slick road.

A window suddenly flew open on the other side of the street and the voice of a grumpy neighbour yelled out, 'Is that you, Roger Kettle? Do you know what time it is?'

'Yes, Bill,' replied Dad. 'It's 2008.'

The family laughed, clambered off the machine, and Dad wheeled the Matchless up the side path and through the back gate. Mum opened the front door and the kids went straight in.

'TV!' yelled Davey.

'Marmite on toast!' said Jack, licking his lips.

'The unique Meissen shepherdess,' Annie murmured, going to her mother's glass cabinet where she kept her favourite ornaments. She found the *objet d'art* and took it out, holding it in her hands reverently, turning it over, studying it. Unique. A valuable piece of porcelain art. Franz must have been able to pass it on to Mum's ancestors – who were also Annie's own ancestors, actually – and the object was then bequeathed on deathbeds until it reached Kate Kettle.

Annie found her mother in the kitchen.

'Mum,' she said, 'do you know this is worth . . .'

'I know,' replied her mother, 'an awful lot of money. But though I've thought of selling it, I find that just at the point of doing so I get this funny feeling that I shouldn't, that it isn't mine to sell. Oh,' Kate laughed, 'you probably don't understand. One day, though, it'll be yours. It's been passed down to the eldest daughter since I don't know when.'

'Oh, but I do, Mum. I do understand,' said Annie quietly, 'You see, it's already been given to me once before, by the countess.'

Her mother stared at her quizzically, and Annie laughed and said, 'I'll tell you later.' Then she carried the object carefully back to its proper home in the living room.

'What's up, sis?' asked Jack, coming over to her. 'What've you got Mum's china girl out for?'

'Nothing,' Annie replied, putting the shepherdess back in the cabinet. 'Just looking. Why?'

Jack shrugged. 'I only asked. Oh, by the way, this was on the front doormat. I managed to pick it up without Mum and Dad seeing it. I dunno why I don't want them to know, but I don't. Do you?'

Jack grinned as he handed Annie a postcard. On the front was a picture of the Charles Bridge and a Prague hazy with river mist. When she turned it over, scrawled on the other

337

side in German were the words 'Welcome home!' It was signed, *Dvorak*.

'Looks like he finally found the secret of everlasting life,' said Annie. 'The elixir. You're right, Jack. Mum and Dad would never believe us. Best keep it to ourselves.'

Dad came into the house by the back door.

'I'll just have a cup of tea,' he said, 'then I'm off to bed. I'm exhausted.'

'Now, no going back on the sly,' Mum warned him. 'We're all safe and well now. Don't let's have any more adventures for a good long while. I think I know enough now about my ancestors — and yours, of course,' she added, nodding at the children.

★

One evening two weeks later, Jack, Annie and Davey heard the roar of the Matchless, as it sped down the wet street outside. Dad was on his way back to another year and place; hopefully this time he would be back in time for breakfast.

Garry Kilworth was born in York on 1941 but has travelled widely around the globe ever since, being fascinated by the folklore, myths and legends of the places he has visited. He has been attracted by various forms of fantasy and supernatural writing but has more recently written a number of acclaimed and much-loved stories for children. Garry has twice been short-listed for the Carnegie medal. For more information visit www.garry-kilworth.com

Find out more about Garry and other Atom authors at www.atombooks.co.uk

INTERVIEW

The Hundred-Towered City contains an exciting mix of magic, mystical creatures, and time travel. Did the idea for this book come to you fully realised or did you have one particular starting point from which it grew?

Books never come to me fully realised. They always start with a small idea that plays on my mind so much I have to do something with it or go bonkers. In this instance it was a visit to Prague. It's such a magical city. Its cobbled streets and bridges and strange buildings instantly enter your imagination.

You've written for both adults and children. Do you find you need to take a very different approach when writing for each audience?

I don't consciously sit down and think 'Oh, I'm writing for kids this time – I'll do it this way'. But certainly children's books allow me to indulge my love of adventure and mystery. I also flatter myself that I can think myself back to that twelve-year-old Garry of yore. I remember what excited me at that age and what sort of stories I liked to read. All right, it may not be what kids today like to read, but someone out there must be like me. Also, when I was twelve I lived in an exotic land (South Yemen), and mystery and adventure were right on my doorstep.

What is it about writing for children and teenagers that appeals to you?

Permission to let my imagination run riot. I'm a member of a book group in my village – adults of course – and the other members are always worried by books in which the imagination is allowed to soar. Not all adults are narrow in this

341

respect, but almost all kids are open to stormy dreams and wild imaginings.

You've written a large number of novels, but an even greater number of short stories. Does the short story format offer you something that a novel cannot?

A short story is the essence of a novel. You can condense the tale into a very hard-hitting piece of prose with great impact. I love the short story form because I can hold the whole tale in my head and sit down and write it in white heat, all in one go. Such sessions fire my writing skills and give me a huge emotional boost. Novels are slow, thoughtful animals that you have to approach with caution and spend time nurturing. Short stories are quick, fierce creatures that you grab with both hands and hold onto while they struggle to free themselves.

Do you have a set writing routine and if so, what is it?

I didn't used to have. Once upon a time I wrote at any time of the day or night, when the urge took me, but certainly every single day, weekends included. Now I sit down at 8 o'clock on weekdays and write until lunch time, sometimes beyond. It's a consequence of having written for thirty-five years. The computer has been a great boon. I used to write in longhand then type up the result. Now my fingers flash over the keys (I learned to touch-type at fifteen) and I can finish a novel in half the old time.

What did you read when you were growing up? Was it mostly science fiction and fantasy or did you have broader tastes?

My favourite authors as a young person were Rudyard Kipling and Richmal Crompton. I loved R. K.'s adventure stories and always wanted to be Kim or Mowgli. Equally I loved the Just William books and believed I *was* William. Yes, I also read science fiction by Brian Aldiss, Arthur C. Clarke and others. And ghost stories – M. R. James – and the weird tales of Edgar Allan Poe and Nathaniel Hawthorne. And Robert Louis Stevenson's stories like 'Dr Jekyl and Mr Hyde' – all absolutely brilliant. I still re-read them now, even the William books.

You moved about extensively as a child – on your website you state that you attended twenty-two different schools in various parts of the world by the age of fifteen. Do you feel that your experience of so many different cultures and peoples is connected in some way to your desire to be a writer?

I'm absolutely convinced of it. Having to move so many times, I was thrown onto my own resources a great deal, and having no TV in those days I read a great deal, and also created my own stories. In those days hardly anyone travelled the world much, from Britain, and the places I was taken to – South Arabia, Africa, the Far East – fired my imagination with their exotic flavours and mystery. I love the Orient and its light-footed wonderful people with fire in their blood.

If you could travel to any place in the world, at any period in history, where (and when!) would you go?

Anywhere in the world at any point history? I think I would like to have been in Athens amongst the Ancient Greeks around 500 BC. They were such brilliant, open-minded people. Failing that, Sarawak (in Borneo) in AD 1840, where Rajah Brooke ruled at the request of the Malays and Dyaks who, rather than take a king from amongst themselves and causing jealousy, asked an Englishman to rule them. Brooke did so, honouring their culture, never exploiting them. Failing that, I would like to go back to the time when we believed in fairies and meet Puck or Oberon or any of those supernatural creatures who have now left us.

Do you think that time travel might become possible one day? Or does the thought throw up too many mind-boggling conundrums for you?

I love time travel stories to bits. I love reading them. I love writing them. I would really like to travel in time myself. However, time is an abstract thing and sadly I don't think it possible in reality. Still, you never know . . .

Your characters are lucky enough to meet Franz Kafka in this novel. Is this an author who has inspired you in your own work?

Most definitely. He's the quirkiest author I know. I love in particular his short stories, especially *Metamorphosis*. Why did he choose a cockroach, I always wonder, for his character to change into? However, I would not like to have been him. He looks haunted. He sounds haunted. I think his dreams must have been pretty dark. Mine are bad enough at the moment. His were worse.

If you were to make a list of famous people from history you'd like to meet, who would be in the top three?

Socrates, Shakespeare and my great-grandfather (who remains a mystery to me – my great-grandmother was a maid in Sherborne Castle in Dorset and was seduced by one of the three sons of Lord Digby. I'd like to have a word with the culprit.).

And finally, what would be your advice to any budding young authors out there?

If you love writing, you'll make it as a writer one day, definitely. It's no good me saying 'Keep plugging away' because if you do love it you'll do it anyway. You'll do it for the pure enjoyment of writing creative literature, as I did and do now, and will always do. It's deep in the blood.